MW01098787

BARRY LEVY

Burning Bright

KWELA BOOKS

Thanks to Michael Rakusin
who showed me the extra mile was far,
but not too far, and to Gael
who was there for every mile

Cover design by Alexander Kononov
Text design and typography by Nazli Jacobs
Set in Fairfield Light
Printed and bound by Paarl Print,
Oosterland Street, Paarl, South Africa

First edition, first printing 2004
ISBN 0-7957-0188-8

For Ian, who didn't make it through

ONE

In the beginning

1

I'm a failure. If I remember my youth it is by those four words:
I am a failure. It wasn't always like that I grant, but it was like
that for long enough. An eternity by the measure of those pounding
adolescent hormones.

To all intents and purposes I came from a decent, loving home and
although my father never said it, nor I'm sure intended it in his continual rantings – *Where's your backbone? Why don't you show some
chrain? What's the matter with you? Don't be such a bladdy imbongolo!* – he implied what I eventually became: a failure.

My mother too, in her own way – with her it was a case of loving
too much, the kind of love that left you wondering whether the true
meaning of love wasn't some kind of oppression – also helped to create what I was to become: a failure.

Although both of them foresaw it, kind of continually predicted it
without ever actually articulating it – that I would become a failure –
what they didn't know of course was the kind of failure I would become.

For me it is all a memory now, a shadow on sunlight, bits of dirt on
clear glass that I sift into the back of my mind. Twisting my parents'
logic – you can forgive but you must never forget – into something I
can personally live with, imploring myself to never forgive, but to forget, forget, forget. Realising somehow even now that the hurt, the
black spot, the bruise remains even as the memory fades. Always to
see re-emerging before me the memory. That memory. It will not go.

Looking back I only wish that I, Danny Rothbart the Elder, could
have been there. To see. To oversee.

* * *

"I feel it in my bones." I hear my voice echoing down through the years, an impish smile breaking on my smooth flesh.

"What makes you so sure?" Chaz Bernstein is replying, his croaky voice breaking into a squeak as it often did.

"I'm telling you, man, I'm telling you . . ."

"Oh yeah . . ."

"Yeah . . . you know how close I've come . . ."

"Then why hasn't she?"

"Her period."

"Oh yeah, I've heard that one before."

"Well I'm telling you, boy-o-boy, man-o-man, tonight's the night. This boy ain't no boy no more."

"Yeah-yeah, we'll see."

I rubbed my chin with the palm of my hand – it was difficult to tell which was the smoother, my palm or my chin, they both felt so soft and pulpy. At sixteen, I still didn't have a hair to shave on my face and while others were broadening out at the shoulders – the hairs on their calves beginning to curl like spiders' legs, black, manly tufts showing on their chests and fanning out from their armpits – nothing much was changing on me. A few extra hairs here and there, but otherwise my body seemed to have reached an awful point of stagnation. If I hadn't grown more than a miserable few centimetres since I was thirteen, people would have still thought I was twelve, asking no doubt: "When's your barmitzvah, sonny?"

"One day you'll catch up to the rest of them. Don't be in such a hurry to grow up," my mother used to say, catching me peering under my armpits or puffing out my cream-smooth chest in the bathroom mirror. But the only thing that seemed to grow on me was the hair on the top of my head, and that my parents nagged at me to get the hell right off. Typical: grow something and they tell you to cut it, don't grow anything and they ask what the hell's wrong with you.

By comparison, my best friend Chaz Bernstein was a man already –

in physique that is. Long, tall, gawky and hopelessly uncoordinated, he at least had a beard to shave. It was an ugly sight really; little black prickles like dark chocolate sprinkles, growing over huge pimply pyramids of pink and red. If I didn't know him so well, I am sure that to me – as to the others who met him for the first time – it would have seemed like he had some fatal disease. But the point was that he shaved and in anybody's language that had to be a plus – especially amongst the girls. At least they noticed you and that could only be a step in the right direction. Prickles on the chin, no matter how like chocolate sprinkles, had to be an advantage.

Those dark thoughts knocking like a loud hammer in my head, I scratched at my silky-smooth face and then for reassurance dug my hand deep into my denim jacket pocket, and there I felt it; the squishy silver-foiled thing. I rubbed it delicately, feeling it between my fingers, telling it: *Tonight! Tonight!*

Seeing Chaz turn away from me – as usual bending down into his hands, cupped over a cigarette lighter – I decided to retrieve the square, silver package from my jacket pocket and transfer it – ready for imminent action – to my pants pocket. Thinking of my Uncle Harold, and his advice on Frenchies and things.

The quick coil of adolescent memory sprang back to the last party, with those new girls from Orange Grove. The ones we met through someone, who knew someone, who knew someone playing all the wrong music: the Bee Gees, I mean the Bee bloody Gees. When there was music in abundance like The Stones, Lou Reed, Bob Marley, The Who, Pink Floyd, Frijid Pink. But there they were, happy little skylarks singing along with the Bee bloody Gees, Donna Summer *Love to Love You Baby* and the ever so risqué Rod Stewart. Did I care? It didn't take me long; a sway of the hips, a sensuous shake of the shoulders – to who bloody cared what music – a joke at their expense, a snide, superior look, a dance and a hug, and then casually walking one of these Grove girls to a room. Chaz's froggy eyes, not to mention Peter's and Aaron's, even cynical Solly's – himself already comfortably on a couch with one of the girls – dripping green envy, that jaundiced "How does he do it?" look. Watching me. Me, chest pumped, swaggering through a door into the dark. And coming so close, oh so close to the finishing line – despite the intrusion of the Bee bloody Gees.

What was it with them? That they led you on so easily and then stopped just short? So abruptly? When all you wanted was for things to go just that little bit further. It was like they knew where the finishing line was and they moved it, every time moved it just that little bit further. Even for me, who they seemed to lead so darn easily towards it. Eventually up would come the red flag, the bloody red flag, like you were carrying some disease. How could they hold themselves back, let your fingertips roam, even undress for you – well almost undress – while the others tried their best in a lounge full of odorous music, sweating those jealous thoughts of you.

My mind flipped back to the time on the train on the way back from the relatives in Bulawayo, with Solly – the only one allowed to come with me on the trip up north at the end of form three – and the Girl Guides, Girl bloody Guides. Royalty – well sort of royalty – from Boksburg, falling all over us. Climbing up onto the top bunk with one of them, stripping off clothes until we were naked. Until I was completely nude with a girl – a first, a first. Solly below sort of squeezing in with the others – shirt slightly ragged, but going nowhere – calling out through the dim-green night light: "How's it going, Danny? When are they going to get out of here?" Knowing I was getting there: a spoiler, placing psychological barriers in my way, just because he wasn't getting anywhere. Anywhere near. Only in form three – well the end of form three – and already getting there, because – and he knew – I had it. So why did she stop at the last moment, suddenly cracking the whip; taming the circus tiger? Oh why, oh why? It could, should have already been. Her period. A real bloody red flag. A little white cotton penis already in there. What did I care what else went in there? So young, with such ambition, such grand ambition – I too could so easily have roamed in there. But still in form three notching a first, a first. And, at the end of those holidays, in my room at home with Chaz and Peter and Aaron, even surly Solly, patting me on the back. Feeling the glow. Sitting there in the midst of them, I glow. Despite the unchanging smoothness of my silky face, I am like a sun; a teenage sun around which they revolve, learn, aspire, grow red with envy. Me. Burning bright. Unstoppable.

"There's something about the air tonight . . . do you feel it . . .? Like something big is going down." Chaz blew a sheet of smoke into the misty air.

"You mean where we're going . . .?" I looked up at him; he was that much taller than me.

"I mean the riots in the townships, people dying, being shot in the streets . . . It's like what if it were us? If it were here . . . now, in our streets?"

I looked straight ahead of me, blowing out a thick funnel of icy mist. Right then it was hard to comprehend what he was on about, that his mind could be anywhere but where mine was.

"Yeah . . . what if?"

"Well . . . what if?" Chaz tried again to break into my thoughts.

"Well, what if what?"

"You know, if it were here, now, us fighting the police. The S-A-P?"

"Oh. I see," I said, waking from my trance, a trance I seemed to spend half my life in. "We'd stand up, man. We'd stand right bloody up, man!"

I saw us, all of us, sitting against the back school fence, standing up and retaliating. Was it really likely? Peter, Solly, Aaron, Chaz, me, really standing up with our big, clean, beak-shaped noses and neatly pressed school uniforms against sjamboks and bullets? Oh yeah we spoke about it alright. We spoke about it. We loathed apartheid, everything about it. Despite the fact that every book about real change, about different social, political and economic systems was banned in South Africa. We had read Bertrand Russell, and through Russell's commentary we had learnt a bit about Marx and Lenin and Bakunin and Kropotkin, whose writings and teachings were banned. We knew about communism and socialism and the true meaning of anarchism, which wasn't what we were constantly told at home and at school: that anarchism was the world run riot because blacks had been given the vote. We had also managed to get hold of a copy of Albert Luthuli's banned *Let My People Go* and now, courtesy my Uncle Harold, we even had a copy of Brian Bunting's doubly banned *The Rise of the South African Reich*. And that really was radical. But what really did we know about apartheid? From our warm, tidy beds that the maid made for us every day, what did we really know about having a different colour skin in South Africa? About being poor, cold, hungry, unschooled? So, yeah we spoke about it, spoke often, Chaz, Solly, Aaron, Peter, me, the crew, the ouens, the manne. We spoke diligently, meaningfully, purposefully about it, like we spoke about sex: constantly, all the time. Rubbed our thumbs in blood like brothers and swore we would do something about it one day. But in the end it was just like sex really: in theory we had conquered a hundred times, in practice all we could do was continue to compete, and dream.

"Yeah, Chaz," I reiterated slowly, almost chewing the words, "we'd stand up, man. One way or another, we'll stand right up, man!"

2

F inally, at the top end of Yeoville, having walked from Berea, we reached an old block of flats on Bezuidenhout Street, where an old squeaky lift that smelled of oil heaved us up to the unit we were visiting on the third floor. Inside the flat, in the lounge, sat two girls on a thick-set, heavily padded three-seater couch that looked well-worn, like it had been manufactured around the same time as the four-storey Second World War building it was now a part of. After exchanging a few words, the girls, who sat close together, seemed to pull even closer together, while Chaz and I sat in armchairs, set apart. The girls eyed Chaz and I suspiciously, whispered secrets and giggled with one another. It always made you feel uncomfortable, uneasy, the way girls whispered and giggled, and I think that was what it was all about: it was their tactic, it gave them a kind of advantage, an upper hand. They knew something you didn't; they held the key to something you wanted and it was in their hands as to whether you were allowed admission into that secret, intimate world. On the other hand – and I don't know that they were conscious of this – it also made you that much more determined to succeed, to break the secrecy, that unwritten alliance between them.

Jessica Shmulowitz – the girl whose flat it was – was fat as a balloon; her round face wet and greasy from all the oils and make-up she applied in an attempt to paint a pretty picture of herself. Remarkably, she had sort of succeeded: there was something crudely attractive in her face, or what the make-up did to her face. I think it was the way she applied the make-up: the thick purple lipstick framed in a thick black pencil line, the heavy brush-strokes of green and brown eye-shadow circling dark mascara. She sat, slumped sideways, leaning towards the girl sitting next to her, one leg tucked under a long purple cotton dress.

The girl next to her, Sophie Street, also had a leg tucked under her, but she sat stiffly, poised, with a sense of natural dominance, blinking her long, black-painted eyelashes hard and often, her speckled silver-blue eye-shadow transforming her blinking into the opening and closing of elaborate theatre curtains.

"So, you just gonna sit there and giggle?" I growled at Sophie Street.

"What's't t'you?" she spat back through plum-coloured lipstick. And when I didn't reply, but merely stared at her: "Well, aren't you going to say something?"

Instead of saying anything, I lifted myself from the armchair I was sitting in, walked slowly, confidently over to her and sat down, hard, in her lap.

"How's this!"

She pushed me off her, but as I fell over, thinking I had played the wrong card, had screwed things up before I had even begun, she caught hold of me and pulled me back.

"Danny Rothbart, you're so cute," she exhaled softly.

Yes, I had made the right move.

As if taking his cue from what I had just done, Chaz, who had been sitting quietly, observantly, smoking away, with one leg folded square over the other, the flares at the bottom of his trousers like mini-sails skewing downwards, now also decided it was time to make a move. He dashed out his cigarette in a red Venetian glass ashtray, unwound his legs and lifted himself slowly, concentrating deeply as his giraffe-like body swayed over to the couch. Without smiling, without even a murmur, he plonked himself down on the couch, next to Jessica Shmulowitz. The two girls looked at one another but no one said a word. And now the four of us, the two girls squeezed in the middle, between Chaz and I, sat nestled uncomfortably, self-consciously, staring ahead, like something out of a Laurel and Hardy movie.

16

After a while, to remedy what I saw as potential disaster, I quickly re-positioned myself between the two girls – pushing Chaz over to the very end of the couch – and threw my arms around both of them, allowing my brashness, my confidence to bubble over, like a monkey on show. Chaz, seeing this as his next cue, the beginning of the action, brought down a bear-sized hand and smudged it over Jessica Shmulowitz's breast. Like a tightly wound spring, Jessica Shmulowitz immediately threw a flat hand into his face and leapt off the couch, a disgusted, tainted look dripping from her oily cheeks. She strode over to the hi-fi, as if having already planned to get up anyway, and changed the record: Lou Reed for The Rolling Stones. One thing about these girls, at least they knew their music. Chaz, flicking his eyes upwards, as if there were something wrong with her, rather than that she had the right to slap his brazen, pimpled face, simply moved into her place on the couch. He stretched himself out like a cowboy in a saloon, so that he was now disconcertingly touching me, leaning against my arm, which was still loosely wrapped around Sophie Street's neck. I knew he didn't mean anything by it, but guys just didn't do that – sit touching one another – even if there was a girl in between them. But that was Chaz, clumsy and awkward and somewhat thick-skinned.

I pulled Sophie towards me, away from Chaz, as though saving her, and looked about the room, thinking of my next move. But wherever I looked I sensed only a room with a stale closeness about it, as though Jessica's parents were somehow there, somehow looking at us from behind the old grey walls of the apartment.

The LP crackled and scratched as it went around. I took in the room, which was filled with Venetian glass ornaments – blue and red, orange and yellow, orange and cloudy white – in the shape of pirouetting ballerinas, fishes and clowns, no different to the ornaments in my own home, caught in an eternal mid-movement; trapped in time. A single book, its pages bent, stood in a mahogany-veneer bookcase filled with copper candlesticks, cheap dolls and ornaments, like a dusty old hobo leaning against a damp toilet wall at a fair. Near the bookcase a faint luminous green light told me where the music was coming from – a hi-fi embedded in the depths of another large wood-veneer cabinet. The room smelled stuffy, of old people from a ghetto, a white ghetto, a remnant of the old country, Lithuania, Poland.

Then it came to me, my next move; it had worked so many times before. I jumped up from the couch, pulling Sophie Street with me, and started dancing around both girls, flapping my elbows like ducks' wings and strutting my way across the room, swinging an invisible scarf through the air a la Mick Jagger. Then I took hold of both girls' arms, forcing their bodies to turn and sway with me. Chaz, by himself on the couch now, sat even more spreadeagled than before. He lit another cigarette, inhaled deeply, then, with tiny cracking sounds that came from his jaw, blew out a series of smoke-rings that followed one another with pin-point accuracy, the smaller rings catching up to and melding with the large initial ring as it floated up towards the ceiling and darkness. The smoke-rings flowing rapidly from his lips now, he looked up at me, soft-focused, a slightly bedazzled look in his eyes. I had seen that look many times before. I marked the look down to three things: first loyalty and then love – not a word you would use openly among guys, but just a sense you felt – and finally hero-worship. Yes, lastly but most importantly, hero-worship. The honest truth was, the way he looked at me made me feel on top of the world. That I was like a prince. It confirmed everything I thought about myself, that I was the benchmark, the leader among all of us, our crew, the ouens, the manne. Modesty was not something that came easily to me.

It was true, I saw now, that Chaz may have had the beard, the maturity, the manliness in his face, and I envied him like crazy for that, but he just didn't have *it*. What it took to get the girls, to hold the attention of a crowd. Next to him, it was easy to see why I was frontrunner in the race among our crew. It was just funny how nature worked: I had everything Chaz needed – the looks, confidence, style – and yet he had all the things I would have killed for – the manly, curling hair that sprouted from his chest, the long-shaven sideburns, the beard and the brains. It was the beard, the beard that especially concerned me. Without the brains you could always get by – you could always get help from private tutors, or simply crib, as I did all the time, especially from Chaz – but with that beard I would really have had them dancing around me. I would already have done it, I was sure, crossed the line into manhood. My biggest failing – I knew it – were the wispy excuses for sideburns that unlike Chaz's broad, definite strokes – that poured like lava down the cheeks – stopped on my head before the ears even began. It was an embarrassment.

Crushing these thoughts out of my head, I leaned over and pulled Chaz to his feet, partly needing to get him off the couch and partly feeling guilty that he looked so left out, so abandoned. Stylishly, I took his hand and joined it into Jessica's. The way I saw it, it was charity from the prince – for both of them – and she didn't step back, just accepted as though I had a divine right. Relishing the attention, I felt the eyes of both girls stroking my cheeks, my neck, my hair, my tiny square shoulders. In this frame of mind, I continued to jump and dance, to sputnik around the room, around both girls like a Russian cosmonaut, until Sophie Street, rolling her eyes, said, "C'mon. Sit down." She said it with such firmness that I just stopped dead in the middle of the floor, my smile stiffening in mid-air, and allowed her to lead me back to the couch.

So now, while Chaz and Jessica Shmulowitz were suddenly left standing facing one another self-consciously in the middle of the lounge floor – Chaz, with yet another cigarette already between his fingers, and blowing out brand-new sets of thick, blue-grey smoke-rings – Sophie Street and I were coiled into the couch staring into one another's eyes. Looking back on it now, I can still feel how uncontrollably driven we were, how quintessentially important it was to be first. It was of only secondary importance that I was in any way attracted to Sophie – to her angular cheekbones, her geisha eyes – to that puckish personality that was mirrored in her full, perpetually puffed-out lips that seemed constantly to say: *C'mon at your own risk.*

Sophie was different to the others. To me, anyway. Despite all her Lisa Minnelli make-up, she was more serious. Deeper. Without talking you felt there was something there, and when she smiled you swam right into her; she just didn't do it too often. Over the past year we had met regularly, at parties, at friends' houses, small gatherings of boys and girls, two-on-two, three-on-three, "overs" as we called them – like this was now, an "overs". And always, whenever she was there, at an overs, we paired off, so that to some extent – though it was never formalised – we were known to most people as a couple. The truth was, each time we saw one another it was more like two strangers with a mild contamination trying to get closer to one another without infecting each other. Although her thickly painted, puffed-out lips said, *C'mon*, it was the *at your own risk* that continually pulled me in, that told me, me, with my special kind of arrogant confidence, that I could break through. Yes, there were no doubts about it, in those pouting lips, there was a voice that was shouting at me: *Just a little more patience, just a little more, and the door will open.*

So tonight, as I leaned forward on the couch without any further ado to kiss her, I half expected her – as was usual – to jerk back and at least feign prohibition. And then the usual pulling and tugging would have us somersaulting, but not really doing that much, or going that far, until it was time to go home, and we would silently agree to begin the battle all over again the next time, at the next overs, or the one after that. But tonight, as my mouth touched hers for the first time, something different happened. Her wet, glossy lips became like a drain, sucking me down. It was like the first time we had ever really kissed. My tongue felt like a tiny fish caught in a maelstrom, in something rich and swirling and firmly in control and for the first time I became really conscious of Sophie's smell; it was like roses, freshly picked red roses. Drowning in this euphoria, I peeped open an eye, to look for Chaz, to see how he was faring, and saw that he and Jessica had now, miraculously, settled down. If you could call it that. They were sitting squeezed up into an armchair; his hand striking out at her breast, her hand lashing out at his cheek, his hand landing on her thigh, her hand pulling a chunk out of his hair. Soon, I knew, even Chaz would have to give up, there would be a truce and they would end up in separate chairs, staring straight ahead in silence, tolerating in quiet discomfort the closeness of each other's presence. Chaz blowing his famous smoke-rings towards the ceiling, or her face; their only escape from one another, watching us – Sophie and me – without openly declaring they were watching us.

I went back to my own furious battle, placing a hand quickly and directly on Sophie's breast – albeit over her clothes, which consisted not only of a shirt but a thick black jersey – expecting her to push me away and tell me – as always – that I had ruined everything by wanting too much, too soon. But tonight she didn't utter a word, not even a squeal of protest. Nothing.

Noting this, I slowly began to pull at the bottom of her shirt until it popped out of the tight-fitting prison that was the waistline of her pants. That achieved – and without protest – I slid my hand underneath, allowing it to move fast, soldier-like, across her smooth, rubbery stomach. Still there was no protest: my blitzkrieg, my quick-as-a-snake, leopard-crawling tactics were working. My head was ablaze. I slowed down, mainly because I needed the rest to think of my next move, to consolidate my gains, and because, based on previous experience, I knew if I moved too fast it would end in disaster. So I stroked for a while, tactically, very cautiously allowing my fingers, like a crab digging a hole, to tickle and burrow into the naked skin around what I distinctly now felt was the bottom of her bra. I felt my eyes spin in my head. Uncle Harold would be proud of me, I thought. Then, with calculated precision – as soon as I had wedged open the tiniest of spaces between the bottom of the bra and her flesh – I quickly slipped my fingers in. Only, as I quickly found out, my fingers would not go in very far, could not get right under. The bottom of this bra was like no other bra I had known: it was like solid steel, a cotton-coated metal semi-circle that clung to her chest. Who could have made her wear such a thing? I had never come up against anything like it before. Was it for real? Or was it some kind of new anti-male protection? I changed tactics, deciding to approach the problem from a completely different angle. I now stretched my hand upwards until it reached the top end of her chest, just below her neckline, then I twisted it back downwards and quickly dug down with my fingers from the top. Up there at least, as I suspected, there was no metal barrier, no steel piping, just the flimsy cotton I had more or less expected to find. Extending themselves, my now twisted fingers reached down into the bra, edging their way toward their target until suddenly, mercilessly, Sophie Street pushed me backwards, and I felt valuable inches slip out of my grasp, like a mountain climber who has suddenly lost his footing. But, like that mountain climber, I was still holding on and now I was even more determined. She had let me in – well, most of the way – and now, come what may, I was going in again. I pushed my way upward and then downwards again, even harder this time, but again she shoved me away. There was no doubt I had to come up with better, more ingenious strategies. I had to find another gear. It came to me quickly. I turned to her lips and kissed her ferociously, forcing my tongue – as she had done with mine not that long ago – deep into her mouth, but for me it was a mere tactic to shift attention, re-focus the mind of the target away from what my hand was doing. And, miraculously, it worked. This time – as I continued to prod the back of her mouth with my tongue – my fingers twisted then slid all the way down through the flimsy material at the top of her bra. And before she even realised it, before she could do anything about it, they were there, at the very centre of her round, doughy breast, feeling that raised bull's-eye that was the goal. But once again she threw me back and my straining, overreaching fingers lost their grip and I had to start all over again.

But I was unstoppable. Once again I went in, using that guerrilla instinct I had developed over the years, supplemented by the lessons I had gleaned from Uncle Harold's books. I began the kissing again, strongly plugging my tongue into her mouth like it was some sort of killer weapon, and again it worked. Only this time as I twisted my fingers back in, I lifted my body to gain more height and therefore more leverage, and as a result more control. I was really thinking now. This time I was actually able to hold onto the target, the mini-thimble, that deliciously hard bull's-eye. Only now that I had it, actually had it there in my contorted grasp, I didn't know what to do with it. My mind suddenly became like one of those banknote-counting machines, maniacally flipping through the pages of Uncle Harold's books as I tried to remember the right pages, the right chapters, the right techniques I had so assiduously been poring over for just such an event. But nothing, nothing in particular, not one particular set of instructions would spring to mind, and as I pored over the pages I felt Sophie Street throwing me back like I was some sort of unwanted carpet.

But I was not to be that easily defeated. So, I shoved back, using my body weight, which luckily for her was not that excessive, to pin her under me. Unfortunately for me, at the same time, by some miscalculation – God knows how these things happen in the midst of battle – I found myself pinned so hard against her that the hand that was beneath her shirt – that was meant to be doing its work to irretrievably excite her – was now trapped, a prisoner unable to move, chained to her flesh, like it was dead. I could feel it squashed up somewhere in the vicinity of her upper chest and lower neck. I must have been strangling her, but I couldn't hear a word of protest from her lips. I was sure I must have killed her. In fright, I moved my weight off her, allowing my hand to slip down and out of her shirt, feeling the bones in my hand straighten and un-crunch. And then I heard a sigh, the noise coming out of her as a kind of piggish snort, but it didn't bother me, she was alive! Alive!

"Not now, Danny, not now."

Searching for composure, I quickly breathed back at her: "It's never the right time, is it?"

"What do you expect me to do?" She rolled her eyes. "Get undressed in front of them? Let everyone have a grand old time watching us?"

Sore and defeated, I lay there, my head pushed into her stomach. Peeking open an eye I saw Chaz and Jessica Shmulowitz; they were sitting there, bolt upright, miraculously still in the same armchair, but in absolute silence.

"We could go somewhere else?"

"No."

"Why not?"

"No."

"C'mon . . . you would if you really loved me."

"Why can't you just be satisfied with what you get?"

"If you really, really loved me, you'd do it . . . for me!"

"Danny . . ."

"You won't be sorry. You'll see, you'll enjoy it too." I looked at her with wet, pleading eyes, ready to try anything.

"Sssssh! Keep your voice down." She clicked her tongue and looked across the lounge. "You don't want them to hear every word we say, do you?"

I stared back at her, as though I didn't care. A look of deep disappointment on my face, like I had been punched in the nose by a close friend.

"Don't look at me like that."

"Like what?"

"Like that! Ag man!" She turned away and then turned back again. "OK then, my boy. Let's go to the dining-room."

There was a loud explosion in my stomach. I think it was atomic.

"Where? Where did you say?" I repeated to make sure I was hearing right.

"Just come!"

3

I could hear my heart beating in my temples as Sophie jumped up and I followed eagerly like a puppy. I looked over to Chaz with a smirk of pride on my lips, but he just winked lazily back at me and took a cigarette out of his top pocket. Jessica pretended not to be interested, not even glancing in our direction, staring past Chaz – whose lap she was still sitting on – towards the little glowing light in the hi-fi.

I took off my jacket and threw it towards the couch; I missed and it fell over like a drunk, but there was no time to worry about it now, I had other things on my mind. I felt into my pants pocket. It was there. I could feel it, the square foil package, squishy between my fingers. *This is it! This is it!* I said to myself as Sophie turned to take a last, conspiratorial look at Jessica, then closed the doors behind us and suddenly the only light in the room was a dim, shadowy gleam that spread like prison bars through the rippled glass doors from the lounge next door.

Inside the dining-room a huge mahogany dinner table filled almost every inch of space; it was incredible how big the table was, or how small the room was. Sophie lay down in a small space between table, chairs and the wall and I immediately dropped to my knees and then wriggled in next to her, or rather half on top of her – even if I had wanted to, there wasn't enough room to fit flat beside her. A cold dampness stroked my back from the wall behind. My body felt like an ironing-board. Nevertheless, a voice kept ringing out inside me: *This is it! This is it!* I could already see myself, behind the school swimming-pool – where the crew met at lunch-breaks – chest puffed, telling of how good it was. Every detail.

Though we were already virtually on top of one another, I suddenly became aware of Sophie looking up at me and now that I realised we were alone, really alone, I felt an irritating kind of twitching in my chest. Somehow, for some reason, nerves had never come into it, into any of my calculations, and I didn't recall any of the sex manuals ever making mention of them either. Nerves. Strange things, strange little electrical impulses . . . but there was no time to waste on useless thoughts like that now. Listening to my own advice, I immediately snuck a clammy hand under the bottom of her still-scruffy open shirt, letting it crawl speedily upwards until it came to rest on that breast that I already felt I had some ownership over. Cleverly, I allowed my hand to stop there. Waiting. And nothing. Not a sound. Not a squeak of protest. Good. Step number one, taken and passed. For a while even I was just happy to have my hand there, as we kissed and held one another.

But it wasn't long before the soldier of fortune inside me was shouting instructions, planning manoeuvres. Screaming out: *Now! Now!* That there was no time like the present, no time to be wasted; and then a voice whispered from below.

"Shall I take my pants off?"

The question took me so completely by surprise, so completely off-guard, that I was sure it was an ambush. She had beaten me to the draw. Taken control. Thrown me completely off-balance. I felt dizzy and could feel my long, matted hair pressing hard against my head like a big, dirty mop.

"Yee," I finally managed to squeak, not intending my voice to break up like that, like Chaz's, but that was the only way I could get any sound to come from me.

But that was all Sophie needed. She immediately jumped up, turned to face the cold, damp wall, and within three seconds flat had torn off her jersey, pants, underpants, and was back on the carpeted floor, close in beside me. *This is really it*, I said to myself, still dizzy from the unexpected speed of everything. *Really, really it.*

27

I rose to my feet, only slower, much slower, and then turned away from her, my nose brushing up against the cold wall, almost banging into it, and began to peel off my pants. Bending over to take my left trouser leg off, somehow, I suppose not surprising given the proximity of the chairs to the wall, my foot caught in a chair and I tripped, hitting my hip hard against the table. I heard Sophie giggle softly, but thank God for small mercies, I remember the thought passing through my head, if the table hadn't been there Sophie would have seen me going right over, perhaps even cracking my skull on the wall, and then she really would have been in hysterics. The word "klutz" shot into my head, suddenly, loudly, like one of those banned Guy Fawkes big bangers, and once the explosion had happened, that was all I could see in front of me: *klutz*.

Small as it already was, the room was shrinking. It was very hot. Very, very hot for winter. I took a deep breath, gathering myself, and finally managed to drag both my feet out of my pants. Compared to the speed with which Sophie had achieved this relatively minor manoeuvre, my antics must have seemed incredibly slow. I felt feverishly white and thin, my knees extraordinarily knobbly. I felt like I had just discovered I was part crippled and now Sophie could see it too. The body of a klutz. I could hear a voice taking over, repeating it, like I needed it repeated, but there was nothing I could do to stop it. Taking another deep breath to gather myself, I found myself holding onto my pants – actually clutching onto them – not knowing what to do with them. I looked around, as though for a cupboard or a hanger, and when I found none, quickly, as though recovering from a trance, threw them under a chair. Now hovering there, above Sophie, I faced my next problem: to take my shirt off or not to take my shirt off? I sort of wished she would take over and tell me what to do, but looking down all I saw was an exasperated expression on her face. And instead of the dark, curly triangular bush I expected to see when I looked at that part of her – just as it was in the pictures in the magazines

Uncle Harold had passed on to me – I saw only shirt, a white shirt that she was stretching with her hands so far down that it covered her entire pelvic area like a trampoline. Her legs – round and ghost-white – rising pudgily up from the floor, were bolted tightly together like clamps, and when she saw that I was gazing down at her she pulled her shirt even further down and glared at me like I had no right.

And then after a few moments a voice came. And it wasn't mine. "Well . . .?"

It did at least have the effect of shaking me out of my indecision. The shirt would stay on, definitely. Now emulating her by pulling my shirt well down, I crouched down next to her on the floor, my knees making creaking sounds like an old man. Then I remembered it, the silver-foiled package. The rubber. *Never, never be caught without a Frenchie*, Uncle Harold's voice breathed wetly into my ear, and I immediately jumped up and dived for my pants, scrambling all over the floor. I had obviously thrown them much harder and further than I thought, and it took a while to locate them. As I crawled under the table, I was wondering what Sophie Street thought of me now. Klutz, schlemiel, imbecile, imbongolo.

Finally, finally, I found my pants, and breathed out a sigh of relief, but in my excitement, as I made to stand up, I hit my head on the edge of the table. I thought I heard Sophie giggle again, but I immediately scratched my head as if nothing had really happened, as if to show I was really thinking, anything but that she should see I was rubbing my head in pain. Remaining kneeling, I juggled my right hand between the two front pockets. Suddenly, when I had been feeling and squishing the damned thing all night long, I couldn't find it. *What if I had lost it? What if it had rolled out when I had thrown my pants so recklessly under the table?* It seemed to take forever before I finally cornered it in the very bottom nook of one of the pockets.

I suddenly thought of Uncle Harold and all the good advice on rubbers and Frenchies and things he had given me. *It's one thing to screw, but it's another thing to screw up your entire life for five minutes' satisfaction because you didn't use a Frenchie.*

Why Uncle Harold had especially taken to me, I really didn't know. I supposed he had always been around, somewhere in the background. He had always been friendly with me and Cyril, always taking the time to say hello to us, ask how we were, how school was going, taking the time to make small talk, letting us in on some of those manly jokes of his. But to us he was still dad's friend, no more than a good family friend, an uncle of sorts, but essentially one of their friends, not ours.

My father had always been a great admirer of Uncle Harold and his admiration had grown still further when Uncle Harold, a few years earlier, had become a Johannesburg City Councillor for the Progressive Party. My parents believing, along with the rest of Jo'burg, that with all his connections, business success and work for charities, Uncle Harold would be the city's next mayor. Only over the dining-room table did my parents admit what they really thought: that Uncle Harold, dad's friend, was far too liberal, far too progressive, far too broadminded. They didn't like it, for example, when he spoke of dismantling apartheid as soon as possible, and they found it distasteful that he had been married twice before and was now living in sin, as they called it, with a new partner Thelma Goodman. Myself, I couldn't give a stuff. If anything it just showed what a broadminded old guy he was.

Cyril and I often heard Uncle Harold espousing to my parents: "Apartheid has to go. It's the only way forward for South Africa. First we get rid of apartheid for Afs with money and education – at the same time, making sure that everyone, from this generation on, receives a decent education. Believe me, after that, given a few years, no one will even remember why we had apartheid in the first place."

Cyril and I always admired Uncle Harold for what he said. I think listening to Uncle Harold was what first opened our eyes to what was really going on in the country, effectively turning us against apartheid and, to a certain extent, against our parents. Nonetheless, my parents, especially my father, saw Uncle Harold – his social responsibility, his great philanthropy – as a role model for us kids. For Cyril and I.

After Cyril had left the country a year or more ago – "to get away from mom and dad and this stupid everything-banned apartheid," as he put it – Uncle Harold had begun to show me an even more personal side, taking on a role as a sort of big brother, or surrogate father. Why me? I really didn't know. Who or what, I asked myself, was I to deserve such concern? Surely to him I was no more than a simple-minded, smooth-skinned teenager with only one thing on the brain? Still, I felt rather privileged to have the city's future mayor taking even a feather of interest in me.

"Come to me any time you have a problem," he would say firmly, warmly, often. "Nothing we say between ourselves is ever going to make it back to the old folks, I promise you."

It felt good to have someone from their world talking to you as an equal, taking you into his trust. It was like you actually existed. A big leap forward from the way my parents saw me: my father as an imbongolo, my mother as the boy she didn't want to see grow up.

One day Uncle Harold had arrived to see my father earlier than usual with a parcel of books he had long been promising. While waiting for dad, he handed over the mystery parcel, saying only: "Knowing the way you think, I'm sure you'll put these to good use."

As soon as he had seen my father and left the house, excitedly, yes I remember excitedly, I unstrung the parcel, not sure at all what to expect. Perhaps books in the line of Dickens, Wells or Dumas – all of which I had gained a healthy taste for through English studies in senior school, and which were seen as good, clean literature. Maybe something in the vein of Ian Fleming (frowned upon), or even Catcher in the Rye (good literature but even more frowned upon), but not,

not, the book I had just pulled from the pile: the thick paperback entitled *The Rise of the South African Reich*. I remember myself scanning quickly through the blurb on the back cover, the chapter titles, Uncle Harold spiralling in my estimation, as page after page the book denounced, with violent vehemence, anything to do with apartheid, colonialism, neo-colonialism. I suddenly began to see Uncle Harold as more than just a Progressive Party stalwart – as he professed to my parents and his constituents – but as a great thinker with a revolutionary secret desire. The book in front of me not just a book anymore, but a kind of medal that I would pin to my chest with pride.

The other books, all four of them, were also a surprise. I can still see them so clearly. Even now their magnificent titles roll before my eyes: *Love Without Fear, The Sexually Adequate Male, The Sexually Adequate Female, Sex Manners for Men*. These books were certainly for me! Books that normally only the tallest of adults had any remote chance of reaching up to on the top shelves of the local CNA. The sort of books that, had it not been for Uncle Harold, I was sure would never have crossed my path in just-about-everything-banned South Africa. Thanks to Uncle Harold, I quickly knew not only that much more about our unjust apartheid regime – from a proletarian, class-based point of view – but also the complete erogenous geography of the female body and much, much more importantly, how to fulfil it. How to fulfil it! I felt superior, like suddenly a world of deep, dark secrets had been opened to me.

In the weeks that followed, Harold Kleinhart – new older brother, person-you-would-like-more-than-anyone-else-to-be-your-father – arrived at the house with other offerings: bundles of hand-typed poetry, dog-eared photographs and magazines. He explained that they were from his own youth and no longer needed, and once again Uncle Harold rose in my estimation.

"The only thing now, Danny, is to get you on the road, lovin' 'em and leavin' 'em, but I'm sure it'll all happen in no time. You'll have the birds flocking, no problem." I can hear Uncle Harold saying it even now, the pictures he gave me still swimming in my dislocated brain – as they did on that first day – worth a fortune, an absolute fortune, a danger just to hold in South Africa. I wasted no time whatsoever in showing them, and the books, to Chaz and all my other schoolfriends, and thanks to Uncle Harold I saw myself rise, or perhaps I should say rise even further, in the rankings of my friends to guru of all things political and sexual. Danny Rothbart. The one to be with. The one to know.

A thick droplet of sweat arrived on my forehead. I looked down at Sophie Street still meekly lying there, wondering if she knew what I was thinking, whether she knew what the hell I was doing. She didn't say anything, but as I met her gaze I saw her eyes somersaulting backwards, and in that instant the room became like a sauna. I wondered if she felt it too, the heat, the extreme heat in the middle of this icy-cold winter?

Still on my knees I thought of Uncle Harold and told myself, if not for anyone else, I had to do it for him. I turned away from her, nearly wiping my nose out on the wall again, and kneeling half-squashed up against the wall I nonchalantly made to rip off the top end of the silver package that clung to my hot fingers. Nothing doing. It would not budge, merely twisted in my fingers like soft plastic. I tried again. Nothing, just more twisting. I clenched my teeth in frustration, ripping at it again, afraid I was breaking the contents, but doing it anyway. Still nothing. In desperation I brought the thing up to my mouth and locked my teeth into a corner of it. I was sure I was puncturing holes in the actual thing, but, again, doing it anyway. Who cared, as long as I had it open and used it, and could tell Uncle Harold – and everyone else – I had. Finally, finally I felt the package opening, leaving a disturbing taste in my mouth of silver foil and powdery rubber – like breaking a filling and swallowing an elastic band at the same time.

Many times before, with my friends, we had unfurled and paraded the rubbers that we had dared one another to buy from the local chemist shops, but with her now, somehow, it was different. I knew, knew straight away, that I didn't want her to see this thing; it looked so long and clumsily empty, especially now that it was completely unfurled, dangling from my fingertips. I peeped over my shoulder to see if she was looking, but once again all I saw were two slanting eyes rolling backwards in her head.

Turning back to the wall, trying to ignore what I thought I had just seen, my fingers – now stuck to this thing – were trying to fit it on. When I looked down at myself, across my thin, ironing-board body, it was hard to tell if there was anything for this long, rubbery, funnel-like thing to fit over. Jesus, what would Uncle Harold say now? I took a deep breath, steadying myself, commanding my fingers to press the empty sheath over my would-be little king, but there was nothing. Nothing. If anything it was shrinking. Shrinking before my very eyes.

Desperately, feeling the moisture sliding down my armpits, I ordered the soldier, the guerrilla in me to fight on, forwards, forwards, until, by some miracle – it could only have been a miracle – the empty thing was firmly attached to me. I looked down and saw it hanging there, sticking over nothing but a few curly hairs. Talk about klutz. This was more than just klutz, this was rachmones: mother's shame. I found myself turning even further away from Sophie, yet again banging my nose against the wall.

"Well . . .?" This time I could definitely hear the frustration, the exasperation in the voice. I had been expecting it all along, had seen it in the backward-somersaulting eyes.

I twisted my face around to her, forcing a smile, as if nothing were wrong, but the truth was that I was drowning. Did I hear a snigger? Another snigger? Was she laughing at me? *So you wanted it, huh? Some guy! Some ouk! Some main man!* Did I hear her say that? Did I actually hear her say that, or was it just the look in her now wildly rolling eyes? I had to do something. Couldn't face this wall all night like I had suddenly turned into a statue and didn't even know she was there. I gave myself three seconds, exactly three, and then like an elastic band projected from between thumb and forefinger, I flicked my body around and sprang. I landed right on top of her.

"Oooof!" I heard the air whoosh out of her lungs, feeling the empty rubber tube still dangling between my legs. I had expected it to fly off at an angle, but it was still there, sticking as if they, the manufacturers, had specially put glue around the rim. I breathed out, relieved, thankful to the Crepe de Chine company.

Looking up at me with a highly irritating combination of bewilderment and daring, I felt Sophie Street open her legs, and I slid down in between them. I knew now, for sure, she was not turning back, not changing her mind, no matter what kind of schlemiel, what kind of klutz I had shown myself to be. I was there, right there.

I pushed hard against her, pressing the ugly rubber tube into her flesh, willing it, willing it to go in. I was praying now, pushing like a water-buffalo and praying, but with every thrust I just seemed to hit up against a wall. Hurting myself against something mysteriously hard down there.

Now I felt a hand groping between my thighs, only unlike the times before, it was hard, knuckly, like the back-end of a knobbed hammer, and it was trying to grab hold of me and pull me into the wall, that wall.

"Uhrrrgh . . . what's that?"

"Keh . . .?" I could feel it slipping, the empty sheath getting stuck beneath me, caught against her thighs.

"Yuk!"

I saw her eyes rolling backwards once again and I buried my face, yes buried it in her chest, deflated, depleted, destroyed.

"Danny . . . are you there? Is something the matter?"

"God, ja . . . I mean wha . . .? No. No."

35

"Sorry, Danny, I'm sorry, I didn't mean to . . ."

Sorry, she was saying sorry! Sophie Street! Maybe there was a God after all? I nestled my head into her armpit this time, staring into the musty darkness of the carpet below. The smell was so bad, of dust and old food scraps, I thought I would throw up, but much as the carpet smelled I could not risk raising my eyes in case they bumped into hers. Stench or no stench, my head felt safer buried in there, only one thought pecking like a hard-nosed cuckoo in my head: *What can she be thinking? What can she be thinking?*

We lay there, like that, for a few minutes, neither of us speaking, neither of us uttering a sound, my heart and head pounding like a row of mistimed jack-hammers. I couldn't believe how loud the noise was in my head and chest, and instead of it growing softer as we lay there, it grew even louder, reaching a kind of crescendo. I thought I would explode. Then suddenly, suddenly, as though possessed by a demon, a monster, I launched myself again upon Sophie Street. In time with raised heartbeat this time, I began pumping, pushing and pumping, pumping and squeezing, between her thighs.

In the room next door I could hear raised voices. Down below, in the carpet, raised voices. In my head, voices. Wherever I turned, voic-es. Instead of roses, suddenly Sophie Street was smelling like the in-side of a gym.

"Why . . . so concerned?" Jessica Shmulowitz's raised parrot-like voice found its way through the rippled glass doors.

"We should . . . concerned." A croaking frog voice responded from a totally separate corner of the room.

"Let . . . bladdy coons . . . themselves . . . more . . . merrier!"

"What makes you . . . superior? They're people . . . your people . . . once slaves."

"Ag man, d'you really . . . save you, my boy, because . . . Mr Chaz poofter deluxe Bernstein . . . didn't . . . names?"

"Oh shit, man . . . point is . . . human beings."

"Kak, man!" Voice rising. "They're bladdy dumb, thick, uncivilised coon-a-jacks. That's why they go around throwing stones and burning down their own bladdy houses and schools!"

"Ag . . .!"

"Creep . . ."

"Disgusting . . ."

"Crap . . .!"

Which summed up, exactly, what I felt about myself right then. Like crap. Disgusting. Worse than disgusting. For a second time I had tried and failed. What had possessed me? Shit! Shit! Shit! As if failing once wasn't enough. I had to go and prove it to her again – that I was a failure. Looking around, I found myself still stuck on her body, stuck like a wet envelope, not knowing how to get off, not, at any rate, without her noticing something was wrong.

And then a voice, a real voice: "Let's just rest, Danny."

Her voice, her words, the reality of her presence, the sudden reality of my own, somehow unsticking me from this glue that was a mixture of her flesh and my hot, dripping, sweaty determination. I breathed out.

"You don't really love me, do you?" she whispered.

I couldn't respond. Nothing, not a word would budge from my throat. There were words there, oh yes, lots of words, millions, zillions of words, but they were all locked in my head. Chained. Bolted. Imprisoned.

"Well . . . aren't you going to say something, for God's sake?"

Even though I couldn't get a word out of my throat, even though I still couldn't turn my head to look at her, the more I thought about what she was saying, the particular words she had chosen, the more her words began to take on a different meaning. Suddenly they began to sound like gold, soft golden nuggets, like the golden footprints of angels treading in my ears. And the reason was simple. The way she had spoken, the tone in her voice, the words she had selected, told me there actually was no blame. There was nothing wrong with me. If there was a problem with me it was that I did not love her, and that, if anything, was her fault. She couldn't get me to love her; therefore she was to blame! Suddenly there was that smell of roses about her again. I could have kissed her, right there and then, only even I knew it didn't seem quite appropriate under the circumstances.

I peeked up from beneath her sweet-smelling armpit and saw her looking at me, distrustful, squinting, yet still boldly half-smiling, and in her smile, her c'mon-at-your-own-risk lips I saw there was still hope. As long as she saw the whole debacle as her fault and was professing love for me, there was still a glimmer of hope, a chance. Spinning with excitement I realised I could still do it. Could still, still do it. How could one, anyway, be so close, so scintillatingly, so temptingly close, and give up? There she was naked, well half-naked, next to me, and there I was, naked, well half-naked, next to her, just letting the seconds, the minutes, my life tick by. The very thought of the crew, the ouens, Chaz, Solly, Peter, Aaron, my friends breathing down my neck, was like a whip to a racehorse. All I could see in front of me was the finishing-post. The photo-finish with my long, proud nose ahead of the field. No, no, no, those misfits were not going to muck up my victory, my day of glory. No way. To hell with Frenchies! To hell with failure! And before I could even breathe in again, I was back on top of her, beating, pumping, drilling. How many times in one night could a man fail? It didn't matter. It didn't matter one iota to me. Even as the vomity smell from the old carpet rose in my nostrils, I knew I could do it, my little buttocks whirring, whirring, whirring, until I found myself praying for an asthma attack, a monsoon, a tornado, a flash flood, an earthquake, any goddamn natural disaster to save me. To save me from this! From sex! Whoever said sex was easy, enjoyable? It was bloody hard work, like trying to fix a flat tyre with a bent spanner. And then, again, it was Sophie, dear, dear Sophie Street, who threw out the liferaft.

"Quick! It's Jessica's dad. He's coming this way!" Her body jerked, throwing me hard against the wall.

"Phew!" I breathed out in pain and with exquisite relief.

I had been saved. I had been saved. To be honest, I still hadn't even heard the faintest evidence of the imminent arrival of Jessica Shmulowitz's dad, but I was only too happy to go along with Sophie, to spring to my feet with her and dress quickly. Out of the corner of my eye, I noted Sophie glancing at me with a mischievous half-smile, but inside my head all I could see was fog, thick, blurry, misty London fog. And now we were up, there was absolutely no turning back, no moving the clock back just a few minutes and starting all over again. Then, before I knew it, we were ready and dressed, and definitely I knew nothing, but nothing was going to give me another chance. I was finished. Sunk. Finis. End. Klaar.

Unlike the eager puppy who had followed Sophie into that dining-room, I exited it, following her like an admonished, injured old dog. And then I remembered it, the Frenchie, that stupid, rubber tube. In my mind I could see it lying there on the smelly carpeted floor, crumpled, unconscious, dead-looking, but no matter what, I couldn't leave it behind. Not for Jessica Shmulowitz's dad to find. Parents didn't exactly take kindly to finding Frenchies on their dining-room floors.

As soon as Sophie stepped into the lounge, I turned back and slipped into the darkness of the stuffy, sweat-filled dining-room and immediately dived down on all fours, feeling for the dead, despicable thing.

"What the hell are you doing?" I heard Sophie call out in a half-whisper, poking her head back into the dining-room.

"I, I, I . . . dropped some money." In the circumstances I didn't know how I managed to come up with that one so quickly, my mind was so muddy, so blocked.

"Can I help you?"

"Fuck! No . . .! I mean no, thanks."

"Alright, alright, I was only asking." And with that Sophie, to my great relief, slipped back into the lounge.

I was in a frenzy, scratching and tearing at the carpet, expecting Mr Shmulowitz to materialise any minute and ask what the heck I thought I was up to under his dining-room table. My neck was ablaze. My armpits were soaked. I thought I heard footsteps and dived flat to the floor, so that even if he walked into the room he might not spot me. Well, at least not immediately. Then I saw it, lying there, the see-through, long-nosed thing, stretched out like a dead, gutted squid, lying in the vicinity where our heads had been. God knows how it had worked its way up there. I quickly cupped my hand over it as if it were a wounded lizard that might suddenly spring to life and skitter away never to be found again, except one day by old Mrs Shmulowitz or, more likely, by the only person who ever got down on all fours in that flat, the maid. Scrunched tightly in my hand, I shoved the thing into my back pocket and then slapped my backside to make sure it was trapped tightly in there, couldn't fall out, could never get another chance to embarrass me again, and then I walked back through the rippled glass doors into the lounge, red-faced and self-conscious.

"Christ! Thanks for honouring us with your presence." Sophie flicked her hair back as I stepped into the lounge.

"Your old man . . ." I said looking at Jessica, avoiding Sophie.

"Oh, don't worry about him, he'd never come in here, he's just busy putsen around in the kitchen."

Sophie looked at me with droopy, cute eyes that said, *sorry for being so silly and getting us into such a mad panic*. She walked over to me and put an arm around my waist, which still managed to make me glimmer with pride. Pride and shame which I hoped Chaz and Jessica couldn't read in my face.

On the stereo the music had been allowed to play out and no one had bothered to change it or turn it off, leaving the record to just go round and round, making a sound that expressed just the way I felt as it wound through one useless bloody revolution after another: ssht, ssht, ssht.

"You ready to split?" Chaz called out the words, a thick barrel of smoke blasting from his nostrils, yet another cigarette dangling from his lips. He was sitting alone in an armchair now, well separated from Jessica Shmulowitz, who was back on the couch, one buxom leg tucked under one buxom buttock. Chaz's jaw clicked, more pronounced than normal, as though irritated, and out popped a suitably resonant ring of thick, wobbling, blue-grey smoke. He clicked his jaw again and a second, smaller blue-grey ring pursued and caught up with the first, the two for a moment intertwining, almost in anger, in argument, then melding, expanding, and dying in the general gloom of the room. Chaz's eagerness to go for once a godsend.

"Ja, OK, I'm ready," I mumbled casually as though unaffected by anything that had happened that night, in that room, under that dining-room table. In reality ready to burst out of the flat quicker than Jody Scheckter from a Grand Prix starting grid.

"Will I see you next week?" Sophie grabbed my arm tightly.

I cleared my throat, hearing for a moment the aimlessly revolving record again: *ssht, ssht, ssht*. I could only look down.

"I . . . I'll phone you," I said, almost a whisper, the shame perched on my lips. Hearing my crew, the manne, somewhere in the background, laughing.

I broke away from her and stepped back into the room to fetch my denim jacket, feeling her eyes following me, as though still trying to get a better answer out of me, something more finite. I found my jacket lying on the floor behind the couch, a dumb, crumpled witness to the crushing early rounds of the evening, when it all just looked like a matter of manoeuvring the prey into the right corner of the room.

I put the jacket on and walked unsteadily to the door. Sophie followed close behind. At the door, before I could even say anything, she gave me a sharp kiss on the cheek goodbye. I looked at her, embarrassed, crimson, flushing. Was it really possible that she didn't have any inkling of what had just happened in there? I couldn't understand why she wasn't as angry as a raging rhinoceros, ready to make me feel small in everyone's eyes. I looked at her, and while she didn't look happy, not happy at all, I saw no judgment in those eyes. While with hindsight I know I should have thanked my lucky stars Sophie was acting the way she was, instead I told myself it couldn't be so. Someone had to get hurt. That was the result of failure. Someone had to suffer.

As Chaz and I walked towards the lift, I waved to both girls, smiling and trying to display the initial confidence that I had galloped into that flat with earlier in the night.

"Yurrrgh . . ." Chaz and I turned to hear Jessica Shmulowitz's voice rising behind us as we stepped into the lift.

Chaz immediately reacted by turning to her with his fingers raised in a stiff, shaking V sign.

Then the iron grilles of the old lift slowly slammed shut and as I watched Jessica Shmulowitz and Sophie Street standing there I suddenly remembered it, the silver condom wrapper. I had left it behind.

"Shit!"

"What?" Chaz looked at me.

"Oh, no . . . nothing." My neck and underarms broke into a powerful sweat, but I decided immediately I wasn't going back to fetch it, no ways, not under any circumstances. Not even the thought of Mr or Mrs Shmulowitz staring blankly at the tooth-shredded silver foil when it gleamed innocently back at them from the dining-room floor could persuade me. I would let fat ol' Jessica Shmelly do the explaining. With her big mouth I was sure she could come up with something.

4

C haz and I, on our way back to Chaz's place in nearby Berea – a flat in a suburb of thousands of flats – walked up Rockey Street, past the heavily secured, bolted wooden doors of the night-clubs and the glass doors of the restaurants, craft shops and trendy dress shops that had suddenly sprung to life in Yeoville and now inter-mingled with the old fruit shops, corner cafes, bootmakers, cheap clothing stores and Indian tailors. Yeoville had become a surprisingly happy cosmopolitan stew of hippies, freaks, new-wave trendies, gays, try-hard-to-be-punks and leftwing radicals living alongside the long-established – mainly still deeply pro-apartheid – white families of English, Scottish, Italian, Greek, German and Russian-Jewish descent, whose numbers had recently been boosted with new lower-middle-class blood of white Portuguese emigrés from freshly liberated Mo-zambique and Angola. There were even a few trendy blacks who had crept into the suburb, though they kept a low profile, their public life in the suburb mainly restricted to night-life and hush-hush night vis-its to political friends. Topping this multicultural potage was an ever-stretching skullcap of Hassidic Jews, with their long black coats and black hats, long curling payers and yarmulkes. Their women, with their blonde and chestnut wigs sitting uncomfortably on their heads like dusty carpets, walked newly born babies in gigantic Victorian prams, while their husbands zigzagged around the suburb, lazily driv-ing over kerbs and knocking down kerbside waste bins in their second-hand Toyota station-wagons. There was a kind of freshness in Yeoville, pressing through the old drabness, that bravely spoke of what the country could be, what life for all could be, that it was possible to mix left and right, black and white, coloured, yellow, brown, Jew and non-

Jew. Even we sensed it, Chaz and I, the cultural flowering that was taking place, and we were children of the drabness.

We walked past a known gay club in the street, and despite the coldness of the night I felt a sudden heat rise in the small of my back. Chaz, for the thousandth time, taunted: "Poofter Palace. Bums against the wall!" I looked the other way this time, as if I had not heard him, was not even with him. It was not exactly what I wanted to hear right then, my mind still spinning from the events of the evening.

Further up the road, on a big red-brick wall in Raleigh Street – an extension of Rockey Street – which used to be the front entrance to the Yeoville police station, but which more recently served as the Yeoville telephone exchange – until, that is, it was burnt down or, as was more commonly rumoured, blown up by political saboteurs – a sign in bold white paint read: *Free Nelson Mandela. La luta continua!* And well beneath that, about three feet up from ground level, in very thin, very shaky, almost childlike white chalk strokes – obviously the work of the white teenage gangs who roamed the streets and scared the hell out of the likes of Chaz and I – was scrawled incongruously: *Spanish fly. Rock around the cock!* Chaz raised his hand merrily in a Black Power salute, and pointing to the childish scrawl below laughed, no kind of wolfishly howled, as we had done a hundred thousand times before. I turned my head; it didn't seem so funny any more.

"You haven't said a word since we left Smelly Shmell-o-witz's pad," Chaz said, his round frog eyes rotating in his head.

"Why, what would you like me to say? That I know ol' dung heap Shmelly gave you a shit of a time?"

"No . . . just like what happened, like, with you! From where I was sitting, it looked like you two were going great guns, man, pumping away . . . for Mother Africa?" He slapped me on the shoulder with a large, clumsy hand. "How far . . .? Oh no, don't tell me, you did it!" He looked at me, eyes popping.

"Yep . . ." Those three letters – Y-E-P – just popped out of my mouth like I had no control over them. I wanted a week, a month, a year to think about it, to frame a well thought-out, face-saving response, but suddenly there it was, the question, shooting through me like poison from a snake, and I had responded quickly, instantly, giving the response I wanted to give, was so desperate to give – thought somehow, after what the night had brought, the hours of sweat I had gone through, I deserved to give – but knew, knew I shouldn't. Even as I said it, the word "yep", I wanted to retract it, somehow slurp it back out of the air, stuff it back into my mouth, swallow it, then confess, tell Chaz everything. The truth.

Instead I lied. Not quite realising what the result could be, thinking only in some murky way that it could be dealt with later. Failure meant far too much. It was easier, so much easier to lie. It is the reason, I see, we become the men we are. Why there is so much violence and abusiveness and mistrust. And all I can think, even now, is that I had to, had to, had to. I was after all trying to be a man.

"You did! You did it! Jesus Christ! Too much, man." Chaz danced around me, literally beaming. He raised his hand into the air, as though getting ready for an arm-wrestle, and I reached out to it, clapping my palm onto his palm and then swivelling our palms until with curled fingertips we clenched our fists together and pulled tightly for a couple of seconds – a variation on many handshakes we'd picked up from watching the black maids and their male friends on our streets – hoping he could not feel in my hand, in my fingertips, the tremble, the quiver, the vibration that was the lie. That the strange vibration in my hand didn't somehow shoot across into his palm and spark something in his mind, because then he would turn around and accuse me, and then I would suffer, then I would know what suffering was. I would suffer forever at the hands of Chaz, socially inept Chaz Bernstein, who probably had little chance of doing it ever, well, until he was married some day. But it didn't happen. The vibe didn't make its way across into Chaz's palm. Chaz could be sensitive, but not sensitive in that way, to another person's lie, another person's bull-shit story. Nothing crossed into his palm, or his fingertips, and instead he simply went on like a madman: "Far out, man! Far bladdy out! No wonder you've been so bladdy otherwise. Shit, man, why didn't you say so sooner? This is incredible! C'mon, man, tell me all about it. What was it like?"

The electrification on Chaz's face was the excitement, the great uncontrollable joy I should have been feeling. I could understand it, Chaz's over-reaction: it was the willingness to share in a friend's con-quest, in a friend's glory – even if, measured in terms of competition, essentially that victory meant your defeat. But of course I hadn't done it, and because of that it was impossible, impossibly hard to show any enthusiasm at all. Instead of behaving like the proud initiate that Chaz was busy congratulating, I stood there looking more like a be-draggled straw guy after all the crackers had exploded, a guy well and truly smoked out and hosed down. I just could not fathom how he couldn't see the death in my eyes, the blank panic, the dark noth-ing. I wanted to be swallowed into the night, into the pavement, never be seen again. I wanted to be dead. I prayed for a terrorist's bomb that would suddenly blow up in front of us, I wanted to end up in hospital, unable to talk, unable to remember, please God, please God, yes defi-nitely unable to remember.

Instead I breathed out heavily in response to his question. "It was alright . . . OK, like . . ."

"It was OK. Is that all? OK?"

"I s'pose I'm still a bit . . . you know, like, shook up myself . . ."

"Jesus bloody Christ, Danny!" He stopped dead in the street for a moment, considering me. His protruding Adam's apple bobbing up and then slowly down like a cork on seawater, and then he said, sober-ly, as though having thought it all through: "I s'pose I'd also still be in a state of shock."

He looked away and from his jacket pocket he pulled out a very short, hand-rolled cigarette. It was a dirty yellow-brown and was three-quarters smoked. He crouched, cupping his large hands around a lighter, finally getting the tip of the thing to glow red. He dragged in very deeply, took two additional smaller puffs, held his breath tightly, so that I thought his froggy eyes would pop out of his head and smoke pour out of his ears, then passed the glowing cigarette end on to me.

"This calls for a gigantic celebration," he breathed out, smoke suddenly pouring out from his nose and mouth like a dragon.

"Ah-hem . . . n-not for me . . ." I said to his gigantic, dragon-like surprise. I was afraid that in my present frame of mind something would happen, something more, something like the rest of the night, something that I had absolutely no control over. Already my thoughts were jumping like a bush full of locusts from one side of my skull to the other.

"Jesus man, Danny, what's eating you . . .? I s'pose you feel all different now . . . all grown up, huh . . .? Huh . . .?"

Suddenly I had this clear vision of my two middle fingers poking out Chaz's froggy eyes, my hands taking hold of him by the Adam's apple and squeezing the cork in there until he dropped dead.

"It's just that I don't feel like talking about it . . . not right now."

"You don't feel like talking about it. Shit, man, I'd be fuckin' shouting it out and dancing in the street!"

He sure knew, even if he had every reason with this one not to know, how to make a person feel bad. I couldn't hold myself back any longer. In front of me I saw only red, and I lashed out at him with a punch that contained every bit of anger that was aimed at myself. The punch connected him exactly where I knew it would hurt most, in the soft muscle of his upper shoulder.

"Ow! Shit, man!" Chaz looked at me, stung, but too hurt to retaliate. He held his shoulder as though I had broken his arm. "What was that for? You didn't have to do that. For shit's sakes, man, I'm only being curious, you know?"

"Shit, Chaz. Shit, man. I just, I just need time, like . . . you know, you know for the experience to sort of filter through . . . like." He looked at me skewly.

"Well, how did it go with you?" I asked, eager to turn the conversation from me.

"A grip, that's it, like, nothing more . . ." He looked at me, eyes honest, lowering, a little frightened. His Adam's apple descending. "Actually it was vile. She's so . . . so fat and disgusting, man. All she can talk about is kaffirs and coons, and how they're killing one another, and how it's their own fault they live in poverty and in tin shanties. It's like talking to a brick wall. All I ask is, please, man, don't ever take me back there. I think I'd rather remain a virgin . . . well, like, you know what I mean."

"Hah . . . ja, ja, I know exactly what you mean." There was nothing like listening to someone else's problems when you were desperate to hide your own. I didn't even have to talk, hardly even had to listen, just nod my head and pretend to be there.

Chaz turned back to the flattened, yet still miraculously smoking scrap of paper left between his fingers. You could barely see the dirty brown speck. Nevertheless he managed to suck one last puff out of it, closing his froggy eyes in the process, and then flicked the remains, if you could call them that, to the ground, where he stood on the invisible thing, mincing it even further into the cement pavement. Such was the fear of being caught. The bravado that underlay it.

"What's the matter, Danny?" he said after a while.

"Ag . . . you know, it's not that there's anything wrong . . . it's just been a huge night, like, you know . . ." I was stumbling. "I'm . . . I'm sure I'll feel more like talking about it in the morning."

We passed under another streetlight. This one had no face, some-one had smashed it with a rock; maybe it had been hit by a bullet? Who knew? Someone was doing a lot of shooting in the country, a lot of breaking.

Chaz, zigzagging in and out of my path, looked at me, his eyes circling. "Don't worry, Danny, it's cool . . . I know you still really respect the chick, like. You don't want to give her a bad name. It's cool, I follow."

I breathed out, relieved. That he had found something to pin my reluctance on. My mind was flicking, spinning and the walk to Chaz's flat, though not that far, tonight felt like a marathon.

Finally, blowing onto our cold, numb fingers, we arrived at the entrance to Honeydew Heights, and caught the lift up to his fourth-floor flat. Chaz shared the three-bedroom unit with his mother, who had a reputation for being even more neurotic than mine – his father had died from cancer a couple of years ago, an event that still brought tears to his eyes – and his older sister, Marcie, who filled all of us with sultry, mouth-watering dreams. She read books by Emile Zola, was slim, yet voluptuous where it counted, and was, unlike Chaz, good-looking. It was hard to even put the two of them together. Chaz and his sister. It was like they were born of different parents. But as for the reality of our dreams, Chaz's sister barely said hello to any of us, barely even acknowledged our presence, not even mine, and I wasn't just Chaz's best friend – I had known him and his sister since Bernard Patley Hebrew Nursery School days.

Chaz's mother was asleep and the chances were his sister was still out as the kitchen light was still burning, the one that was always left on, to scare off black intruders, until the last person was home – except Marcie always switched it off, whether she was the last person home or not.

As we entered the flat, we veered off into the kitchen, and Chaz set straight down to making himself a chocolate drink, stirring four heaped spoons of Cadbury's Drinking Chocolate powder vigorously into the milk. Then, on top of that, he added a further thick layer of chocolate, which he allowed to spread and settle on the top before scooping it out of the glass with his spoon and into his pouting mouth. My stomach turned just watching him. It was like he couldn't get enough of the stuff. Despite his pimply skin condition and constant warnings from his mother and doctor that chocolate was the root of it, he slurped at the drink as if he had no fear. Once Chaz had scooped down the top layer of chocolate, he vanquished the rest of the drink without taking a breath, his Adam's apple careering up and down.

Looking at Chaz finishing his drink, I suddenly thought I should tell him the truth, before it was too late. Before there was no chance of retrieving the situation. Now was a good time – when the lion was full and satisfied and less likely to pounce – but something in me just couldn't do it. Telling him, I saw then, would not only completely crush me, it would crush him. It would change his whole world-view. Just the thought of him viewing me as just another run-of-the-mill failure, a loser, a nerd, a nebbish – the people we laughed at in the streets, at school – was just too much, too much for me. That was the thing about this kind of lie, it revolved around surface features, the gloss on the outside of the mirror – image, looks, ego, personality – everything that I was built on. How could you admit you were dead afraid when the people around you saw you as a lion-heart, a leader of the pack? Suddenly I could understand all the people who had ever lied, who had ever cheated. I knew them from the inside. I saw what they were hiding and I understood why.

"Urrrh," Chaz belched and, instinctively, I felt like I had made the right decision. I saw in Chaz's burp, in the gross way he glugged down his drink, that there was nothing, absolutely nothing he could do to help, to offer advice, to conjure a remedy. He just didn't know about these things. Not enough. Was too inexperienced. More inexperienced than any of us. And the chances were, behind my back, he would tell the others and laugh. On all fronts I was finished. I looked at him, and swallowed. It was better to live with the lie. Chaz patted his stomach and then placed the brown-speckled glass on the draining-board for the maid to wash up. Meekly, I followed him out of the kitchen to his bedroom.

Chaz's bedroom was small and the bed I slept in whenever I stayed the night was a fold-out, placed at right angles to Chaz's bed, against the wall behind which was Marcie's room – not that it meant much, but it did give a kind of skin-tingling feeling of close proximity. Once in bed, Chaz started muttering again, almost drunkenly this time, about my night's triumph: "Shit, man, Danny, that's great! Too much, man. Far out. Far fuckin' out, man . . ." But then suddenly it was like he was gone, like he had been transformed into an obedient bear, and all I could hear was a light snore, like a cat's purr, like the Chaz I wanted him to be.

Usually I could take Chaz's snoring – he always snored – or if I couldn't, I would shout at him or throw a shoe or some other nearby object at him, and usually it would be enough to get him to shut up, at any rate long enough for me to get to sleep. But it wasn't long before his snore tonight – soft and even and cat-like as it was – became intolerable. I felt like throwing not just a shoe but a whole cupboard of shoes at him. On the other hand, tonight I definitely didn't want to risk waking him; the last thing I could bear was Chaz, in his present frame of mind, waking up and raving on about how great I was. *Too much, man. Far bloody out, man. You should be dancing in the fuckin' street, man.* So I tried as best I could to ignore his snoring, but the more I tried the more his soft nasal vibrations became like a roadworker's drill. Chaz's room, though small, had never felt so compact, and the longer I stayed awake the more agitated I became. Soon my heart was palpitating like I had just run a hundred-metre dash; my stomach, on the other hand, though swirling, felt empty, like it had a hole in it. I thought I was going to bring up, with or without Chaz's snoring.

Finally, I couldn't take his snoring any longer. I grabbed a shoe from the floor and threw it at him, hard. Enough was enough. It hit him right on top of the head, and for a moment I thought I had done it, had fully woken him up instead of merely stopping his snoring. But in the end, an extremely befuddled Chaz merely raised his head as though he couldn't understand why the hell things might be falling on him from the ceiling, and without a word, merely a stunted croak, he put his head back on his pillow and went back to sleep. But this time in silence. In beautiful, blissful silence.

At last I could hear my own thoughts, terrifying as they were. It was like a cat-fight going on up there. One thought scratching, clawing, shrieking over the other.

"Sweet sixteen, sweet fuckin' sixteen," I remember mumbling, actually mumbling loudly, berating myself, "and pathetic! Crippled! Lame . . .! Impotent!" The word *impotent* unfurled in my mind like a giant banner across the sky for all the world to see. Instead of *Danny Rothbart First* emblazoned across the school hall, as I had once imagined, I now saw *Danny Rothbart Impotent* emblazoned in its place. I couldn't believe it, the gross Divine Injustice of it, I who had read all the books, who knew everything about love, romance, erogenous zones and coital ecstasy. I gulped in a deep breath, telling myself to remain calm, to analyse my situation rationally, but every time I thought about it, everything went crazy up there. I felt like smashing my fist through the wall.

And then I heard Marcie coming home. Unable to sleep, and with nothing better to do, I traced her steps, first to the kitchen where she switched off the light without even bothering to come and check whether Chaz was home yet. Then to the toilet, where after a while I could hear a flushing sound followed by a cranking noise in the building's cold metal pipes so loud I was amazed it didn't have the neighbours screaming out to tell her to shut it down. Thankfully it didn't wake Chaz; he must have been used to it. Next she shuffled into the bathroom, where I could hear a tap running, the sound of a toothbrush fanning teeth and finally a gargling sound, before she spat and dragged her feet into her bedroom and we were separated by a wall. A mere wall separating my body from Marcie's.

Through the wall I could hear the ruffle of clothes being peeled off, or at any rate that is what I imagined was happening, but once I had imagined that all sorts of thoughts began to trapeze through my mind, and I began to wish that it was Marcie I had been with rather than Sophie Street. Marcie, with all those extra years, all that experience. I imagined her in her room, her firm, round breasts staring out at me, and then I saw her moving off to examine her breasts in the mirror. She rubbed her soft, slender hands over them, caressing them and tilting her head coyly at the same time. In the reflection in the mirror I saw her looking between her legs, concentrating on that black velvet patch of fur; the velvet that was lost beneath Sophie Street's shirt that was pulled down to the top of her thighs like a trampoline. The velvet I had seen in all the magazines. Now she was whispering to me to touch her, almost begging, and I felt myself coming alive down there. It really was alive. Yes, still alive.

Then I heard a light click off, abruptly, like she had suddenly become aware of someone watching her and she was angry as a result. Her face transformed in my mind into that scowl she more often than not greeted me and the others with and suddenly I seemed to lose all feeling down there, my hands automatically moving up to my chest. Marcie was lost in her own dreams now, and the events of the night came back to me, crushing me under their weight.

I was confused. For years it had been there, alive, boundless, a genuine jack-in-the-box, uncontainable. Even in class, at school, behind your desk, at the oddest of times, you would suddenly feel it rising, as if it were obeying some teacher of its own; suddenly your biggest fear being called up to the blackboard. The only problem was getting it to relax, calm down, chill. But tonight, when you needed it to be normal, defy gravity, the laws of nature that it defied so readily every other five minutes of the day, oh no, suddenly it becomes a pacifist, a rebel, a peacenik. It did not make sense.

And then I remembered it, the still empty, crumpled rubber thing, waiting in my pants pocket for a decision about its future. Shit! I flew out of bed and began rummaging through my pants, keeping an eye on Chaz in case he should wake, in case I should suddenly have to jump back into bed as though I had been sleepwalking or something. But, snore or no snore, when Chaz slept he slept. Maybe it was the drinking chocolate?

Standing in the middle of the room, pants in hand, I pulled the dead Frenchie from the back pocket of my jeans. I looked at it for a while, pulling a tongue at it like an angry child. Cursing it like it was something alive, something you could speak to, blame. I curled my fingers around it and squashed it, as though to make sure that it really was dead, that it could not spring back to life. Then tiptoeing lightly, I quietly opened a window and threw it out, knowing it would fall all four floors into the building's little garden below, more than likely to be found one day and pondered over briefly by the building's black gardener, and then tossed out again.

I crept back into bed, but still I couldn't sleep. I saw around me only mountains, mountains of brick and more brick and more brick. It seemed there were no options. I had no choice but to keep it to myself forever, my secret, my lie, which would probably kill me. Just the thought of life without sex, without being able to boast just once was unthinkable to a sixteen-year-old who had built his whole life around doing it, had measured every success and failure around getting there.

The thought dawned on me that I could seek help from my older brother, Cyril. It was a possibility, a real possibility; we used to tell each other almost everything, especially about sex, even though mostly it was him bragging: I did this and I did that, and now when are you going to do this and when are you going to do that, nincompoop? But the plain truth, anyway, was that he was just too far away, too, too far away to present the sort of instant solutions I needed. Plus with Cyril there was always the risk that he would simply lie back in older brother fashion and laugh his head off. Definitely, I couldn't go to my parents. I could just see my father clipping me over the ear and calling me an imbongolo; and then grounding me for life. And then it came to me: Uncle Harold. Uncle Harold who had always offered a hand, who had given me the books to read in the first place! Almost ready to spring out of the flat immediately, I decided that first thing in the morning I would make some or other excuse to Chaz and then head straight off to Uncle Harold's shop. Nervous as I was to tell anybody about any of this, at last I saw in front of me a wonderful glimmer of hope.

5

I was up early next morning, eager to get out of Chaz's way, out of his claustrophobic flat, eager to breathe in some fresh air, to get into the city before I lost the little courage I had left altogether. I told a still groggy Chaz that I did not feel too well, and that I had to go home anyway, to finish work on an English assignment for class on Monday. Rubbing puffy, red eyes with big, anaemic looking fists, Chaz walked me to the front door, a sort of ambivalent look on his tired face. On the one hand he seemed to still be peering down at me with the infatuation of the night before, and on the other there was disbelief that I could have done the wondrous deed and still be so reluctant to even talk about it, let alone boast about it.

By the time we reached the door Chaz already had a lit cigarette dangling from his lips and was breathing out funnels of smoke from his thickset nose. Despite his mother's neuroses about almost everything else, Chaz was allowed to smoke at home. In fact he was, in not so many words, encouraged to do so by a chain-smoking mother who saw cigarettes as a terrific nerve-settler, a "natural" tranquilliser.

At the door, Chaz patted me on the shoulder and in a smoky haze winked exaggeratedly. I nearly doubled over in pain. I knew, I knew exactly what Chaz was saying with that wink. It was forewarning, a forewarning that screamed: *Don't worry, Danny, by Monday morning all the ouks will know. You'll be a hero.* I wanted to shout back at him: *No, please, don't! Please, please, don't!* Chaz's wink reminded me only too well that come Monday morning I would have to face up to a circle of friends wanting to know every last detail, every hand movement, the intricacy of every touch, the length of every kiss. What it felt like. How long it lasted. How good I was. Blast! Blast them all!

I swore to myself. But I knew from Chaz's look that there was no escaping. My only option was to somehow rebuild myself sufficiently to carry off the story, to be able to look them straight in the face come Monday morning and spout how magnificent, how superb I was.

Without another word I turned away from Chaz and walked to the lift. He half shouted, half groaned something in the background, but I hardly heard a thing, feeling only his eyes on my back as I was swallowed behind the steel doors of the lift.

Of course, instead of making my way home to my house in Bellevue, as I had told him I was going to do, I walked down an already fairly busy Louis Botha Avenue and hopped onto the first bus into town. I looked through the bus window over the little natural wonder in the middle of Johannesburg that was The Wilds, thinking how Chaz and I used to often go there on weekends, to smoke cigarettes, to pretend we were in the veld, to pretend we were miles from anywhere.

Feeling dizzy I jumped off the bus near the City Hall, at the terminus in Loveday Street. Almost as soon as I landed on the sidewalk I was confronted by a wire-thin black boy, who looked no older than eleven or twelve. Dressed in soiled, baggy khaki trousers and a thin grey jersey full of holes, he doffed a dirty grey cap at me. Looking away from him I immediately put my hand into my pocket and came up with twenty cents, which I tipped into the cap.

"Thank you, leetle baas. Thank you," he said in a cracked voice that sounded far older than the age his body suggested.

I walked on, down a couple of long city blocks, until I arrived outside one of the much larger of the second-hand furniture shops that crowded into the lower part of town. The old colonial buildings were no higher than four storeys, squat and obstinate-looking; they were built of red and grey stone and were dwarfed by the city's new towering silver-blue glass office blocks. Just to look at these new shiny edifices made me feel small and useless and grey. They leapt so slender and high into the sky it was as if they were striving to penetrate it, while below white families dressed in their Saturday best, black delivery men, black beggars, me, shivered in their cold, permeating shadow.

At the entrance to the shop I was about to step into, an old square neon sign bubbled dustily: *Golden's New & Used Furniture.* Just above the sign the company's motto, in ornate gold age-flaked paint read: *Golden by Name, Golden by Quality.* And pasted all over the shop's large glass windows, long blue, white and orange posters, emulating the colours of the South African flag, read alternately: *BARGAINS GALORE* and *STOCKTAKE SALE.* These same posters, or very similar ones, had been pasted on the shop's windows ever since, reaching no higher than his knees, I could first remember being brought to the shop by my father.

Under the fuzzy neon sign – even during these times of rioting and troubles in the townships – a black man with a big toothy-white grin dressed in black pants, white evening shirt and a thick red bow-tie danced and crooned to the mainly black passers-by, half clown, half jive: "Hello mama, hello baba, step inside, see our bargain furniture now. Something for everyone. Buy now-uh, pay late-uh!"

"Come inside, leetle baas. Step right in." The crier's voice followed as he waved me into the shop. Self-consciously I waved back, as I passed under a musty-smelling, yellow-stained armpit, but he had already turned away, singing to other potential customers.

Looking in from the street, you could barely see what exactly was behind the posters. Inside the shop all you could make out were rows and rows of wooden and aluminium tables, chairs, cupboards and, right at the back of the shop where they were almost impossible to get to, an assortment of heavy, squat, battery-operated portable record-players and radiograms that looked like they had been rescued from a World War Two bunker, but which were very popular amongst the blacks – the shop's main customers – because there was no electricity in the townships.

Inside, I saw three or four black customers wending their way through the maze of furniture, opening and shutting cupboard doors and knocking with their knuckles against items of furniture, as though testing whether they really were wood. Eyes downcast, I eased my way in and out of the maze, past these few customers, looking for the boss of the place, Harold Kleinhart, Uncle Harold. At last I spotted him in an aisle not too far away, pen in hand, standing leaning against a wooden desk. Despite an easy, relaxed stance, he kept pointing his pen purposefully at two black customers, an old, greying couple, who stood before him. Not wanting to disturb him, and still afraid to actually announce my presence, I stood back and watched as he waved and motioned, always winding up pointing his pen in the face of the elderly couple, who continued to look up into his eyes as though up to a deity.

I heard him explaining about a document that had to be signed and monthly payments that had to be made; the pink shirt that stretched tightly over his paunchy stomach shaking as he spoke. The shirt had a white collar that was stiffly bound to his fleshy throat by a yellow tie that now skewed sideways in line with his casual stance. His head, bald except for a few wispy strands of brown hair that crept over the back of his shirt collar, was large and round like pictures of Ancient Roman emperors. Like them, he exuded power; you felt the waves of it streaming from his body. You also felt it in his eyes, which exuded both a depth and a firmness. Looking into his eyes you saw, definitively, why he and not his opposition from the National Party was sitting on the Johannesburg City Council, why he and not his opposition within his own party was poised, at any rate strongly rumoured to be poised, to take over as mayor of Africa's richest city.

Gaining courage, I walked a little closer, to make my presence felt. It took a while, but eventually he spotted me, and while still poking his pen forwards and holding the attention of the couple in front of him, he called out loudly: "Danny! Howzit! Good to see you, my boy. What are you doing here?"

I was trembling at the knees; the complete opposite of the Danny

Rothbart who had danced into Jessica Shmulowitz's flat like he owned the place only a matter of hours before.

"Just thought I'd pop in, like . . . say hello," I managed to say.

"Good. Loverly," he called back, almost singing. "I'll just get rid of these people, and I'll be with you." His face alight for a moment like that of a young boy.

He waved over to the other side of the shop and a dull, teenage-looking junior shop assistant walked slowly over to him. He explained to the assistant where they were up to in their dealings and, winking sideways at the boy, said, "Maat, it's just a case of showing them where to sign." Smiling he waved to me to follow him.

"Here, take a seat," he said as we arrived at a cluttered desk near the back of the shop. He threw himself into a chair on the other side of the desk. "Good to see you, Danny. Really, loverly," he repeated about three times. "It's not often you come in here – to see an old friend?" He smiled widely. "In fact, I don't remember you ever coming in here without Stan the Man." He meant my dad.

It was true, in all the twelve or so years I had known Uncle Harold I had never ventured into the shop without my father, but then again, I never really felt easy about coming into the shop alone. Uncle Harold was still, after all, only an old family friend, and that basically meant Dad's friend. The handing down of books, pictures, poems, magazines and advice had really only started over the past year or so, and it was always done at home, usually at odd moments, when Uncle Harold called around to our place early and had to wait for my father to arrive home from work. Often, at those times, he invited me to come and visit him in his shop, and although I always said "yes", when push came to shove, I never felt I could comfortably barge my way into his shop and simply say: *Hi, Uncle Harold, I'm here to say howzit.* Today was different. I was desperate.

"Well, what've you been up to? How are ya, Danny, my boy?" Harold was leaning forward, trying to make me feel at ease.

"D-d'you think we can talk . . . a-a-lone, like?" Next to Harold's booming, singing voice I felt like I was talking in a squeak.

"Of course! Right here," his eyes lit up. "Why, is there something the matter?"

"No . . ."

"Yes . . . There's something the matter, isn't there, I can see it?"

"No . . . Well, ja." I could feel the sweat on my forehead, but there was no point in holding back now.

"Well, c'mon then, let's go into my private office," he said, pulling himself up out of his chair.

Harold's private office was set still further back in the shop. It was built of thin masonite partitioning which stretched from floor to ceiling and – unlike the rest of the shop floor, which was covered in speckled blue and red vinyl tiles – the office floor was covered in carpeting, thin, dusty-looking and turquoise, but carpeting nonetheless. The office was more than a comfortable size, but other than the carpet and Uncle Harold's large, expensive-looking wooden desk, was exactly the same as the rest of the shop – cluttered with bits of broken furniture and clusters of old, worn lounge cushions. It was hard to match the office to the man who could be the city's next mayor.

Harold's desk, huge and solid, stood out like an island amongst the rubble, and that was where we sat now. On the desk was an unlit silver study lamp – its long, narrow face pointing straight into mine – and three small, ornate silver picture frames that pointed into the middle of the table so that even from where I was sitting I could see the brightly smiling faces in them. I had the feeling they were specially positioned like that: so that anyone who came into Uncle Harold's private office could share his proud view of them.

The picture closest to him was of a very pretty blonde: Thelma Goodman, his latest partner. I often heard my father saying to my mother that Uncle Harold had sworn never to marry again. That he would rather live *in sin*. Sometimes I thought I saw a glint of agreement in my father's eye, but my mother would simply glare at him until the glint turned into a more agreeable furrow of disapproval.

The middle frame contained a picture of Uncle Harold's two grown-up children from his first marriage, one of them in a cream-coloured dress-suit and the other, with long flowing brown hair, in a black graduation gown.

The third picture showed off two widely grinning young boys, one with no front teeth. These were Thelma's two young sons from a previous marriage, but who Uncle Harold always said were like his own. He gave them everything they needed, maybe even more than his own children, but, as my father always said, that's how big Uncle Harold's heart was.

"No need to feel embarrassed, Danny, you can talk to me." Uncle Harold nodded warmly. "There's nobody around here who can hear us. I promise you."

"Eh-hem." I cleared my throat.

"Yes, go on, don't be afraid. Remember, Danny, whatever it is, I'm here for you, I've told you that many times before . . . "

I really didn't know where to begin. I became aware of my clammy hands clasped together in my lap; my neck was hot, stinging. I had thought about this moment so many times through the night and now I felt like I should have gone for rehearsals.

"Yes . . ." he coaxed again.

"Eh-hem." I tried yet again, my throat sandy and rough, knowing I really couldn't just stop and say nothing now. "I-I . . ." I began badly and then tried again. "Eh-hem, I, well, I had my first . . ." And then my throat completely stuck, clammed up just like that, like it didn't belong to me. In response he nodded, encouraging me with those deep-set, brilliant blue eyes of his and finally I managed to get my voice to re-engage. "I . . . I had my first real, my first real chance, you know, like . . . last night . . ."

"Ye-es . . . and . . .?" Harold looked for a moment genuinely baffled.

I guessed that what I was trying to say was not exactly a part of his everyday vocabulary. Nevertheless, having begun, I had to go on.

"I was with, you know, Sophie last night . . . you know, Sophie Street, the one I've mentioned to you before . . . the one I told you I had a chance with . . ." He nodded his round head, pointedly, serious. "Well, last night, like . . . well, she took her clothes off for me, like . . . but I couldn't . . . I-I couldn't, you know, like . . . get it . . ." I looked into his eyes and felt my entire body flush. "No matter what I tried . . . it just, you know, like, it just . . . wouldn't work . . . you know . . . I just couldn't . . ."

"Ye-es," he said, nodding, "aaand . . ."

"I-I even tried, you know, to put a Frenchie on. You know, like . . . like you always . . . but, eh-hem, noth-noth-ing . . . I feel . . . I dunno . . . you know, shattered, like. Absolutely . . . shattered."

"Easy Danny, easy now, just slow down, take a deep breath and re-lax," he said, and clasped his hands under his chin as though in deep contemplation. After a moment of silence, he looked up and said, "You know, it's very brave of you to come in here and tell me something like this." He looked at me as though he was trying to see something deep inside me, something beneath the flesh. I looked down. "Have you told anyone else . . .?"

"No." I looked up again. "You're the only one. I-I wasn't sure—"

"Good." he stopped me dead in mid-sentence. "I don't think anybody else should know about this. This isn't exactly the sort of thing you just go and tell anyone about." I blinked. It felt like at last somebody understood and was taking control. For the first time I began to feel more confident about my decision to come to Harold Kleinhart, about lying to Chaz.

"You know, in all the years I've known you, Danny," he said, "I've always felt you would never come to me of your own accord, and that's exactly why I've always come out to you. This is no light matter, I know, and I'm pleased, very pleased you've come to me. It shows character,

real strength of character just to be able to talk about these things."
He suddenly smiled, and offered something that really made me feel
a thousand times better. He said, "Don't look so glum, boychik, it's not
the end of the world. There are solutions, you know." And that was
exactly, exactly what I wanted to hear.

"You know, it's all . . . everything . . . it's all . . . everything, like.
Everything in me. Crumbled. I dunno . . . I just dunno." I felt like I
was choking.

"C'mon Danny, c'mon, my boy, everything's going to be alright."
He said it like someone holding a grieving person and trying to make
them laugh. "Don't feel so down-hearted. I'm sure that basically there's
absolutely nothing wrong with you." He raised his almost invisible
eyebrows and leaned forward in his chair, speaking softly now, as
though in strict confidentiality. "Just remember, Danny, there is always a way out. Always. I can tell you that, because that is probably
my biggest lesson in life. There is always a way around things and it's
not always as difficult as it looks. In fact, as Napoleon put it," he
raised an arm into the air, "'The only way round is through.' And that's
what we're going to do with you, Danny, we're going to find a way
through."

My heart gave a loud drum-roll. He was speaking the language I
wanted to hear. Just the language I wanted to hear. Instinctively, I felt
I had come to the right place. In front of me I saw a man with the experience to put me back together again. I saw for the first time why,
despite everything, my parents respected him.

After considering me for a while, he said in a calm, relaxed tone,
as though he could have been talking to my parents: "Tell me, Danny,
do you play with yourself?"

I nearly fell off my chair, at the same time unsure that I had heard
right, whether he really meant what I actually thought he meant. I
wanted to say: *What do you mean, do I play with myself? Do you mean,
am I a loner? Someone who plays by himself, like with make-believe*

friends? But the way he looked at me, the man-to-man look that was inscribed all over his brow now, over his wide forehead, told me that he meant what I had not expected him to mean, but what I knew, deep down, he must have meant. I was shocked. What did playing with myself have to do with it? What did it have to do with anything? Uncle Harold, anyway, should have known the answer to his own question – why else all the sexy pictures and poems and magazines handed to me from his own past, his own youth? Did he not play with himself? Ever? In his whole life? I felt my face redden like it had been forced into a pizza oven.

He winked at me. "You don't have to be shy with me, Danny. You should know that by now. What's more, you've just done a very brave thing by confiding in me. And I mean *very* brave. I was also young once, you know. Looked at pictures, read magazines and things like that."

"Yeah, I know." I pulled my fingers back and cracked my knuckles nervously, only half-looking at him.

"Well, the only reason I bring it up now is to make you aware that sex is natural, as completely and utterly natural as playing with yourself." His voice, deep and reassuring, maintained an evenness, an unbreakable control that made me look up at him. "It doesn't give you headaches, you know?" He looked at me and I looked back at him to show that I had read the books he had given me and I did know. Acknowledging my look with a smile, he went on: "You know, Danny, there's nothing, absolutely nothing to be ashamed of in it. Everyone does it. Everyone." He paused. "Even birds, you know? It's just old hogwash that there's anything wrong with it. You don't ever have to feel guilty about playing with yourself, Danny. It's like going to the toilet, natural. But if you feel guilty about it, it can be painful. Very painful." Uncle Harold sat forward in his chair again. "What you have to realise is that birds want it just as badly as guys. Oh yeah, they may protest, but they want it just as much." He pointed his index finger at me. "It's not a one-way thing, you know, else there wouldn't be such a thing as sex."

"Ja . . ." I nodded – as if I too were an expert – thankful that he was talking to me in this way, because other than the books, I had no idea.

"You know, Danny, guys your age aren't meant to be taking on the whole world. I know you, Danny Rothbart, I know you more than you think I know you, and I know how you feel about politics and people's suffering. I know from what your parents say about you, from the little conversations we've had in the past, and just from observing you, but guys your age aren't meant to be worrying about these things. Not the way you do. Guys your age are meant to be going to parties, getting pissed, getting off with birds. Your whole problem is that you worry too much, create mountains out of molehills. I know, I've had a lot of time to observe you over the years . . . and I think that's where your problem lies, always making big things out of little things. Making big g'vald out of little g'vald. Danny, you've got to learn to relax, to accept life for what it is, for what it dishes out. In the same way, you've got to see that sex is just a natural act, as natural as . . . yes, as I said before, pulling yourself off, going to the john, as eating or drinking."

I sat there in silence, looking into his eyes, grateful. Even with Chaz and the guys, whenever we spoke about these things, it was mostly in a show-off fashion, as a challenge: who would be first, how far had we gone. And it was true, what Uncle Harold had observed, I did worry about everything. From my parents suddenly dying on me – getting killed in a car accident or something like that – to the way blacks were treated in everything-banned, half-starved, only-for-privileged-whites South Africa. I worried about school and about exams – I had already messed up my June mid-year exams, and now I had to do extra well at the end of the year to make it to varsity. If I did not, there was no hope, absolutely no hope of avoiding the army.

And under no circumstances, no circumstances at all, was I going to end up in the army, pointing a gun at blacks anywhere in defence of apartheid, in defence of a country that banned John Lennon – I mean imagine banning John Lennon and The Beatles from the state radio waves because John Lennon had simply said what was probably true: that The Beatles were more popular than Jesus. And absolutely not for a country that didn't even allow nudity – or even the slightest whiff of sex – on its movie screens. Often when I couldn't sleep at night I wrote poems about what was going on in the country. Poems about the cold brutality of whites. Chaz and I had made a pact on it, that if we couldn't delay the army by going to university first, we would skip the country together. But currently it looked like I was going to be the only one skipping, because Chaz was so bright, so extraordinarily bright at school, while I was languishing well below the average. Bordering on failure. Ironically, when it came to sex, I hadn't really worried about it at all, the only worry being when, with whom, how well.

"You have to understand," Uncle Harold shook me out of my thoughts, "that we can't spend our lives worrying about everything. Life has to go on. If you don't live it, nobody's going to live your life for you. Other people will look after themselves. You, Danny Rothbart, like the rest of the world, have got to look after yourself. Have got to see yourself as number one. At your age there's no need to put anybody before you. Believe me, Danny, there's plenty of time for politics, for righting the wrongs of this world, plenty of time for worrying about the rest of the planet."

"Ja, but . . ."

"You see, there you go." Uncle Harold stopped me short. "There's no 'ja-buts' about it, Danny, you've just got to stop fretting about everything. You've got to learn to take yourself and the world around you less seriously. You've got to lighten up, boychick, learn to take life more in your stride. Take it as it comes, with all the ups and the downs.

Believe me, you'll find there's lots more ups and downs than you think, but by taking things in your stride, by going with the flow, you'll find your problems won't seem so big." He smiled that reassuring smile of his. "Don't look so downhearted, my boy, I promise you, we'll get you right . . . Remember under every dark cloud there's always a silver lining. Always."

I shifted in my seat. Something inside of me telling me that there actually was hope. That here in my father's friend Uncle Harold's shop I might well find a cure, a remedy, a treatment. I only wished that it could somehow all be more magical, more instant, that after all this talking, he would simply click his fingers and I would be fine again.

"Danny, you know, I'd like to talk to you much longer about this and about everything else," he said, raising those invisible brows. "But maybe now isn't quite the right time. If I'm not out there on the shop floor this place falls to pieces." He lifted himself out of his chair and walked around to me, placing a warm hand on my shoulder. "I really think we must spend more time, perhaps an entire morning or evening some time, talking about this." He paused. "Look, I know this is serious, very serious to you, so how about tomorrow night, Sunday. Are you doing anything?"

I cleared my throat, sorry that nothing definite was being done right now, no instant magic, but Sunday, tomorrow night, was not too far off, not too far off to offer a chance to retrieve myself, to reinvent myself for Monday morning when I faced the guys.

"No . . . just schoolwork," I said. "Tomorrow night will be good."

"Good. Loverly. How about I pick you up just after supper, say about seven? Just tell your old folks I'm taking you with me to visit a customer, showing you a bit of the business."

"Yeah . . . fine."

As to the old folks, as Uncle Harold called them – as though he were one of us, the ouens, the crew – I was sure they would not stop me from going with him to learn about the world of business that, to their great disappointment, I had shown absolutely no interest in up until now.

"Will you need a lift home?" Uncle Harold asked.

I shook my head.

"C'mon, I told you, Danny, you don't have to be shy with me . . . here, I'll get you a driver." He immediately stuck his head out of his office door and shouted: "Petrus! Petrus!" Until a thin, greying black man, stooped, hands tucked into his stomach as if in pain, arrived in the office.

"Ja, Maste' Harold?" Petrus said in a small voice, his tiny, raisin-dry eyes lighting up in a smile.

"Will you take the young boss here home. You know the place, Big Boss Rothbart's . . . there in Bellevue."

"Ja, maste'." Petrus smiled at me with patchy, nicotine-stained teeth.

"In the meantime, Danny, have a good look through some of those magazines. I'm sure it'll help to put a bit of perspective on things."

I smiled back at Uncle Harold, appreciatively, and then followed Petrus out of the office and out of Golden's New and Used Furniture. In front of me a beam of white winter sunlight, streaking through the city's tall silver-blue buildings, looked like a ray from heaven. I crossed my fingers, and drew in a deep breath of smudgy city air.

6

I arrived home to one of my mother's specials.

"Danny! Darling! Where have you been?"

"I told you yesterday afternoon, I was sleeping at Chaz's." I clicked my tongue.

"Oh, I must have forgotten. You know, you could have phoned or something, just to make sure we knew."

"But I already told you."

"Well, alright, but don't you think you'd better get yourself into your room now, you've got exams coming up soon . . . and you still want to make it to varsity, don't you?"

"Yes, yes, for Christ's sake, don't have a bladdy cadenza!"

"Danny, you know I'm only trying to help. Now come here and give me a big hug hello."

"Shit!" I exhaled under my breath. There was nothing like coming home from a night out with the guys, the crew – a night of rumbling on the couch, a night of near initiation and in this case near suicide – and then being cuddled by your dear, sweet old mother like you were still a little boy.

"There, now just a kiss, and off you go."

"Shit!" I swore under my breath again, but it was too late to escape and I pecked her anyway, as was the custom – and had been the custom ever since I could remember – twice on the lips. I felt a strange piercing heat rise through my body. A kind of irritation.

"Was that so bad, to give your mother a little hug and a kiss hello?" I stared at her blankly, not saying a word. "OK then, off you go and do your homework. And just remember next time to remind us when you're going out for the night. You're my only boy now, I don't want to lose you too!"

I clicked my tongue and turned away, heading straight to my bedroom. I wanted to avoid any further nagging, which came easily to my mother. In any event, the only place I wanted to be right now was alone in my bedroom. I certainly didn't want her to see me in the state I was in, moping and brooding about the house. That, no doubt, would elicit questions and she was sure to have something to say on all of them. *Too many late nights! Too many girlfriends! That's all you care about. Girls! It's time you spent more time at home, concentrating on your schoolwork. And when are you going to come with us to visit your bobbe? She hasn't got much time left, you know. I think she'd like to go to the other world knowing she's still got a grandchild!*

It wasn't that I really hated my mother, despite that instant feeling of uncontrolled heat that seemed to rise whenever she wanted to smother me with her hugs and kisses. It was more a case of wanting her to realise that I had grown up, that I wasn't her little baby any more. It made me squirm the way she wanted to hold on. Yes, I knew she, rather than my father, was always the one to run to when there were problems at school, problems with other kids, problems with your older brother, problems with dad himself. And then she would cuddle you into her arms and you would enjoy it. But the problem was that when it came to real problems, problems like this, I knew I could never talk to her. Not about this, not the problem I had just been to see Uncle Harold about. There was no way in the world I could talk to either of them, mom or dad, about that. About anything like that. Just the way she mentioned girls was enough to make me feel bad about having dates, about going out with them. Even if underneath it all I did sense a certain pride in her that they were at least interested in me.

So shutting my mother – as far as that was possible – out of my mind, I locked my bedroom door behind me and then stripped out of my jacket and pants. I switched on my little blow-heater because it was very cold in the room, and in the silence that settled on me, I lay on my bed allowing the past day or so to filter randomly through my head. I remember thinking to myself, over and over, that it wasn't even twelve or so hours ago that I was *that* close. *That* close. That by now I could have been a man. Number one. Relative even to my own short life, it was like seconds, mere seconds ago.

There seemed, right then, to be no room for miscalculations in life. None whatsoever. On the one side there was the possibility of success, happiness, on the other destruction, suffering, despair, pain, failure. It was amazing how long the list could be on that, the negative side of the line. And the barrier between the two worlds was so thin that it almost didn't exist. One tiny mistake, one teeny-weeny misstep, and life was black, black as hell. And there was no stepping back and seeing things in some sort of perspective. There was no such thing as a molehill. Everything was Mount Kilimanjaro. Everything. Despite Uncle Harold, with his bigger, wiser, older shoulders, it seemed impossible not to make mountains out of molehills, not to make big g'vald out of little g'vald.

The thought crossed my mind that perhaps I was being punished. For what? By whom? I didn't remember being particularly bad or sinful, certainly not the way you read about some kids, especially in America. Overdosing on drugs, dropping out completely and totally, holding up their teachers with knives, shooting one another in gang wars. Cheeky, yes, I was that, full of myself, yes, I was, but surely not cheeky or full enough of myself to bring this punishment down upon me? So the question was, if I was being punished, why was I being punished? It could only have been for my thoughts, the way I thought. Were my innermost thoughts, my fantasies, really that bad? So bad that God had singled me out, out of everyone else in the world, for a gigantic smack on the head? The word impotence popped back into my mind. Impotence: the abject failure to turn theory into action. No, worse than that, it was an abnormality, an abomination! I hated the sound of it, hated it, hated it, hated it.

72

Then a thought crossed my mind: had my circumcision something to do with it? That little snip at eight days old that you had absolutely no say in? Could that little shaving of the wick, my wick, have disconnected something in there that made it operate? Was that possible? Was it?

It was time to test the waters. Yes, I had to gain perspective. I struggled to my feet in a kind of fuzzy daze and scraped under a pile of winter shirts in my cupboard, feeling first my once trusty, now virtually discarded flick-knife, and then sliding out from under it one of a small pile of creased, yellow-stained magazines.

Magazine tightly in hand, I shuffled back to my bed and began to flick through the pages. I was trying to be rational, as calm and rational as I could. What was it that had scared me? What was it that had made me so tense and nervous and stiff in all the wrong places? Maybe, truth was, I actually was allergic to the female body? Just as I remembered we always used to say in nursery school: "Girls give you germs. Don't kiss them, they'll make you sick." And yet my eyes had roamed these pages so many times before, with such electrification, such deliriousness.

Then another thought rocketed through my mind. Was this, was this thing that was happening to me, was this the time when boys, the time when boys began to question, to question whether they really were, really were? I couldn't even finish my own question. My hands were shaking. I could hardly hold the magazine. The only contact I had had with boys like that was to point fingers at them – the one or maybe two at school. There were probably dozens more, but with attitudes like ours there was no way they were coming out of their closets.

"Bums against the wall, here he comes Johnny Twinkletoes, that rabbit, poofter, queer, homo, arse-rammer! Let's get out of here!" We didn't even try to whisper it, the idea being – if I remember correctly – to let them know that we knew they were rabbits, homos, poofters, and that because of that we were somehow better, cleaner, more normal than they were. Just the thought of those taunts had my head wheeling.

Thursdays, for some unknown reason, were known as "Rabbits' Day". The one day of the week specially reserved for homos, queers, rabbits, gays, poofters, to date, hang out and breed. To say to a friend that you would meet him on a Thursday never failed to evoke a knowing glance, a derisive laugh, a sarcastic accusation. And now I was asking myself if Thursdays weren't also my day? I felt the sweat rolling down from my armpits, and when I looked down at my few sparse hairs under there, it seemed to confirm everything.

With the magazine still somehow upright in my trembling hands, and having decided there had to be another true test of manhood – other than actually doing it – I set myself my own little test. If the pictures brought on a reaction down there, I was OK, if not I was done for, one of them, a rabbit.

I began to turn the pages, slowly, my jaws tightening; hit first by the Italian magazine's business section – slick cars and suave dark men in silver suits. I turned those pages – any pages with men in them – quickly, like they didn't exist, like I had not seen them. Sweat was dripping between my thighs; they were so hot I had to flap them open and closed like a fan. I turned another page and suddenly, without warning, without a hint of build-up, my eye hit it: a naked, crocodile-brown, sunburnt figure, slithering out of the page. I blinked and turned another page. This time the same sunburnt figure was lying backwards, away from me. Yes, this was the picture; this was the test, the real test. I looked closely at the page; the breasts were extraordinarily large and shaped like light-bulbs, the sort of light bulbs you put into floodlights in huge football stadiums. She held them up, in her white palms, like they were great weights, mammoth pawpaws, her yellow eyes looking menacingly coy as she slid her hands over the length of her breasts, as if offering these mighty mounds as a gift to the hungry.

Now I made my way down to her legs, which were stretched out on the blue satin sheets, slightly raised, spread apart, just the way you would want them. Tensely anticipating a reaction I allowed my eyes to steer over the oily body, slowly turning my eyes, like headlights, over every curve of the brown, sunburnt skin. Surely by now if I was what I thought I was, what I claimed to be, I should be feeling something? Something? A flicker? I gritted my teeth, feeling my skull about to burst, but as to a reaction down there: nothing, not a twitch.

I felt sweat drip from my forehead down my right temple, mixing with my hair. I breathed out and laid the magazine down on my chest, deciding to take a short break, turning my eyes to the ceiling in prayer. Then, I lifted the magazine up again, giving myself a second chance. This time, calmly, at any rate more calmly, I allowed my eyes to navigate the page, until there, right there, in the midst of all this mushy flesh, my eyes collided with it: the oily, brown, sunburnt figure's wild bush of curly black hair. And there, right there, stood this Gothic creation, a brilliant pink cat's eye staring back at me. Although my eyes had roamed these pages so many times before, suddenly now, it made my stomach jolt and flinch. It was like I had never seen this picture before. Not quite like this.

In my chest I felt a drum-roll. I blinked, my eyes wet with worry. So, what was I? I couldn't be. Just could not be! I had to try again. Perhaps I had approached from the wrong angle? Concentrated on the wrong aspects? Was too tense, too critical, too unappreciative? What was the matter with me? The sheet beneath me was soaked in sweat. I had to lean over and switch off my little blow-heater.

I decided to try again, this time taking in the naked body – the spreadeagle thighs, the extraordinary breasts, the coy, yellow eyes, that pink Gothic cat's eye – as a whole. And when I did this – saw it as a thing in general, not a thing in its parts – to my relief, to my great relief, a warm, fuzzy feeling flowed through my body. But that was all, just a warm, goodish feeling; otherwise, not a sign, not a twinkle.

So was I or wasn't I? On the face of it, the evidence was looking bad. I was confused. Brutally confounded.

I was driving myself crazy now and I knew I was driving myself crazy, but there was nothing, absolutely nothing I could do about it. I was digging a hole, and for some crazy reason I just wanted to burrow in deeper and deeper. Talk about making mountains; I was digging holes, and not just ordinary holes, but massive meteoric craters. And I had no idea what any of it meant, except I was in it, deep in it, and it looked like the end of the world. I looked up again at my dull, white ceiling, and this time I shivered. I blinked my eyes, hearing myself breathing in and out rapidly. I thought I was having a thrombosis.

Suddenly there was a banging on my door. I jerked my hands up to my chest and quickly crumpled the magazine under my pillow.

"Daaa-nyyyy! Daaa-nyyyy!" The unrelenting voice of my mother. "Luuunnch is reeeadyyy."

"Alright!" I screamed back. "Don't lose your hat. I'm coming!" She really had a sense of timing, that woman.

There was no choice; I had searched every corner of my skull, and could find no way out. I would just have to leave this entire mess for Uncle Harold to sort out.

7

A t exactly seven the next day, Sunday night, Uncle Harold arrived at the front door. "Never be late for an appointment," he
once told me in one of the rare lessons he gave me on business, "you
could lose the ballgame." Even our rotund, normally surly-faced maid,
Faith, who answered the door put on a wide grin for Uncle Harold.
Actually he almost bowled her over as he bounced, full of energy, into
the lounge. Freshly shaved, his face shone as he stood under the
brightly lit chandelier in the lounge. I, by contrast – at the dinner
table with my parents in the adjoining dining-room – sat sullen and
depressed. I had to rub my eyes twice when I saw the way Uncle
Harold looked, colourfully dressed in his red Dean's smart-casual,
box-square pants and mustard turtleneck jersey. Nevertheless, I did
feel a bit special that tonight Uncle Harold was not here for my dad,
or my mom, but for me.

My father, on seeing Uncle Harold, took a heaped spoon of his
custard dessert and, shovelling it into his mouth, leapt up from the
table with a broad smile on his face and an outstretched hand to greet
him. My father, Stan, slow and getting on in years, but still broad-
shouldered and strong, tugged vigorously at Uncle Harold's pink hand.

"Good to see you, Harold," my father beamed, his large shoulders
expanding as he continued to shake Uncle Harold's hand. "I understand you're going to be showing the boy a bit about the business
tonight?"

"Yes, yes," Uncle Harold smiled back proudly. "I want Danny to
come along and meet some of my contacts, show him exactly what
can be achieved in a weekend of socialising. Show him a bit of the
real world." Uncle Harold looked sideways at me and winked, at the

same time waving a hand at my mother, eager to show he had not forgotten her.

"Any time spent in your hands is always time well spent," said my father, pointing to a chair.

As Uncle Harold sat down, my mother called my father back to the table to finish his dessert. Reluctantly, he lumbered back to his seat at the head of the table, and after a couple of mouthfuls he was scraping the plate. My mother took that as her signal to ring the small brass bell that was shaped like a Victorian damsel with a long, starched dress and hair in ringlets. The bell, during meals, was always placed at my mother's end of the table. A few seconds later Faith appeared, waddling into the room with a big wooden tray, and began to clear the table.

Both my parents rose at the same time, my father still wiping the corners of his mouth with a white linen serviette, which he threw back, crumpled, onto the table, before they both went to join Uncle Harold in the lounge. Feeling anxious and uncomfortable, I remained at the table, sitting low in my chair, still slowly dabbing at my dessert with my spoon as Faith, her face having re-established its usual thick scowl, mopped up around me.

"Hau Danny, how long you going to be?"

"OK, OK, I'll bring my own plate into the kitchen," I said, glaring at her. She looked at me exasperated, but carried on clearing the table around me.

From where I was sitting, facing directly into the lounge, I could see my mother sitting alone on the vibrant orange and gold-specked three-seater couch. Despite her frail physique and her delicate cheeks, which hung on her thin face like sunken muscles, she still managed to retain a certain elegance, an attractiveness. And if you believe, as they say, that worry gives you grey hair, my mother proved them absolutely wrong. Despite constant worry over everything – ninety-nine point nine percent of it trivial – she still had a full head of wavy, undyed chestnut hair that was the difference between her looking well into middle-age – which she was – and old. Her thick hair also gave her otherwise ragged body a sense of presence, a kind of quiet assertiveness. To my embarrassment she would often remind people proudly how they used to say she looked just like Judy Garland.

"C'mon then, Danny, you better finish up there and grab a jacket. I'm sure Uncle Harold hasn't got all night," my father, who was now standing with Uncle Harold in the middle of the lounge, hurried me on.

Immediately I threw down my spoon and left the table.

"Don't bring him back too late . . ." I heard my mother's voice as I walked to my room. "I don't want him turning into a tsotsi."

That, in effect, was a slap in the face for Uncle Harold. No one, but no one cast aspersions on Harold Kleinhart. I knew that my mother admired Uncle Harold for the way he had built up his business and political career, rising, as she and my father had often told me, from a poor home and tiny second-hand shop in the goyishe southern suburbs. But she also made no bones about her disapproval of his broken marriages and the fact that he was now living in sin.

"Look at him," she would often say to my father, "flits from one marriage to the other the way some people eat the k'naidlech in their matzah-ball soup." Of course she would never say that directly to his face, but she said enough to put Uncle Harold on notice that she didn't approve of everything he did, just because he was so well regarded in the city.

I arrived back in the lounge with a heavy, three-quarter length, navy-blue sailor jacket hanging off my shoulders, but my mother immediately drove me back to get a jersey. "It's freezing outside," she said, "you'll catch double pneumonia."

I rolled my eyes, but went back to my room anyway.

Behind me I heard my father appealing to my mother: "Stel, let him be. Let them go already. It can only do the boy the world of good to learn a bit about business. He could do with a bit of saichel."

I returned to the lounge, now wearing the jacket and the jersey under it, to see my father winking at Uncle Harold. Uncle Harold nodded to my father in acknowledgment, and said, "There's absolutely nothing to worry about, Stel, I promise you. We won't be late. There're just a couple of business friends I have to see. I think Danny can learn a lot from listening to them, and then it's straight back home. I promise you."

My mother twisted in her seat, looking at me, I thought, with a sense of misgiving, like she was hoping that I would only learn the good lessons that were to be learnt from life.

"Danny, where did you get that jacket from?" she said. "It looks like a dog used it to sleep on." I could immediately see what was on my mother's mind – that I would embarrass her while I was out with Uncle Harold visiting his friends. "Put something else on, Danny. Quickly, while there's still time."

I turned and opened my mouth to say something reasonably loud in my defence, but Uncle Harold winked at me, and the message came through loud and clear that this was not the time. Consequently, instead, I just stood there looking at my mother, feeling ashamed that she still treated me like a child. Had treated me like a child in front of Uncle Harold, who was going to help me unravel problems bigger than Mount Fuji, problems the nature of which she could not even begin to imagine.

"OK then." She looked at me despondently. "Go. Wear whatever you like. You won't listen to me anyway." She said it with a kind of concealed affection rather than anger, I think embarrassed to pursue the matter further in front of Uncle Harold.

I shrugged, and Uncle Harold winked at me again. I waved goodbye to both my parents and headed straight for the front door. Behind me I heard my father's voice directing itself to Uncle Harold. "Cheerio, and just take your time," he said. I could hear how proud he was that I should be learning some lessons about the world from Uncle Harold and at that moment, for just a moment, I don't think he thought I was such an imbongolo.

Outside the house, despite the overriding darkness, Uncle Harold's shiny red sports car still managed to gleam. Next to it, as he walked around the car, his red pants fused with the car, an identical red. The car was a 1975 E-type Jaguar, making it only a year old. Uncle Harold once told me and my father it was the very last of the E-type models to roll off the factory floor.

Inside the car, Uncle Harold's huge frame pressed against the miniature racing-style steering-wheel. Looking at me over his outstretched arm, he said, "You know your old folks only want what's best for you, Danny. I can understand how you feel, but they're another generation. You've just got to take what they say with a pinch of salt. Basically, they're very good people, you know."

I nodded, smiling, nervous. Feeling the car rev, then purr as we sped off at high speed, my feet pressed to the floor as though to apply the brakes.

I thought of telling him about what had happened when I looked at the magazines, but then decided I didn't want to make a fool of myself and would only tell him if he asked. But he never did. I think he must have forgotten his advice to me.

As we drove along, he announced: "Look, there is someone I have to see on our way. It won't take a few minutes and then we'll go straight on to the shop." I looked up at him questioningly, thinking we were going to his house in Kew, and he said, "It'll be easier to talk there, at the shop. At least at the shop there's no one to disturb us. It's completely private."

I nodded, stiffly. I could feel a tight knot in my stomach.

"Danny, you know, you look as if the world's coming to an end?" I nodded yet again, struggling to breathe, and he smiled. "I already told you, Danny, don't worry so much. If there's one thing we do, we'll get you right." He looked at me, fatherly concern in his eyes, the slick nose of the glimmering car steering us through the dark suburban streets like the Batmobile.

The house in Lower Houghton, where Uncle Harold stopped off, was a stately, southern-American colonial-style mansion with Hellenic pillars holding up a broadly curving balcony under which we had to drive to get to the front door. Inside the house a black male servant, dressed in a white jacket, led us through a passage with a white marble floor into a sunken lounge where I was introduced to a youngish couple: Harry and Freda Silverman. The couple were smartly dressed – tie, suit, black evening dress – and, I surmised, either worked on a Sunday and had not changed since coming home, or always dressed in their own home as if they were on the verge of going out somewhere posh. It was not the way I wanted to live, ever.

Soon after we arrived in the lounge, a maid, in a stiffly starched white apron, led two young, shiny-faced children into the room. The children unleashed themselves from the maid's hands and began to dance around Uncle Harold, while she merely smiled, curtseyed and left the room. They shook and pulled Uncle Harold's hands boisterously, punched his stomach and pecked him on the cheeks as he leaned down to them, saying: "Howzit! Howzit! Howzit!" The children, a boy of about five and a long-haired girl of about six, kept jumping up onto Uncle Harold and butting their heads into his stomach like it was a soft ramming cushion. While the children were doing this, Harry Silverman offered Uncle Harold and me: "A whisky . . . ? Tea, coffee, biscuits, cake, dinner, anything, anything at all?" To all of which Uncle Harold, looking at me and then smiling at Harry Silverman, said, "Naa, naa, naa, ta, ta."

I discovered something now I had not known before. As the children jumped up and down and carried on around him, they kept referring to Uncle Harold as HK, and Uncle HK. "Uncle HK this," and, "Uncle HK that." There was obviously a section of people, close to Uncle Harold, perhaps children only, who referred to him simply and affectionately as HK. The initials suited him, like the epaulets on the shoulders of a great commander.

After a while, with the children still spinning berserkly around him, their parents watching, grinning broadly, Uncle HK literally picked up each of them in turn, like they were mere paperweights, and then placed them on a well-cushioned Idaho couch, telling them with a friendly finger in front of his lips to "Zip it!" They laughed and screamed: "HK. Uncle HK!" But in the end they zipped it. Then he and Harry Silverman left the room, Uncle Harold telling me they'd be five minutes, and Harry Silverman telling me to make myself perfectly at home. I sat down quietly on a heavy, immaculately white armchair, feeling like just by sitting on it I was somehow dirtying it, while Freda Silverman glided out of the room, in another direction, telling me not to worry as the kids would keep me entertained.

And this they did, plying me with a hundred questions: What school did I go to? Did I play soccer? Tennis? Chess? Did I support Highlands Park? Did I have TV? How many sets? And asking me if I wanted anything, anything at all, because if I did: "We'll just ring for the girl and she'll bring it for you."

I was thankful, even if it was more than half an hour later, when Harry Silverman, followed by a smiling Uncle Harold, arrived back in the room and Uncle Harold immediately announced our departure. The children, seeing us to the car – now my friends as much as Uncle Harold's it seemed – jumped up and down shouting: "Bye, Uncle HK. Bye, Danny." Finally the car's wheels spun on the pebble driveway, and we zoomed off through the Silverman's high wrought-iron gates.

"What was the visit for?" I asked as we drove through Lower Houghton's wide, tree-lined streets, where the houses sat in leafy gardens, set well back from the road, like miniature country estates.

Uncle Harold thought about my question for a moment, and then said, "Danny, it's called keeping up alliances. Footwork. You know, Harry Silverman is a big macher in the Prog Party. He's a hard worker and big donator, and his support is going to mean a lot to me in the future. We also do business together. He's a furniture manufacturer, one of the big ones, so I always make sure I buy plenty of stock from him. You see, it cuts two ways: he massages my back, I massage his. But, really, I have known Harry and Freda a long time, since they were teenagers, and they've always known Thel and her kids. A loverly couple, really. Nothing's ever too much for them. And they're true Progs, you know. They have African friends, wealthy Afs who would join the party tomorrow if they could. Harry has literally given away a small fortune to build African schools in the country."

"Oh . . . it's good to know there are rich people like that," I said nodding, showing Uncle Harold that I approved. He smiled back at me, but there was still a tight knot in my stomach.

* * *

The streets outside Golden's New and Used Furniture were empty, the black tar road running by it like a big, dark river. Town on a Sunday night, especially this part of town, was like a deserted Aztec city – short, squat buildings surrounded by tall skyscrapers, but with no hint of a people to breathe life into them – the myriad black passers-by that filled the streets by day reduced to shadows.

Outside the shop door, Uncle Harold pulled out a heavy bunch of keys from his pants pocket. Crouching, he began to open up the various locks on the door, slowly working his way upwards, one by one. The door open, he waved me inside before putting his hand out and switching on a row of fluorescent strip-lights that illuminated the row upon row of wooden and aluminium tables, cupboards and chairs. And then there was silence, something in that brightly lit silence that was eerie; under the strip of light the jumbled furniture looked like the preparation for a giant Aztec sacrifice.

Uncle Harold locked the door behind us and told me to go to his private office at the back of the shop and switch on the table lamp in there, the one that stood next to the pictures of his loved ones. When I had done as he asked he switched off all the fluorescent strip-lights and joined me in the office, pushing the head of the table lamp down low so that it cast our shadows like giant shadow puppets over the masonite walls.

I felt jumpy, anxious, like a child called into the principal's office for something he had done wrong, now waiting to explain, waiting for the principal's reaction. Of course, I had been looking forward to this meeting – was relying on it, was pinning all my hopes on it – but now that it was actually happening, I felt half-petrified. My stomach felt mushy. I didn't know what more I could tell Uncle Harold, what more I could say. Not knowing what to say or do, I stood there frozen as Uncle Harold moved in closer to me and looked deep into my eyes as though wanting to elicit from them a sign of my backing, my trust. I looked back at him, I hoped communicating to him that he had all of the above, and I saw his eyes soften.

"You know, Danny, what you told me yesterday was a very honest thing. You were very brave." He was more or less repeating what he had told me the day before.

"You always said to come to you if I had a problem . . ."

"Yes, yes, and I'm glad you have, Danny. Very glad. To come with this sort of problem, you know, shows a lot of character. Great courage. And I promise you, if there's one thing we do, we'll find a way through."

I wasn't sure how to tell him that what he had just said was exactly what I wanted to hear, that all my hopes now rested on him, that more than anything I wanted to be able to walk into school the next morning and at the least, at the very least be able to smile when I faced the guys. But even though I had put my faith in him I found it hard right then to say something corny like: "Uncle Harold, I'm pinning all my hopes on you." So I just stared back, waiting for I don't know what. The remedy, the miracle, the magical words to drop from his lips.

Instead, he simply looked at me with a kind smile, and said, "You're tense, Danny. Much too tense for someone your age. You've got to learn to relax more. You'll see, my friend, alles sal regkom, in the end, alles sal regkom." There was something very soothing in his voice that made me feel reassured.

"Do you feel shy with me?" he continued.

I shook my head, as if to say "no", but Uncle Harold obviously saw through my lie, no doubt because of the deep crimsoning in my face, and he said, "You know, Danny, you don't have to be shy, not with me . . . not with anyone. I think that's a part of your problem." I nodded, shyly, but he was beginning to talk my language, was reading me. "You see, Danny, this is what I want for you. I want you to be a normal ouk, a normal guy who goes out with the birds, who has a good time, and never has to feel he is shy or embarrassed in front of anyone. I think you are capable of that. Well capable. It's just that there seems to be a wall, this wall that you always put up in front of you, that you constantly hide behind. And that I'm sure was the problem the other night. Well, now I want you to climb over it, I don't want you to spend your life hiding behind a wall." I nodded, and he said, "If you want to get ahead in this world, if you want to be yourself, you have to be prepared to speak up, be heard."

I looked up at him, swallowing, wishing someone, even my older brother, had spoken to me like this a long, long time ago.

"Danny, you know, you're no ordinary kid," he said, surprising me, surprising me that he could see beyond ordinariness in me, and for a while, as he continued, I wasn't sure which way to turn, only recognising that it felt good to have someone notice these things in you, especially when you had as good as thrown in the towel on yourself. "You're different," he went on, "you have a very creative mind, and I think because of that you're very sensitive. Maybe too sensitive. Things are going to turn out great for you in the end, that I can see, but you have to remember what I started telling you yesterday: you can't take every problem in the world and put it on your shoulders. At your age, especially at your age, you have to put yourself first. The rest will follow. You've got plenty going for you, much more than most, and you've got plenty time. Just don't waste it tied up in problems that aren't yet your own." I looked up at him, feeling incredibly small and innocent, like I was a child looking into a brand new world. "And remember, you should never have to feel guilty about anything, like you owe anyone anything. Or that what you do, whatever it is, is wrong or sinful. It's all normal stuff. All normal stuff for a young guy. Look, Danny, I know the books have told you most of this, but it is you who has to believe it. You. In there," he said, pointing to my chest.

I looked up at him, a small child unleashing admiration on an adult he suddenly discovers really understands small people like himself. I felt I was experiencing a new zone, a world where it was okay to discuss your inner thoughts, yes, even sex, or any of the sorts of things for that matter my friends and I would discuss – but only on a more mature level, without all the giggling, the bravado. I felt like I was really seeing Harold Kleinhart, Uncle Harold, Uncle HK, for the first time, and I wondered for a moment how he ever got along with my parents.

"I want to show you something tonight that I know will help," he said after a pause, and my heart leapt. I mean really leapt. He looked away from me and I thought he was about to walk away, to fetch whatever it was he was going to show me, that would bring me back to life, but then he suddenly turned back and looking at me intently, seriously, said in the softest but most controlled of voices: "Danny, I want you to take your pants off."

I nearly farted.

"My pants?" I asked, shocked. It didn't sound one iota like the correct conclusion to what we had just been discussing.

But all he said in response was: "You're not shy, are you?"

I shook my head.

"Well then," he said, "remember what I told you, there's no need to be shy, and definitely not with me."

I felt stunned, like someone had shoved a club in my face, but when I looked up into the calm in his eyes and thought about all the years my family had known him, thought about what we had discussed the day before, the books he had been giving me, I saw no reason not to think anything but that what he was proposing was, as he himself said, good for me. It was just a shock that it was this, this sort of thing that he was asking me to do, and we were two males. Males. I felt a spasm run through my stomach as it suddenly crossed my mind that this could really be the beginning of some bizarre Aztec ritual. Who knew, with the books Uncle Harold had read, the knowledge and wisdom he carried around in his larger-than-life frame, what remedies he may have in mind? Perhaps this was some new therapy I had never heard of, but that was being used all the time in the world out there, the world I was just discovering? The world banned in South Africa? Perhaps this was the next step in growing up?

"Danny, honestly, there's nothing to be afraid of, this is only to help you," he said as though reading my thoughts. "What we are going to do is completely and utterly for you, you'll see."

In all honesty I was afraid, but I looked into his eyes and saw such gentleness, and behind that gentleness the promise of the cure to the most debilitating problem a man could have. Seeing this concern and the promise of what could be, I actually began to feel encouraged and started – albeit very slowly and very, very shyly – to unbutton my fly.

He turned away, I knew to make me feel easier. And I appreciated that. Uncle Harold's sensitivity.

When I was completely naked, he considered me, a slight smile on his lips, but as if not one bit interested in my undressed state. It was more a smile to tell me I was doing fine, and he said, "Here, I'll put the heater on . . . that'll make you feel warmer." And he raced off, returning with a small blow-heater.

"Thanks," I said, dragging it out of the back of my throat. In the back of my mind unwanted thoughts suddenly flashing about perverts and deviants and queers and things, but when I looked at him, I saw no reason not to believe. Not only that, I wanted to believe. I thought for a moment as I faced Uncle Harold of my father, and knew that if he saw me now he would be furious, shouting that I had no backbone, no chrain, was like gefilte fish; an out-and-out imbongolo. I nervously patted my clothes – which I had neatly folded on an office chair – like the poor guest at an expensive dinner-party, not knowing what to do, how to act.

Looking up at Uncle Harold, he seemed so much greater, so much more cultured than me. His eyes looked somewhere in my vicinity now, I thought trying to show me his presence was of no great consequence, other than that of helper, guide, counsellor. And when I looked back at him, seeing how busy and important his life was, how significant and essential he was to those around him, how absolutely small and insignificant I was, I saw that he did not have to be taking this kind of time with me.

"How do you feel?" he asked tactfully.

I looked down over my knobbly knees.

"Ah-hem . . . O-K." I could barely breathe.

"Good . . . you see you don't have to be shy in front of me, and that's what I'm trying to show you, Danny, you don't have to be shy in front of anyone. There's nothing to be ashamed of in your body and that's what you have to keep telling yourself. There's nothing to be ashamed of." I looked up at him and he stared down at me, gently drawing me deeper into his eyes. "Danny, I just want to assure you that what happens here is not what others might take it to be. You know me well enough. I don't need other guys, especially young guys, or dolls for that matter. And if I did I wouldn't be here with you, there's plenty out there. But, Danny, you've come to me with a problem and now all I want to do is help." Once again I looked up at him, giving him the reassurance I think he needed from me.

"Good," he said. "Here now . . . lie on the top." He patted the top of the large wooden desk. I looked at him, a little confused, and he said, "Oh yes, of course, give me a hand and we can lay out some of these old cushions . . . it'll be a lot more comfortable."

Feeling clownish in my undressed state and still wondering about the thing he had asked me to do – lie down on his desk – I neverthe-less bent down alongside him, and began picking up cushions and making a bed of them on that desk.

Strangely, in all of this to-ing and fro-ing, this fetching and carrying of cushions to make a bed on top of his desk, there developed between us a kind of camaraderie, a kind of bond, a closeness that only two people involved in the same secret mission can have. I even managed a half-smile, venturing to ask when the bed on top of the desk was ready: "Which way should I lie?"

Uncle Harold smiled back and good-humouredly threw his hands into the air as if to say it did not matter in the least, was close to a stupid question.

But the truth was I was unsure of myself, like a child on a nursery school gym. Awkwardly I crawled over the top of the desk and lay down.

"No, not on your stomach, on your back," he said.

I turned over.

"That's it," he said. "Remember, Danny, with me there's absolutely no need to be shy."

I felt a warmth flowing from his voice, but nevertheless looked straight up at the ceiling, too afraid to look directly at him. I sensed him positioning himself at the side of the desk, alongside the region that was the source of this entire episode. The table lamp, pushed to a corner of the desk, now shone over his face like the light on a sur-geon in an operating theatre.

He touched my skin lightly, delicately, skimming his fingertips over my thighs and my stomach, telling me to relax, that everything would be alright. That I would feel better afterwards, that everything would be alright in the end, that I would arise strong and confident. I looked up at him a little hesitantly, but he looked down at me with such striking poise and directness that I immediately felt certain. He told me to think of girls now, naked girls, "birds", as he called them – rather than "chicks", as we, my friends and I, called them – and to think that I was lying next to them, about to put it in. Birds or chicks, whatever he called them, he was talking my language, and it made me feel good, like I was among my own.

And then suddenly something popped and it was like a shaken Coke bottle had burst, and the gas was spurting through the closed steel top. It was like I was fully awake again, bright white-light shooting in my forehead, and Uncle Harold was looking down, with a large smile on his face, asking how I felt.

The strange thing was I felt relieved, like something in me had been released, shaken off, cast out. I felt like a kite – light and breezy, floating on air – and I told him this.

"Good," he said, "that's how you should feel. It's how you should feel with the birds too, Danny. You know . . ." He looked at me, as though seeing a flicker of doubt in my eyes. "This has got absolutely nothing to do with guys going with guys, just remember that."

I'm sure I must have sighed, because he smiled and winked at me. "Danny, what this is about is getting rid of inhibitions, showing you that sex, pulling yourself off, being with birds, is normal, just normal activity for young guys your age, and you don't ever have to be shy, or feel guilty about it."

Remarkably, at that moment, I felt I could have taken Sophie Street in my arms and straddled her with ease, right there and then, Frenchie and all. If only I had come to Uncle Harold sooner, the thought kept running through my mind as I lay there looking up at him. Then he moved away from my side and bent down on the other side of the desk, searching in a drawer.

He came up with a handful of white tissues and handed them to me with a kind of fond motherliness. Then he glanced at his wrist-watch and it was like everything came crashing down.

"Holy hell!" He clapped a hand against his chest. "Your old lady will throw a fit! We'd better get going, boychik."

At the entrance to the shop, watching him secure the locks on the door, the cold air hit me like a sobering shower. It brought with it a new reality, a reality that I felt like a new-born calf in – shakily struggling to my feet. A reality where I was not sure what was real, had actually happened, but which I somehow, unfathomably, felt incredibly light in, like I had lifted a great weight from above my head and then suddenly let it fall to the floor.

"At least we've made a start," he said, as we slid down into the soft leather comfort of his low-slung sports car. "I'm glad you came to me when you did, Danny. Soon you'll have nothing to worry about. You'll be cruisin'. Lovin' 'em an' leavin' 'em."

"Yeah . . ." I nodded, my voice so soft I could hardly hear it.

* * *

Pulling the car up outside my house, he said, "Danny, what you've got to learn is to let go of yourself. You've got to tell yourself to lighten up, get the most out of life. You know what Oscar Wilde once said?" I shook my head. The only thing I knew about Oscar Wilde was that he was gay, and therefore suspect. "Well," Uncle Harold said, peering down at me, "he said: 'The trouble with youth is that it's wasted on the young.'" Harold considered me for a moment and when he saw no immediate response, he smiled and then, looking straight ahead at the road again, said, "Never mind, Danny, never mind, we'll get you right yet. That's the main thing. It'll all fall into place. You'll see."

Now looking up at my house and the single light that was still dimly burning to show there was still someone due to come home, he added: "You must remember, Danny, there is absolutely nothing wrong with what we did tonight. It is only because of the way the world is at the moment, because of the narrow way people think, that what happened tonight should remain strictly between us. That's not the way I want it, but I'm afraid that's the way it is going to have to be." He waited for a moment, and hearing no verbal response, said, "I want you to promise me you'll never tell anyone about tonight . . ."

"Ja. Of course," I felt the words dripping almost immediately off my tongue. "I won't tell anyone, I promise." It felt so easy. At last I felt like I was getting somewhere, I had found someone who knew what to do, who wasn't afraid to take action, to do whatever needed to be done. I felt encouraged, and thankful. As to telling anyone else about what happened, in reality, I didn't think I could anyway. No one would have understood. Not Chaz, not my brother Cyril, not any of the guys, not Sophie Street. I was sure that I held in my hand a secret, a handsome secret that very few, if any, had tried or knew about, and that was daring, daring like sinking a bottle of wine or smoking a pack of cigarettes underage. It made you a cut above, different, someone to be looked up to.

"When will I see you again?" he asked, obviously satisfied with my response, but I could only shrug my shoulders.

"Well, how about not this Wednesday, but next Wednesday night then? About six, after I've closed the shop? You can tell your old folks you're going to be helping me with some stocktaking. I won't get you back late. How does that suit? I'll pick you up?"

"Yeah . . ." I nodded, still excited that even if not quite by magic, things were happening. The situation was being taken under control.

I breathed in and opened the door to get out of the car.

"You'll see, Danny." He stretched over, calling through the window. "Everything is going to work out. Just go with the flow, my boy. Just go with the flow. Alles sal regkom."

8

Monday morning hit like a hangover. While I was sure I was getting somewhere, I still had to convince everyone else that I was already well off the ground, already a man. Without Uncle Harold at my side it would have been back to square one. Shivering with foreboding I met up with Chaz – as was usual during our school lunch-breaks – on the tarmac in front of the cold, red-brick Victorian school building, the building that sat so square, so smug, so prohibiting, and that I swore now looked exactly like a surly Queen Victoria. I could hardly walk upright, but somehow Chaz didn't seem to notice. We ambled along the outer fringe of the sacred rugby fields – it was prohibited, at fear of the headmaster's cane, to walk across the hallowed turf – to the very back of the school grounds where the swimming pool was. Behind the southernmost pool wall, on the grassy mound we visited almost every lunch-break, we loosened our bottle green and red striped school ties and sat against the picket fence that marked the King Edward VII School boundary.

Around us gathered our closest schoolfriends, Solly, Peter, Aaron: the crew. Chaz and Aaron immediately lit cigarettes and began to compete at blowing the biggest and best smoke-rings. Click. Click. Click. Ring after ring. Big ones. Small ones. Round ones, wobbly ones, failed and broken ones. It was Monday midday and everything about the day had Monday written all over it. Still tired and grumpy from late weekend nights, we stared through the eternity of the week to when it would be Friday again. The talk, too, had a Mondayness about it – the usual chatter and banter about setbacks and advances; usually quickly mentioned setbacks offset by boastful talk about advances which, more often than not, amounted to no more than wishful thinking.

The competition among us was fierce. The objective was to get over the line, first if possible, but get over the line at all costs, and they, the girls, were the opposition, the other side, the enemy. It never really crossed our minds that perhaps you had to get over the line with them – that it could be an experience that was shared. And that's why Uncle Harold's remark of the day before – that I had to realise that girls wanted it just as badly as guys – had come as such a revelation. Did any of the others realise that?

I sat there, in our circle, shivering. I no doubt looked pained, leaning back against the picket fence, my mind still suffocated in a weekend of experiences that were reshaping the entire universe; cruelly destabilising what I once saw as a smoothly oiled, finely rotating galaxy. I sat there and listened, amid their smoke-rings, not contributing anything, keeping silent, for a brief moment believing that because they had not yet mentioned anything, I could escape the net. And yet, and yet if things had worked out differently I could have been sitting there smiling, unable to shut my trap. Instead, I found it impossible to so much as twitch a lip, but I could tell from the way Chaz kept looking at me – out of the corner of a winking, fast-moving froggy eye – that I had to keep trying, had to show some sort of inner radiating glow of success. If only he could keep it to himself, but of course I knew he couldn't. You could see it in the momentum of his Adam's apple, rock 'n rolling up and down his neck like Little Richard, about to twist, shake, explode. And finally it did explode.

"You know, Danny scored. Friday night!"

"Shiiiit, reeeally!" All eyes suddenly on me.

I looked across at Chaz, his spotted face suddenly seeming somehow pinker, splotchier, more mucousy, uglier than ever. I could have strangled him, but I knew deep down that he had only done what he had to do, what any of us would have done.

"Yeah," I said nonchalantly, knowing I had to respond, and fast. My voice distant, somewhere outside of me.

Then Peter, sticking his freckled nose into the air, looked around and pronounced: "Shit man, you don't say. That's great. You must be in heaven!"

It was like the official opening of the floodgates.

"So, Danny, why the scowl?" Cynical Solly, my closest rival in the race.

"Yeah-yeah," Aaron, nodded, agreeing, blasting tubes of smoke out of both nostrils. "You should be glowing, man, like Jesus, not looking so bladdy miserable."

I nearly shrank into the collar of my school blazer. Despite the cold, my neck and armpits were like fire. I looked around to Chaz, appealing for support, but all I received in response was a hero-worshipping wink. At least he, Chaz, was still convinced.

"Who with?" Cynical Solly.

"What's't to you?" I snapped, and immediately saw myself on the run; but in this instance, by luck, could have only been luck, my curtness paid off, at any rate had the desired effect. I was protecting my chick after all, and seeing my aggressive response it was like suddenly they were now all convinced, and their tone changed.

"Hell, Danny, you can tell us, we're not going to spread it around . . ."

"Yeah, c'mon . . . we're not going to say anything . . ."

"Well, OK then," I conceded, as if I was doing them a great favour. "Sophie . . . you know, Sophie Street." My throat was lumpy, tense, the fire in my armpits raging.

"Well, how was it?" Solly was sitting slumped now, hanging his thick, curly head of black hair, his cynicism transformed into disappointment. But his enquiry only unleashed a chorus of "yeah-yeahs", as they all chimed in behind him, ears cocked, leaning forward, almost into my face.

Keep your cool. Keep your cool, I told myself.

"It was, well . . . O-K," I started, breathing in. "I mean, like, it was cool, like . . . like fan . . . tastic, really."

"What did it feel like?" Aaron, glassy-eyed, like Chaz, always wanting to know the last detail, making sure he'd heard it all.

"Yeah, what did it feeeel like?" Solly, now also with a cigarette dangling from his lips, breathing out smoke. A dragon. All of them dragons around me. Solly the hardest dragon to look in the eye, somehow the most dangerous, capable of frankly, cruelly exposing the truth to everyone, to the whole school.

I took in yet another deep breath. "Like . . . like it's hard to describe. You . . . you'll see . . . You'll know when you've done it. Like you'll just know. Know what I mean . . .?" I was getting braver. "It'll come, don't worry. Your turn'll come."

"C'mon Danny, don't be such an arsehole." Solly put a blunt perspective on the matter. "What the fuck's got into you? Why the sudden hush-hush, secret-secret stuff? She's only a chick, you know. Not the Queen of bladdy England."

"Yeah, c'mon, man," Chaz breaking in unexpectedly, making the hairs on my neck prickle. Now that he had the whole crew behind him, he had turned. He smiled, pressing me.

"OK, OK, calm down," I said, trying to give myself breathing space. "I just didn't want . . . I just didn't want . . . Look, actually, it was fuckin' great . . . All like moist 'n great 'n orgasmic-like." I could feel hot sweat trickling down my neck.

"C'mon, everything! How did you get her undressed, like? How did it really feel?" Aaron again.

"Fuck you, Aaron! You think I'm gonna give a chick a bad name just because you want to know everything . . .? I still have respect for her, you know. I'm not about to dump the chick just because she let me!"

They all fell silent, not sure how to react. I think Peter even grabbed for a sandwich, buried his freckled nose in it. I seized the moment, springing to my feet.

"Shit, I just remembered my history book's still in the library . . . check you ous in class later."

As I turned, ready to run, holding back, not wanting to show I was running, I heard Peter behind his sandwich, pointing his straight, freckled nose towards Chaz: "What the fuck's got into him? Thinks he's bladdy Lord Byron now!"

"Shit, I dunno . . . just dunno . . . been like that all weekend . . ." I heard Chaz's reply trailing behind me.

"What an arse . . ." I'm sure I heard Solly beginning to add.

I hurried towards the school building, half-walking, half-running, knowing full well I was really going nowhere, feeling their voices, their remarks cutting like a butcher's cleaver into my neck, my eyes, my groin. They couldn't be trusted. If – no, not if, *when*, when they found out, they'd string me up. They'd draw blood. They'd have my testicles. I was done for. But I knew I would have acted the same, exactly the same, and that's what made it worse, that much worse – to know that you would have done exactly the same to the very people whose razor-blade eyes, whose slicing tongues you now wanted to tear out. And what about Uncle Harold? What if they found out about him? They would never understand what was between us. What it was doing for me. Just thinking about it was too much to bear: one day hero, the next day faggot! Bloody faggot!

I couldn't breathe, and as soon as I reached the low-set sandstone wall that formed the perimeter of the school tarmac in front of the red-brick Victorian school building, I sat down on it, my head swirling.

Little form one kids were suddenly running around me and I couldn't understand what all the fuss was about. I even grabbed one, a very small one, by the collar, but he looked at me, eyes spinning curiously, like I was completely mad, and I let go of him, drawing only a crowd of innocently spinning little form one eyes, threatening: "Big prick!" Which of course, if only they knew it, was true, and yet nowhere near the truth.

Sitting at my desk, in a classroom now, I felt tense. The air was thick and the room smelled of sweat. I could smell my own sweat, something I could never remember being able to do before. I remember thinking I should be smiling. Smiling, for God's sake! I forced a smile and my lips cracked. I'm sure they cracked. I could hear them cracking. Could taste blood on them. I felt like pleading illness, asking to be allowed home early, but though I did truly feel sick, I couldn't risk drawing any more attention to myself. I would just have to sit there and suffer.

The class I found myself in was the weekly period of R.E., Religious Education, a class that as a Jew in a Christian school I didn't even have to attend – Solly, Aaron and Chaz never attended – but which I attended anyway, to show I was no different to anyone else, not an arrogant Jew like the others, unwilling to hear about other religions, or because my parents had told me not to attend. I didn't want to be seen as a cut above. Lord Rothbart, master of politics, guru of sex, wanted to show, at base, he was no different to anyone else. Now I felt like pointing my beaked nose into the air and proclaiming: "I am a Jew and I demand to be let out of here!" But it was too late and with no other choice I used the period to think and pray.

As long as they, my friends, did not know, I argued to myself, I was still first across the line; a hero, no matter how suspicious, how cynical they remained. But if they found out, I was as good as on my way down the Via Dolorosa. Only for me not even a cross to bear, more like one of those big black trucks full of coal, and definitely no resurrection. No candles burning. No followers. Only stones. Big, brown, testicular-looking stones being thrown at me.

At last the final bell and I whipped my canvass knapsack over my shoulder – Hot Stuff the Little Red Devil, with his trident drawn so mischievously on the back – and hurtled out of class like a missile, racing for the bus stop, hoping to avoid anyone and everyone. Behind me I gradually became aware of thumping footsteps, sharp, rasping breath. It was Chaz.

"Have you . . . have you . . . forgotten about the Afrikaans you wanted me to help you with?" He was holding onto my knapsack, Hot Stuff the Little Red Devil clasped in his hand, pulling me back, looking out of breath.

"Oh shit, yeah . . . shit-yeah." In my delirium I had completely forgotten our long-made arrangement.

"Shall I . . . shall I still come home with you then?"

Shit! Shit! Damn! Damn! There was no way out. I needed Chaz's help in this assignment. Knew I would not get through, maybe would not even be able to do it without his help, and that meant worse trouble: Mr Nothnagel's thick cane swiped across my sensitive, paper-thin backside – *Die Hand van Here God*, as he always put it. The memory alone was enough to bring back the smouldering sensation inside my pants.

"Ja, of course ja," I felt my lips cracking into a smile, knowing already all the stupid questions he would ask me.

9

It was about a block's walk from the bus stop to my house in Isipingo Street. I had been told one day by one of the servants in the street that the word "isipingo", a Zulu word, meant adultery or unfaithfulness, and I wondered how anyone in their right mind could call a street "adulterous". But that was the sort of country I was growing up in. Nothing made any sense.

Above us, as we walked from the bus stop, the old Yeoville water reservoir at the top of Cavendish Road looked terrifyingly like a huge maroon testicle balanced atop its rusty pyramidal frame, like it was about to spin off to another galaxy, or at any rate simply fall off. Only, like everything else in this place, it was never going to take off, or even fall off. It was going nowhere. Just like the country I was living in. Just like my life.

Chaz, knowing he couldn't smoke in my house, immediately flipped a cigarette into his mouth. He looked at me, cigarette dangling from his lips, eyes eager, but I knew I couldn't say anything, definitely nothing about why I was suddenly seeing the rusty old water tower as a giant testicle about to take off or fall on top of us. Even Chaz would think I had flipped out. So I just turned away, until I felt his eyes finally drop from me, concentrating on inhaling his cigarette and blowing out smoke-rings.

"Chaz's here for lunch, Fay," I announced to Faith, who opened the front door for us. "But don't worry, we'll make something for ourselves."

"Hau, Danny!" Faith looked at me, rolling her eyes. "You know what a mess you always make in the kitchen. Ho-no! I'll make the lunch: eggs on toast?"

"Alright then," I said, secretly thankful. Swearing for the hundredth time under my breath that the day I moved out of home would be the last day I ever had a maid wipe up after me.

After lunch Chaz and I went to my room and sat at my little red and yellow study desk facing the window which used to look out on to a tree-lined street but now looked out on to our new concrete security wall. Nevertheless, because our side of the street was elevated, I could still see the tops of the jacaranda trees that lined the pavements and the red and green, triangular, corrugated rooftops of the brick houses opposite. More and more, houses in the suburbs were beginning to lie hidden behind tall fences or grey concrete security walls like our own – to allay a growing paranoia about burglars and tsotsis, and talk of a spiralling number of break-ins.

Chaz loosened his school tie and let it dangle halfway down his shirt; I took mine off altogether and dropped it to the floor where it lay like a red and green striped carpet snake. *Original Sin*. Then we began on the Afrikaans composition I had to have ready for school the next day. The title of the composition, Mr Nothnagel said, had to be: *'n Ondervinding met 'n Spook*. An Experience with a Ghost. When the country was violently turning, spinning, burning, everything around you collapsing. Black kids revolting over the kind of education they were getting – if you could call it an education at all – revolting over the Afrikaans language itself. The threat that it was to be decreed the official language of instruction for many subjects in black schools, showing how it was possible to come to hate the sound of a language – like my parents had taught me to hate the sound of German, a language once associated with high poetry, deep thinking, philosophy, the high sciences.

Fortunately Mr Nothnagel held Chaz's compositions in lofty regard. I knew, because I always did well with them. Basically my only part in the feat was to nod and agree, and whenever there was a lull in Chaz's thought processes, to proffer sprinklings of conversation on subjects like politics, movies, prospective dates and, of course, sex. As a result, my silence was soon smashed.

"You sure there's nothing wrong, hey Danny?" Chaz looked up at me after only a few minutes at work, his voice breaking into a squeak, his Adam's apple bobbing up and down.

"Yeah, 'course . . . just this . . . this crappy composition. Just want to get it done and out of the way."

"Eh-hem." He swallowed. "There's something else, Danny, you can't bullcrap me . . ."

I had to think fast. Very fast.

"Ja, I know, Chaz . . . I just can't help thinking about the riots and thinking that next year we could end up with a gun in our hands." To me, at that moment, it sounded so fake, so hollow, but somehow he immediately fell for it.

"Shit, yeah," he said. "No ways. There's no ways I'm going." Then he swallowed and looked at me closely. "But we'll do what we've always said we'd do, like: we'll split the country. Whatever happens, I'll go with you."

I nodded my head. "Yeah, I know . . . it's just that . . . like we should . . . like we should be doing something now. It's like we're all, it's like this whole bloody country is impot . . ." I don't know how that word arrived on the tip of my tongue, probably because it was now permanently pasted there, but suddenly it was dangling half in and half out, and I couldn't quite get it all the way out. Not in front of Chaz. Not in any context. I was finding it hard to breathe, let alone talk. I cleared my throat several times.

"We're like, we're like . . ." Short of breath, I finally managed to get out the next best word that came to mind: "pathetic!" Chaz looked down, as if genuinely ashamed of himself.

I looked back down at the book, and like an obedient child he shifted his head back to his work.

Around eight minutes later, the average time I had read somewhere that men could go without thinking about sex, his head was up again.

"Are you going to be seeing Sophie Street again?"

I could have strangled him.

"Eh-hem . . . yeah, why? 'Course . . . Probably."

"Tell me, have you lost respect for her?"

"Nah . . . 'course not. Why should I?"

"So how was it, then?" He looked at me as though following the question down my throat. I could feel the heat rising in my collar, my throat constricting. "I mean, did she just like, just like take all her clothes off for you, like that!" He clicked his thumb and middle finger loudly in the air.

"Shit!" I heard my voice somewhere outside of me. There was a tightness in my chest, like a locked vice. Perhaps now was the time to come clean, tell the truth, confess. I thought of Uncle Harold and I gulped in a bubble of air and unexpectedly belched. Inside of me I felt like Krakatoa, like I was going to fragment.

"What?" he said.

"Oh, no. Nothing . . . I told you before, man, she couldn't keep saying no forever . . . and then just like that . . ." I coolly, deliberately, snapped two fingers together in the air, but unlike when Chaz had done it no sound came from them, not even a slight noise. "Just like that," I tried again without success to click my fingers together, "she took her clothes off." At least that part rang true.

"All of them?"

"Well, like, just her pants." True.

"Wow, so you weren't, like, completely naked . . .?"

"Ja? . . . huh? Naaa . . . It was sort of strange, like." Also true. Too true. "We both still had our shirts on, like . . ." True. Very true. At that point my voice faltered and completely dried up. Once again I looked back down at the book, to get Chaz's attention back to the task, to that very important experience with a ghost, but he wasn't really looking at me any longer, he was kind of just still staring down my throat.

"So what did it feel like, hey . . .? I mean, you know, Danny, like I'm not exactly going to be splabbing it all over the show." His Adam's apple was really pumping now.

"What's this?" I suddenly shouted back at him. "Some kind of inter-rogation?" There was only one way to deal with the situation. Lies. A raised voice, and lies. That was the way to deal with Chaz, but right now not even that seemed to scare him off.

"I won't say anything, won't ever ask again, promise!" He wasn't budging.

"OK, OK, it was uh, you know, like . . ." I tried my best to remem-ber the details from the books I had read, the stories I had heard, the rumours that had circulated. "Like sort of soft and squelchy, like . . . like Vaseline." I looked up at him, seeing his eyes circling.

"Shit man, that's great! That's great! I was only asking, like."

"Well there, now I've told you! But just remember I still have a hel-luva lot of respect for Sophie, and that's as far as I want it to go."

Lies. Lies. Jesus, it was just so hard to maintain the lie, and yet it was the only thing keeping me going, keeping me in with Chaz, the guys, keeping me up on that grand old pedestal. Without it, without the lie, I was done for, finished, klaar.

He winked. "Yes, man. Don't get so freaked out, I understand."

I wondered what he would do if he ever found out the truth . . . if he ever found out about Uncle Harold and me. I felt myself flush, just thinking about it.

"You don't have to get all pink-faced like, I just wanted to know," he said, and I nearly punched him in the shoulder, just to take his mind off things, but just in time he looked back down at the exercise book and asked: "OK then, where would you stick the verb in this sentence?"

I breathed out. The interrogation was over, for now at any rate. All around me, a prison closing.

10

Wednesday night, as my life stood then, was the only thing to look forward to. The days at school were grey, foggy, accusatory; the nights alone with my parents like wearing a rough woollen jumper over naked skin, uncomfortable, itchy: *Do this! Do that! What you doing now? Tidy up! What do you think this place is, a shebeen? Stop brooding! Forget the girls! Study! Work! Get a haircut!* They meant well, but most of the time they came across like jail warders. My bedroom, the closest thing to a sanctuary, had become just like another chamber of my smogged-up mind: a place to walk in or set myself down, but not necessarily a place to find peace.

As far as possible, I had even given up looking into my bedroom mirror, the long mirror on the inside door of my wardrobe, the wardrobe where I hid Uncle Harold's pictures and poems and magazines and my flick-knife. It was amazing to think how often I used to look into that mirror and what I saw reflected in there: a tall, dark, high cheekboned, long sideburned rock-star belting out throaty, whisky-coated numbers. A vast, endless audience in the shadows below; a front row of girls stripping out of bras and panties, throwing them up to me. And now I was nothing, less than nothing. When I looked into the mirror now, I saw only a schmock, a schmendrik, a rachmones. The crowds disappearing, melting like the audience after a late show into the darkness. The show was over. I had no more use for the mirror in my bedroom. Any mirrors. Harold Kleinhart, Uncle HK, my only way out.

Wednesday evening I found myself sitting on a couch in the lounge with my parents, who had not long arrived home from work, waiting for Uncle Harold. They sat there, in the armchairs in the lounge, facing one another, yet managing not to actually look at one another.

My father's big frame set well down in the bright orange, gold-speckled armchair, his socks, already peeled off his feet and crumpled into his shoes, emitting a light grainy odour.

My mother was sitting as she always did, skewly, in her matching bright orange armchair, which was tonight placed directly below the room's magnificent centrepiece, the Tretchikoff print. Set in an ornate gold-lacquered frame, it showed the colourful top half of a traditionally dressed Eastern woman, who, with her striking black hair and alluring narrow eyes, was veiled behind a demure Mona Lisa smile. The print, in hues of green or orange, depending on the predominant décor of the room, was to be found hanging in the suburbs, on the walls of hundreds of lounges just like ours. Our Tretchikoff, needless to say, was orange, and my mother was forever moving it around, along with the other glowing furniture in the room, to make the most, as she put it, of the room's appeal. The painting shone in the strong light of the room, lighting up mother's thick bush of brunette hair, but at the same time the woman's Mona Lisa smile contrasted sharply with the drawn look on my mother's face. Every now and then she mumbled something about her sore back and moaned that it was because of the cheap second-hand chairs her boss insisted on buying.

"Bladdy schnorrer wouldn't buy his own wife a decent chair to sit on," she groaned, to whoever might be listening. Then turning very definitely to me, she said, "You know, you haven't even given me a kiss hello today? Come and give your ma a big kiss hello."

I grunted under my breath, but in the end I knew I would have to get up and give her the ritual kiss hello. It wasn't so much that I minded kissing her, it was the way she demanded it, making me feel small and chained, that irritated me.

"Two kisses, please, you know I always like two," she said after I had quickly pecked her once on the cheek and turned away. She pouted her red, lipsticked mouth and I leant over again and kissed her twice, quickly, this time on the lips. As usual, it sent strange waves of hot and cold through my body, only tonight it seemed worse than ever. I was trying to be grown-up, show that I was my own person, a man, or near-ly a man, and there was my mother reminding me that as far as she was concerned I was a child she still had under her control.

"That's better," she said. "Remember, I'm the only mother you have, and I love you no matter how many girlfriends you have, and even if you turn your nose up at me, mister."

I felt myself colour, like she had seen my rejection as I turned away and wiped my mouth, but she didn't say anything more. Back in my seat, on the couch, I looked at her in the bright light of the room, un-der that ornately framed centrepiece, the Tretchikoff print, and felt a strange affinity. I saw in her a pride that did not easily tolerate failure, a pride that I also recognised in myself. And yet despite that pride, encouraged no doubt by her Judy Garland look-a-likeness – which she went on and on about to her friends, not to mention my friends – the fact was she had achieved little in life, had to settle for the average to the less than average. And in the bright light of that room, under the ornately framed Tretchikoff print, for one awful moment I saw myself in her chair, growing old, skew, empty, my dreams squashed up against the back of that bright, gold-flecked orange armchair. I felt a shiver run through me and turned to my father who was staring straight ahead of him into his own dreams, reliving his own missed opportunities, in silence, waiting for the maid to ring the bell for din-ner. I knew definitely I didn't want to be like them, but in front of me now I saw only them, the four walls, the brightness of the room, and the Tretchikoff print that kept us united in a sort of helplessness. A bit like cows in a pen waiting for the signal that would allow them out to pasture. Only the signal never seemed to come.

And then the bell rang, not the dinner bell but the one at the front door.

"I'll get it." I immediately jumped up.

It was Uncle Harold, of course, wearing his mustard turtleneck jersey and carrying a wide smile on his freshly shaven face. He shook my hand and then bounded into the bright light of the lounge. As he entered the room, I saw my mother look quickly, squarely, at my father, as though trying to remind him in that flash of a second about what he should instruct Uncle Harold in relation to me, but my father looked back dully at her, like he didn't have the faintest idea of what she was on about. Instead he jumped up with outstretched hand and said, "Howzit, Harold. Howzit. Good to see you. Good to see you again."

Just then Faith arrived in the dining-room and gave the old brass bell a heavy shaking. Even though we were only a matter of feet away from her in the adjoining lounge, she had to shake it, and it brought all conversation, all thought, to a halt, sort of like a final theatre call.

Then, as though coming to, or suddenly remembering something, my mother turned to me: "Aren't you forgetting something?"

"What?"

"To give your mother a hug goodbye."

It caught me off balance. I had only just hugged and kissed her hello! My first reaction was to look at Uncle Harold. He nodded to me and immediately I obeyed, slowly walking up to my mother and quickly hugging her, but she clung onto me.

"And a kiss, or are you too ashamed? Harold's not a stranger, you know, I bet he still kisses his mother . . ."

Uncle Harold nodded. "Of course I still kiss my mother, whenever she sees me she expects me to kiss her," he said, much to my mother's appreciation.

"See." She looked at me.

Slowly, feeling deeply embarrassed, I stepped up to her and pecked her quickly on the cheek, but even in front of Uncle Harold, or maybe it was because of Uncle Harold, she demanded what she always expected.

"Two kisses, please," she said. "I always like two of everything, you know that."

I felt so deeply hot and dismayed I thought I was going to melt into the floor. There was no choice now. All eyes were on me. I bent forward and kissed her twice on the lips and then quickly broke from her grasp.

"That's better," she said, looking at Uncle Harold. "You know, whatever happens, he's still my baby."

Uncle Harold smiled.

"Yes, I know, he'll always be your baby, even when he's a zeide one day with a dozen grandchildren, he'll be your baby . . ."

My mother looked happier with that farewell than she had in a long time. My father just waved us out of the door, like we had to urgently make up for lost time. For a change, I was thankful for his materialistic world-view.

In the car, as we drove off, Uncle Harold said to me: "You know your mom's no different to any other mother. All she wants is the best for you. My mom's exactly the same. No different. They're all the same . . . still calls my younger brother, and he's forty-two now, her baby. She's a good woman, your mom, you know that . . . a bit strung out, but a good woman." He looked down at me, across his driving arm.

"Yes," I told him, "I know." In the back of my mind thinking how reassuring it was to know that I wasn't the only one. Though the thought of her doing it until I was forty-two was harrowing. I didn't know if I could put up with it, like Uncle Harold and his brother.

After a silence, Uncle Harold patted me lightly on the knee. "Don't look so glum, Danny, I promise you, my boy, everything's going to be alright. Remember always to look to that silver lining."

I blinked my eyes and smiled up at him.

* * *

In Uncle Harold's cluttered private office, I stood naked as I had on that first occasion, meekly in the shadow of the table light, ready to

110

create with Uncle Harold a new world, new horizons, new planes, and put myself back into one proper piece. Once again, we both bent down and, recreating that sense of camaraderie, that bond of friendship, together prepared a bed of cushions on his huge desk for me.

"You know, soon you'll be wondering what all the fuss was about," said Uncle Harold, breaking into my thoughts. "You'll see, soon it'll all fall into place, Danny."

I nodded, appreciative.

Then, as before, he patted his hand on the wooden desk, and I climbed up. Without asking this time, I lay on my back, the desk lamp hovering above me, the light shining in my eyes.

"Relax, Danny, just relax. Everything's going to be alright. There's no need to be shy, no need to be shy."

I felt my cardboard-stiff body sigh, beginning to relax; lulled under his soothing voice and now so light, sensitive touch, somewhere in the back of my mind wondering if I would ever have the courage to ask where, from what book, he had learnt this particular approach. Was I still too young, too immature to read that book?

Lying there, looking about me, I noticed for the first time, to my left at the very back of the office, a dark wooden cupboard. It loomed there, leaning slightly as though over-packed, somewhat ghostly in this light, and I wondered what my Afrikaans teacher, Mr Nothnagel, would have made of all of this. I knew the response without having to think about it: he would have clamped my head under a shelf in that cupboard and given me six of the best – Die Hand van Here God – and called me a moffie. What would my father have made of it? Would he have slapped Uncle Harold on the back, and said, "Well done. Thank you for showing my boy the real world,"? I think he would have put an assegai through Uncle Harold's head, but that was the difference between my father and me. He was an open and shut case, if he couldn't understand what stood before him, he shut the door on it, ridiculed it. I couldn't expect understanding from him. He would never comprehend. My mother, on the other hand, I was sure would show at least some understanding, would at least try to understand the reasons why. And while she would definitely not agree that I should have been trying these things, any of these things yet, she would in her way understand that I was only doing my best. But the reality was, in the end, she would take my father's side, and I wondered if they, either one of them, would ever talk to me again if they saw me on this desk.

"Danny, you're losing it. You're losing it. Just relax, relax! What's going on?" Uncle Harold perceived my preoccupations. "Just clear your mind, clear your mind. Think of birds, just think of birds, naked birds. Don't think about anything else. Just think of yourself with a bird, her legs wide open, and she wants you, she wants you to put it in, think that you're just about to put it in . . ." I felt reassured not just by the calm, steady tone of that voice but by the language, the language of that voice. That we had the same fantasies on our minds, the same hormones jiggling in our brains. "That's it, that's much better." I looked up and saw him smiling now. "I can tell you, you have absolutely nothing to be ashamed of." And I felt much easier. Almost proud.

Then a rush of waters, upstream, dropping onto my stiff body, and then everything was still. Perfectly still. A pond of silence.

I looked up at him. His eyes were aglow. And in that moment I saw not Roman emperor, city elder, or surgeon-psychologist, but proud father brimming, glass overflowing with a sense of adulation reserved for a wife who has just given birth. And I felt secure, that someone could feel like that about me. Inside of me sure that I could take Sophie Street in that moment, overcome by that strange new lightness of being, like I was floating on air.

"You see, Danny, it's not so bad, nothing to feel hung up about," said Uncle Harold. "You're already well on your way. Maybe you should think of taking Sophie out again?"

I swallowed, and in this lightness, in this elated mood, I saw that without a doubt I would one day soon, one day soon with Uncle Harold's help, become a man.

"Yes," I nodded. "For sure, Uncle Harold. A good idea. I will."

Now with my back turned to him, I dressed as quickly as I could. Looking up to see that he was not even looking, but stacking away the cushions, re-organising the photos of his loved ones.

There was a big smile on his face now. "You should've seen how far you shot. Over your head onto the desk." I looked around seeing him cleaning, with a tissue, a spot on the desk. And I laughed with him. Two men with a mission. More than convinced now that I had pulled in at the right hospital, asked for the right doctor.

He looked at me, embracing me in his eyes, telling me, without having to tell me, that everything was going to be alright, alles sal regkom, as we walked back out into that sobering chill of the city night, that Aztec city darkness. Only now I was feeling taller, prouder; the city's partly glittering skyline no longer so threatening.

* * *

Uncle Harold pulled up outside the house, only this time instead of a pep-talk like the last time, he leant across me towards the glove-box, opened it and drew out a bunch of keys.

"These are the keys to the shop. They're yours to use any time you have a bird and don't have a place to take her."

I looked up at him. I could hardly believe it, that he would trust me with his shop. The entire empire. That I would have my very own keys to his massive store. I wondered if anyone else would believe it. I slipped the heavy bunch into my jacket pocket. Having a place of your own, more than half the battle.

"Thanks, I'll put them to good use, I promise." I smiled widely.

"Remember, Danny, any, anytime, I'm here for you. Just call, I'm never far away. I just want the best for you. That's all, the best. I have absolutely no doubt you'll soon be up and running again." And then, like a friend, one of the crew, he invited me over to his place for dinner some Friday night. "Come past the shop after school, and then we can go to my pad for a graze. You know Thelma, she's a great bird. Don't be shy. You're more than welcome. She really likes you."

I nodded enthusiastically. "Yes, of course, I'd like that, thank you." Thanking him this time with my voice rather than in my head, thanking him for his time, his patience, his kindness. Thinking, if only, if only I had Sophie Street here right here and now.

Inside my room, in bed, I had a quick look under my arms to see if there was any extra growth there, as if the events of the past few days could have shocked an extra few hairs out of me. But it looked about the same, a few sparse strands. Something was happening, but no matter how hard I tried I couldn't quite put a finger on exactly what. Everything was new, unfamiliar, confounding. Who could have guessed that just few days, a week or so ago, I could have come so close, that close, and then completely and utterly mucked everything up?

I wondered what it was really like, how good it would really have felt to be able to say, honestly, that I had done it. Aside from Chaz and the crew, I would have loved to have written my brother, Cyril, and told him all about it. That I had caught up with him, that now I knew what he had been raving on so irritatingly about. I wondered if perhaps Cyril was the one person I could tell everything to, even about Uncle Harold. The distance, the fact that I would have to write it down, might even make it easier.

Inside of me there was this bursting feeling that someone had to know. Even just some of it. Someone aside from Uncle Harold. And perhaps Cyril, with his increasing experience, his ever-growing worldly wisdom was that person?

11

T he very next day I resolved it was time to take up Uncle Harold's suggestion and call Sophie Street again. The shop was the ideal place where Sophie and I could be alone, not only without fear of interruption, but with masses of space to loll around in without being squashed up against walls and tables and chairs. Even Uncle Harold's desk was bigger than Jessica Shmulowitz's dining-room. Things were, for the moment anyway, looking up.

That afternoon, immediately after school, riding high on my resolution, I called Sophie Street, and in my most casual voice asked her if she wanted to come out with me that Friday night. Of course, she immediately asked where. Prepared for the question, I said to a movie in town, but I would let her know for sure which one when I picked her up. She sighed and breathed out heavily, as always not entirely happy, but in the end said she would just have to check with her dad. Knowing her relationship with her father, in which she, as an only child, called all the shots, I mean all the shots – from dictating the time they should eat their meals to what time he should go to bed at night – I think she was just giving herself more time to think, to decide whether being with me was what she really wanted. I breathed in deeply, suddenly despondent as she put the receiver down. I listened intently for any signs of conversation, other voices in the background. There were none. Eventually, after a good couple of minutes, she returned to the phone, but to my relief, she said, "Well, OK. "

I felt like singing. Immediately after the call I phoned Uncle Harold at work to tell him my good news.

"Excellent. It's good to hear you sounding so chirpy, so full of beans," he said.

"Ja, well, just so that you know, like . . ."

"Anytime, Danny, anytime. And I mean that, the shop is all yours."

"Thanks. Thank you."

And then came the real encouragement: "Just remember to relax, Danny . . . Go with the flow. Forget about the troubles of the world, forget about what happened the last time. Just think of yourself as though. . .as though you were alone. No inhibitions. Nothing to be afraid of. Just let go. And remember what I've always told you, don't forget a rubber. I really mean it. It's not worth the hassle for five minutes' enjoyment."

I felt my neck and face go red, happy with all the advice, but wondering what I would do about the rubber. Just the thought of it made my throat constrict. But there and then I resolved that I wasn't going to let any dumb Frenchie get in my way.

As I replaced the receiver I looked up at the Tretchikoff print and despite the condescending smirk on the perfectly dressed face, I felt a rush of optimism.

* * *

No sooner had I arrived at the front gate of Sophie Street's paint-flaked house in Observatory East than she opened the front door, looked at me, and laughed.

"What's wrong?" I felt like retreating through the front gate.

"No. Nothing!" She clicked her tongue and flicked her head to the side as if to say I should have known what she was thinking.

"You don't like what I'm wearing?" It struck me that Sophie Street, with her always meticulously matching tailored clothes, was laughing at the way I looked or, more precisely, at what I was wearing: faded blue jeans with a brightly coloured paisley shirt, over which hung an open grey trenchcoat that I had to sneak out of my house in case my mother saw it and forced me to take it off.

"Just tell me where we're going," she said, ignoring my question and leading me into the lounge.

Failure tonight would kill me. We hadn't even set a foot out of her front door and already it seemed to me we were starting out on a bad one.

"Well, don't just look at me like that, are you going to tell me where we're going or not?" she asked, squinting.

"I'll tell you when we're on the bus," I said quickly.

"Listen, Danny, I've got to say somewhere to my father. I can't tell him you'll tell me when we're on the bus. He'll blow his top!" I looked at her sceptically. "C'mon Danny, I have to say somewhere."

"Tell him we're going to see *Towering Inferno* at the Kine Centre." Remembering the plan. Actually this was Plan B, if it looked like Plan A – to get her to come to the shop with me – was going to fail. To me it was already looking like Plan B. And I could see us sitting together in a movie house, if I was lucky, our hands coming together and staying stuck together until they became hot and sweaty and sort of voluntarily fell apart. When I could have been in the shop, sword drawn, initiation, manhood, victory, just a matter of a stab away!

She turned and left the lounge, her skin-tight black jeans making a sound like a distant howling wind as she walked away.

I sat down on a heavy brown sofa that had faded images of young ladies in extravagantly long dresses sitting on swings printed all over it. A thin brown carpet struggled to fill the centre of the small room, stretching from the squat wooden legs of the sofa I was sitting on, to the squat legs of two matching, equally faded armchairs that sat opposite one another, neatly angled into the middle of the room. I wondered how Sophie Street could afford the fashionable clothes she always wore. She never spoke of money, or the lack of it. To my irritation, she also seldom, if ever, spoke about politics, about the plight of blacks in South Africa. At least she never looked down on black people like Jessica Shmulowitz. That much I knew, because she never said anything about them. In the background I heard a fairly high-pitched grumbling which proved she really was talking to him, her father, and

117

picked up through the strong Eastern European accent that perhaps, despite what I thought, he really did have some say in her life.

"Ver . . .? Vot time . . .? Vot kind off film is zis . . .?" I heard the run of questions, which were followed by Sophie's solid replies: "Yes. Ag, please dad . . . For heaven's sake, ag dad, please, don't worry . . . Of course not, we won't be home late. What the heck d'you think we're going to be doing there, it's only a flippin' movie!"

I had only seen the old man twice, each time dressed in a thin dark brown cotton dressing-gown that tied neatly around his thin waist. His hair was completely white and he looked more like Sophie's grandfather than her father. Sophie never spoke much about him, or any of her family for that matter. Nevertheless, she did once tell me that her father had immigrated from Russia and that their name was a shortened version of their real Russian name, which was something like Stretskovsky. Apparently, when her father arrived in South Africa, everyone laughed at the name and had difficulty pronouncing it until finally people simply started calling him "Mr Street", or just plain "Street". The name stuck and eventually he even changed it legally. So now they were Street.

About a quarter of an hour later Sophie returned to the lounge, her face freshly powdered and painted, and out we went, my heart pounding but in a relatively steady way.

"So now can you tell me where we're going?" she said as soon as we were upstairs on the bus.

"No, it's a surprise."

"A surprise?"

"Yeah."

"Well, it had better be a good one, my boy."

She eyed me unhappily, but willing, I thought, to go along for the ride. Now that the time had come, I really didn't know what to say to her, about where we were going. It was hard to explain. I was relying on the belief, or rather the hope, that once I got her there, it would be too late for her to turn back and she would just have to put up with it. Who knows, she might even find it exciting? Fat chance. But I had my hopes.

"Why do you always have to play silly little games with me?" She was squinting again.

"I'm not playing games."

"Bullshit, Danny, you're always playing games with me."

Whether I was playing games with her or not, I didn't really know myself. My mind was so full of strategies, so full of plans, tricks, connivances, tactics, desires, that it was difficult to know which was which, what was what.

She stared at me, square in the face.

"Danny you're such a shit!"

I just looked back at her as she continued to stare at me, and for a moment I thought, Sophie Street, I do, I really do fancy you. Her eyes, glaring through shiny straight black hair that curved towards her neck, were slicing like a knife right through me. I felt uncomfortable, but something in me responded to the way she stared at me.

She turned away and sat stiffly, looking straight ahead. Not even the jerky motion of the bus could rock her. A few moments later, still looking straight ahead, not even blinking, she took my hand and placed it in hers. Shocked, I breathed out a very, very silent sigh of relief. I was still in there with a chance.

"Why are you looking at me like that?" she said, suddenly turning back to me.

"Was I . . .? Oh . . . I didn't realise." I turned away, looking straight ahead, still holding her hand.

She didn't respond.

As the double-decker bus grumbled along, the thought of her, undressed, lying on the floor, perhaps the desk, popped into my head. I tried to wipe the thought from my mind, but it was like a fly that wouldn't go away. My hand fidgeted inside hers; it was growing hot.

I hoped she was not noticing, that it was my hand growing hot, not hers. Why she still wanted to be with me, I just didn't know. You know what they said about opportunity – that it didn't knock twice – but for me, maybe it did. For a moment I wished that I was a girl, I was Sophie Street, and our positions were reversed. Then I would be, I don't know? But certainly not saddled with this problem. All you had to do was just lie there! *Tell yourself to relax, Danny, just relax. Just go with the flow*, I heard Uncle Harold's voice encouraging me as the bus slowly drew up to a stop and we hopped off at the terminus in Loveday Street.

The city, deserted on weeknights, breathed with a little more life on Friday nights, as young white couples and small groups of smartly dressed white people darted across the streets, into nightclubs, movie houses and restaurants. Eager to be off the streets. The streets in Jo'burg at night not a place to be. The streets a place where skollies hung out. The streets a place where you seldom saw any of those skollies, except occasional groups of young drunk white ones. The number of blacks on the street you could count on the fingers of one hand. Keeping safely to the shadows.

"I suppose you're going to blindfold me now?" Sophie Street brought me back to our own little circle of reality.

"Hah, oh yes. Just turn around!" I exhaled, expecting some or other retort, but fortunately she smiled and left it at that.

Finally we arrived at the entrance to Golden's New and Used Furniture, the neon light above the door, for some reason tonight, still bubbling away. Perhaps Uncle Harold had forgotten to switch it off? Or perhaps he had left it on especially for us? Standing there, in the dowdy light created by the dusty neon tubes, the tall buildings surrounding the shop seemed to reach up twice their size. Without saying anything to Sophie, and suddenly somewhat embarrassed about holding such a big wad of keys in my hands, I bent down and then slowly began to work my way through the locks, seeing above me the shop's fading motto – Golden by Name, Golden by Quality – recalling how Uncle Harold had once, recently, told me the name really belonged to his mother, it was her maiden name: Golden.

"Fits perfectly, don't you think," he'd said proudly. I remembered nodding, wishing I had a surname like Golden or even Kleinhart rather than Rothbart, which meant nothing.

As soon as I had undone the last lock, she said, "This is where you're taking me? To a used furniture shop?" She looked at me, incredulous.

"Ja . . ."

"You've got to be kidding!"

"No . . . this is it."

"What . . .? Are we pulling a job or something?"

"Of course not . . . the shop belongs to Harold Kleinhart. You know, the city councillor? He's an old family friend . . . said I could use it any time I liked."

"Jesus Christ, Danny Rothbart! This place is disgusting! What do you think I am?"

I could feel my heart folding in on itself, actually collapsing. This could already be the end of it, all my strategies, plans, tactics, mental rehearsals, sessions with Uncle Harold, come to nought. Zero.

"I've never brought anyone here," I said after a while. "This's the first time . . . you're . . . the only one." At last some honesty. But even as I said it I couldn't help but see the shop through her eyes and it actually made me feel queasy. Only I could not, not under any circumstances, admit that to her.

"Well, c'mon, c'mon inside then," I said cheerily, reaching for a note of optimism.

"It's dark."

"Yeah, well, I'm just about to put the lights on . . ."

Groping across the wall I found the light switches and switched on the fluorescent tubes that hung from the ceiling, the entire shop suddenly firing up like a factory. Then leaving Sophie by the door I dashed to the office to switch on the desk lamp.

There, on the desk, I immediately spotted a piece of white paper sticking out from under Thelma's picture. It looked new and stiff, like it had been purposely left there. I picked it up and was surprised to see it really was intended for me. "Make yourself at home. Good luck!" it read. I smiled – truly surprised and truly thankful – crumpled the paper up, and threw it in the bin. Noticing as I did that on the floor, to one side of the office, two rows of flat, neatly laid out cushions lay side by side like a mattress. I smiled again. Uncle Harold had gone out of his way for me. I hadn't expected anything like this.

I dashed back again to switch off the big fluorescents. I was out of breath by the time I had finished, but I tried to make out as if there was nothing to it.

"Just follow the light." I smiled, pointing to the office at the back of the shop, breathing silently but heavily in my chest.

"God!" she breathed, but followed anyway.

As we walked she bumped into tables and chairs.

"Shit, what the hell is this? Christ, Danny, Christ! What the flip have I hit now!" she kept muttering and swearing. By the time we got to the dimly lit office she was fuming.

"Never, never again!"

"It's not that bad, is it?"

"Not that bad? What do you think I am, one of your little hippie whores?"

"Eh-hem . . ." I cleared my throat for what felt like the hundredth time since we'd entered the shop. "I'll get a radio, that'll make the place seem a bit better."

I walked into the shop, bumping in the darkness into the corners of all sorts of furniture until I found what I had come after: one of the many portable radios that were stacked at the back of the shop, in between the rows. I returned to the office, delighted with my find, switched it on, and tuned it till it picked up some vaguely decent music. Although the pick-up was not good, and the radio crackled and

122

hummed, I was hoping the sound would breathe a touch of life into the place, breathe a bit of warmth into Sophie.

"Make yourself at home." I swept my hand across the cushions, making a show of it, switching on the charm, and then took my coat off, casually throwing it over Uncle Harold's desk like I owned the place, like this was my empire.

"All you ever want to do is screw me, Danny Rothbart!"

"Ja . . . I mean no, no," I said, not thinking, feeling the chill on my back, my mind ashamedly preoccupied with just that thought.

"Can't you ever think of anything else?"

"Ja, I've been known to," I tried to joke, sweating, doing my best to make light of her aspersions.

"It's eerie in here." She shivered her shoulders. "Are you sure there's no one else in the place?"

"Yeah, of course." I looked about me as though to make sure. I even strode off to the big cupboard in the corner of the office and boldly, exaggeratedly, flung open the doors, for a brief moment scared myself that something, some monster might jump out, and when nothing did, I bowed and said, "See, señorita. Nothing!" Then I walked back to her, and noticing a faint smile, I was sure I saw a smile there, I took her hand and pulled her towards me, smelling her perfume: that strong smell of roses. Holding her, more than half expecting her to throw me back, I felt how soft she was, how like a girl she was, even through her thick winter clothes. And when after a few moments I saw she was not going to protest I pulled her down onto the cushions with me.

"You always get your own way, don't you, Danny?"

"What do you mean?" I looked at her innocently.

"Nothing!" She flicked her jet-black hair back and, typically, said nothing more.

Tonight, I told myself, whatever I did, I was going to ignore her defensive airs. I pulled her closer to me and began to stroke her ankles – she was sitting close to me, her knees bent, pulled tightly into her chest, her ankles about the only naked spot close enough for me to grope.

"You don't give a damn about other people's feelings, do you?"

For a moment, I didn't know why, all I could see in front of me was Mr Nothnagel shoving my head into the back of that cupboard in the corner of the office and readying himself to give me six of the best.

"I do . . . of course I do care!" I said finally.

"Oh yes, all you're interested in is one thing!"

"You always say that. But if you really loved me, it wouldn't matter," I said, putting on the face and voice of some older, wiser man who knew all the answers.

"Yeah, and then that's the last I see of you?"

"But I'm here, I'm back already, aren't I?"

She looked at me, exasperated. I couldn't tell what was going through her mind. I only hoped, from how she was talking, that somehow she had chosen to forget the last time. There was no way I could open up and talk to her about that. The girl I was supposed to have done it with! Success tonight, my inflamed, agitated mind told me, would be like the first time never happened, was just a very, very bad dream. Success tonight would be liberation, freedom!

"Do you really love me, Danny?" Her voice came as though from a distant room.

"Huh?" What a question! "Yes . . . of course, yes, of course I do." At that moment I was willing to agree to anything. Anything.

"But, when I let you, that'll be it, you won't want me any more."

"Of course I will! I will . . . I promise I will . . ." Then and there, swearing that if I did manage to do it tonight I would, I would, I would until the day I died, for ever and ever.

"You're so full of shit, Danny Rothbart!"

I just stared at her. I was done for. I knew it. She was like a cobra, strong-headed, slippery, wise, and I just didn't have whatever it was I needed to raise her trust, to capture her mind – to charm the pants off her, as I might have put it at that time.

124

Then a miracle happened. I don't know what possessed her, but she pulled me to her and began to lick my ear, to suck on it like it was a sweet, something edible, something warm and nourishing and tasty. It sent tremors down my spine and immediately I became conscious of a loud booming in my chest – pah-doom-pah-doom – like someone was striking at my chest with a hard rubber hammer.

Now we were lying down, in just the position I had imagined us in from the moment she had said "yes" to coming out with me. Immediately my hand was stretching upwards, in no time reaching that critical area between her legs. To my amazement, there was no sign of protest, no abrupt pushing away, no stern looks, not a word, not the faintest whisper. It was like she wasn't even aware of what I was doing. I felt my heart pounding faster, but her pants were hard and thick, like stiff-pressed denim worn for the first time, and perhaps, I had to admit it to myself, she couldn't even feel my hand.

I put my hand on her zipper, let it rest there, just to test if there was any reaction, and when there wasn't any I began to jerk at it nervously. Another miracle: it came shooting down, sliding, quickly, like it was never meant to be up, like it was always meant to be down. That was a first.

Now I grabbed at the brass button that held her pants around her waist. I tried to hold it firmly between my thumb and index finger, to pop it open. But her pants were pulled so tightly around her plump waist that I could hardly get my index finger between her stomach and the buttonhole. Suddenly, from a more or less relaxed state, my fingers were working hard, fast, twisting this way and that, but it was taking too long, and I was getting hot – I thanked the heavens she could not see my puffing cheeks – so much for a first – and I was beginning to wonder whether she knew what was going on down there? Or whether knowing how clumsy, what a klutz I was, she had chosen to simply ignore my frantic, battling fingers. Was I just too uneducated in these things? I felt a bead of sweat drip down my neck as though in response, but I would not be defeated. Would not, would not, would not.

"Ouch!" I heard her scream, and suddenly I felt my index finger crack.

"Einaa!" I screamed out without being able to help it.

"Shit!" I heard a voice come back as a sort of echo. With no other choice – my finger injured – I placed my damaged hand on her stomach, resting it there. The only thing I saw in front of me was what I had feared all along, a cul-de-sac. I was finished. Dead. Kaput.

And then, and then those magic words again.

"Do you want me to take my pants off?"

I gawked at her like a stunned parrot, gazing, amazed, into her serious, dead-serious eyes. Just like that, once again, offering herself.

"Eh-hem." I swallowed, at first unable to talk, and then managed my usual squeak: "Yee."

She didn't even so much as blink, just continued to lie, staring ceilingwards, and I wondered whether she had even heard me. It seemed like minutes, many, many minutes, of me staring in wonder, confusion, into the air, at the desk legs, at the scary cupboard in the back corner of the office, at nowhere in particular, but definitely not at her, when finally she said, "Well, don't just lie there. Look the other way!"

Instantly I rolled onto my side and stared intently at Uncle Harold's blank masonite office wall. I heard her stand up, but unlike the last time when she was out of her pants in world record time, I heard her wrestling with that brass stud. But still, it wasn't long before I heard her pants brushing down over her legs, and I turned back to look.

"Not yet!" she snapped. And I immediately and obediently turned back to the wall, hearing her fold her pants and then place them over a chair. A few moments later her cold body was lying down beside me.

"Well . . . aren't you going to turn around?" she asked.

I was flabbergasted – first ordered this way, then that – I felt like the school dunce, but who was I to argue? She was giving me what I wanted; it was hardly the time to hold a debate. I didn't even know if I had the voice for it. Slowly, cautiously, I turned to face her. As with the time before I found her lying on her back, stretching her shirt down towards her knees. From where I was looking, I still couldn't even make out if she had pubic hair like the women in Uncle Harold's magazines.

I put a hand over her stomach, which meant sneaking my hand under her arm – which was stiffly stretching out her shirt – and then sort of pushing forwards. Once there I stroked her abdomen like I was in no hurry, no hurry at all – all the time my fingers ready to charge forward – while in my stomach, a voice, no thousands of high-pitched voices, were singing out like a veld full of insomniac cicadas. Finally, with a thudding jerk, she released her shirt and turned to me. Inside of me the rubber hammer beat, rolled faster – pah-doom, pah-doom, pah-doom, doom, doom. *Shit!* I swore to myself. *No, no, relax, Danny, just relax! Everything will be alright. Just let go*, I heard Uncle Harold's voice, like it was my own, coaching me. And I wished he could suddenly manifest himself to show me how.

Then a real voice sprang up from my side: "Well, aren't you going to take your pants off?"

As if it were possible, I felt my chest tighten even further. Shakily but determined, I struggled up like a cheap puppet on a string. Once up, I turned away from what I was convinced were her staring, bemused eyes and began to work on my pants. For once, thank God, they seemed to slide off easily. That was a good sign, a good sign. But when I stared down at myself, at my killer spear, my sword, my once and future little king, all I could see were thin, knobbly, moon-white legs. I stood there too mortified, too shocked to even turn around. Like her, I pulled my shirt down as far as it would go, briefly wondering if I should take it off.

I peered down at her.

She peered up at me.

It was like I had on a skullcap made of steel and I felt like my temples were going to burst. If the room grew any hotter I would need a cold towel to wipe myself down. Then, shirt still on, like a shy, cumbersome clown, I twisted myself around and not wanting her to see anything, nothing under my shirt, I sky-jumped right on top of her.

"Ooooof . . ." She exhaled sharply, but lay still and I began to think, once again, that I had killed her, this time by other, more violent means. Finally, an eye opened, blinked at me: she was alive. What's more, she was sticking a hand under my shirt and running a long fingernail down my spine. I felt a shiver tingle down my back and suddenly I was alive. I, I was alive.

All that remained, I told myself, buoyed by my discovery that I was really alive, that I could actually feel her tickling fingers running down my back, was to press it in, just press it in and I would be there. There. Wherever there was? I heard the radio crackle, a faint voice inside singing: "Major Tom to ground control. Major Tom to ground control . . . This is ground control to Major Tom . . . Ground control to Major Tom . . ."

But as with poor, lost, gravity-less Major Tom, there was no connection, no connection. I was lost in space. That smell of hers, of roses, just too sweet, just too, too sweet.

Remember, Danny, no matter how old you are, no matter where you are, you'll always be my baby, a voice swam through my mind. And behind that voice, very close behind it, there was this Second World War army sergeant yelling: *C'mon, my boy, c'mon, what kind of man are you? No chrain, that's the trouble with your generation.* And behind that yet another voice, steady and booming: *You're a normal ouk, Danny, believe me, a normal ouk, just let go, don't think about anything . . .* The voices circled around in my head like a cloud of dizzy flies around a half-finished Coke bottle. While my heart raced – pah-doom, pah-doom, pah-doom. I could feel the sweat breaking out all over my body, and I wondered when she was going to call out for a towel or just shove me off in revulsion. Convinced now more than ever that in this subject, as with bloody Afrikaans and maths, and science, and Latin – in fact you name it, you just name the subject – I needed extra lessons, needed outside tuition, would need to sing out to Uncle Harold again, and again, and again. I wondered if he would even have that kind of patience. Generosity? How would he run the city with me still squealing for help at his side?

Then a vaguely familiar voice came from below: "It's me, isn't it?"

I breathed out, at first confused, but then realising that once again she was saving me from disgrace.

I looked into the face below, as though in sympathy.

"It's alright," I whispered. "It's alright."

And she turned away. That mild scent of roses rising, pleasantly.

I became aware of the radio again, now for some reason hopelessly out of tune, crackling mercilessly in my ears. I stretched over and turned it off.

Below me Sophie's slit geisha eyes stared hard at the roof.

"This place is spooky."

Her words suddenly made me think again of Mr Nothnagel. What would he say of tonight's episode? *Skrik wakker, man! Kom by! Your little man walks around like it's in a permanent dwaal!* And then, of course, it would be at least two of the best on the backside just to get me to wake up.

"Ja . . . it is kind of creepy," I agreed, thinking perhaps if I were not brought up in this damned country – where everything was banned – maybe it would be different. How the hell did anyone over here ever learn to do it? It seemed to me right then that there could be no worse fate than being born in South Africa – where government, religion, laws, nature and nurture all conspired against you. I recall myself remembering on that cold floor that I had read somewhere that if a male chimpanzee before the age of six was denied sexual knowledge through watching sexual acts, he would never be able to do it with a female chimpanzee no matter how receptive or helpful she might be, because, when it came down to brass tacks, he simply would not have the foggiest notion what to do. *Like me*, I remember thinking bleakly, *like me in this everything-to-do-with-sex-banned country of mine*. On the other hand, I had read that in the life of the chimpanzee's close cousin, the bonobos – where sex was a very natural part of childhood – sex remained as a relaxed activity that worked as a perfectly normal social cement. That is to say, the bonobos were doing it all over the place, all over the bladdy place, anywhere, anytime, anyhow, no problems at all. *Unlike me*. I recall thinking, albeit cloudily, that being in South Africa was like being consigned to primate hell! The only monkeys to be found here were chimps like me.

"Danny . . . Danny, maybe this just isn't the place . . .?"

"Wha . . .? Oh, yeah . . . Maybe . . . maybe if we . . ." But my voice just shut down, completely shut down and I was left with no other choice but to roll off her, thinking, *God, what a mess I've made of it, what a fuckin' mess*. I had taken a bad situation and turned it into a complete and utter disaster. I was blind from the sweat, but Sophie Street just lay there, I think a little comatose, but unbelievably patient, a fingernail under my shirt again, meditatively drawing mandalas with the sweat that was pouring from my stomach.

"Let's get dressed," she said. "I want to get out of here."

I immediately jumped up, relieved to be dismissed from the floor and quickly made a grab for my clothes. My legs, wobbly like a boxer's after a solid beating, caved in as I tried to put a foot into my underpants. I looked back to see if she was watching, but fortunately she was too busy with her own dressing to even notice the fool at her side. She was slightly bent over, I saw, drawing in a heavy breath to get that shiny brass button on her pants to squeeze through the hole.

Finally, both of us dressed, Sophie stood stiffly, placing her backside against Uncle Harold's desk, as I moved the cushions into a neat pile against the office wall. I didn't bother to ask her to help, I didn't want to risk the answer.

Amazingly though, when I was through with my manoeuvrings, she turned to me, eyes dropping, and – as though to confirm what she had said earlier – said, "I'm sorry."

"What! What for?" It just spluttered out of me. I couldn't help myself.

"It's me, Danny. I know . . . I know you don't really love me."

I just gawked and gulped. Even if I could have found a response, I couldn't have found a drop of saliva in my mouth to get it out with. My heart was pounding, I couldn't believe that she was taking the blame. Why was she protecting me? Why? If I were her I would have been giving me the flick, telling me I was wasting her time, that I was nothing but a useless, impotent schmek.

"I, I . . . do . . . like you," I finally managed.

"Jesus Danny, you're so full of crap!" She looked the other way, impatiently tapping her fingers against the desk.

Almost in a whisper, I asked her to walk out to the front door and switch on a light there. She clicked her tongue as if in refusal but, I think in her eagerness to get out of the place, obeyed anyway. I heard her swearing as she bumped and knocked into tables and cupboards and chairs.

I peered at the family pictures on Uncle Harold's desk, at the dark cupboard at the back of the office, sort of wondering what they thought of the evening's events, if they had even noticed. As soon as she flicked on the lights I switched off the desk lamp and walked to the front door. I switched off the main lights, including the neon light outside, which was still merrily bubbling away, and in the darkness outside the shop I made sure that I secured all the locks. All the while Sophie Street was standing behind me, tapping her feet, heaving, "Never again, my boy. Never again."

131

12

B ack at home, in my room, I sat on the bed for a while, blaming myself, wondering what kind of saint Sophie Street was to still want to hang around me. Then suddenly I sprang up and changed out of my clothes. I switched on my little blow-heater and then sat back on my bed in underpants and vest. I felt my heart racing, but as though in slow motion, taking a long time between beats – the beat loud, hard. Rather than thinking of Sophie Street and what kind of pathetic dweet she must have thought I was, I was thinking of Harold Kleinhart. Uncle Harold's plan – to try to be cool and philosophical – hadn't worked. Well, not yet. I obviously needed much, much more treatment. What would Uncle Harold say when I told him? He would be upset, deeply, deeply upset.

I recall being so alone that night, that out of sheer desperation – knowing I could not, no matter what he said, call Uncle Harold at midnight – I decided to write to my brother, Cyril. Perhaps he, together with the help I was getting from Uncle Harold, could bring me back? Salvage the wreckage I had become?

Yes, Cyril, always ready and willing, in his sarcastic older-brother way, to reduce the serious, the critical, the drastically urgent, to the easily overcomeable, the easily conquerable. Always ready to sort things into black and white, make them easy to understand, or throw them overboard. Sort of like Dad, but only with some intelligence. Yes, he was definitely my next best bet after Uncle Harold.

Because of the distance and because of his laziness – he hardly ever wrote to me – it was a long shot, I saw that. But I knew once he realised the seriousness of my situation, he would respond, would supply answers, would, in his unflappable way, reduce the complex to the simple. Just what I needed. Only even to him, I knew, I could not mention Uncle Harold, well, not entirely, and definitely not in the first letter. From such a distance he was sure to misinterpret what was happening. I dreaded the typical Cyril reply: *Have yourself seen to, kleinboet!*

But Uncle Harold aside, I knew I could tell Cyril everything. He was sure to have answers. Practical answers. No doubt, several answers. Enough, with Uncle Harold's guidance, to put me back on track again. Surely Cyril would not neglect me now? Surely? I jumped up, taking the two steps it took to get to my red and yellow desk, and then, staring into the darkness outside my window, picked up a pen. I felt suddenly illuminated, like my problems were in the process of being solved.

J'burg, I began at the top right edge of the page, *fog, smog, serious sweat, and all things flaccid.* And then I started my letter, my SOS:

> Cyril, old brother, how things? Long time no hear. This is not quite the letter I wanted to write you. But it's the only one I can write right now. I wanted to write of conquests and triumphs. But I am afraid, for me, it looks like that's not to be. The days here are grey, misty, bleak. Actually Cyril, my mind is black. Black all around me. I reach out but there is no one there. Wherever I look no one. And when I do feel a hand coming across to me, I manage somehow to screw it up, shake it off like a badly fitting glove. I don't want to sound melodramatic or anything, but a tragedy, no make that a double tragedy, has struck me. And I need your help. Fast! Urgent! Quick, ou boet! Here, in a nutshell is what happened.
>
> The other night I was with Sophie Street, remember her? The one with the China doll eyes. Well, anyway, she's a pretty good chick and the other night, well, she let me. You know what I mean. Only something wasn't quite ticking properly in me, I don't think my blood was flowing right or something and . . . I'll be

blunt – I couldn't get it up. Yes, you heard me, I couldn't get it up! I know this may sound weird to you, but she was lying there on the floor without her pants on waiting for me to do it, but as I said, I just couldn't. I don't know why? It was like I was suddenly crippled or something. I even tried putting a Frenchie on, but that only made matters worse. Shit man, you should've just seen me with this empty, dangling bag hanging from my ball hairs! Only it wasn't so funny at the time. It's still not funny!

And if you think that's bad, to make matters worse, it's happened again tonight, yes tonight. With Sophie again! Remember Uncle Harold, dad's friend, well we've become quite good friends lately. He's been a real help to me without you here, but anyway he gave me the keys to his shop – free run of the entire shop – to take chicks there whenever I need a place. How's that! Not bad, hey? Anyway, there I was with Sophie Street tonight, the shop all to ourselves, and shit, shit, shit! Nothing. Nothing doing. Same as before. I don't know what's wrong with me? You can imagine how I feel. And now I don't know what to do? I know it's a crazy thought, but do you think my bris could have something to do with it? Its all I can think about these days – my bris – that something may have gone wrong, that the wrong piece of skin, or maybe too much skin was snipped off or something? Is there anything, anything that you know that you think I should know? Please, please . . . now's the time to tell. I should repeat: you can imagine how I feel – like drek, like crap, like death! Anyway, I don't want to go into too much detail, except to say again, help! Please write and let me know what you think – or more importantly, what I can do. I need your good advice – urgently! This is an SOS.

Oh yes and when you reply DON'T address the back of the envelope, otherwise ma and dad will open it without even looking at who it's addressed to (you know what they're like). I couldn't handle them having even a whiff of this.

Anyway please ou boet, please help! I need some answers. I don't know what's happening down there! I'm confused. All messed up. Please write SOON!!!!

Your troubled, dying boetie

Desperate Dan!!!

I went to bed feeling somewhat better for letting my brother – no matter how far away – into my deepest secret, even if not quite all of it. I couldn't wait to get to a post box to mail the letter. There was a life at stake and if anyone could turn the situation around I knew it was Cyril. I looked up at my dull, white ceiling, somehow confident that I was drawing on all the forces around me now, namely Uncle Harold and Cyril. Most people, I thought, would be envious – what they would do to have a team like that on their side.

13

ncle Harold called early next morning, waking me out of a shallow sleep, my only sleep for the entire night.

"Is there anyone there . . . is it safe to talk?"

"Yeah, you can speak. They're in their bedroom. Actually I was going to get hold of you as soon as I got up."

"About last night . . .? I was hoping you had some good news for me?"

"Eh-hem . . . actually . . . like, shit, I dunno . . . It wasn't good . . . actually bad, very bad . . . like the first time . . . terrible."

"Danny, I can hear, you sound helluva down. I'm sorry."

"Yeah."

"C'mon, boychik, look up. Just don't take it all so seriously. Put it down to experience. I've told you before, whatever we do, we'll get you right. Tell me, did she say anything?"

"No, actually she, like, blames herself. Says I don't love her or something . . .? I'm amazed, really, she doesn't seem to realise . . ."

"That's good, that's very good. She obviously fancies you."

"Or she's a complete idiot."

"C'mon Danny, take it easy on yourself. I told you these things happen, they happen to the best of us. And I think she's obviously mature enough to realise that. The point is, if it wasn't this time, it'll be the next time, or the time after. But it'll happen, don't you worry, you'll see. What you've got to believe and understand, Mr Rothbart, is that there's nothing wrong with you . . . absolutely nothing wrong with you. Look, I can see we're going to need a few more sessions?"

"Yes, I think so. I feel truly . . . screwed . . . Completely down, like."

"Look, what about tonight? I know it's Saturday, but around seven, we'll just go to the shop for about an hour or so, try to sort this little mess in your head out and then I'll drop you back home?"

"Yes, that'll be great." I was incredulous at how he was still willing to put himself out for me. All I wanted to be was just like the other guys – normal – and deep inside I knew he was the only one capable of doing anything about it. Aside from Cyril perhaps, whose letter I hadn't even posted yet. Would post today. For sure. I didn't know how I could have ever thought of myself as better than anyone else. Let alone ahead. Above. Now all I wanted to do was come up to scratch. Just be the same.

Almost exactly ten minutes after we'd said goodbye, Uncle Harold called back. He was puffing.

"Good God, Danny . . . I don't know what I was thinking . . . I nearly forgot . . . I have an important Prog Party meeting tonight. At the City Hall . . . You may have seen some of the posters for it around . . . To protest at the Government's inaction over black education . . . But don't worry, we don't have to let the meeting get in the way. In fact, perhaps it's a good chance for you to come to one of our meetings, see what we're all about, and then we can go to the shop afterwards?"

"Yes," I said enthusiastically, sure that my parents would be happy to see their son go with Uncle Harold to a Progressive Party meeting.

As it turned out, my parents were happy and proud too, my father saying that now I was "going places", even though he himself never voted Progressive, and regularly called them "a bunch of namby-pamby, pansy-wansy imbongolos". My mother too was proud, even though she did say, "Why politics? At your age? Harold should know better than to get you involved in his politics?" But I could see a look in her eyes that said, *my son, mixing in the right circles*, and she relented a little and said, "Well, I'm sure that at least from this you will learn something."

Uncle Harold arrived that night smartly dressed, but not over-dressed. He wore a well-tailored light grey jacket and black pants that flared slightly over black leather shoes. But he wasn't wearing a tie; instead, he had on a black turtleneck jersey that crept under his chin. He looked like some suave rebel leader, perhaps from a South American country. His face gleamed, shaven, rosy, and he smelled of Old Spice.

Although my parents had already gone out to an early show in town, my mother had made sure that, given my determination to wear denims, they were at least my new ones, and that I had on my brown corduroy jacket – the one that she had bought me for special occasions such as weddings and barmitzvahs, jahrzeits and funerals. Even Uncle Harold, who had warned me on the phone to dress up a little, winked approvingly as soon as he saw me.

Arriving at the City Hall I was incredibly surprised. Rather than the protest meeting I had imagined – with an angry crowd throwing stones and chasing police as we saw in the townships – it was like the opening night of an opera, and if there were any police there they must have been in plain clothes because I couldn't see them. Outside the squat, sandstone City Hall building there were parked an array of Mercedes Benz, XJ6s, Alfa Romeos and large Ford Fairlanes, like well-lit luxury cruisers berthed at a dock. Then there were also, of course, the mayor's black Rolls Royce and Uncle Harold's shimmering red E-type Jaguar, which brought a torrent of stares.

Having parked the car in a specially reserved zone outside the City Hall, Uncle Harold smiled at me enthusiastically and led me into the crowd waiting outside the building. The crowd was mainly made up of middle-aged people. The men elegantly silver-haired and thinning on top and the women, well nearly all the women, attired in long black dresses with sparkling sequins, diamond pendants on gold chains clinging neatly to their necks. There were also a few noticeably older women, who looked like they had come to see what their now middle-aged children were doing, and who, though shorter than their children, stood proudly erect, their buffed up hair tinted candy-floss blue and pink. It was a relief whenever I saw a more casually dressed person with an open collar and even more of a relief when I spotted a batch of denim-clad varsity students who made me look over-dressed. Incongruously, it seemed to be they who were directing and ushering people into the hall and making everyone feel at home. I also recognised one or two kids from my school, with a clean-showered look, standing somewhat awkwardly with their very upright and decently dressed parents. My appearance there was probably just as much a shock to them as theirs was to me.

As soon as Uncle Harold and I arrived at the top of the wide cement stairs, a loosely held knot of people rucked around him, including Harry and Freda Silverman, who looked like they were still wearing the same posh clothes that I had met them in at their home. They were obviously the sort of people who never changed into casual wear. Then arrived a small circle of press, who seemed to have a string of questions ready for Uncle Harold. Following closely behind them was a three-man SABC TV crew, who with their extra equipment lumbered along slower than the rest. As soon as they reached the top of the steps, everyone, including the reporters and their camera-flashing photographers, automatically made way for them, as though for a bride and groom on their wedding day. That is except one.

As the television crew puffed up to Uncle Harold, a reporter with hair that curled slightly over his ears, wearing a crew-neck shirt and corduroy sports jacket, stood his ground in front of Uncle Harold, continuing to ask questions as though oblivious of the presence of the SABC TV crew. When the television crew impatiently nudged him in the back with their equipment, he turned around and told them: "Wait your fuckin' turn," which drew applause from the other reporters.

During this little mêlée, I was pushed to the back of the crowd and watched Uncle Harold as he continued to answer questions and shake hands with people, radiating like a star.

Inside, the hall was filled to capacity, and the smell of after-shave and perfume hung so thickly in the air it was like being in a hairdressing salon with my mother on a busy Saturday morning. On the walls were draped blue and white Progressive Party banners, as well as posters that read: *Together into the future, Justice for all* and *Equal Education = Equal Opportunity*.

I took a seat towards the back, squashed in between a row of younger-looking, less dressy people, but I still sat stiffly, feeling out of place, watching Uncle Harold – seated right beside the fat, chunkily gold-chained mayor – looking easy and at home in the centre of a long white-clothed table on the stage.

Then the speeches began and it was good to know that there were white people, even well dressed white people, in this harsh country of mine who were willing to stand up and speak out against the Government. When it came to his turn, Uncle Harold showed himself to be the most eloquent and inspiring of them all. He spoke loudly and roundly in a finely controlled, sandpapery voice that had to be listened to. Mainly he spoke about how despicable it was that a government in a bilingual country – he was referring to English and Afrikaans – should force the majority of its people to be taught almost exclusively in Afrikaans, a language that was not even their mother-tongue and that had no value whatsoever outside the borders of South Africa. He received a loud round of applause for that and used the moment to take a sip of water from a tall glass in front of him while he surveyed the appreciative crowd. He received another round of applause when he said that unless blacks were given an equal education to that of whites, including the opportunity – if they could afford it – to attend private white schools, we would end up in a generation or two with peasants for leaders and "an economy as red as the reddest in Africa, with only our physical labour left for barter". Then, pointing to his own stomach and face, he said, "How would the Government like it if schools only accepted children with big boeps, double-chins and beaks for noses?" and made the entire audience laugh.

"No person's freedom should mean the freedom to exploit or abuse any other person, no matter what the colour of their skin or their standing in the community," Uncle Harold boomed from the stage, tightening his jaw. "What we here in the Progressive Party also say is that no person's higher standing in the community gives any person the right to use that power to abuse or run roughshod over any other person. That is what we in this party stand for," his voice evened and softened, "dignity, respect, humanity. Even the lowest person on the street is entitled to basic human rights. And we at the top, we whites with control over education, must use that education, that intelligence, to give respect and dignity to our fellow beings and not to take it away from them . . . not to use it to trample and enchain them."

Then briefly stroking the saggy skin on his chin with an air of finality, he said, "Recognising the great differences in our peoples, the great divides that still have to be bridged between white and black in South Africa, I say the only road to solving the problems of our country lies not in simple solutions like one man one vote, as though we were a pack of donkeys, but in . . . one educated man one vote. Or as I always say: one smart man one vote. Power must go to the educated, whether they are black or white. Only in that way will we be able to overcome exploitation and the abuse of power, be it black power or white power. And that is why I say: one smart man one vote. That is the way forward to a free and fair and dignified South Africa."

Next to me, I heard a young man tell his wife that Harold Kleinhart was: "just the man this country needs". And it gave me a thrill to know the intimacy I had with this man, and what he was doing for me.

Afterwards, when we met outside on the stairs, after Uncle Harold had said his farewells to a number of people, including the Silvermans, he looked electrified, like a boxer after winning a title bout, and he grabbed my hand and shook it exuberantly, I think forgetting for a moment I was just plain old Danny Rothbart – kid with a problem.

And then we walked down the stairs to his car and in the darkness I was surprised when he asked, "Well, what did you think?"

I told him that I thought it was good, and that he especially was very good.

"Great, I'm glad you got something out of it," he said. "It was a tremendous turnout. Good for the party." He looked away from me, at the grand stone walls of the City Hall, his head, I was sure, still in there, centre-stage.

Then we were in his E-type Jaguar and within seconds we were outside the shop, opening the complicated set of locks to another world.

* * *

Inside, sitting in his private office, he looked at me for a while and then with a slight, warm smile, said, "You know, everything that was said inside that hall tonight, all the grand sentiments and aspirations, are not as important as getting you right. All I want to see from you is a bright smiling face. I want you to be a normal ouk, one of the guys again. I know that person is in there, but for some reason I think you have just blocked him out. It's like there's a blocked drainpipe or something in there." I nodded in agreement.

After considering me for a few moments in silence, he said, "One thing I want you to be sure about, Danny, and that is that what we're doing here, whatever is wrong with you, has nothing to do with being queer, or having feelings for other ouks or anything like that. All I'm doing is trying to help you clean out whatever it is that is blocking that little mind of yours." I moved uneasily in my seat; of course that had been bothering me, that this might be something more, but I was more than immediately happy with his reassurance. Almost feeling a smile on my face. Once again, as though reading me, he said, "You're feeling better within yourself, getting closer all the time, aren't you. . .?"

"Well . . . yes, I suppose . . ." I nodded, always feeling better in front of him.

"Good. I can see you're still unsure, but slowly, slowly, Danny, I think you can see we're unblocking that pipe?" I nodded. "And that's all we can do, little bit by little bit. I was hoping things would happen much faster, would turn around much quicker, but sometimes, with some people, it just takes a little longer. It doesn't mean there's anything more wrong with Danny Rothbart than anybody else. That idea you've got to get right out of your head. It just means you're a little bit different, in your case a little more sensitive. Too sensitive." I nodded again. "All you've got to do now, Danny, is learn to relax, learn to slow your mind down, not to think of everything at once. And when you're with a bird you've got to realise, as I've told you often before, she wants it just as badly as you want it. Maybe more. That it's not a sin. Like God is going to strike you down dead or punish you or something. That's all old hogwash. There's no need for guilt. Never. What you have to do is get yourself out of this mind-set of yours. Youth is too precious, you know. The world will look after itself; we can only do what we can. At your age, Danny, you don't want to be losing sleep over anything. You've got a whole life ahead of you for worries and responsibilities, believe me. Right now the most important thing is getting you right, bringing that bright smile back to your little face. And we will. Danny, you'll see, we will." I looked up at him, feeling comforted, as a baby is comforted, and he said, "I want you to get undressed now and this time, remember, Danny, just relax and enjoy. Don't think about anything. Nothing except birds. Just let yourself go, relax. Completely relax."

And that night, under his tutelage, under his eyes that didn't put me in their spotlight, that didn't make me feel my raw nakedness, I did feel easier and more relaxed than I had ever before. Sophie Street's comments – from only the night before – that to her this same shop appeared so cold and sinister were gone and forgotten. Under Uncle Harold's shadow I felt warm and consoled, like an infant rising after a long illness, like it all could be turned around.

It was hard to believe how someone could feel so differently with two people. With Sophie Street: so tense, so self-conscious, and finally so ashamed. With Uncle Harold: like the shop was a warm, secure shelter or nursery, where there was nothing to be afraid of, where my body worked like a finely oiled machine. And yet strangely, perhaps ironically, it was still Sophie Street with whom I felt more comfortable. More natural. It was her I wanted to be with, who I wanted at my side, and I'm sure Uncle Harold would have agreed, would have told me that was because that was the way it should be.

And once again, as usual, after that night's session, I felt that incredible feeling of lightness, a burst of confidence, that now I was ready, that my problems were over, or would be soon. As once again he told me: "You see there's no need to worry, Danny, I've told you a hundred times before, alles sal regkom."

But there was something different. Something different happened that night. After I had dressed, he looked me in the eyes for a good few moments, intently, as though studying me, as though staring right into me, and then after a while he stepped up to me and hugged me tightly. I hugged him back, unsure what I was meant to do, and then he released me, once again looking at me with an incredible intensity, like he wanted to extract something from me, some truth.

After a while, his eyes visibly moistening, he said, "I love you, Danny. I love you. I just want you to know that."

I was taken aback, completely taken aback, unsure how even to respond. Something in that office had changed. Skewed. Suddenly I was treading water. Needing oxygen.

Looking back now, I still ask myself, what did I think as I heard that confession? I didn't know, I still don't quite know what to make of it. I had never had another male tell me something like that. So it was beyond me. If Chaz had said something like that, I probably would have punched him. Yet coming from an older man who had taken my problems and worries upon his shoulders, who had taken them into his heart, it was kind of a compliment, a magnificent show of faith that I couldn't believe was really coming from another man's lips, from another man's heart.

I could see the love in his eyes as he said those words, I could hear it in the soft vibrating tone in his voice, and yet despite the great compliment it made me feel awkward and self-conscious. I didn't know what to say in return, how to act, I didn't even know if I could return that love. Whether I needed to? I was confused. Perhaps I should have read it as a sign, like signs that people once read into comets – of disaster, a bad omen, of the end of the world approaching – but it was difficult to see, to feel, to sort out. It is difficult anyway, I think for anybody, to turn up one's nose at love. And what I saw and felt there was love. But at the same time it scared me. Just knowing there was love there still scares me. And when, at that time, I couldn't respond, he simply said, "Perhaps one day, perhaps one day, Danny, you will understand." And he looked away, and I felt left alone to look into a future I truly could not fathom.

* * *

Driving home Uncle Harold didn't say much, just sort of looked down at me over his arm and smiled every now and then, a kind of inner glow flickering around his face, his deep-set eyes shining but steadfast.

Arriving outside the house, he put his hand on my hand, and holding it firmly, he reiterated, "Danny, I just want you to know that you are a normal ouk. You have nothing to fear. One day you'll be able to look back on all of this, secure with a wife and kids, and laugh. The only thing I wish is that we could be open about our friendship, about what we're doing, about your problems. But the world just isn't open to that yet, people would never understand." And as he spoke I swam into his arms, and he held me there, telling me: "everything will be alright, yes, everything will be alright."

Walking into my room, a distinct smell of Old Spice about me, I heard a dog howl like a wolf at a moon I couldn't see. The dogs in the neighbourhood always seemed to be barking these days – chained up behind the houses, the growing security walls – barking, howling at moonless shadows, at ghosts, at nothing.

The next morning my parents told me they had seen Uncle Harold and myself on the late TV news. Uncle Harold talking briefly into a camera frame and my face somewhere to the side, at the back. But they had seen me, and they were proud. Proud of their son on the country's newly launched and only channel, on SABC TV, proud of their friend Uncle Harold who had a voice the country listened to.

But inside of me, there was just this incredible feeling of loneliness. Complete and utter loneliness. The future circling before me, like the phantoms that had the neighbourhood dogs barking at everything, everything, yet nothing.

14

S aturday night. Already. Another Saturday night that once had the gonads puffing and pounding. Finding myself now, alone, waiting for Chaz to come over and pick me up for a party in a neighbouring suburb, waiting like a religious person, skullcap and prayer shawl weighing on the head and shoulders, waits for a miracle.

Uncle Harold had called during the week for another session, another talk, and I had immediately told him about the party, the party that I was – as was normal these days – feeling despondent about.

"In that case you must go!" the voice on the other end boomed, concerned. "You have to go out and enjoy yourself, Danny. That's the only way you're going to feel better about yourself. You can't sit at home brooding. A young guy like you, good-looking, the dolls are waiting for guys like you . . . Have a good time for a change. Get drunk. Get smashed. Just make sure you enjoy yourself."

"Shit, I dunno . . ."

"What do you mean, dunno? Don't talk like that, Danny. This is just the sort of language you have to avoid. Be positive. Tell yourself that you're OK, that there's a whole world out there waiting for you. Even if you're feeling down, Danny, you must go. Nothing will ever happen if you stay at home moping. Nothing. Danny, go, and you'll see. I know that sometimes you just need a bit of a push, but go after it and you'll get there. Mark my words."

"Ja . . . but maybe, like, we should meet again first . . .?"

"Yes, yes, OK . . . I think that may be a good idea. What say, I pick you up Thursday?"

We met again that Thursday night. Once again he soothed me with his assurances, and once again, as was becoming the usual now after our sessions, he hugged me and I clung to his body, unsure of what to do, feeling like a tiny bird swamped by a bear, but nevertheless appreciating the warmth, the security, the closeness. And even though on this occasion he didn't speak of the love, the love he had told me he felt for me, I thought I could see it in his eyes, in the moisture that filled his eyes when we hugged.

"Even if you never love me, I will always love you," he told me once, and though it made me feel like a small king to be loved so grandly by such a powerful figure, it confused me and confuses me still. How could someone love like that? How could he love someone so inadequate? So unable to love back? What, anyway, I thought in my boyish mind, did it have to do with the therapy?

But I came home that night with a feeling of surety, feeling like I always had somewhere to turn, always had someone who would be there for me, someone to hold me when I needed to be held.

The aching, gravelly voice of Leonard Cohen stirred me from my thoughts. One consolation was that my parents were out. It was always such a relief when they were out and I was left to myself. The house ceased to belong to them; became mine. Having them constantly about was probably what blacks in this country felt like, always having a pair of eyes hovering over your shoulders, telling you where to be, where to go, how to mind your manners, what to say, what language to say it in. So now, without my parents in the house, there was this great sense of space, of air. Even though right now, as usual, I was finding it difficult to breathe.

I looked about the lounge, not quite sure what I was looking for: perhaps some helpful angel from another world who had witnessed my life and who would arrive now, magic potion in hand, to make me whole again? But the lounge, with its bright orange sheen and its plastic chandelier hanging from the middle of the ceiling like an illuminated box jellyfish, didn't exactly encourage such higher energies. Worse, in the centre of the wall opposite – it had been moved again –

our orange glowing Tretchikoff faced me, looking down like she understood everything but refusing to do anything, simply refusing, just opting to remain on the wall and smirk and ridicule.

Cyril, I began to think, would have long received my letter by now. What did he think? Why was he taking so long to reply? I was almost tempted to write again, to impress on him the urgency of it all. The absolute urgency. I imagined him scribbling away, having thoroughly researched the problem. Posting the letter, or rather trying to post the letter that was by now the size of a book. I imagined him pushing, bending, twisting the manuscript, trying to squash it through the narrow Royal Mail post-box window. And, somehow, at that moment, I felt sure it was on its way, or would be soon. Patience, as Uncle Harold often said to me. Patience. Everything will come in its time.

Lethargically, I dragged myself from the armchair and draped myself over the couch, out of direct view of our Tretchikoff, the omniscient, all-knowing Tretchikoff, that offered nothing but the self-satisfied smirk of foreboding. In the background Leonard Cohen droned on, sinking to lower and lower depths of despair.

In this frame of mind, I decided Uncle Harold was right: I had to let go. I just had to somehow make the effort and get the most out of life. Live, enjoy. Conquer! With this thought in mind, I jumped up and began to pace the room, at first shaking my hands and legs as if in exercise, and then in a definite dance. It didn't matter what the music was, suddenly I was dancing, dancing before the Tretchikoff woman, saying aloud to myself, to her, "I can, I can, I can," until the words on the LP told me: "So, is this what you wanted . . . to live in a house that is haunted . . . by the ghost of you and meeee . . .?"

I raced over to the stereo and flipped off Leonard Cohen, replacing it with The Rolling Stones. Now I was really dancing, my thoughts flying, surging, lifting, soaring, as my body bounced and my hands smashed the dull air with a drum-roll. And then there was a crashing sound at the front door, snapping me back to reality.

Chaz. I opened the door as he flicked his cigarette-end into the garden. He lumbered into the room, blowing out one last smoke-ring and swinging a green wine-bottle in his hand. His blotchy, pimple-specked face ruddy from the cold and sprouting a little black beard that resembled the hairs on moulding fruit, but which made me look up to him in envy.

"Looks like you're ready to jol?" His voice pitched and cracked, as he held up his hand for me to slap and clinch.

"Yeah, Yeah. Ready to hit it. Anywhere. Anytime." I slapped his hand hard, heartily, clinching his fingers tightly, then turned, thrusting my pelvis forward with two sharp jabs, my right hand on my hip, like Elvis.

Seeing my mood, Chaz dashed into the kitchen for a bottle-opener. He returned from the kitchen with the bottle opened but no glasses. With a wide swinging arm he took a long swig from the bottle – his Adam's apple swashing frighteningly against the tide of the liquid going down – then he passed the bottle on to me.

"Mmmmm . . . better than the usual," I said – the wine didn't cut my throat like the vinegary wines we were used to. "Where d'you score it?"

"My old girl, she was given a case by my uncle visiting from Cape Town. There're so many bottles, like, I don't think she'll notice one's missing. It's a blanc de blanc."

I held the bottle up to the light, watching it glint.

"Ohhh yaars . . . the tex-chaah . . . the boo-kay . . . now this is what you call a blank der blank. Geen nie-blankes hier, geen nie-blankes daar . . . geen nie-blankes any-bloody-whaar."

Two sips and Chaz and I were roaring and suddenly it felt like a good time to let out the truth, to come clean once and for all. But as I prepared to speak, to make my confession, I looked up at Chaz and my jaw hardened and froze. The truth was just too hard.

Chaz took one more swig and popped the cork back in the bottle, ready to go. I switched off the stereo and all the lights in the house, except the hallway – the one left on for burglars. I would normally have taken one final glance at myself in the square gold-framed mirror in the hallway, above the phone table – usually in approval, or else I'd dash back into the bathroom to get my hair right, even if in essence that meant more messy, more natural-looking – but tonight I walked right past the mirror. I had to haul myself back at the last minute, telling myself, as Uncle Harold had coached me to tell myself: *Everything will be alright, everything will be alright.*

I caught a fright when I saw myself – my spring-mattress brown hair that my mother always said was so handsome and curly, my dull, groggy brown eyes that my mother always said were so wide open and beautifully bright and serious – but there was no way now that I was dashing back into the bathroom to touch up. No way!

As we walked out of the house Chaz's fingers dived straight into his corduroy jacket pocket and retrieved a packet of cigarettes and a lighter. He flipped the top open and pulled one out with his teeth, like the tough lone-star in the Marlboro ads or the super-cool racing-car driver in the Lucky Strike ones. As for me, instead of cigarettes, or even Frenchies, these days I was carrying chewing-gum. I took out a packet and threw two of the white peppermint pieces into my mouth and then offered the pack to Chaz. He shook his head, a smoke-ring funnelling out of his warbling mouth.

Out in the dark, fortified against the cold – the wine soothing to some extent the tightness in my stomach – I could see in Chaz's determined gait the way I used to feel on my way out on a Saturday night; out to prove, in my father's fine, imaginative language, that I was a man not a mouse.

"It's so cool, your not being a virgin, man. Maybe we could arrange something for me now, like?" Chaz.

I had to say something.

"Yeah, yeah, of course, like, I'm sure we can do something." I felt my throat constrict. "Some time. Some time soon. Who knows, maybe even tonight?"

"Yeah, as if . . . But maybe, like, we could arrange for Sophie to come over to my place with one of her friends, like . . .? Just not Jessica Shmelly again. Never, never again. Anyone but the Shmell."

I nodded sympathetically, chin and nose in the air, like I was the wise, experienced one.

"Yeah, OK, Chaz. Definitely, I'll see what I can do. I'll speak to Sophie." Shit, would he ever let up? It was like he knew something, like he knew and was purposely making me suffer. I looked up into the tight, black skullcap of a sky and thought, Why would anyone so great want to shape us the way we are? Make life so good, so damn easy for some, so completely terrifying for the rest? That poem, that poem that we had to learn off by heart at school, running through my head, the words already warping: "Tyger, Tyger, burning bright, In the forests of the night; What immortal hand or eye, Could frame thy *awful* symmetry . . .?"

"Ja . . ." Chaz, scratching a pimple on his chin with his cigarette hand, looked at me and said: "And you're the one who still thinks there's a God?"

Chaz Bernstein had read my thoughts. Just what I'd always been afraid of. That he would see it in my eyes, read it in my head, and announce it through his megaphone mouth for all the world to hear.

I didn't answer him, instead saying, "Don't we take a left at the next street, into Observatory Avenue?" Life wasn't a lost cause, it was a battle of losers.

* * *

Arriving at the front gate we looked up a stone walkway that led up through a sloping garden of shrubs, trees and rockeries. Faintly we heard music and laughter. This was a different side to the Observatory where Sophie Street lived, this was not Observatory East – where

152

the houses were almost joined to their front fences – but Observatory proper, where the yards were like mini botanical gardens, and the houses, set well back into the gardens, were solid-stone mansions serviced by a small team of full-time servants. One servant just to look after the garden and act as back-up in case of an emergency, and another two or three to care for the mansion itself: to cook and make the beds. The big double-garage beside the house itself a mansion to the Soweto families some of them came from.

It was only when we reached a short flight of stairs hewn out of the rock at the top of the garden that we caught sight of some young people hanging over a stone veranda above our heads and we knew for sure we were in the right place; hadn't wasted our breath chuffing up the endless path for nothing.

As we arrived in the main part of the house, where the music was blaring and most people were hanging out, I heard a girl whisper behind me: "There's Danny Rothbart." It took me completely by surprise. It was the voice of someone who had obviously noticed me. Why I should still have fans I didn't know. But for a moment I felt myself lift two feet off the ground, my head expanding like a balloon. Then thinking about it, my life thus far, I wondered what they would say if they knew, and immediately I felt my head shrink, my ankles lock, my feet slamming back to earth. The old knot was back in my stomach. *No, no,* I scolded myself with Uncle Harold's voice, *don't think of such things now. Take it easy. Lighten up. Just go, go with the flow. Relax, Danny, just relax. Don't always try to think of things from all angles.* I felt a little soothed.

At the other end of the room, in a large doorway, a shadowy presence flickered a dark golden brown, just out of the candlelight: Sophie Street. My heart leapt. And there next to her hovered the plump, over-painted face of Jessica Shmulowitz, ol' Shmelly, whispering, I saw it, the word, "Danny". I waved, but as I did so I saw Sophie girlishly grab hold of Jessica's hand and both girls turned, out of the door-

153

way, out of the candlelight. I felt a strong urge to run after her, but the presence of my friends, the crew, around me prevented me. Fuck! She could be so aloof, so cold. And to think with one tiny word from her plum-coloured lips she could wipe me out. I shivered, but it was too late to do anything now; the guys – Solly, Peter, Aaron – had formed a circle around Chaz and me. Chaz was offering the wine-bottle around, and then flipping a cigarette into his mouth he immediately began to click out a series of tyre-thick smoke-rings. Aaron tapped the side of his cheek with his middle finger, trying to match Chaz, watching his much smaller rings float a short way out of his mouth only to melt too soon into the dim air. When it came to smoke-rings, there were no two ways about it: Chaz was in a league of his own.

In loud voices, we began to shoot down whoever fell into our path: this one for wearing floral bell-bottoms that were ten years out of date, that one with the shiny black boots and couple of orange streaks through his hair for thinking he was some punk trendy, this one for singing to himself as he danced, that one for flicking his fringe back like Robert Redford, thinking all the girls fancied him. As if. My eyes wandered about the room, still looking for Sophie. I spotted Jessica Shmulowitz surrounded by a ring of black and purple-clothed girls and pointed her out to Chaz, watching as he stuck his middle finger deep into his throat and then wriggled his body: expelling a loud, invisible waterfall of puke.

But even as we laughed snidely at those others I was wondering what they thought of me. What did Solly, Peter, Aaron think? What did they know that they weren't saying? I could feel it, feel them feeling me trying to feel them. I was coming apart; could feel my flesh, the very seams, fraying, tearing open. Jesus, and there was nothing, absolutely nothing I could say or do. I wished I could have Uncle Harold in my pocket to put me back on track whenever I fell off.

Then out of the corner of my eye I became aware of her, a wiry, white-haired girl standing in the shadows by herself, staring from time to time, at me openly eyeing me from that dark spot in the corner of the square room.

Suddenly feeling a rush of blood to my head – probably from the wine – I dropped back from our circle and walked up to the girl, taking her hand, feeling her come willingly. Willingly! My heart gave a loud bang and I threw my body round to the music, wildly pulling her towards me, then throwing her backwards. She followed my pulls and shoves like they were ballet steps, like we were two sputniks whirling around one another, as between us a kind of warm, woollen space filled with sparks. Totally inspired, I was jumping up and down like I was on a pogo stick, feeling her eyes lifting me. Feeling happier than I had for a long time. *That's it. Just let go. Lighten up. Relax, Danny, relax. Just take it nice and easy and it'll all fall into place.* I thought I spotted Sophie Street, but it didn't matter now, not now. I was high on the moment. In the background becoming aware of my friends, even Solly, clapping their hands to our beat, yes, our beat, whistling and shouting, urging us on. This was the old Danny Rothbart. The Danny Rothbart I thought I was.

Finally growing tired, both of us growing tired, we swayed out through the open French doors onto the stone patio outside, followed by the envious stares of the crew, Chaz and Aaron's open thumbs up. And there we leant, exhausted, against one another, looking out over the wooden railing onto a garden that looked like a perfectly manicured miniature jungle.

Outside we exchanged names, hers sounding like some sort of starship: "May-Ann . . . May-Ann Cruise . . ." She already, pleasingly, knowing mine: "Danny . . . Rothbart." How she knew, she wouldn't say, but I was more than happy to let it slide.

She put her arm through mine, lifting me ten feet off the ground. Boldly, I looked into her face, studying it: the tracing-paper-thin skin, smooth, soft, milk-white; the eyes, small, bright, elfin, unmade-up, natural. Unusually natural. Gazing back at me, unabashed, she told me that she would soon be leaving the country with her family for London: "Because there isn't a thing anyone can do, South Africa will never change, everything will remain separated, banned, and soon the country will be drenched in blood." As if it were not already. But I didn't say it; I didn't want to spoil a night like this on pedantic details.

Her face lit up as she spoke of how exciting it would be to live in London, to be part of the real world, to be at the very cutting edge of art, movies, music, fashion, all that was happening. To be unchained from everything-restricted, nothing-to-do Jo'burg. A world apart from the kugels at the party, the imported Vogue and Cosmopolitan clones who only thought: *How do I look? What should I wear? How can I be better than . . .?*

I was amazed, more and more amazed, that she had chosen me. In return I told her how Chaz and I planned to leave the country at the end of the year to avoid the army, and she with twinkling eyes, responded: "It'll be magic. Absolute magic. To meet in London Town . . . How about checking out this wonderful lush jungle below?"

"Ah-maaazing . . ." Her voice a fairy's song, her elfin eyes a mystery, this garden: Eden. She pirouetted, her long white hair, her soft blue dress flowing around her like a high-school girl's thin cotton uniform.

"We have a garden just like this at home." she sang the words, sang them. "Only it is even more beautiful than this, fuller, wilder . . . I'll miss it . . . Wouldn't you just love to live in an old English castle . . .?"

Nodding enthusiastically I tripped over a rock. *Klutz,* I thought. *Was I always such a klutz?* She smiled and grabbed my hand, pulling me down through the garden. *Just go with the flow.* I heard Uncle Harold's voice coaching. We came to a sweeping, bowing tree like a willow and sat beneath it on the cold, damp ground. Neither of us saying anything, happy to be hidden from the house by the tree and the bushes and the wilderness that surrounded us. Involuntarily I placed a hand over my stomach, to smother a rising commotion in there, then realising how it must look I threw my hand to the side, leaning back casually, smiling.

156

We just sat there, holding hands, staring straight ahead at the leafy shadows, the sky our roof. But in my head the guerilla was busy getting down to the business side of things, working out tactics, lines of action: How? When? With what words? What signal? What kind of kiss? What kind of embrace, exactly? Hearing the crickets, unstoppable, flapping in my belly as I mulled over the moves, feeling a nose sliding slippery against my nose, a forehead fixing against my forehead, eyelashes clashing like a loud clout of moths' wings, lips crashing, tongues colliding. Then all of a sudden I felt myself stirring, stirring down there. It was moving. I couldn't believe it.

And then I felt her hand on my crotch and the world was out of control, spinning, faster, faster. *Don't be a bloody schmendrik,* I told myself, using my dead zeide's words. *Just make the most of it, lie back, boy, enjoy.* I wished I could be relaxed, relaxed like I was on Uncle Harold's great desk.

"Yu-uk, what's that?" Suddenly I felt her unceremoniously pushing me backwards.

I had forgotten about the chewing gum in my mouth – the chewing gum I kept in my pockets instead of condoms these days – hidden between cheek and back teeth. But I suddenly felt it now, soft and mushy, caught up against her front teeth.

"Just a bit . . . bit of . . . gum." I drew it back with the tip of my tongue and swallowed it.

"Urgh," I'm sure I heard her moan, but to my surprise she continued and I felt myself falling.

Just relax, Danny. Relax. Just go with the flow, I began to repeat over and over in my head – finding, upon analysis, that really, perhaps, it was she that I was trying to tell to relax, to just go with the flow, to be soft and gentle, to have some consideration for the battered and bruised and inexperienced among us. But of course I could not get the words out of my mouth, not those words. Suddenly feeling us down on the damp ground, sweat pouring from my armpits like a spring. They say lightning, as I had noted somewhere before, never strikes twice, but here I was under that bolt again. Yet again, incredulous receiver of yet another golden bolt. I must have something, some attraction about me, some attraction that I just couldn't understand. Thinking. I remember thinking. For all of my crew, the ouks, the manne, what was happening here akin to coming face to face with the Messiah: a dream, a revelation. For me: a time bomb.

She ripped off my jersey, adeptly unbuttoned my shirt, and then pointed coyly with those lovely elfin eyes at my pants. Instantly I obeyed, and she helped, seeing the klutz in me. I am sure, seeing the klutz in me. Then leaning back on my elbows on the cold, wet ground I saw her kneeling, looking at me with those tiny, peeping eyes as she unbuttoned that flimsy summer schoolgirl dress, lifted it like an unwanted rag and threw it, a wobbly Frisbee landing behind us. Still looking at me, she began to undo her bra. Her bra! Jesus, if only the guys could have seen me. I felt a liquid heat explode in my forehead and spread through my body, right down into the tips of my still sock-covered toes. I wriggled my toes just to test that they were there, that they still did really belong to me, but as I was busy contemplating my toes, she was suddenly on top of me, spine arching, hand reaching down. I thrashed my legs like an insect and she rolled over, laughing, pulling me on top of her.

And then like the mighty bellow of God from Cecil B. DeMille's *Ten Commandments*, I hear a voice blast forth in my ears: "THIS IS IT! THIS IS IT, DANNY!" Inspired, I make my first thrust. One, two, three. But the more I thrust, the more I know I have felt this before and the truth is: THIS IS NOT IT! THIS IS NOT IT, DANNY!

"Shit!" I heard a voice cry out as though from the moon, shocking me back to reality, the reality that there is actually someone else there. Her elfin eyes, wild and green now like a goblin's, turning in her head. "Are you drunk or something?"

"Huh? Oh, me? No!" I swallowed hard, feeling anger, feeling like stabbing myself. Instead, because there was obviously no knife with which to stab myself, I sat up, slapping my hand sharply across those oh so delicate, oh so subtly beautiful, tracing-paper-thin cheeks. The moment it struck, this way and then that, I noted the horror rise in the sunken face. Panicking, I breathed out: "Sorry! Sorry! I, I didn't really do that." Screaming inside myself: *Did I, did I really do that?*

But the once white, now deeply pink face was glaring up at me, eyes wounded, stunned, declaring: "Oh shit, man! Oh shit!" And then she sprang up – grabbing clothes and underclothes – leaving me in the woods, lumbering through the only thing there was for me to lumber through, my thoughts. *What has come over me? What? Am I now becoming a monster? As well? On top of everything else? Is this the pattern? Failure . . . Loser . . . Molester . . . Killer . . . Serial failure . . . Serial killer? Oh my God, oh my God.* Even if I told Chaz the exact truth of what had happened now, he would never have believed me. None of it. Not a blinking word. *So much for magic meetings in groovy London Town,* I thought as I dressed and made my way up through the shrubs, the shadows, to the house.

As I approached the top of the garden, grand stone mansion in sight, wondering who by now knew, a thick-set boy, manly black stubble that I immediately envied prickling darkly out of a jutting, gorilla-sized jaw, stepped in front of me like a werewolf. Without even a nod or a wink he grabbed hold of my jersey at the shoulder, jerking me up to his wide flaring nostrils, peering down at me with yellow, red-specked eyes. My eyes spun as he lifted me, dangled me in the air; his shoulders curling like he was in a gym exercising. Behind him my revolving eyes made out her goblin eyes, her too-thin frame, her arms folded stiffly over those oh so amazing breasts. I wanted to smile in recognition. Say I was sorry, sorry. But instead I felt my top lip twitch into a curve and then both my lips, my entire face wobbling as this half-boy, half-wolf thing in front of me shook me backwards and forwards, forwards and backwards. Then the hot misty breath from his mouth shot into my nose as he barked, "Fucker! Stupid-dumb-thick-good-for-nothing-prick!" As if I didn't know, as if I didn't know. Behind him I saw her nodding in agreement, as he threw me backwards and caught me, solidly, in the face with a tightly clenched fist, first right and then left and then right again. Strangely numb I crumbled to the ground. Like I was the man my father always said I was: a frightened little rodent with no backbone.

I lay for a while, perhaps a minute, two minutes; and then, struggling, I managed to sit up. I looked down and felt my nose – my fairy princess and her dragon slayer already dissolved into the night – my fingers returning from my nose strangely wet, my blurry eyes confirming they were soaked in something, something black?

"Shit, man! What's out? What's happened to you? You OK, like?" Chaz's cigarette-breath was suddenly around me. Solly, Peter and Aaron also in the vicinity, looking on, heads darting, fists clenched, looking for the bastard who did this thing to me. "We just saw this big ou bouncing you one, like, then he was gone." Chaz, Marlboro Man, to the rescue. "Else we would've planted him one. Maybe we can still find him now?" Me shaking my head, vigorously. *No, no, no, no.*

"Shit, go clean off your face, there's blood everywhere." Solly looked down into my face, aghast, like it was a badly painted image of someone else's face.

Chaz and Solly held me between them as I limped to a tap in the garden. To one side, Aaron looked at me, even as we all walked together, like he was studying a ghost, a bloodied ghost. Peter looked away from me, like he didn't want to know a ghost. Bending down I felt the icy water wash across my face, completely refreshing, sobering, as all of them stood around me, muttering revenge, retaliation; but in the end none of us even went back to the party. Instead we retraced our steps through the miniature jungle and walked home. All talking loudly, at the top of our voices, parting one by one, heading off in our different directions to the suburbs, until, as per usual, just Chaz and I remained.

When we had all been together and they had asked what had happened, how I had ended up in such a bloody mess, I told them I had no idea. There was just this big guy who took an instant dislike to me. Bumped me in the garden as I made my way back up to the house after making out with this May-Ann Cruise chick, and then he had smacked me one in the face completely out of the blue. They all found the story plausible. It happened all the time at parties. At some parties in the nearby suburbs – Highlands North, Orange Grove, Sydenham – it was so bad you had to be careful of the way you swished the fringe on your hair, or the way you glanced at some of the guys. Because if they didn't like the look of you, or the way you looked at them, before you knew it you ended up with a broken nose, broken ribs, a smashed-up face.

But now I was alone with Chaz it was different.

"Danny, what really happened, like?" Chaz's Adam's apple bobbed up and down excitedly, dryly.

"Really, I don't know, like . . . I know it may sound bizarre, but really, like, I don't know." I sniffed what I thought was blood back up my nose.

"Why didn't you punch him back?"

"He took me from behind. When I wasn't even expecting it, like. You saw for yourself."

"Who was the chick, anyway?"

"Oh, her? The chick? Eh-hem, May-Ann . . . May-Ann Cruise."

"And . . . anything?"

"Shit, you've always got to know everything, don't you? Why the hell do I always have to tell you every bladdy little detail?"

"Shit man, Danny, what's with you . . .? All I want to know is what happened."

"Actually . . . like I came pretty close, hey."

"And . . .?"

"She took her bra off for me, like . . . What a pair, man! What knockers! And then, like, after a while, she just said she had to go. Got a hand-job though."

Chaz looked down at me gaga-eyed. Placing me on that pedestal.

"Shit man, you just seem to have it. You always seem to get the chicks to do whatever you want. A hand-job, hey? Fuck. Lucky prick!"

"Yeah, well . . . no . . . shit-yeah."

Lucky prick. If only he'd known. Prick indeed. Prick, penis, whatever brand name you gave it, came to the same thing: *noun, pl. penises or penes – the male genital organ of higher vertebrates, carrying the duct for the transfer of sperm during copulation.* According to the Oxford English Dictionary, *the* Oxford English Dictionary no less, I did not have one. Chaz would have laughed his head off. Solly and Aaron would have gone berserk.

And then, thank God, we parted. At last I was alone again, alone and safe. Sullen, depressed, bashed, bruised, but at least alone and safely out of the way of their questioning eyes.

I couldn't sleep that night and when finally morning came I pulled the blankets over my head, hoping to block out the daylight, but my head throbbed, my mouth was desert-dry and the pain, like my thoughts, just wouldn't go away. Finally, thirsty as hell, I forced myself up and limped to the kitchen. My father – just the person I didn't want to see – was already sitting at the breakfast table, leaning over what looked like a row of eggs staring roundly out of his plate, yellow and runny-eyed. Worse still, a distinct smell of fried liver pervaded the kitchen and around the edge of his plate I could see little burnt balls looking like scorched cicadas. For a moment I thought I was going to pass out and began to reverse, but it was too late.

"Jesus Christ, Danny, what happened to you?" I watched him swallow with difficulty the huge mouthful he had been chewing.

"I got into a bit of a fight last night . . . at a party . . . it's nothing."

"A fight, eh? You know that's some shiner you got there? Maybe we'd better take you to a doctor? Just a check-up? Can do no harm."

"No, really, I'm OK, it's nothing."

"So how did it happen?"

"I don't know, just this guy, this guy sort of took a dislike to me and came at me from behind."

"Took a dislike to you? For no reason?"

"Well I think, without knowing it, I was dancing with his girlfriend earlier in the night."

"Oh. I suppose that kind of thing can happen. And you didn't defend yourself?" Silence. A long, loud silence, and when there was no response forthcoming, "You know how to use yourself?"

"Ja, I did, I tried, but he was big . . . much bigger than me."

My father, half rising from his chair, took on the demeanour of sports coach. "I've told you this before, don't be frightened by size. It's not size that counts. It's how quick, how fast you are. How quickly you get in there. You know the old adage, the bigger they are the harder they fall?"

"I tried, da'. I really tried."

He looked down, at the kitchen floor. "Danny, you've got to learn to use that little kop of yours." He sat down again, I could see, my defeat hanging on his curled shoulders like I had somehow let the family name down. "Well, are you OK?"

"Yeah . . . thanks for asking."

"You know, in my day I could use myself. It didn't matter how big they were. In-out, jib-jab, one-two, and down they went." He sucked in a remnant of egg from his upper lip. "I thought I taught you how to look after yourself. All that judo and karate and boxing and stuff I took you to."

"Yeah, well . . ." I glared at him, remembering all the self-defence classes. I hated most of it, especially the boxing – the hot runny eyes from being punched flat in the nose – always protesting that I'd be too tired when I finally arrived home to do my homework. My mother protesting, on my behalf, that I would get hurt, could maybe even be disfigured for life.

163

"Well, never mind, never mind," he said, turning away from me, "the army'll make a man out of you yet."

I turned to leave the kitchen, without my water, and walked slap-bang into my mother.

"Oh my God. Oh my God, Danny. Just look at you! Your eye . . . what's happened? It's all blue and swollen. Were you in an accident or something? My poor baby. What's happened to you?" She was pulling me into her arms, kneading me into her chest like I was dough. "What happened to that lovely baby face of yours?"

"I was just in a fight, that's all."

"A fight!" She let go of me, eyes wide and shocked. "Who would want to fight with you? Who would want to do such a thing to my baby?"

"It was just some guy at the party."

She shook her head, her hair sticking up like unbrushed coir from its heavy early morning application of hairspray. "I don't want you going to any more of these parties, I don't want to see my boy getting hurt. If you want to go to a party in future you can rather just have a few of your friends over here. You can enjoy yourselves then . . . in the safety of your own home. Only last week there was that story in the paper of how those gatecrashers, Lebs or something, smashed up that nice young Jewish girl's home in Highlands North. Beat up the father, too . . . Lucky the police were in the area."

"It was just a bit of a mishap, ma. I'll be OK."

"Well, that party in Highlands North was also just a bit of a mishap . . . Here, I can't stand to see your face like that, give me a hug."

Seeing in her eyes that she was deeply thrown, that someone could want to do this to her "baby", I walked into her outstretched arms. I saw it was a chance for her to caress and mother. If only she knew the truth. That her son, her baby boy was not only hurt and badly bruised, but that he was now going around hurting, bruising every-one else. I wondered what she would do? Would she still want to hug

164

me, still be so ready to love and mother me? Or would she want to see me locked away in some institution and punished? A blight on the family, a family she had raised to be straight and stand tall. How could I ever tell her, either of them, the truth? The truth could be so cruel, brutal and confounding. It was better to live with a lie, a thousand lies, with cover-ups and disguises. Facing those you love – even those you despise – and telling the truth is hard. It is easier to face yourself in a mirror and lie.

Hugging her, I now – as was expected – kissed my mother twice on her pale, dry lips. The strange thing was I knew she believed me, trusted me absolutely. I could tell her a thousand lies and she would believe me. Tell her the truth, and I don't know, I didn't know what might happen. I could already see in her eyes the famous lines that said, *Tsores. Such a young boy and already such tsores*. I felt her releasing me.

"Tell me, was it a Jewish boy?"

"Stel, for God's sake, leave the boy alone." My father quickly to the rescue. "Jewish boys do these things as well, you know. Danny just came off second-best this time around. He's just got to learn to look after himself better, that's all."

"Well, if you don't mind, I don't want there to be any more rounds, no more first or second, or any more rounds!" My mother turned around and stormed off wet-eyed, as though up against a wall she could not crack.

My father threw his arms up into the air, pronouncing the old saying I had heard him pronounce a thousand times before: "What can you do? Life with a wife . . . twice as bad without one!" And then, taking me into his confidence, he said, "I don't know what it is, Danny, women just never seem to understand. One day you'll see for yourself. It's not that easy. Just look after yourself, my boy, and enjoy yourself while you can."

I nodded and smiled. At that moment I could see why he and

Uncle Harold were friends after all – even if politically they were poles apart; there was something in their language that was the same. There was something, somewhere, in their thinking that was alike. My father winked at me, friendly, as if we were two men who understood one another, and then he went back to his breakfast. Still without my water, I retreated to my room and lay back on my bed, hands over my eyes, seeing only black. I wondered if I would ever have a woman, any woman, even one like my father spoke of, one who never seemed to understand. Praying for a miracle. I knew I would have to get hold of Uncle Harold soon, as soon as I could.

15

"Christ, Danny, you're a mess!" Uncle Harold's head flicked back as I walked into his office. He was sitting, unusually relaxed, with one leg lazily stretched over a corner of his desk. His hands were folded across his stomach and he was leaning well back in his chair. I – sitting on the opposite side of the desk – sat slouched in silence. The desk lamp glowed softly between us, throwing a dull light over his loved ones in their little ornate silver frames.

"Danny, don't look so morose . . . I've told you a hundred times before, it's not the end of the world. There's always a way through." Uncle Harold's eyes glazed over, as though my failure was somehow his failure, saying, without saying it, *It's OK, Danny, lean on me.*

"Well, I think . . . you've got to admit . . . it doesn-doesn't look . . . too good . . ." I began, mumbling.

"So what?" He threw his arms into the air and swung around in his chair, nearly taking the family pictures with him as he dropped his leg to the floor. He steadied the pictures, looking intently at me. "Danny, that's the way it is sometimes, that's just the way it goes. That's life. OK, so you got a bit of a zets, had another bit of a bad experience, but it's not the end of the world. Like I said, there's always a way out, always a way through. Danny, what you've got to start doing is taking a more positive, more realistic look at the world. Don't take everything on your own shoulders, like it's always your fault. I would have also been hurt had some girl said to me what this Mary-Jane—"

"May-Ann," I corrected.

"Well, this May-Ann or whatever her name is, said to you. The thing is not to let these things get to you." He lifted his finger. "Frailty thy name is woman!" Then he pointed his finger at me and smiled wryly.

"Danny, the one thing you can be sure of in this life is that you'll never understand them. Girls. Birds. Women. Whatever you want to call them. They're a breed of their own. One minute they love you, need you madly, will do anything for you, next they accuse you of not caring, being selfish, and you can't do a thing right. Sure, we need them, but it is not our wont, not in our make-up to understand them, so don't even try, especially not at your age." I nodded and he pointed his index finger at my chest. "Danny, things may look grim now, but remember, after the night must come the day. Never forget that. Night must always be followed by day. The trouble with you, Danny, is that you're always looking for the night, a deeper meaning, a deeper side to everything. Always a way to dig yourself into the darkness, into the hole rather than out. Well, let me tell you this, there isn't always a deeper side to things. Sometimes things just happen. We don't want them to, but they do, and all we can do, all we must do, is accept. We can't always go around questioning and changing things, sometimes we must just accept things the way they are, and slowly, slowly, as we come to terms with them, so we will work our way through them. What it comes down to is this: you take your chances when you can get them. And if something goes wrong, if you mess up, well, it's not the end of the world. It's not as if you're a freak or something. Danny, you're a normal guy. Everything will be alright in the end."

I looked up at him, wanting to say something, something wise, but in the end all I could get out was: "Maybe I should be seeing a psychologist or something." It just sort of flowed out of my mouth, like a waterfall.

He waved his finger in the direction of the ceiling, nodding his head. "Psychologist-psyshmologist. What could a psychologist do for you?" And when there was no reply, just my eyes searching for an answer in his face, he said, "Look, I'm not saying a psychologist couldn't help, but it would take years. Years of delving into your childhood, delving into your parents' childhood, bringing up a load of stuff about whether your mother and father really love you, when you and I know very well they do. No, I think you realise by now there is a block somewhere in there, somewhere in that little kop of yours and once we get through that block, you're going to be fine. Just fine. I know your mom and dad don't always understand what's going on with you, what's in that head of yours. But that's what I'm here for, Danny. I want you to speak to me, never be afraid to speak to me about anything." He paused for a moment and studied me carefully, examining my face the way perhaps I had examined May-Ann's, the way I often wanted to examine Sophie Street's – if only she would let me – and then he said, "You know, Danny, with your looks and your brain, I can tell you, you're going to have the birds running, birds galore. We've just got to work our way through this little block in there and then I can promise you you're going to be on the road again. Ultimately, you've just got to learn not to be so sensitive."

"Yeah . . . but it . . . it's just that . . . it's all . . ."

"It's all what? Danny, remember whatever you say will never go past this door. I promise you." He motioned with his eyes to the office door behind me.

"It's just that . . . well, for one thing . . . whenever I leave here after one of our . . . sessions . . . I feel like, better, elevated, you know, like . . ." I could feel my armpits growing clammy, the hairs on my head prickling as I marched towards a truth, my truth; but in the end I couldn't do it, couldn't admit my fears, my real fears, and I chose another tack instead, telling him only a half-truth. "But when it comes to the real thing, well, you know, I still get so damn . . . so damn anxious . . . I just sort of lose track . . . for-forget what I'm doing."

He laughed almost boisterously and said, "What you mean isn't forget as much as remember. Remembering too much, being too mindful, too focused on the outcome, rather than forgetting the outcome, forgetting what's happening and just lying back and enjoying the ride."

I looked at him and nodded.

"Yes, I think you're right. That's true . . ."

He looked at me softly now and after a moment of deep silence, he said, "You know, if it's being queer you're worried about: don't, Danny, don't! Let me tell you this, and I've told you as much before, if there's one thing you're not it's gay, or queer, or a faggot. I mean, be honest, although things didn't work out for you on Saturday night, did you feel absolutely nothing?"

"No," I responded almost immediately. "I did feel, I think I was closer than ever, and then . . . just . . . I don't know . . . I just sort of started thinking and got all uptight, like."

"Exactly, you just for some reason blocked yourself off again . . . or did you feel like being with another guy?"

"No . . . No!" I responded again, trying to look him in the eye, seeing through his eyes that I was as usual exaggerating, being unbelievably foolish.

"There, you see," he confirmed, "it's got nothing to do with you being queer, or your having feelings for other ouks." His eyes were intent now, as though searching through the darkness in my head. "It's simply a blockage, a neurosis in there. Something in you that you won't let go of. That keeps hiding behind a wall. Well, we'll get there, we'll find what and where that wall is and we'll bring it crashing down, Danny, unlike some psychologist who doesn't know you from Adam spending hours upon hours delving into your childhood and not getting anywhere for years . . . Danny, I'm telling you it's only a matter of time. Soon you're going to be fine. Absolutely fine . . . Like any other normal guy, enjoying life again." He smiled warmly.

I smiled back, feeling like he had reached into my core, like some ice in me was being cracked open, melted. At that moment I wanted to talk about that love he had confessed to me on several occasions now – the residue of confusion it always left behind: What did it mean? What did I mean? Really? To him? But since he hadn't mentioned anything about his love, I felt maybe I couldn't; maybe it would just open out onto new waters, waters I could not handle, waters even deeper than I was thrashing in now. Then I heard him softly, almost cautiously, say, "I've already told the staff to go off early, and Piet, my floor manager, will lock up, so why don't you start getting ready now. I'll lock the door."

I lifted myself slowly from my chair and looked away, half-turning my body as I undressed. Pulling my pants and then my underpants off, I half-looked back to see if Uncle Harold was watching. As usual, he was doing anything but watching, scrambling around the office placing the bed of cushions on the desk, not showing the slightest interest in me. Then when all was ready, he said, "Relax, Danny. Just relax and enjoy." And in that now familiar way of his, he stroked my stomach and my thighs. "Remember, Danny, there is nothing to be shy or ashamed of. You're a normal guy, a normal ouk. Just think about birds, birds lying back with their legs open waiting for you to put it in."

Then he moved very close to the table, so close that I could feel his body touching mine. I felt myself flush and looked up briefly, only to find him staring off into the big dark cupboard at the back of the office like it held something he had lost and was trying to find. Die Hand van Here God? Then seeing me looking up, he looked down at me, a flicker of a smile over his lips, and I closed my eyes, knowing that he was just about to tell me to. He reminded me again to think of birds, naked birds, and then he did something he hadn't done before: he took hold of my right hand and twisted it gently backwards. I wasn't sure why he was doing that, but after a few moments I felt my hand touching something that felt like cotton and after a few moments more I realised that what I was touching was his pants. I wasn't sure why he was making me touch them, or what he was doing exactly, except that I now felt something bulging, something that felt like a tumor, or a boil, and my stomach shrank. Then he moved back, untwisting my hand to make it more comfortable, and when he seemed to have himself gained a more comfortable position, he started to rub my hand against his pants more firmly.

Something in my stomach felt like it was being sawn in two. Only the wood or whatever it was that was being sawn in there felt hollow, like ants or some other insects had eaten the insides. But it was like the ants or those other insects were still busy chewing away in there, even though there was nothing to chew on. I knew what was happening now, was fully aware, wanted to sit up and protest, say something, but somehow I couldn't utter a word. I think now, in retrospect, perhaps I didn't want to know, didn't want to believe what was happening was really happening. Was afraid of what might happen if I did protest. I had no idea, absolutely no idea, but I feared the worst: that I would be abandoned, chucked out like dirt, struck with violent blows. My head felt thick, like one of those blue-grey fogs you see on the moors in English horror movies. I felt suddenly claustrophobic, muzzled, like there was a sack over my head.

I heard his zip slide down, and he said, "Hold it." Words I thought I would never hear, words that only ever entered the ears of others, others who wanted it to happen to them – the moffies at school. The word betrayal formed in my head like a giant tower mushrooming out of the ground from nowhere.

Professing his love, that was one thing that maybe I could have grown used to, come to terms with – especially considering the help I was getting, the patience, the generosity, the dedication – but this, this was not what I was expecting, this was what gay people did. This was everything he had assured me I was not.

Too scared to open my eyes, I felt my hand meekly enclose the enormously thick, rubbery-soft skin. Even though I knew what it was now, I refused to look, too embarrassed, too ashamed. I felt like I was there, there at the beginning, discovering the real serpent, the real evildoer in the Garden of Eden. It was this snake, this rubbery-soft thing.

"Pull it, pull it up and down, just like I'm doing to you," a voice instructed from way above.

My head was pulsating; it was hard to believe my body could feel so hot. I felt like a child entering a world that was not meant to exist; that I had been told, told time and again, didn't exist. Now I was like Isaac, being blindfolded, keeping the faith. This man, this great man who I had put so much trust in, who had professed his deep love for me, was taking me where he said I didn't belong. Where I was so, so afraid I might.

Reading my panic, he said, "It's OK, Danny. It's OK. I can assure you, there's nothing to be worried about. It's only natural. I'm not going to make you do anything you'll regret." He paused. "Just let go . . . think of a bird. Just think of a naked bird with her legs wide open . . . That's it . . . that's it. Ah yes . . . that's it, that's much better . . . and remember to keep rubbing . . . yes, like I'm rubbing yours . . . that's it, that's it . . ."

For a moment as he spoke I almost forgot about it – the thick, rubber-soft truncheon I was clutching in my baby-white fingers, was holding onto like it was a lifebuoy.

"Ah there. Yes, that's it, that's it." Harold breathed out shakily, and for a moment I felt like a young girl, just like one of those girls I had forced to touch me at an overs, even as she shyly pulled away.

"Softly now, softly, slow down, slow down . . . that's it. That's better."

"I think, I think . . . I'm . . ."

"A bit higher. Yes, yes, keep it there."

"I'm trying . . ."

"Good. That's it. Keep your hand on me . . . slowly now . . ."

"I think . . . I can't . . ."

"OK now, pump, pump, pump into my hand!"

And before my eyes the world shook, broke open, thunder, lightning, sheets of soaking rain bucketing down on tin rooftops – onto my forehead, my chest, into my belly-button – then nothing.

Uncle Harold looked down at me smiling, eyes enquiring, but I said nothing, just lay there, still settling accounts with my own thoughts, feeling my way through what seemed to be only one more blocked drainpipe.

"Well . . .?"

Truth was, I was thunderstruck, but not in the way he probably thought. I looked up at him and though I could not get a word out, I managed to smile. And seeing me smile, he looked happy, and joked, "Danny, moenie so worried-looking wees nie, one day you'll invite me to your wedding. Only just don't make it too soon!" And then he asked again, "Well, how was it?"

What could I say? There was this whole new universe in front of me, this whole new world that I had never wanted to be a part of, and yes, I had enjoyed it. Hated it. Enjoyed it. Hated it.

"Tell me, Danny," he said calmly, amid this storm, as usual reading me only too well. "Tell me, Danny, have I ever done anything, forced you to do anything you didn't want to do?"

" . . . no . . ." It took a while to get out, but I couldn't think, in that moment, of any other response.

"I wouldn't, you know. You know that. Believe me, you've got nothing to worry about. You're not queer or a faggot or anything like that. And you know that I certainly am not. This is just a natural thing between friends, Danny. Good friends. A natural evolution of friendship." He paused briefly and I looked up half-nodding.

Then as if he had gained my confidence, he went on, "There's something I want to tell you that you must never tell anyone else, and I mean anyone . . ." I nodded my head in agreement. He looked down at me, almost looking inward. "I used to do this with my own best friends, you know. And don't get me wrong, they're all happily married guys today, with grown-up children of their own. Successful businessmen and professionals in their field. But this is what I want you to understand, what we are doing is just a way of friends showing their feelings for each other. It has nothing, absolutely nothing to do with being gay or queer or anything like that. But it's also not something you do with just anyone. It's something between real friends, Danny. Real friends. Like you and me."

He looked at me: a master explaining to his pupil the natural, the perfectly natural world, natural concepts of an ideal world that I didn't know. Had never heard about. Not like this.

I nodded, my head swimming in an ocean that was so big there was no end, no shore, no beach, no landing, no railings. Looking up into his eyes at that moment I saw how he reigned over people. I had seen it that night in the City Hall on that podium – in his eyes, in his voice – and I saw it now.

"Danny," he said, "I want you to understand, this is not something I take lightly, not something I have entered into for the pleasure. Yes, I enjoyed it, just as you enjoyed it, but I think you realise I'm doing this because, more than anything else, I want to see you up and running again. Danny I want to assure you this is for you. And only for you."

He stroked my face and I felt something shift in me, a strange warmth and at the same time a strange pain flowing through me, as I tried to unravel all of this in my head, trying, yes, to love him the way he loved me.

He rubbed my hair.

"Danny, I'm serious when I say what I say to you. I have never felt like this for any other guy, not for anyone before. And I don't think I could ever feel like this for anyone again." I looked up into his moist blue eyes and felt a deep comfort and suddenly an irrational confidence poured over me, a feeling of having someone who, despite everything, is always there for you, always there to love you. Much as I felt like running, it was a difficult feeling to run from, it was too strong, just too strong.

As we stepped out into the street that late afternoon, the last tinges of sunlight were just managing to break through the cloud, giving to the sky an almost unnatural sulphuric pinkness. It looked to me like two worlds colliding: the one full of fire and new, unknown boundaries, the other full of bleakness, bleakness of the night that inevitably follows the day.

Arriving at my house, Uncle Harold put a hand on my shoulder and said, "Danny, give your mind a rest, just let life take over for a while, don't try to define and analyse everything. Remember this: 'There is nothing either good or bad but thinking makes it so.'" And when I looked up at him – dumbly searching in my mind through the Hamlet we were reading at school and that he was quoting from, unable to come up with a quick reply – he pursed his lips and said, "I really think we must meet again, soon. What about Friday . . .? I'll let the staff off early again. There's not much happening anyway . . ."

I nodded my head, not having the chrain to even say, "another day."

Still confused but smiling, I climbed out of Uncle Harold's car, and was quickly left behind in the grey, fumy embrace of the exhaust from his E-type.

The last of the day's strange pink light was fading. I looked up towards the old Yeoville water tower. The Wellsian thing was standing out in the dying light, as usual these days, like a huge red testicle poised to roll over and crush us meek Lilliputians in the world below. The way I felt right then, to see the world crushed by a giant rusty old testicle didn't seem like such a bloody bad idea.

Then suddenly – as though I, simply by thinking that thought had caused it – all hell broke loose in the street. Housemaids – their fat hips wobbling like rubber tubes – men with hats on, the old, the young and even the crippled, suddenly running, hobbling: scattering in all directions, jumping over fences, slamming and hiding behind gates. At first, caught in the panic – still convinced that in some bizarre way my thoughts had ignited this chaos – I made a dash for it. Trying to get behind my own fence, to hide in my own yard in case they – whoever they were – came looking for the culprit who had set off this frantic commotion. But as I struggled with my front gate and looked about me, I noticed that the only people really stampeding were black. At first I thought it was one of the usual fahfee raids on our street, but when I saw a policeman grab hold of one of the maids, searching through her apron and pockets as she pleaded with him – a grim, crushed look on her face – I knew it was a pass raid. As usual it was a surprise attack, launched by police with truncheons in hand and heavy guns round their waists, who sprang from the back of a Black Maria, as the khaki-coloured police vans were known. Looking to arrest anyone who didn't belong – didn't have the papers to be on our suburban streets.

Each time the raids had that same feeling of steel about them, of cold metal twisting, of skin tearing, of people being separated from the little they clung to, by force. The police grabbed whoever they could, whoever didn't realise in time the danger, or who simply didn't have the pace to get away. Partly hidden behind my front gate I watched all this running, noticing the half-run, half-limp of a balding old man I had seen lately on our street corner. He stood out mainly because he looked so sick, standing on the corner against a house or wall, stooped, with a gnarled hand set just below his jaw like he was constantly coughing. Despite always being doubled over with sickness, whenever he saw me he was always ready with a short wave and a wide, toothless smile. Now even this dilapidated old man was running for his life. I wished I could somehow run out and rescue him, but I remained stuck in my hiding-place behind the gate watching him run, or rather hobble, until one of the heftier maids lifted his entire rickety frame off the ground and drove him forcibly through the small opening of a front gate.

Within a couple of minutes, the streets were completely empty, except for three policemen, two white and one black, who emerged, each of them with a black captive held by the scruff of the neck. They marched their prisoners to the Black Maria, which was parked almost opposite our house.

177

Inside the van, I could make out the round white eyes of the prisoners inside – probably from a previous raid – the gnarled black fingers clinging through the khaki iron grilles, like prisoners of war.

The back door of the van was opened and into the black square hole that appeared went first the prisoner of the black policeman, followed by the black policeman himself, who sprung into the van with an athletic ease, as though used to the procedure. Then one of the white policemen pointed a thumb into the van and the defeated black woman in his charge, dressed in a smartly pressed blue maid's outfit with clean white apron, struggled up the step. This time the policeman didn't follow but stood to one side with the serious but satisfied look of a bookmaker having just accepted a punter's money. The third policeman, the biggest of them, a heavy-boned man with short, wavy blond hair, shouted at his prisoner: "Kom nou, kaffir, spring in!" But instead of obeying, the wiry middle-aged man suddenly pushed the policeman backwards, protesting bitterly, "Aikona, what you think I am?" Immediately the policeman gave his reply. It came in the form of a fist that landed flat in the middle of the black man's face. As though a fountain of some sort had suddenly been discovered in the black man's delicate features, blood gushed from his nose, rushing in a torrent over his upper lip and into his mouth. The black man swayed for a few moments and then fell like a drunk onto his back on the tarred road. The policeman bent over and at first it looked like, seeing what he had done, the damage he had caused, he was going to give the black man a hand up, but at the last moment, as though having second thoughts, he straightened, pulled back, and shot the heel of his boot into the black man's cheek. The skin on the black man's face tore wide open like a stretch of earth that has been dynamited. Even from where I was standing, I could see a raw pink moisture running through the middle of the broken flesh. The man curled up like a foetus, his hands covering his head for protection, and once again I felt like rushing out to stop this carnage on our street. But looking at the size of the two policemen and the wild stare in the eyes of the one who had done the damage, I couldn't get my body to move even an inch.

Now I saw the policeman bend over, and this time he did pick the black man up. I suddenly felt a little easier about everything – it was at least all over now – but as the black man struggled to his feet, the policeman held him at a slight distance and began to strike his head, rapidly, over and over again, like it was one of those small, springy punching-bags in a boxing gym. Blood was now pouring from every hole in the man's face, but the policeman, in his fury, didn't stop punching until he lost his balance and nearly fell over backwards – his colleague eventually having to step in to hold him up. The black man, drenched in sweat and blood, slumped over the back step of the van, just barely able to hold on. The hefty policeman who had been punching him wrenched the half-unconscious man up and screamed, "Donderse houtkop!" into his face, before throwing the black man into the back of the wagon. I heard the dull clunk of flesh and bones against steel as the man landed on the floor of the khaki van. The policeman locked the back of the van, dusted himself off as though preparing to go out to a special appointment, and climbed into the front of the van with the other white policeman. Then they sped off; the police van's tyres screeching down Isipingo Street, leaving tyre marks so thick and black I thought they would mark their imprint on the history of our street forever.

I stood there cemented to the ground in the now darkness of the evening, feeling an empty swirling in my stomach, berating myself for not being able to do something, for being too frightened to even step forward and shout something out, anything. Just anything. Gradually, like someone recovering from the shock of an accident, I became aware of myself – who I was, where I had just been, who had just dropped me off – and as I walked up the path to my front door, the complete safety of my own white walls, the thought of all that had happened that afternoon, the confusion, the blood, the unfathomable love, flooded back like an extension of what I had just witnessed.

179

16

At that time my dreams tended to be strange, very strange, but the dream I had that night was the weirdest of them all. I don't think I will ever get it out of my head.

I was in my bedroom, as I had been when I went to sleep, covered in blankets up to the tips of my ears, alone in thought. The door to my room was locked, but somehow my mother, wearing a flimsy see-through nightie – her hair heavily greying and dishevelled – had managed to slip through and sat on top of my yellow-topped desk. Although her nightie was see-through, I was deeply conscious of not wanting to see through it – I felt embarrassed, I didn't want to see her in that way. After a while she rested her chin on the palm of her hand, her elbow digging into her knee. In a strange way it looked like she was watching over me and for a while it felt comforting.

I looked at her, trying to fathom the real reason for her presence, but as I did so her hazel eyes turned to green onyx, hard, piercing, and I became uneasy. I followed her eyes to my bed and saw the reason why. There was a young girl on my bed. When I looked at her, this girl on my bed, she was like no one I could remember, but she had the feel of May-Ann Cruise about her. She was bending over me on all-fours and was dressed in tight-fitting denim jeans and a short white lacy top that showed off a flat, neat little abdomen. Her hair was long and golden-brown and fell straight down, sweeping my face.

I felt conscious of searching through other dreams to see if I could recognise her from some other time, but although it was on the tip of my tongue, I couldn't quite bridge the gap of identification. She appeared totally oblivious of my mother's presence, or just didn't care. My mother, on the other hand, looked deeply concerned and the more

I looked at the girl the more my mother appeared offended. After a while, when it was obvious the girl wouldn't get off me, my mother, with extreme agility for her age and physical condition, stood up on the table, turned around, bent over, flipped up her nightie and began wobbling her naked bum at us. She began to groan in one of those deep, throaty early-morning voices of hers: "Kush mich in toches. Gai in drerd arein! Kush mich in toches. Gai in drerd arein!"

She repeated the Yiddishe sayings over and over, her bare, pink bum waving at us all the while. I was hot and embarrassed, but it was a long time before the girl even became aware of my mother's presence, and when finally she did, she merely glared at my mother as if to say whatever was happening between us had nothing to do with her.

Then the girl, with a stylish flicking movement of her hands, slipped out of her jeans and showed off a thin, soft brown wedge of pubic hair. In spite of my mother's presence I became faintly aroused. I put out a hand to touch the brown curling wedge of hair, but as I did so, out of it grew a tiny, circumcised penis like an asparagus-head. I was horrified and found myself saying aloud: "So this is what's inside? So this is the little man in the boat?" I looked at my mother and she turned her head to me, annoyed. This time she joggled her backside and yelled: "So now you know! Now kush mich in pupik!" It pained me to see my mother like that, but more than anything I was still curious about that little penis. Eventually I couldn't hold myself back and touched it. It did not change in size, but it grew stiff and felt incredibly dry. Then there was a loud, official-sounding knock on my bedroom door and I turned to see Uncle Harold barging his way into the room with his own key. He was elbowing off my father, who, it dawned on me, had been standing guard over my door. My father eventually gave way and, sort of apologetically, went to stand back outside the door, mumbling something like: "OK . . . but no more. No more . . ."

Uncle Harold, now standing in the centre of my bedroom, looked brilliantly clean-cut and his round face was shining like there was a torch inside his cheeks. His stomach, though bulging over his pants, was tightly tucked into a sparkling silver evening shirt. He excused himself to my mother, saying he had an important meeting to attend, but didn't so much as remark about the position she was in on my desk. She had to poke her head around her arms to see him. Then Uncle Harold looked at me and at the girl, a sage veil over his eyes, and in a calm voice said that this was the way things were. Just like this, the way this girl was showing me. Whether I liked it or not, I just had to accept it. This was where the power lay, he said, and there was nothing to be afraid of. The girl now stood up and made strange poking movements in the air with her little stiff member. I felt confused and began to sweat heavily. The little penis seemed so natural, yet so unnatural. My body grew so hot that I wrenched at the blankets and pulled them off me. As I did so my mother turned around, regained her original sitting position, and made to open her mouth. Although I could hear no words coming from her lips, I could see she was calling out to me, it was more a dry-retching cry than anything else and I found myself doing exactly the same, crying out, but no voice would come. Everyone in the room now, including my mother, looked somehow misshapen and threatening, and when I looked up all I saw was this May-Ann Cruise-like girl with her stiff little asparagus-head motioning in the air. I felt strongly I couldn't breathe and I began to scream, just one long loud rush, but again no word, no sound whatsoever would come from my mouth.

I thought of my brother Cyril, who was somehow now standing guard at the door with my father, but it was like neither of them would come to my aid. Inside of me the scream became so loud and the threat of the people around me so great that I thought I would explode and die. But in the end I just lay there paralysed, unable to lift a bone in my body.

At exactly that point, when I couldn't move and thought I was about to literally burst open like a smashed fig, I awoke. I was soaked with sweat and panting heavily. So acutely aware was I of my mother's presence nearby that I half-expected her to be sitting on my desk. When I saw no one around me, I wiped my eyes and the sweat from my forehead with my sheet to make sure I really was awake and then, as I lay there still half-clouded in dream, I wondered whether girls really did have little penises. The thought scared the hell out of me, but there was nothing I could do to shake the image from my head. There were no two ways about it, I concluded at that moment, the human body was a cruel place to be. That poem, that poem we learnt in school again warping in my mind: Tyger, Tyger, burning bright, In the forests of the night; What immortal hand or eye, Could frame thy *hideous* symmetry . . .?

Finally, sure I was awake and not dreaming, I put my head under the blankets and tried, without much success, to get back to sleep before my mother came rattling the door, as she always did, to wake me for breakfast. To strengthen me for the life I more and more wanted to bludgeon into eternal sleep, into a black hole, into a deep dark black hole; that I at least, at the very least, wanted to burn and re-fashion like Vulcan into a new world. A world without human bodies, without human form, a world without penises and Frenchies and any other kinds of little asparagus-headed monsters. A world that would be free.

17

That week at school was blurry, one-dimensional, a fuzzy linear trance of walking, zombie-like, from class to class, from Dickens to Shakespeare to Blake to the elemental make-up of hydrogen and oxygen and salt, to the breakdown of an atom, to the magic of Pi, destruction of the Holy Roman Empire, rise of nationalism. Hiding in cold, dark shadows, behind solid brick walls. Every nerve-end in me piqued, ready to react. The truth was, nothing we learnt seemed capable of digging me out of the mess. No amount of science or English or geography or history. Not even Latin, language of our great learned precursors. What indeed was this *tail – Latin root word: penis –* I had? This ridiculous, ritually snipped tail? Neither Einstein, nor Pi, nor E, nor knowing all of Newton's laws could change anything.

Even when Chaz approached me I avoided him, sneaking behind doorways, under desks, into toilets. I knew everyone was looking at me, everyone was saying it – especially the crew: Solly, Peter, Aaron – *What's with Danny?* From centre of circle, from great articulator on all topics from politics to the psychology of life to sex, I had become a laughing-stock. A nothing.

Occasionally when I couldn't avoid them I tried with great effort to sound normal, to joke my old jokes, but I think, without actually saying it, they knew, smelt that something somewhere had gone horribly wrong. Fortunately for me, Chaz, at least Chaz, still held onto the old loyalty, the old belief in me.

* * *

Then it was Friday afternoon and I was making my way downtown still dressed in the remnants of a school uniform. In this case that meant tight-fitting grey flannel school pants, which reflected the incoming punk fashions – fashions which, after years of opposing hippie flares and bell-bottoms, had teachers screaming and howling for their return. Over my tight grey pants I still had on my white school shirt – hard to cut anything fashionable out of a white shirt – and my bottle-green school jersey, but no tie and no jacket, which placed me firmly, and cane-ably, outside the school rules.

It was a mild day and the city looked busier than it had for a while. The intensity of the rioting in Soweto and the other townships around Johannesburg had fallen off and most of the workers were back at their positions, though their children's schools still lay empty and mostly in ashes. The pavements as usual were cloaked in a grey sheet of semi-darkness, cast by the city's towering office blocks. It was hard to find a spot of sunshine, except in the middle of the roads, or at the lights on street corners.

Even as I walked the couple of long blocks to Uncle Harold's shop the streets were filling with black workers and the garrisons of black unemployed. In my mind I saw these straggly black columns as the survivors of a great campaign, like Napoleon's Russian Campaign of 1812. Now these heroic troops, coerced into battles they hadn't created, never even dreamed of, were trudging their way home from yet another humiliation, another defeat – and they did, as the black and white pictures in my history reader at school showed, look utterly cut, torn, ragged, near to death, just like Napoleon's depleted armies. Having done their day's labour, or unable to find any labour at all, they were still expected to pay their own way home, well away from the protected white streets of what my parents and their friends frequently referred to as still the cleanest and safest city in the world. Standing in long queues, the columns of black people were eventually whisked out of town in big black taxis, marked and unmarked, vast battalions of kombi vans in various states of disrepair and big green government buses that juddered and choked along like old castaway cattle trucks through the city streets.

185

When I reached the dustily flickering neon sign at the entrance to Uncle Harold's shop, the crier appeared in unusually high spirits. He was singing and kicking his feet into the grey cement of the sidewalk in a rhythmic tribal dance, almost oblivious of the passers-by he was meant to be wooing into the store. Perhaps he had already been told the store would close its doors earlier than usual – on account of my visit – or perhaps even he was relieved that with some return to normality in the townships he was no longer under so much pressure to boycott work and forfeit wages. He greeted me with a wide smile, showing that front row of long, jagged, nicotine-stained teeth that all the criers outside the shops seemed to have.

"Hallo, my leetle maste'," he said, waving me into the store.

And once again I passed under those musty-smelling armpits, responding with my usual half-wave, half-smile, which as usual the crier didn't even notice. This time when I entered the store I was immediately hit by a peppery-thick staleness, a coldness in the air that I hadn't noticed before except when I had been with Sophie Street and had seen – for the briefest of moments – the place through her eyes. I decided to ignore the atmosphere and walked right in, trying to be cheery.

Seeing Uncle Harold was busy I didn't go up to him but walked straight into his office. Even there, at the back of the shop, I could still hear his booming voice, even if I couldn't make out the words. His arms were threshing the air and his head was bobbing meaningfully, like he was a senator in the Forum delivering an important address. As he spoke to his customers I came to understand – in the way they looked up at him like ordinary citizens without any power but to listen – a little of how I had also come to look up to him.

Sometimes it was hard to believe that there could be anything between us. He was so much older, of another generation, and even if he had much more modern ideas than my parents, he was also tied to a sort of uniformity concerning marriage and settling down and having children and making a decent living that didn't quite fit with my desperation to break away, to do things differently.

Yet watching him now from across the shop I could see why it was so difficult to turn away. I could feel that aura of confidence, of certainty rippling off his flesh; like a powerful Roman senator, even from this distance.

I continued to watch as he finally showed the elderly couple he was addressing to the front door, their bowing figures slowly disappearing out of the shop. Then I sat down as I saw him striding back to the office.

"Whew, what a bummer of a day," he breathed, as he panted into the office and sat down at the desk. "Sometimes they expect the world from you, these people." And when I looked at him with confusion, he said, "What can you do? I don't mind helping them out where I can, but there's really not much you can do if people don't tell you the truth, buy more than they can afford and then hit Dung Street and can't pay back. Then they look at you like you're some cruel tyrant when you have to tell them it's not on and you're going to have to repossess their furniture. It's going to be the undoing of me. Bad bloody debts."

"Bad debts . . .? I didn't realise."

"Well, it's not as rosy as you think, my boy. In fact, not looking rosy at all at the moment."

"But I thought you were doing so well . . .?"

"Yeah, well . . ." he looked genuinely confused himself, as though he had not yet quite worked out why things were the way he was saying they were. "Ja, we've done well over the years, Danny, but the whole political situation now isn't good for us. People are out of work and don't have money. You feel sorry for them, but we've reached our limit and it's not looking pretty at all." He pursed his lips. "But we'll recover, by God we'll recover, the good times will come back." I looked at him, wondering if the optimism he was reaching for was real. Seeing me looking at him, he said, "Just like with you, Danny, the good times will come back. It'll all come back again and everything will be fine." He laughed. "You know, Danny, business is like a marriage. There are the good times, the bad times and the flat times, but it always works itself out in the end . . ."

Impulsively, I said, "But you got divorced. Twice!"

"Mistakes, Danny. You know, we all make mistakes. At least we're not Catholics. There can be nothing worse than having to stay together when two people don't love one another. I know many in my generation who have done exactly that and it doesn't work. It's worse. Children are sensitive, they pick up on these things. Bad vibes around the house all the time. It's not good."

"My folks always ask why don't you marry Thelma?"

"Ha," he laughed shortly. "Your folks would ask that. They're such a traditional, stable couple. Even with your father's hard-headedness your mom has always remained loyal. But Thelma and I will get married. In fact, soon. It's just that today . . . well, you can road test a bit." We both laughed. "And it's a better world for that, I can tell you. That's why I always say, Danny, you must play the field a bit before you marry. And hopefully soon, when everything's right, you will." He lifted himself from his chair and walked around the table, closer to me. "One day you'll see, you'll know what it's like to have a bird you really want to be with."

I looked up at him, having to force a voice from my breath, "Do you tell Thelma what's happening here, with us . . .? That you're helping me?"

"No, of course not!" he threw his head back. "Well . . . not exactly." He looked down at me, staring, taken off balance. "I couldn't tell her, you know that, not everything. I think you appreciate that. She wouldn't understand. You and I, what's between us, is something different. She doesn't need to know."

He looked down at me and I nodded, clearing my throat. "Eh-hem

. . . You know I, like . . . like I appreciate what you're doing for me, I really do, you know . . . it's just that . . . it doesn't feel . . ."

"Danny, stop right there," he said, putting a hand up. "I know exactly what you're going to say . . . I know you don't like it when I say I love you." I twisted in my seat, wondering how he had hit so very close into the heart of it. "But I do, I just do . . . I can't help it." He leaned over me, eyes moistening. "Perhaps one day you'll understand this thing between you and me. This thing I feel for you." He looked into my eyes, his voice coming now from somewhere deep inside his chest. "It's . . . it's just like . . . a light that automatically switches on in the mind, or a cupboard door that suddenly opens in your chest and you can't shut it again, can't ever quite get it to close again. It's something that just happens, just clicks on, opens up, and then you have no control over it. I only wish society could understand. I only wish that you could feel the same as I do . . ." He stopped as uncertainly as he had started and looked down at me, a sadness in his eyes.

For the first time since I had known him I felt sorry for Uncle Harold. Like I really owed him something. Like I should be giving him something. I stood up, stepped up to him and hugged him. He held me, his face on my shoulder, then stepped back, smiled, his eyes pink and glinting. He looked happy, like I had crossed a threshold. Then he said I should get undressed while he went to see if everything was locked up properly.

With Uncle Harold out of the office I undressed as quickly as I could, wondering, as usual, what Mr Nothnagel, my Afrikaans teacher, would make of all this – two cuts on the backside for sure – and then made a rush for the cushions, placing them neatly on the desk. Just as I had positioned the last cushion, Uncle Harold arrived back in the office.

He stood there, a shy smile on his face, something like the smile on the face of our Tretchikoff woman, only where she was dressed up to the chin in some beautiful and exotic oriental silk tunic, he stood there stark blistering naked, except for a tiny Hawaiian grass hula skirt that looked like it was about to bust open at the sides. Under his naked right arm he proudly held one of the store's old maroon and cream portable gramophones.

I gawked at him like a parrot whose cage has been rocked, completely befuddled. Seeing me so flustered, he smiled, then advanced and swept the family pictures aside, carefully placing the gramophone down on a corner of the desk. Now he shuffled over to the big, dark cupboard at the back of the office, bent down, looked around and popped back up holding an LP. Delicately placing it on the gramophone he immediately pressed the curved cream-white plastic arm onto the record, which slowly scratched to a start. And then suddenly there was music, loud music in Uncle Harold's shop as he, Uncle Harold, Uncle HK, began swaying his hips, this way then that, rhythmically, energetically to what turned out to be the sound of The Beach Boys. Chunkily, he twirled to the left, and then twirled to the right, lifted his arms like a glamorous hula dancer and snapped his fingers in the air. Shaking his backside like Chubby Checker, he did a shake, then a twist and called out: "C'mon, Danny, live! Try to live a little. Dance! Dance, while the night is yet young!"

I looked up at him, actually past him, avoiding the commanding, now sparkling eyes, but unable to block him out, seeing how he looked so surprisingly loose, so surprisingly relaxed, his big beefy stomach undulating in almost perfect time to the easy beating sound echoing through the office. My pink praying mantis body so taut, so like a dry stick, that if I bent even slightly I knew it would snap in two. Then he wheeled and spun, throwing out a dancer's curling hand and called out again: "C'mon, Danny, live! For once in your life, live!"

But instead of moving, which I couldn't do, not even for Uncle Harold, I felt my jaw drop so that my mouth, I am certain, was shaped like the 'O' in the mouth of Münch's Scream. Where was *The Rise of the South African Reich* in all of this? Where even were the sex manuals? The *Sex Manners for Men? The Sexually Adequate Male? The Sexually Adequate Female?* I didn't understand. Didn't understand him.

I could feel my eyebrows involuntarily twitching like upturned earthworms as I saw Uncle Harold's outstretched hands coming out towards me, his mouth crooning as though into a microphone, *"Tell the teacher we're surfin' . . . surfin' U.S.A. . . ."* He looked at me, encouraging me, smiling widely. Then suddenly his eyes fell from my face and his body turned completely out of rhythm, as he pulled the gramophone arm off the record with a short, loud scratch. Then there was silence. Absolute silence.

Sweating a little, Uncle Harold said, "I'm sorry, Danny." His face looked sunken. "I'm sorry, I just thought you might enjoy it. Enjoy something a bit different for a change. Something more your scene. A bit of pop music."

I looked up trying to reassure him that it was alright, but saw that he had already seen in my frozen eyes it wasn't.

Uncle Harold walked straight over to the big cupboard, stripped off the hula skirt, shoved it somewhere into the back and then turned to me naked. The sight made me turn away quickly, flushing crimson, embarrassed. And then he walked out of the office and when he returned he was fully, normally dressed. It was like landing on Mars without having the foggiest idea you were even headed there. Another normal day turned into a Martian experience.

"Lighten up, Danny. Lighten up." He looked directly into my eyes, his hands crossed in front of him. "C'mon, Danny, let's see you smile."

I felt my lips crack, reshape and widen into a half-line across my face.

"That's it. That's much better. That's the way I like to see you, Danny. That's the way it should always be." Then he patted his desk. "OK now, on the table. Lie down and relax. Just relax."

I climbed up and lay there – as I was well used to by now – stomach up, peeping at him, seeing his eyes float over me, pink and glowing. Noting in them, despite everything, an incredible devotion, an incredible love; his eyes studying me as an art-lover might study a Van Gogh, or a Gauguin. And then he was busy twisting my hand around again, towards him. I felt that material again, only this time it was already unbuttoned. I felt sweat break out on my forehead, and I wondered what the outcome would have been if I had danced with him.

* * *

Uncle Harold dropped me off at home and I felt light as usual, but dizzy, unusually dizzy, and in the car, before I jumped out, he considered me carefully and said, "Danny, you know, you must always be a leader, don't simply follow others, let others follow you, never the other way around."

"Yes," I agreed, because I did agree.

"Good, Danny."

I think he thought I was finished, but I looked down, determined. "But somehow, like, when I'm with you . . . it's different, I feel like I am always . . . following . . . it's like there is a step-a step-a stepladder . . . of leadership and it changes with different people, different circles . . . Sometimes it's like you can feel you are leading, but then with others . . . you feel like you are . . . following . . . just following . . ."

"Ha, yes, that's true, Danny, a good point," he said, and his eyes lit up, "but as far as possible, Danny, as far as possible, you must always be the leader. Even with me, don't just follow."

"Ja . . ." I agreed, unable to press the point further, wondering if there was anyone, anyone at all, Uncle Harold followed.

And then he said, "Why don't you bring a bird over for dinner next Saturday night . . . may be a chance to ask Sophie, an excuse for a date?" I looked fuzzily at him, a bit unsure. "Truly Danny, Thelma'd love that, she likes young people, she likes you and I'm sure she'd love to meet Sophie."

Immediately, without wanting to, I nodded. "Ja . . . no, that'd be great." And he squeezed my hand.

18

S ophie Street's immediate reaction when I invited her to Uncle Harold's for dinner was: "What? To the owner of that shop? Are you crazy? Can you imagine what he thinks of me!" But after I pleaded that it wouldn't be so bad, that he hardly knew her name, or that I had even brought her to the shop, she finally relented, saying, "Only because it's you, Danny. Only because it's you." Restoring in the process some lost faith in myself and giving me hope that, with Sophie Street at least, there still remained a chance. Increasingly, disaster or no disaster, Sophie Street was becoming the girl I wanted to be with.

* * *

"You'll see, he won't say anything, it's not like he even knows you were there," I reiterated what I had said on the phone as we walked through the high wrought-iron gates that had been opened to allow us in. This time Sophie did not respond. She simply looked straight ahead, ignoring me.

As we walked up the long pathway to the front door, she appeared unimpressed by, or certainly was purposely ignoring, the Kleinharts' lush garden, including the specially-lit heart-shaped swimming-pool that dappled a glowing turquoise-green to the side of us and normally evoked some sort of response even from those who had walked by it many times before. The pool, with a dense rockery surrounding it – giving dimension to its heart-shape – was written about in every newspaper and magazine in the country, the latest an article in *Scope* magazine entitled: *Alderman Kleinhart's Wet Dream*. A daring headline at the time. But looking at Sophie Street, it was as if she didn't want to show that anything that belonged to this man who had given me the keys to that shop was worthy of attention. As if she wanted to reinforce rather that she was there under duress. Only for me. Hard as she was to tolerate right then, I liked the only for me part, it made me feel wanted, kind of sought-after, like someone other than Uncle Harold was willing to go out of their way for me. You couldn't ask for much more than that from any girl, I thought, let alone a girl like Sophie Street. I felt chuffed.

"He'll probably offer you the keys to his house next!" She finally spoke, blinking her sparkling silver-blue eyelids.

"C'mon Sophie, calm down. Just take it easy, cool it." I tugged at her arm, as we followed the soft garden light that led us up to the front door, and I looked nervously forward to what lay ahead.

In the end dinner at Uncle Harold's was, I suppose, as I should have predicted, very proper, very sociable and not really worth noting. Sophie, come to think of it, not only ignored the lavish, spectacular garden but also didn't show any interest in the finely presented food and drink that was served up on fine pink Royal Doulton plates and in impeccably clean crystal. She left her perfectly pink, three-inch-thick prime fillet virtually untouched, which fortunately – in Thelma's eyes at least – was quite acceptable, because they both seemed to be on a similar diet. Unlike Thelma, though, she hardly even picked at her salads and refused completely the oysters that we began the meal with, and which I had to carefully watch Thelma and Uncle Harold pick out of their shells with tiny forks, so that I did not make a complete fool of myself by using my fingers, or worse, a meat-knife and fork.

Come to think of it, despite the friendliness and smiles all round the only time I saw Sophie smile was when Uncle Harold, who was bouncing around filling everyone's wineglasses and telling stories of his youth, told one about how he and a couple of high-school friends were nearly expelled from school for hanging a row of water-filled condoms off the front of their goggle-eyed science teacher's lab bench. They hung the condoms up to look like they were a row of test-tubes the teacher had specially set up as an experiment for the students to view and analyse.

But other than that, Sophie sat mostly silent and intent, if anything maintaining a slightly annoyed look, and other than a first half-glass of wine, refused any other drink Uncle Harold offered.

However, after dinner, despite Sophie's continued cutting looks, Uncle Harold somehow managed to get her out onto the white marble patio that adjoined the lounge by way of a pair of French doors, leaving me alone inside the brilliantly lit, brilliantly white lounge with Thelma.

"What's been going on in the townships is just too terrible," Thelma said by way of conversation. She spoke as though the passage of her voice was almost entirely through her nose. Then she put a hand to her cheek, and added: "You know, Alexandra Township is just down the road from us. Grace . . . our girl . . . her brother lives in a hostel there, but she hasn't been able to visit him in weeks. Sometimes he's even been staying here, it's so bad, you know?"

"Yes, the situation is bad," I nodded. "I don't know how they expect blacks to learn everything in Afrikaans when they don't even expect it from white kids. And on top of that blacks hate the language, it means oppression to them."

"Yes, that's true and it's not fair," Thelma said, "but children forcing their parents, who can hardly afford it, not to go to work is going a bit too far, don't you think?"

I swallowed, suddenly finding Uncle Harold and Sophie's closeness on the patio highly irritating, and said, "If it wasn't for apartheid, none of this would be happening in the first place. Their parents are just as much victims as they are." The thought crossed my mind that Uncle Harold and Sophie Street could be discussing me, and I felt flushed.

"Uh-oh!" Thelma looked at me like I had fed her a stale chocolate or something. "You know freedom, independence and equality are things that have to be earned, Danny? It's not something that comes overnight. It's not something you boycott school and work for and then think it should all come to you just like that."

"But there's nothing to earn. It's theirs. It belongs to them, has always been theirs. They just want it back." I felt myself redden, embarrassed at what I was saying, or rather how I was saying it, never expecting to find myself in a position like this – arguing with Uncle Harold's "Thel".

"Oh yeah," she said, "if it was left to them, they'd still be out there grazing their cattle, there'd be nothing in this land, just miles and miles of mielies and veld! Who do you think built Jo'burg?" Her chest with its diamond pendant and big breasts shook and I had to look away, only to find myself staring at the patio, where Uncle Harold and Sophie Street seemed to be getting on like they were old friends: Uncle Harold swinging his arms and Sophie Street nodding her head like she was one of those Victorian tin dolls.

Inside, Thelma continued, "You know people get what they deserve. We've worked bladdy hard for what we've got and we're not about to give it up just because they want it. If they can show they deserve it, then yes, I'm all in favour. I don't mind having black neighbours. That's never been a problem for us. Ask Harold. But they have to show they've earned it, my boy."

"But how do you earn it if your salary is a tenth of that of your fellow white workers, or you aren't allowed to go to school because there is no school for you, or . . .?"

"Ja, well . . ." She cut me off, flapping a hand in the air and then tucking it thoughtfully under her chin. "As Harold always says, everyone's entitled to their own opinion . . ."

There was silence; then she suddenly and bewilderingly changed tack, and said, "Do you ever go to any of those clubs, you know, those gay clubs that seem to be springing up everywhere these days . . .? You know, like Shappa, or Stiffer-Stifferelli's or whatever it's called . . .?"

I shook my head, feeling a little shocked, like now suddenly she was casting aspersions. What should I know about gay clubs? Clubs, any clubs, weren't exactly what we, me or my friends, were into. If she saw the way Chaz and I reacted every time we walked past the Rockey Street clubs, she may have understood.

"No . . . I don't really know them," I said softly, almost losing my voice. "It's . . . it's not really our . . . scene." I squirmed, self-conscious. "Anyway, you have to be over eighteen."

"Oh well, I suppose I'm really thinking of my nephew, Darren, my sister's son," she said to my relief. "But, of course, he's a bit older than you. Twenty. He's forever in those clubs, you know. Every weekend, Friday and Saturday nights. Dusk till dawn. And she just doesn't know what to do. How to stop him." She looked at me as though I could somehow help. Immediately I shook my head, not really knowing how to respond, still jumpy that there could be some underlying insinuation. I looked outside, to the patio; I would have done anything to be out there with Uncle Harold and Sophie Street. Inside Thelma went on: "I've told her to ask Harold to have a talk to him. Put him straight. As you probably know, Harold's good at that?" I nodded my head in the affirmative, wondering how much she really knew, still suspicious of what she was really driving at. If she was driving at anything at all. Outside the very sight of Uncle Harold and Sophie Street talking to one another began to pain me like a bull-ant biting into my flesh. "You know, you've just got to be there all the time for your kids these days," Thelma said, and I wondered if she was casting aspersions that my parents weren't always there for me, and that was why Uncle Harold had to come to my rescue. "I just don't know what I'd do if my kids grew up to be funny, you know, like Darren," she went on. "The way he's going, he's not even going to make it to his twenty-first. I think Harold would kill my boys if he saw them going that way.

197

It'd certainly kill me. Anyway, at least I can rest assured he'd put them straight. He's good at that, you know . . .?"

I nodded, feeling like I was toasting. Suddenly as I looked around me, I saw myself on that giant desk, Uncle Harold at my side. I felt the whiteness of the Kleinharts' white walls around me, like they were somehow much cleaner, much shinier than I was, and felt soiled and accused.

"Maybe you and Darren should meet some time? It might help him. Even if you're a bit younger, at least you're interested in sports and books . . . and normal things, like girls . . ." she said, making me feel suddenly a whole lot cleaner, that I could actually help the sick and smitten of this world. Or was she being sarcastic?

I breathed out. And then in. Unsure.

"Yeah, maybe, some time." Suddenly, again, I was so hot I thought I was having a nervous breakdown. I felt the sweat pepper my forehead and then thankfully, mercifully, I saw Uncle Harold and Sophie Street stepping back inside.

Sophie, as soon as she stepped into the room, winked at me, but I was not quite sure what she meant by the wink. She sat down on the couch with me, but at a distance. Uncle Harold poured himself and then me another liqueur, Sophie refusing yet again, and then he sat chatting for a while, before somehow managing to get me out alone onto the patio with him.

As soon as we were safely on the patio and out of hearing-range, he said, "You know, Danny, Sophie's a really, really loverly girl . . . Once you get speaking to her – really intelligent, you know, and I think she has a good understanding of you, maybe better than you even think . . ."

I felt my neck prickle. "You, you didn't say anything . . .?"

"Of course not! Jesus, Danny, what do you take me for? Would you doubt me?" He looked at me, disappointed. "That's just between us, between you and me . . . what I mean is she is sensitive like you and obviously realises the sort of person you are; how the slightest of things upsets and worries you . . ." He took a breath. "Oh yes, I did tell her she obviously had very good taste!" He laughed aloud, spreading his arms wide, and for a moment I thought he was actually going to hug me, out there on the patio in front of everyone. Instead he put his arms down at his sides, and said, "So you see, Uncle Harold isn't such a bad guy, is he?"

I shook my head. "No, of course not."

"I sometimes think you think that, though?"

I felt the colour drain from my face. "Well . . . it's all . . . like, you know, everything that's happening . . ." I couldn't even get a full sentence out of my mouth.

"Danny, how many times have I told you, don't worry, relax, everything will turn out alright in the end . . .? You'll see . . . we shall overcome, my friend." And for a moment I did not know if he was talking about my situation, or our situation, or even the political situation. His voice was calm yet his eyes were aglow as he put a hand on my shoulder and led me back inside. As we stepped through the French doors I heard a moth smash into the light, the sound of the collision jarring something inside me.

Soon after, to my relief, Uncle Harold insisted on driving us home. At the front door, Thelma smiled graciously, like a queen, managing somehow not to look directly at either Sophie or me, but rather into the luminescent heart-shaped pool behind us, like she was Cleopatra or some film star on a movie set. She told me she would definitely tell her nephew, Darren, about me and give him my number. I involuntarily shook my head, left to right, to which she simply smiled and said, "Thanks, Danny, thanks, I'm sure you'll be able to help."

At the car, Uncle Harold insisted that Sophie and I sit in the back, while he played the humble chauffeur. As soon as we were out of the drive and on the road, he shifted gears smoothly and softly, and then suddenly took off like he was trying to show us how quickly the car could accelerate or like he was trying to set a new land-speed record between Kew and Yeoville. The good thing about it, though, was that it had Sophie clutching fearfully onto my arm, which I enjoyed no end. Just the heat of her hands, never mind the speed of the car, had my heart pumping.

Outside Sophie's paint-flaked house, Uncle Harold drew up to a surprisingly smooth and quiet halt, as though suddenly showing a deep respect for the neighbours. It was probably the first time such a car had ever been parked in her street, I thought, as I walked Sophie up to her front door, conscious of the gleaming red sports car purring softly behind us. If it was during the day I had no doubt the neighbours and their children would have had their noses pressed against their lounge windows, whistling and rolling their eyes at the dazzling machine that was temporarily glued to their sun-cracked street.

At the front door, out of sight of Uncle Harold, I had to let it out.

"You were pretty friendly with him in the end?"

"Well, I didn't really have a choice, did I?" She glared at me.

"OK, OK, just remarking. But obviously it wasn't so bad after all, then?"

"It was alright, O-K."

I looked down, realising I wasn't going to get anywhere like that, and she looked down too, I think because I looked down, then we both looked up at exactly the same time, kind of peering into one another's eyes as though for explanation, some meaning, and then we both smiled. Then laughed. It was like in that moment we were seeing one another as different, but not really saying it or able to explain how come, and as we looked at one another and laughed she pulled me to her and kissed me on the lips. I felt my heart pole-vault out of my body.

"I love you, Danny," she whispered loudly, and I wanted to hold her there, just her and me in each other's arms, but a moment later her front door had been miraculously opened and closed and she had been swallowed inside. Completely and utterly befuddled, but still happy with the outcome, I nearly skipped back to the car. If it wasn't for Uncle Harold waiting there, I think I would have skipped all the way home.

* * *

"Give me a call during the week and let me know how you're doing," Uncle Harold said when we were parked outside my house, suddenly looking emotional. He stroked my shoulder.

"Here, Danny, hold my hand for a minute." He put out an open hand on his thigh and I rested my hand on it. He squeezed and I immediately felt my hand lost inside his chunky white palm. Just before freeing my hand so that I could climb out of the car, he gave it a final short, sharp squeeze that was so full of intensity, so full of reassurance, so full of love that I thought he was going to cry. Inside of me, I felt something tear and rip, like I was splitting in two.

19

I woke next morning with a head that felt like it had been placed on an anvil. *Too many liqueurs*, I thought, and wound the crook of my arm over my eyes. My head throbbed. I could hear my heart beating like a machine-gun and there was a tight ball in my stomach; it felt like the thousands of elastic sinews tied together in a golfball, and right in the middle of this ball was the sac, the poisonous sac; it was the taste in my mouth, of badly rotten apple. The thought came to me that this was not a hangover from too much to drink at all, rather it was a hangover from holding too much down, too many untruths, too much failure.

In love. Yes, I had not forgotten. I was still high on my feelings for Sophie Street, but somehow it was like it was going nowhere, I had no control. It wasn't like we were a couple, or anything like that, and I was able to just call her and meet with her at my whim. It was still something that had to be worked at, strategies had to be schemed up and I still feared what she knew and wasn't saying.

In the bedroom next door, as if lending credence to my war-torn thoughts, I heard my parents talking over one another. My father's deep slow groans, my mother's assertive rasping voice; but I couldn't hear what they were saying above the din that was going on in my own head.

I took my arm away from my eyes; in front of me zillions of coloured spots collided with one another, making me dizzy. I put my hand under the blankets and felt the doughy thing that was still, without a doubt, at the centre of my misery. That was driving me crazy. It was lying there, as it always was these days, folded over like a rag-doll.

No longer able to face the ceiling that was staring blankly back at me, I turned over onto my left side, but that felt no better either, and when I opened my eyes they were hit by my garish yellow and red desk. It seemed to glare back at me, reminding me of that freakish dream of the other night, and for a moment I saw my mother once again on that desk, her naked bum wagging in the air, chanting: "Kush mich in toches. Kush mich in toches." And again I experienced the claustrophobia of that night, the unanswered questions, the vision of that girl's dry little asparagus-head that made no sense at all. To break the spell, I quickly turned onto my right side, to face the blank wall.

What if I really am . . .? I found myself asking the blank wall for the millionth time. I rolled straight back onto my back. Impossible! How could it be? How could it be that one day you were on the brink of initiation, manhood, a hero among your friends, first among peers; and the very next day, next minute, did not know, if you were Arthur or Martha? Danny or Daniella? *Why were we made so fragile, so break-able?* I asked the ceiling, feeling the sweat begin to well on my fore-head. One minute on top of the world, the next right at the very bot-tom? It didn't make any sense. No sense at all. And if they found out, your friends, your parents, everyone around you, if they saw where you had been, what you had done and not done, what would they say, what would they make of you, what would they call you?

I heard my parents' voices rat-a-tat-tatting through the house, firing away like World War I fighter planes dogfighting for domestic su-premacy. And lying there I asked myself: *Would death, my death, end their war?* So many of their fights seemed to be about me or my broth-er. One of them giving support when the other was shouting, and then reversing the roles, fighting over what should be done about us. *But more importantly*, I asked myself, *would my death end the artillery bar-rage going on in my own battered skull?*

I recalled a question from one of the self-help books I found in my father's little bedside library. This one was from Dale Carnegie's *How To Win Friends And Influence People*, where Carnegie sets out his plan for better, smoother, more positive living that did leave an impact. This – paraphrased – was his view on suicide:

Before taking the drastic action of doing your little eagle-nosed face in, take the time to ask yourself who would come to your funeral, and then see if it was still really worth it. See whether you were not just biting off that big, fat eagle-nose of yours to spite your smooth-skinned little puss.

Scanning through the book at the time, still so cocksure, I nearly laughed. Who would be so absurd as to even think about such things? But now, dumb as it seemed, I found myself compiling a list, coming to the conclusion after only a short while that, since there were so few who would come to my funeral, this in itself was all the more reason why I should do myself in. Deciding in the end that what was important wasn't who I would leave sobbing, or laughing, or whether there was no one there at all. What was important was that I was gone. No, even more than that, that it was I who had decided, that it was I who had chosen.

"Daaa-nnyyy! Daaa-nnyyy!" a shrill cry followed by a sharp rattling on my door made me start from my bed.

"Yes . . .?"

"It's Chaz on the phone, for you . . . Chaz!"

Startled, I said, "Say I'm not here, for Godsake!"

"Oh now, just listen to that . . . I'm sorry, I've already said you were."

"Alright, alright," I dragged myself out of bed. "For fuck's bladdy sake!" I swore loudly to myself.

"What?"

I hadn't realised my mother was still behind the door.

"Uhm, nothing. I just said, 'Shoes. Where're my friggin' shoes, for Godsake?'"

"I hope that's all you said. You'd do well to watch that tongue of yours, mister."

I shook my head; it wasn't my tongue that was the problem, but I couldn't expect her to know that. If only she could, if only my mother

204

could, I'm sure she would have hugged and held me, for once because I needed to be hugged and held. Simply because I needed to feel that parental warmth. But I knew it was more than I could have expected.

Now Chaz was breathing down the phone, into my ear, like we hadn't seen one another in years. "Shit man, we must do something next weekend. I tried to call you a couple of times during the week. Didn't you get the messages?" As if we hadn't seen one another at school. Then again, I had probably been in hiding.

"Nope," I said.

"Oh, I spoke to your mom . . ." Silence. "Anyway, how things with Sophie, man? You still seeing her?"

"Yep . . . 'course," I managed, wishing I could change the sound of my voice and stop the call, saying *Sorry to interrupt, the line's faulty and will be cut off until further notice.*

"You sound like something's up . . .?"

"Oh . . .?" My heart was suddenly beating double time. "Do I . . .?"

"Yeah, well, you sure everything's still cool between you and Sophie, man? Like, are you still . . . getting it together, like?"

I swallowed like I had a rock twice the size of Gibraltar caught in my throat. Back to the big lie. "Yeah . . . everything's cool, like, like fine."

"You're so lucky, man. Shit, I wish I had a chick like that."

"Yeah, meaning?"

"Meaning, like, having a chick who always comes back . . . like, who's always there for you, even when you get off with other chicks."

"Huh . . .? Oh . . . I see. Don't worry, Chaz," I felt my voice faltering, "your day . . . your day will come yet."

"Oh yeah? Like with who?"

There was just no placating him. He was obsessed. I suppose, in the end, like I was obsessed. Like we were all obsessed in those days. I had to think fast. "What about that . . . uh . . . that Zilla chick? You know . . . Zilla Tabatznik. The crazy one who's always dancing around and says 'howzit' to us at parties . . . you know, with the long brownish hair, who always hangs around with those Kensington ous?"

"You really think that she'd look at me?"

"Ja, well. Worth a try. She always seems to be checking us out, like."

"You mean you, or Solly?"

"No, I mean, like all of us."

"Yeah . . . shit, yeah. Maybe, maybe. Jesus, I just wish . . . I just wish it all came as easily to me as it does to you."

If ever I could have swallowed my tongue it was then.

"You alright . . .?"

"Ja . . . just like swallowed the wrong way."

"Oh . . . Well, what d'you think I should do, like . . . do you really think there's a chance with her . . .?"

"Chaz, it's worth a shot, who knows? It's always worth a shot." I couldn't believe I was saying that. Giving out free Dale Carnegie classes.

"You really think so?"

"Yeah, 'course, I really do!" I wouldn't have had the courage to say anything else.

Now, immediately, he was scheming.

"Maybe, like, we could have Zilla and Sophie over at my place, some time?"

"Yeah, maybe, sounds good to me." I was ready to agree with anything, just to get him off the phone.

"You don't sound so sure?"

"Well, I am."

"I bet it's Sophie. She's really got you, hey?"

"Yeah Chaz, that's right, I worship every step she takes." He really knew how to dig in when he wanted to. Which is just what I was afraid of. "Now bugger off, will you, and leave me alone!"

"OK, OK. Take it easy, man. Don't get so uppity, like."

That was the truth, but Chaz, fortunately, was a bit like a pillow, once you struck him hard he always fell back, dented. As expected he immediately changed tack.

"You know, I scored some good stuff yesterday. Some poison, like. Like, it's time we had a bit of a smoke together."

"Yeah . . .? OK. Sometime." The furthest thing from my mind right then was Durban bloody poison.

"Check you tomorrow, then," he said, and finally put the phone down.

Thanks to Chaz, awake now, fully awake, I had lived to see another day; reminding me I had not yet, not yet decided on an exact date for my demise, my imminent self-execution. Wondering if there was still even the most meagre of chances before I did so to unravel my monsters, to commit my Original Sin; to even for a fraction of a second become a part of that side of the species that called itself Man.

20

A couple of days later it finally came – the golden missive I had spent weeks waiting for – the letter from England, from my saviour: my brother Cyril. Solution to my problems. Answer to my prayers. Salvation. At last, salvation. As I had asked Cyril, there was no return address on the back, but as soon as I saw his handwriting and the stamp from England on the front of the envelope it struck me that whether he put his address on the back or not, my parents would still have known the letter was from him. Fortunately I spotted the letter before they laid eyes on it, but even Faith, who had retrieved the letter from the post-box, recognised immediately who it was from.

"Ho-so, a letter from Cyril. Hau, that brothe' of yours, Danny, he does not write enough. Your mother is always worried."

I only hoped she would trust that I would automatically show it to them and therefore not say any more about it. I grabbed the letter off the kitchen table and scrambled to my room. I was so excited that my hands were trembling. At last, at last, the answer. The solution. The magic formula.

I felt the edges around the thin airmail envelope and it began to strike me just how thin, just how almost ironed flat the envelope really was. Nowhere near the two-volume-size package I had imagined Cyril struggling to squeeze into an old, red Royal Mail post-box.

Perhaps, I thought, actually growing quite confident now, his advice was so good, so precise, so unbelievably wise and expert that there was no need to go into long, contorted explanations and solutions to my problem. Just a quick, simple formula, an easy-to-follow five-point plan, a neat set of how-to instructions – which was just what I wanted – and everything would be right again. Thank you Uncle Cyril. The very thought had the blood pounding in my chest, swirling in the back of my skull. Sitting at my little red and yellow desk, I held the envelope up to the light in the window. I couldn't make out much, but I took it as a positive sign: obviously the advice was crammed in, hidden from ma and da's prying eyes. Taking a ball-point pen I slowly cut away at the edges with the tip and pulled out the contents, still somehow half expecting those contents, their post-card thinness, to magically expand, transform into the size of some-thing much larger, perhaps a pop-up book. But then there it was in my hand, the flimsy postcard with a picture on the front of it and some writing on the back. I stared at the card, back and front, front and back, checked and re-checked the envelope – tapping it on the table like some hidden parcel might still suddenly drop out – but all I ended up with was what I was holding, an empty envelope and this paper-thin postcard with the crammed writing on it.

With no choice now but to read the card, I slowly took in the pic-ture on the front. It showed a window lit with pink fluorescent tubes, a bra and panties hanging in mid-air behind the glass – I supposed inspired by *The Invisible Man*, only this was *The Invisible Prostitute* or something like that. In the top left-hand corner was a small in-verted pyramid bearing the words: *Soho – Adults Only*. Very appeal-ing. I could see why Cyril had chosen the card. At the bottom edge of the postcard my eyes now took in a small, faint drawing in blue ballpoint pen, very obviously Cyril's ballpoint pen. The drawing was of a small male stick-figure and right in the middle of the figure, between the outwardly angled, cowboy-style legs, was drawn a long thin line with an arrowhead at the end of it. The arrow stretched straight up to the panties that dangled in mid-air, sort of colliding with them. A comment, circled above the smiling head of the stick-figure, read: *Me. Window-shopping*. I laughed, reminded of Cyril's humour, and flipped over to the back of the card, still somehow hopeful.

The few crammed lines on this, the blank side of the card, read:

Danny, m'young lad, don't worry. Just hang in there. No, actually look up! And it will too! Just a temporary setback, I'm sure! Don't take your eye off the goal, as they say, or rather the goal-mouth, if you know what I mean. Things here going great guns. Make that blazing guns. Chicks not half as stuck up as in Joeys. You'll see when you get here!!! At the end of the year? Though I may be in Spain, or Italy by then!! Don't be a schmo, bro', stay loose! See ya soon, your ou broer – Cyril.

Then there was a cramped, difficult-to-read P.S., which as best I could make out, read: *With all the shit going down in SA, I'm fuckin' glad to be out of the place.* There was also a line with the word *Harold* at the end of it, but I couldn't make out quite what, perhaps something along the lines of: say hi to Uncle Harold?

It didn't matter, I was angry as hell. Was this some sort of cruel hoax, one of Cyril's big-brotherly jokes and the real letter was still to arrive? My heart was plummeting so fast I felt like I was in a lift where the cables had suddenly snapped. I sat there bolted to my seat, unable to move, ready to hit concrete-bottom, my hands and knees shaking, wanting to rip the postcard up into a thousand tiny pieces and then set fire to it. I felt my eyes moisten. A lump formed in my throat like a dry bubble. I was all alone. I might as well be an orphan, I thought, and wished something large like a great big steel bank vault would suddenly fall out of the grey London sky and bash Cyril right on the head. Then maybe he would wake up and see. Too bloody sure of himself, that was the trouble. That was always the trouble with him. Never had a setback in his life. And now his big head only seemed to be getting bigger.

I sat back, breathing jerkily, tempted to write back immediately to tell him exactly what I thought of him, what was rampaging like a rogue elephant through my head, when it struck me the letter would take him at least two weeks to receive, that it would be at least another two weeks before he even bothered to reply, and then another two weeks for me to get the reply, and I lost my feeling for saying anything. It was no use. I would just have to face up to the fact that I was lost, and getting more and more lost. One problem had become two, three, four. I had stopped counting. I needed a map, and not just some ordinary sort of road-map, but a map showing every square centimetre around me. That letter was like a punch in the face, the sort of punch that lands you flat on your back. After a blow like that, either you begin to see or else you become even more fogged up. Typically, I was not one of those who *saw*, not one of those who a blow to the head wakes and makes *see*. I would wait for fate to finish me off completely, or bring about the miracle I still saw – believe it or not – still saw as possible, see-sawing somewhere between Uncle Harold and Sophie Street.

My life was decided. I had no further say in it. I gave up, surrendered, prepared to take whatever was dished out. Angrily, I ripped Cyril's postcard into thousands of tiny little fragments and watched them drop into my black metal wastepaper basket, landing like a mound of multicoloured mini-scrap.

21

By the following weekend I had managed to put everything and everyone off – even Chaz and his wild ideas; his Durban-bloody-poison, his Zilla-bloody-Tabatznik and Sophie-bloody-Street dream-overs – and I was back at low-point, which is to say, about normal.

After Sunday lunch with my parents, my parents of all people, I felt I just had to go somewhere I could be alone. Somewhere where I could just sit and think, sit and consider, sit and philosophise, sit and unravel my dumb, gross life; perhaps even finally decide where, and when, to end it. Funnily, or maybe not so funnily, the only place I could come up with to be alone in was Uncle Harold's shop. Jo'burg was like that. You just didn't do it, go to things alone in Jo'burg. There weren't even any neatly tucked-away rivers, or little-known hilltops to sit and hide on. Not in my part of town, anyway. In Jo'burg there was nothing, absolutely nothing, only people, rivers of people, and to show you were anything – in public at any rate – you always had to be with other people, even just one other person. Otherwise, for all the whispers about you, you might as well lock yourself up in your room and never come out. So at least there, in Uncle Harold's shop, I knew, despite everything, despite the shadows, despite the ghosts, I could be alone. Totally isolated, in a vacuum, cut off from the world – the normal world that is – the world of people and judgments, the world that I used to belong to, had been an avid partaker in.

As usual, I found myself telling my parents I had to go to Chaz's to get help on an assignment that I needed to do well in to get through my matric, an explanation they always found plausible, if not pleasing. At least with Chaz, they believed I was getting somewhere, that I might make it beyond high school.

"Do you think you could be back around teatime? You know, Uncle Abe and Aunty Fanny will be here, it's a good chance for you to see them."

"I'll try."

"Please, Danny, do, you know you always seem to be out, or doing other things, when it comes to your relatives; it's hard to get you to even visit your own bobbe these days. I don't want you running off like Cyril . . ."

"I'll try, ma. I will, I'll try. But I really must be going now . . ."

"OK then, but aren't you forgetting something?"

Yes, yes, I was forgetting something, something I wouldn't have to do again if I chose to end it all. Would she regret it? Miss it? Would she blame herself? Have a nervous breakdown? I braced myself, knowing if I didn't do it right the first time, I'd have to do it all over again and I didn't want that, not the way I was feeling. I walked up to her chair and leaning over I embraced and then kissed her twice on the lips, feeling that strange hot-cold feeling rush through me, but telling myself to ignore it, ignore it, ignore it.

As I let go of her, she looked into my eyes, sort of unexpectedly, like she hadn't really done in a long time, as though trying to see something inside me.

"Danny, you must look after yourself," she said.

"Yes, don't worry, ma. I'm looking after myself, doing fine." And I thought for a moment that she was seeing, actually seeing something inside me. Perhaps knowing something was wrong without knowing what. Testing to see if I might open up and tell, finally say something, finally tell them something a bit more intimate about my life, my private thoughts. But I couldn't. Just couldn't. Close as we might have seemed at times, especially to others outside our family, there was no history of saying what was there, in our hearts, not in this family. The closest I had come to that was with Cyril, but that was all gone now, all gone. I looked over to my father and saw that he too was waiting, wanting to touch me just that little bit deeper. But I couldn't, I just couldn't, it would have broken their hearts.

And so I turned, albeit for once slowly, feeling their eyes following me, trying to comprehend my mood swings, my hours of heavy Sherman tank-like silence, and found myself on a dull Sunday afternoon, furniture-shop keys bulging in my denim pockets, at the bus stop in Cavendish Road. Above me the old red testicle of a water tower hovered as I waited impatiently – spinning around, kicking the ground and banging the bus stop shelter – for a bus to get to Uncle Harold's shop so that I could be alone. Completely alone.

Nearly an hour later, I was still at the bus stop, still impatiently kicking the ground and bashing the aluminium structure, watching the empty streets, looking up to the old crusty water tower that was only growing rustier and rustier, more and more like a giant old testicle. I imagined it gazing down in amazement at the growing number of high-walled houses in our suburb, watching people cutting themselves off from neighbours, protecting themselves from the black ghosts that they saw prowling. I was thinking of pictures I had seen of the rows upon rows of matchbox houses in Soweto, where there were no high walls for protection from the streets, where the streets were the place to be, the place where everyone seemed to play and cavort and make friends and enemies, where the battles with police were still raging. Remembering now it was Sunday when everyone was meant to be in church, and there was no sport, no movies and very few buses.

By now I was ready to pack it in, admit defeat, go home and plan my end from there. I knew I should have walked, it would have done me good, no matter the distance, no matter what people said. And then I saw it – a lonely dusty red and cream-coloured double-decker bus juddering its way up Cavendish Road.

I was the only passenger on the bus, the only one sitting up there on the top deck, alone, alone with my thoughts. I saw the Hillbrow

Tower whiz by and wondered what had happened to the revolving restaurant at the top that was once so popular and why the Brixton Tower was now the new all-important tower.

And then I was walking past the pet-shop in Loveday Street, the one I always walked past and peered into on my way to Uncle Harold's shop, the dog and cat hutches in the windows empty now; the fish, silver, gold, rainbow coloured, still trapped, flicking, darting round and round, going nowhere.

At Uncle Harold's door, Uncle HK's empire. Looking up I saw the dusty, paint-flaked motto above the now dead, unblinking neon light: *Golden by Name, Golden by Quality*. As I unlocked the door I noticed that Uncle Harold, negligent Uncle Harold, hadn't locked all the latches, but I quickly stepped inside, happy, happy to have this dark haven, this ghostly refuge to hide myself in.

How many people my age in Jo'burg had a place like this all of their own? It was a holy refuge, a therapy room, a love-nest, and here, in blissful, tormented isolation, I could think through every little conundrum, until I reached the other side, that mythical place of salvation. Where the grass was not just green but gold. Where that word failure did not exist. Where sex, as for the bonobos, was the most natural, simple thing in the world. And there were no hung-up girls and nothing was banned, absolutely nothing banned.

Suddenly, jogging me from my thoughts, I heard a noise right here in the shop, a squeal like the high-pitched whinny of a horse. No, more high-pitched than that, like a cat. Then again, this time deep and throaty, like a warthog. I could hear it clearly now, a sigh, a human breath, a cough, a gasp, no a grunt, coming from where I was headed, right there at the back of the shop. Could it be, could it be intruders, burglars? Nervously, I fixed a sweaty fist in self-defence, wishing I had my flick-knife with me. Hoping I wasn't called on to use it, my fist – my already shaking fist. Seeing myself running. Already running. I heard the sigh again, only sharper now, then low, low like a grunt, then high again like a squeal, then a sigh, a deep sigh. No, no, those were not ordinary breaths, that breathing couldn't be burglars. It sounded more like what I had seen glimpses of in the movies, before the inevitable cuts, yes, like passionate love-making, sounds I dreamt, dreamt all the time, that I might one day hear myself making.

Then it hit me, Uncle Harold, it was Uncle Harold, bugger, he'd brought a woman in here – Thelma perhaps? A refuge from the children? I couldn't blame him. I said a silent, gulping prayer, too scared to intrude, and decided to turn like an angel and leave, to leave Uncle Harold and his wife, his secret lover, to themselves, alone, as I should have been, as I desperately wanted to be. But on second thoughts I turned back again. Just a glimpse, a tiny peep, and I would have something over him. For once, something over him. Something only I knew about him. I crossed silently, on tip-toe, into the office doorway, the inner sanctum, and peeped in.

The room smelt of a mixture of stale sweat and sickly-sweet colognes and on the corner of the desk stood a half-finished bottle of Bells. I knew it was Bells because my father always drank Bells, always had it on the dining-room table on weekends. The table lamp was on, facing down onto the flat desk, the silver framed pictures pushed over, facing dull wood.

A sneaky smile began to form on my face as I saw a half-naked body, pale round legs spread lusciously wide apart, smooth and white as baby skin, and between them, bouncing flabbily, a backside; clumpy heels lifting off the floor, white shirt ruffled around a broad back. The sight of the wide-open kicking legs stirred life in me, involuntary, unstoppable flickers of life. I felt a swelling, there was life in there. Life! Then suddenly that awful squeal again, that sharp cat's cry, rising into a yell, and I saw the head that belonged to the lusty, life-sparking legs crane around those lumpy Roman shoulders and I felt the life in me blow out like a candle. I felt sick. Recognising beyond a shadow of a doubt that the face was Sophie's. Sophie Street's.

"Danny! Danny!" Yes, it was her voice, only shaky-contralto, tremoring.

"Gosh, Danny!" A male groan, his head turning, cheeks coal-stove red, eyes burning. I felt myself turn and run, smashing into wooden chairs, aluminium tables, cupboards, gramophones. Reaching the front door I pulled and pushed at the dead-lock, my hands trembling. Feeling them behind me, feeling their sweaty hands touching my back, my skin searing hot. Turn key, turn! Determined to get out, to kick down the door if necessary, to smash my worthless body through the glass – the blood, the injury nothing compared to what I had just seen. I heard a shrill screech – the sound of a cat caught in barbed wire – Sophie Street right behind me, yelling my name, and felt the key turn, finally turn; their damp fingers coldly slipping off me; the shrieking, the crying, the hoarse panting fading behind me.

I ran through empty town. Jo'burg, city of churches, steeples and shuls. Down Bree Street I hitched a ride with one of the sporadic Sunday-afternoon drivers; sightseers, doing nothing, seeing nothing, hearing nothing, eyes dead open. Climbing into the car I was faced by an anaemic blotchy figure sitting bent-shouldered behind a stiff collar, a thrust of straight brown hair swept from one side of his head to the other. He winked at me and asked my name, offered me a cigarette from his shaking hand, asking whether I preferred long, hot summer days or cool, cosy winter ones, half-moons or full, mysterious bewitching ones. Then suddenly he began to confess, confess to a sickness, an injury, a boil on the skin beneath the trousers, telling me tearfully to feel, feel for myself. I felt it for myself, on his upper thigh, near the pocket, yes, a boil, a big hard round boil. Just like his, like his, like Uncle Harold's, and I suddenly knew I had once again been duped. I felt the car slow for a streetlight and reached for the door-handle, tugging, tearing, ripping at it until it broke right off and the door flew open. Air, fresh air rushed in and my body rushed out, I fell on my knees, ran on my knees, got up, scrambled towards a blurred vision of temples and steeples before making out in the distance my suburb. The old testicle-shaped water tower now like a boil, a boil I had touched, about to burst, to infect the population below. On a street corner, three men in smart grey suits, eating with concentration the jagged, thin-boned skulls of sheep, sucking in the last remnants of boiled flesh on the grey bone.

Stumbling down the hill, Cavendish Road, the dogs, the neighbourhood dogs, Alsatians, bulldogs, little yappy chihuahuas, toy poms, no longer friendly at all now, growling, howling, barking at me, like I was the enemy, the intruder, the black man in their streets.

Arriving in Isipingo Street, my faithless, upside-down Isipingo Street, I burst through the security gate, careful this time to go around the house, through the back door, the servants' entrance, to evade my parents – but instead banged right into Uncle Abe and Aunty Fanny. I had completely forgotten that they might still be there.

"Just look how you look," my mother cried, "how could you go out with shoes like that? Your pants are torn at the knees!"

I looked down and saw that my shoes were dirty and dusty and the laces had come loose, like pieces of unwanted string. My shirt was sticking out, ragged, from under my jersey, and my denims were torn at the knees from falling and crawling on the road.

"Chaz," I began. "Chaz . . . and I were just playing a bit of football in the park, and I fell, that's all."

"But I thought you went there to study?"

"It was just a short break. We needed a rest."

"Leave it, Stel, leave it. You know what boys are like . . ." said my father, smiling at my Uncle Abe. "Well, aren't you at least going to say hello to your Uncle Abe and your Aunty Fanny before they go?"

I looked up at my wrist-watch thin yet immaculately pressed Uncle Abe and my opulently round but always sweet, smiling, giggling Aunty Fanny and grunted hello with a quick, short wave of my arm. Then face to the ground I raced to my room. Once inside I turned the key and held onto the door handle, pressing against it, breathing heavily, as though they might try to follow me, burst their way in, interrogate me.

But they remained at the back door, just around the corner from my room, where I could hear my mother saying, "Sorry, so sorry about Danny, that he has to come in like such a vildergai, and not even greet you."

"Don't worry about it, Stel, they're all like that," Aunty Fanny replied. "The kids of today lead such fast lives it's hard to keep up. Frankly, I've given up trying." She laughed. "Anyway, don't worry yourself, just say goodbye to Danny for us."

"As if it's not bad enough having one son, for who knows how long in some Godforsaken foreign corner of the world, now we have to have him, always out, girls ringing all the time, and he never tells us a thing. Not a thing." My mother again.

"Danny'll be OK once he gets into the army, you'll see." Dad, of course my dad, probably to Uncle Abe. "They'll knock the bullshit out of his head!"

"Stan, don't be so hard on the youngster." Uncle Abe. Always worrying.

"Never mind hard, the army'll give him hard!" My father again.

"Don't be so unreasonable, Stan. He's in matric, and he's under a lot of pressure." Mother.

"Yes." Aunty Fanny, being supportive; she really was sweet. "Trouble is that the kids of today think they can do everything, and all at once. They think they're somehow invulnerable. There's all that peer-group pressure and things, and they're just bombarded with so much more than we used to be. Anyway, how's he going at school, Stel? That's always a telling factor."

"Who knows, don't ask me, he never says anything."

"I'm sure he's just going through a phase," Aunty Fanny, of course. "They all go through phases, but they get over it. They all get over it in time."

Head on pillow now, feeling it like a warm, padded handkerchief on my face. It was like a mother to me, that pillow, like the way you would like a mother to be: something soft and cuddly and accepting. Instead, in front of me I saw a fire-hoop, another sneering, snarling hoop of fire.

22

L ater. A rat-tat-tatting at my door. Mother.
"Danny, dinner."

"Please, sick . . ."

"Sick?"

"Yes. Sick, ma . . ." *Yes, sick again, ma.*

"OK, can we help with anything, get a doctor?"

"No."

And later.

"Danny, phone. I think it's one of your girlfriends."

"Say I'm not here."

"But I just said you were."

Damn.

"Thanks, ma."

As I flopped down onto the chair next to the phone I swear I saw the Tretchikoff woman blinking, no winking at me. *Bitch!*

A voice. Ah, it's you. Sophie, Sophie Street. Witch. Wicked witch. First of the beasts.

"Danny, I'm telling you he was forcing me. Trying to . . . trying to . . . screw me. You don't have to believe me, Danny, that meshuggene creep city councillor bigwig friend of yours was trying to rape me," she whined painfully.

"Then how come you don't go to the police?"

"What are they going to do?"

"Arrest him, of course. What d'you think?"

"Oh yes. The police are going to take my word, Sophie Street: schoolgirl from Observatory East . . . over that pig from City Council. You don't even believe me!"

"Me?"

"Yes, you."

"But it looked like . . ."

"You see? See what I mean. You only saw what you wanted to see."

It was true. I was confused now about what I saw and what I made of it. Unsure of my own vision. I, the only witness to this apparent crime. And yet no witness at all. Only seeing, as always, as Sophie was seeing now, what I wanted to see. And when the police began their interrogations, whose witness would I even be? Hers? Or his? Was she not just defending herself? Exaggerating out of embarrassment? Rape? What was it? What was it anyway? The nature of rape? I didn't really understand. It didn't happen to anyone you knew. It was sexy. We dreamed about it. Saw it in the papers, and dreamed.

"What about the alcohol?"

"Danny, you know I don't drink. And not *that* stuff. If you think I'm going to sit down with some weirdo fat-arse and drink, then you've really got the wrong idea of me."

"But you were there!"

"To discuss you! Because he said you were so low and depressed, and if somebody didn't step in to help, who knew what you might do. And old idiot me said, 'Yes, sure, if you really think so, maybe I can help . . .' He was so keen, he even came to pick me up to talk."

"And did you talk?"

"Look, Danny, I'm not asking you to believe me." Her voice was prickly, almost rasping. "I just want you to know the truth. I don't date older men, and I certainly don't allow men nearly my father's age to put their grubby hands all over me . . . Has the gall to tell me the truth lies at the bottom of a bottle. More like craziness. I'm telling you Danny, that man is meshuggene . . . massaging my shoulders, old fart, telling me to relax. Telling me what a sensitive guy you are. He's mad, Danny, I'm telling you, mad! Listen, Danny, just do me one favour, one big favour before I hang up. Wake up to yourself. Just look around you, open your eyes."

Left alone again, to open my eyes, sift through the new lies, the new deceptions, half-truths. In my room, the crook of my arm over my eyes again, lying down, thinking. If it were true, what she was saying, how could I ever look at him in the eyes again? I was convinced at that moment, more than ever, there really was no one you could tell anything. There was no one to trust. Everyone, the whole of humanity was built on a lie. I had seen it again and again. And I was right at the very centre of it. The biggest lie. We were all just flying in circles. My parents, my relatives, me, aiming for some sort of depth, for communication, for feeling, but finding only the circle, always only traversing the wire-thin, feelingless edge of the circle. Honesty. How did you ever recognise it?

My door rattled again.

"Danny, it's for you! Uncle Harold . . . said he just wants to have a quick word with you about helping at the shop one night this week."

Fuck.

"OK, I'm on my way."

"Tell him for God's sake you've got schoolwork. You can learn the business when you're finished school. At the end of the year when you've got more time!"

"Ja, ma."

Back to the phone. Madame Tretchikoff smirking.

"Danny . . . I'm, I'm . . . sorry."

I wanted to slam the phone down.

"Just, please, please, listen to me. It's not what you think."

Nothing was ever what you thought. Not ever.

"Listen, please, Danny. Just hear me out. OK, I was drinking, and I shouldn't have been. Not with her. But she was sitting there, telling me how much she fancies you, and that you just have too much on your mind, and sort of coming on to me at the same time. You know yourself she can be pretty, well, deceptive . . . And she kept sort of waving her shoulders at me as she spoke . . . and yes, I'm sorry, because of that, Danny, things did get out of hand. But it wasn't just me. You've got to understand that. Maybe I misread it. But not altogether. All I wanted to do was discuss you. Just find out more from her about you, from someone your own age, someone close to you. Believe me, Danny, there's no reason why I need to go chasing after young birds. Any birds for that matter. Those days are long gone. You know that. I have a decent business to run and I'm an alderman with responsibilities now. I need to go chasing after young birds like I need a hole in the head. I don't need it. You have to believe me, Danny . . . I was just trying to get another perspective on you, to help you. I can assure you there was absolutely no other reason why I would want to bring her to the shop."

"But she says . . ."

"Listen Danny, I'm telling you, believe me. The lady doth protest too much. What she says is not true. Maybe I did misread. I know. But not like that, not altogether. Yes, I think she's nice and could even be very good for you. She's still young and naïve, but at the same time, it seems to me, she knows what she wants. Exactly what she wants."

"But she said . . ."

"Yes, I'm sure I know what she said. But remember, Danny, in any event, it takes two to tango. Two."

Two. No one ever blameless. Not even the antelope that is eaten by the lion?

"Just think about it, Danny, think. Woman – get thee to a nunnery . . . Wise men know well what monsters you make of them." Silence from my end. "Look, I'll call you during the week. I think we have to speak more about this. No, actually, better still, why don't you just come into the shop . . . I've got something I've been meaning to give you for a while now . . . a book . . . a banned book. It's very good. I know you'll appreciate it."

"I've got schoolwork." I was determined this time to say no, to take control. But at the same time I couldn't help wondering what the book was.

"I think you'll find it worthwhile, really . . . What say I pick you up Thursday afternoon? Around four?"

"Well, I d'no, maybe . . ." Thursday again, why always a Thursday?

"Danny, we need to talk, we really do. And I know you'll get something from this book."

I thought hard again for a minute, then heard myself speak, unsure, stilted:

"OK . . . then."

I hung up the phone, ready to hold my breath till I died, ducked under the snide gaze of pretty Miss Know-It-All-Tretchikoff and dashed back into my room, telling my mother I was sick, really sick, but refusing help, all help, thinking only through the blur of Harold, Uncle Harold and his latest offer. Wondering what was really in it for me, what really he could now say to me, what was in this book that he hadn't shown me before. Was this the book that Cyril should have been sending? What was I to do? What?

23

My mind bleak and mushy, I climbed into Uncle Harold's car on Thursday afternoon, and as he sped off I could see nothing, absolutely nothing in front of me other than his flabby, half-deflated buttocks bouncing between Sophie's immaculately smooth, round thighs. I felt like I should rather be at home smashing myself over the head with a 20-pound hammer.

This time, arriving at Golden's New and Used Furniture shop, I hardly even saw the great white toothy welcome of the bow-tied crier at the front door, didn't even remember waving my usual half-embarrassed hand in response. And once inside the shop I felt enveloped in a dark shadow, like someone had forgotten to switch on all the lights. For the first time I noticed a thick dustiness about the place, creeping up my nostrils, like a wind had blown years of unswept dirt and cobwebs through the place. I felt claustrophobic, but I pressed on, thinking of the book, the banned book he had promised, praying, still praying for some magic that would save me.

As we sat down in his office, Uncle Harold immediately began replaying events between himself and Sophie. He spoke calmly, steadily, and I sat there nodding, sort of wishing that his words, the controlled tone of his voice, the absolute certainty of his reasoning, could somehow infiltrate my own being and lift me into that winners' circle that people like himself seemed permanently to reside in.

"Danny, what happened in here," he explained, "is just something that happened, that got a bit out of control. We started discussing you, and I must tell you, if you think there is anything drastically wrong with you, she certainly doesn't know it, and if she does, she certainly isn't saying so. And I think if it's the latter, that's very mature, a very mature sign."

I nodded, feeling a little better for the inside information.

"But the problem started when she began to speak about herself. I could see she needed help just as much as you, and I tried to explain to her that all she needed was to be more relaxed, just be herself, as much as you needed to be more relaxed and just be yourself. Then, I don't know, one thing led to another, but I must tell you, Danny, and you have to believe me, I didn't intend anything to happen, and I don't think she did either. As you know, nothing did happen in the end, anyway."

I nodded, tensely.

"And that's why I think if we just see this whole episode as one of those mistakes that happen and put it behind us, then we can move on; we don't need to let it destroy our friendship, what's between you and me . . ." He looked up at me and when I nodded again, this time like I was trying to understand, he said, "I want you to be sure, Danny, that what's between us is something special. To me, it will always be special, and I don't think, being honest with yourself, you would get this sort of help from anyone else . . . I just don't think so."

"Yes, that's . . . true," I managed with some difficulty. "It's just that at the time . . . and Sophie is angry, really angry, and says she didn't want to . . ."

"Yes, I know that, Danny, and I want you to know that I think she's right . . . but just not altogether right . . . there's a difference . . ." He looked up at me again, as though asking me whether I knew the difference, and when I nodded, he said, "Good. I just want you to be sure there is a difference, but I also want you to feel that you can continue your life, and be friends with her just as before." He raised a finger and pointed it towards himself. "The point that I'm trying to make is that you should put this whole thing behind you. Don't make it any bigger than it is, just put it behind you."

I think I must have looked close to tears, because he then walked up to me and hugged me as I sat in my chair.

227

"Danny, it's alright, it's alright. As I have always said, Alles sal reg-kom, don't worry, my boy, alles sal regkom."

"Yeah . . . but rather sooner than later," I said, actually managing a smile, and he laughed, and then we both laughed together.

Now, his hand on my shoulder, squeezing it, he told me to start preparing a bed on the desk while he checked that everyone had left the shop and everything had been locked up. Unsure of myself, but feeling better for having spoken to Uncle Harold, for having discussed what had happened between him and Sophie, I did as he said, and began to undress and place the cushions on his desk. Wondering as I did so if he even remembered the book, but somehow not wanting to ask and thereby disturb the balance, this balance between us that he had recreated.

When everything was ready and he was back in the office, he started off at first as though disinterested, standing as he always did, be-side me, coaxing me, encouraging me. And then, as had become the practice, I heard the zip of his fly coming down as he re-positioned himself.

And at the end of it, when I was sitting up, dazed as usual, his eyes lit up, and he said, "I love you, Danny . . . I just want you to know that. I will always love you. All I have ever done is only to help you." He looked at me for a while, as though waiting for a response, an ac-knowledgment. Eventually I smiled, and he stroked my shoulder, and said, "There, that's much better." And he took his hand off my shoul-der to allow me to get up and dress.

Having stacked the cushions away along the office walls, which he did as I dressed, he walked over to the big dark cupboard at the back of the office.

"Don't worry, I haven't forgotten the book," he said, and now I re-ally and truly smiled.

From an even darker drawer inside the cupboard he pulled out a key, and then opened a drawer in his desk. Out of the drawer, he lifted a somewhat bleached-looking red, hard-covered book. Walking back to me he handed over the book, and said, "Keep it. It's yours. I'm sure you'll find it very interesting. It has some very interesting perspectives. Just don't let your old folks find it."

I smiled, and felt my heart skip a beat as I held onto the red book tightly, like it was a royal jewel that could easily slip through my fingers. Something in me, some deep intuitive spot telling me that this was it, this was the book that held within its red covers the solution, or at any rate a much, much deeper understanding of my problem, and thereby eventually a solution. In my head I compared it to Mao Tse-tung's "little red book" that I had heard so much about but never actually read or even laid eyes on. What Mao's book was to the Chinese peasantry, I thought, so this book would be to me: my own little red book. A book that was going to save me, resurrect me, give me a new life. In my own mind, it was as if I had at last graduated from the foundation phase of Uncle Harold's treatment and now he was handing me the key to the next and, hopefully, final stage: the stage that would make me the man I had already bragged to the world I was. In this book that I was holding on to so tightly, I was convinced there was magic. I could still make it over the line, and first. First. So far, come to think of it, I was still in front.

As I looked at Uncle Harold trying to communicate my thanks, the expression on his face suddenly changed – he went white and tears welled up in his eyes – and it looked to me as though he was about to kneel down and make a confession. He opened his mouth a couple of times like a fish, as though to speak, but nothing came out. Then, as though thinking of something else to say, he said what he had said to me often before: "Perhaps one day, Danny, you'll understand . . . this thing I feel for you . . . I only wish that you could feel the same as I do."

For the second time ever, I looked back at him, and felt sorry for him. I stood up and hugged him. He squeezed me back, and I still felt there was something more he wanted to say, but he didn't say it. Instead, smiling warmly at me, he asked if I minded catching a bus home, saying that he had some urgent business to attend to. The truth was I didn't mind at all. I was more than happy. It was just what I needed, a little walk through town, time to think, time on the bus to start looking through my little red book, and with it to plan my life anew.

Outside the shop I was caught in a twilight world. I saw the magnificently tall buildings of the city above me, a luminescent sky that looked trapped between winter and spring, between old and new; the darkening pinkness in the sky like a layer of old skin the world was ridding itself of. That I was ridding myself of. I felt good, light, in a bubbly sort of way, and gripped tightly onto the red book as if someone might try to snatch it from me. Looking up into that sky I thought, for the thousandth time, how all I wanted now was just to be like other guys. Not above, not below. Just the same. Well, no, actually that was a lie. I did want to be a bit more, I still wanted to be first. In my heart, I still wanted to be first. I wanted others to look up at me, just once, like I was on a stage. And just once I wanted to feel proud, not muddle-headed, downcast and ashamed like I had been on that day I told them my good news. Right then, I believed, with this book in my hands, and Uncle Harold's help, I could still do it. There was time yet. And I could. I could.

Clutching the book firmly against my chest, against my loudly beating heart, I looked ahead and realised that I had missed, somehow walked past, Loveday Street. I had taken a wrong turn, yes, a while ago, and was now a good couple of blocks up into the centre of town, on the fringes of another world. In front of me a huge crowd had gathered at the bottom of one of that part of the city's higher office blocks, waving and shouting and looking upwards.

As I looked around, ready to head straight back to my bus stop, I realised there were actually two crowds, separated by several metres and a cordon of police. The one crowd, the one I had stumbled into, was ninety-nine percent black, myself and two or three other whites making up the one percent; the other crowd was one hundred percent white.

When I realised where I was and what was happening I backed away, holding tightly onto my book, and took up a position somewhere in the middle, between the two crowds, close to the safety of a group of journalists, who were excitedly recording the entire episode. The day had now grown completely dark and two police spotlights picked out, on top of the office block, a black man dressed in white overalls. He stood on top of the building like a famous star waving and holding a placard that was impossible to read. Crouched to the side of the black man, looking like he was pleading with him, was a policeman in regulation blue peaked cap. In the darkness and with the spotlights wavering around the black man it looked almost as if the white policeman was bowing before some black superstar. But it soon became evident that the black man was threatening to jump and that the crowds had been there for a long while watching the event unfold.

The white crowd was very vocal, screaming from time to time, almost in a rehearsed unison: "Spring kaffir! Spring!"

On the other side, the black crowd had a chorus or rather a kind of dialogue of their own going with the man on top of the building. Every few minutes the man on top of the building would raise his fist and placard and scream: "Aaaa-maaan-dla!" And the crowd below would respond: "Aaa-weee-thu!"

I was mesmerised by everything that was taking place around me. It was difficult in the unfamiliar atmosphere, with the crowds, the spotlights shining and the man threatening to jump from the top of the building, to believe that I was on this planet.

And then suddenly someone in the white crowd screamed: "Spring King Kong!" And everyone on that side laughed.

231

Wherever I looked now there was something wrong, something abnormal happening, something going in the opposite direction to the way life was meant to be.

Then just as the white crowd started crooning, "Spring kaffir! Spring!" once again, the man took a giant leap forward, sailing through the air, his momentum carrying him forward, causing him to pirouette elegantly as he sliced through the night air; the police spotlights fighting with one another to follow his spiralling descent. Unlike the crowd below, there was something breathtakingly graceful, dignified in the motion of his body as it glided through the spotlit darkness to the grimy pavement below. The man looked like a ballerina or a famous trapeze artist, slight, delicate, dancing through the night. And in those few moments, as the man's body danced through the air, there was recognition of his bravery, and it was shown in the complete silence of both crowds; even the white side standing dead-still, their breath caught – in exhilaration, in amazement, in horror – between their ruddy, bloated cheeks. And then there was a dull thud and a crack, like someone loudly crushing chicken bones between their jaws, and although I couldn't see it through the crowd, I knew the man had hit the ground.

Then, like a broken movie starting to wind up again, the white crowd stepped out of its trance and began slowly and then more vigorously to clap and cheer. Among the black crowd there remained a stunned silence, but then someone in the black crowd began to chant, a deep, stiff voice that finally broke into a booming, steam-train sounding incantation – a-choof-a-choof-a-choof – and the black crowd began to follow the chant and dance to its rhythm. The very rhythm of the crowd's movement was immensely powerful and threatening, and the police, seeing the danger, pushed the white crowd backwards until, in the face of the ululating, dancing horde, the whites began to disperse. I, too, saw this as my time to leave. My head was like a warplane fuselage struck by enemy fire, bursting and shooting in all directions.

If only I had a fraction of that black man's courage, I thought, as I redirected myself to my bus stop in Loveday Street. Compared to that black man, I felt like a speck, nothing more than a miserable piece of dirt whirling haphazardly in an enormous universe. Everything suddenly looked colossal around me, the buildings, the night sky, the people still left in the city. All I was doing on this planet was going round and round in circles, like dust blowing in the wind, like the fish in the pet-shop window.

Still shaken by what I had seen, I found myself almost unconsciously climbing onto the bus. I sat upstairs, right at the back, as usual as far from people as I could get.

Unlike that black man, what I needed – I tried to look as honestly as I could at myself – was not just passion, courage, commitment; it was something more, something like the tablets my mother took for her nerves. What I needed was a quick-fix, a do-it-yourself solution, a single pill, a single mantra, that could solve all my problems. And then I became aware of it again, the red hard-cover book that I still had clamped tightly in my right hand, tucked beneath my heart like it was something sacred, like it was some holy text.

I released my grip on the book and placed it on my lap, looking down at it and for a moment feeling a great surge of strength from the fact that I had this book, that I had someone I could always turn to, who I could talk to about almost anything.

I looked carefully for the first time at the title of the book, somewhat hard to see on the bleached cover. It seemed to read, yes, it definitely said, *The Sixth Man*. This was confirmed on the title-page inside. *The Sixth Man, The Sixth Man*, it went round and round in my head. Is that what I was? The sixth man? That in every six people there was only one like me, someone different, someone special? I knew it was the case, I knew it.

Eagerly I began to skim the pages, starting with the introduction, reading a few words here and there, moving quickly on, not sure that what I was reading was really what I was reading. The more I skimmed, the more I went into the book, the more I was not sure, the jungle of words throwing up a puzzle of black and white before my eyes; until the puzzle began to fall into a shape, a pattern, and it became evident that this book was not even vaguely what I imagined it was.

I began to perspire, persisting, reading on, just, just in case. In the hope. In the faintest of hopes. But it didn't seem to matter how much I read, nothing changed, it only grew worse. After skimming almost the whole way through the book, it was obvious the book didn't even mention my problem. This was definitely not a book about getting it up, well, that is to say, not in the traditional sense, because from what I had read, this was a book about getting it up alright, but each and every chapter was about doing it in a different way – being happily and unashamedly gay – from birth to adolescence, to coming out of the closet, to forming stable relationships, to growing old and grey and remaining happily, pinkily gay. Everything, everything I didn't want to be.

Was this some cruel joke? No, I should have known better. It was all falling into place. I had been betrayed. Bitterly and undeniably betrayed. And even then I found myself arguing with myself, asking myself why I was reacting this way – like a betrayed, immature, ungrateful fool. But inside of me there was nothing I could do about it, just this feeling that I had been taken up a tall building by a close friend and, once at the top, just like that, pushed over. Inside of me I felt something piercing and hot, like a blister, growing, about to burst.

I looked over and over at the chapter titles, lest I had missed something, missed the pages where the magic formula was hidden. Looking even for some code, but of course there was none. I knew at that moment that I would never let anyone see this book. Ever. Not my parents, not my friends, not anyone, least of all Chaz, and definitely not that cynical bastard brother of mine, Cyril. Never. Never.

Sitting there on that bus, I felt bilious, like all the events of that day, of my recent past were suddenly being sucked into a whirlpool in my stomach. Everyone was looking at me now. Everyone. I was sure. But this time I didn't bother to turn away. I had murder in my heart. I was so bitterly disappointed and I wanted them to know it. If Uncle Harold had been in front of me then I would have taken his neck and wrung it like a kosher chicken until it bled dry.

As soon as I arrived home, I went straight for the medicine cabinet in the bathroom, yelling out to my mother and father that I had a bad headache and was going to be sick. I locked the bathroom door and swallowed six headache tablets. That at least I knew they would understand. Everyone in the house was a tablet-taker, my mother bought them in bottles by the hundred, like tissues or toilet paper.

I could feel my mother's silent presence at the door, but I wouldn't come out until she had left, replying to her question, "Are you alright?" in the calmest voice I could: "Yes, yes, I'm fine now, ma."

Even later, when my parents came into my room asking how I was, offering to call a doctor, I refused to lift my head from under the blankets, shouting back into the muffled darkness: "Please, please, just let me be!" Hearing them pass out of the room, whispering to one another: "Talk about a mood . . ."

Later, much later that night, when all was quiet and the house was perfectly dark, I switched on my bedside light and shuffled into the kitchen, badly in need of water. In the kitchen I opted for milk, the white creaminess of milk, and drank it down, straight from the bottle, feeling the sweet thickness passing through my throat like it was draining through me, somehow cleansing me. Feeling hungry, I opened the pantry cupboard and spotted the Cadbury's Drinking Chocolate, which my mother didn't often buy. I lifted the tin from the shelf and opened the cutlery drawer to get a teaspoon to dollop it down with, telling myself that, unlike Chaz, the pimples wouldn't come, well not with the same vehemence. Seeing in the drawer not just spoons, but forks and knives. Knives! I felt them hot, hot and cold, in my hands. Then I spotted the long, sharp chopping-knife that I so often saw in Faith's hands, mightily chopping away, and I saw it suddenly in my own hand, chopping into Uncle Harold's shoulder-blades, as I re-played, in my head, the cracking sound of that black man's bones as he hit the street. And then I thought of Sophie Street dangling over that desk, and thought of my own flick-knife, the one that was out-lawed, that I still kept hidden in my drawer.

Back in my room, foraging through my drawers, I felt the smooth, glossy paper of the banned magazines, the magazines he had given me – the magazines that always felt so shiny and exciting and yet dirty and greasy in my hands – until finally I had it in my hand, the banned weapon, the flick-knife. Yes, just like Brutus, I was going to stick my knife right into the middle of the emperor's back. In the mid-dle of his shop, in front of everyone, yes, right there, in the middle of that rich ghostly empire.

24

I stayed home from school the next day, sick, unable to face the world, and by midday I could not hold myself back any longer, I had to go. My body felt tense, stiff, wound up like a spring, and in my head I heard a voice: *What are you made of? Are you a man or a mouse?* Yes, definitely my father's voice, only now it went deeper, now it was right inside me, it was my voice, part of me.

That voice rattling in my head, I dressed quickly and then grabbed the flick-knife from where I had put it – under my pillow, next to my ear, next to my head, so that it could be there in my mind, a part of my every sleeping thought – and slid it into my pants pocket.

Sitting upstairs on the bus I gripped the knife in my pocket and felt its mechanism, testing its motion. I felt like a member of one of the Yeoville gangs I was so afraid of. Looking outside I noticed that despite the grey, the grey-red in my head, just what a remarkably blue day it was. It was like there were two distinct worlds, the one outside – all clear and sparkly, just like I wanted to be – and the one inside me – the one I hated, that was all brown and muddy and murky.

In the city I hopped off the bus, the brown shadow of the tall buildings reflecting the claustrophobic darkness in my mind. Briefly I stopped and gazed in at the pet-shop window, and immediately I saw myself – for one brilliant moment – smashing fish tanks, cutting open mouse and hamster cages, dog and cat hutches, liberating all the animals from their prisons, their cutesy circular ladders, their jangling, jingling balls that went round and round and round. I blinked, yes, it was possible, I could do it. I could, I could.

About a block and a half from Uncle Harold's shop, I became aware of a strange smokiness in the air. As I walked on, the smoke became thicker and for a moment it crossed my mind that the smoke could be from Soweto, from the thousands of domestic coal-stoves that I knew burnt there every day, or perhaps from black schools and government beer-halls that were now, even as I walked to Uncle Harold's shop, being burnt down in a new wave of protest. I felt a tickle of doubt. Maybe I would not, after all, be able to do it – look Uncle Harold in the eye and lunge at him with my flick-knife. I clutched the knife and flicked it open in my pocket, feeling the blade half-open against my thigh, wondering. Thinking of ways I could approach him from behind. Ways I could avoid his eyes. Ways I could get into the shop and move around so that he wouldn't see me. Then I would spring up, and the deed would be done. And I would just run for my life.

As I rounded the corner into Uncle Harold's street I felt a speck of ash blow right into my nose, and this seemed extraordinary. An actual fleck of ash blowing right up my eagle-nose, all the way from Soweto? Then, suddenly, right in front of me there were hundreds, no thousands of flecks. They were flying and swirling and diving all around me, almost like dirty-grey snow twirling and dancing through the air, and then I saw it: thick smoke billowing out of the windows and doors of Golden's New and Used Furniture. It was amazing. Uncle Harold's shop was on fire and huge crowds of people, black and white, had gathered in the streets to watch the smoky, blazing spectacle. The immediate area of the shop and street was cordoned off by police and a row of firefighters in big black boots stood with their legs wide apart like tin-helmeted cowboys, shooting great bursts of water from heavy black hoses.

I slowly squeezed my way to the front of the crowd and, like everyone else, stood there watching as the firemen fought their battle. Judging from the thick, deep purple colour of the smoke, the twisted, smashed windows and the blackened walls, it looked like the fire had already claimed the better part of Uncle Harold's shop. Inexplicably,

I became anxious, unsure of myself, feeling as though I should be doing something, that I should not just be standing there like everyone else. I should be in there, helping to save the shop. It was a strange feeling. A minute earlier I had felt such hatred, such betrayal, that I had been on my way to draw blood, to kill, and now I was standing there feeling like I should be lending a hand, that I should be in there helping to save the very soul I wished would fall into hell.

At that moment a man broke through the police cordon, running into the middle of the street where the firefighters were so courageously trying to save Uncle Harold's shop, and immediately began shouting and motioning frantically.

From my position, to the side of the building, and with the air now a smoky green haze, it was at first difficult to make out who this man was with his charred white shirt, torn and uncuffed. But as I shifted my position, it became more and more obvious that this unruly man in the middle of the street was none other than Uncle Harold, the man I had come to kill. He looked shorter and fatter and older and the bald patch on the top of his head had a black smudge running around it like a child had painted over it with a palm full of soot. He was swinging his hands in the air and swaying around, shouting: "Look what they've done to me. Look what they've done to my shop. Just look. God, just look! Noble bloody savages, everyone. Noble bloody savages, the lot of you!" Uncle Harold, Uncle HK, Harold Kleinhart, top Johannesburg city councillor, looked like he had gone completely berserk. For a moment I thought I knew what he was on about – remembering the debts he spoke about, the business problems he began to intimate he had – but it was still so hard, so hard to see why he had flipped out like this. It dawned on me slowly that maybe I had put myself in the hands of a maniac. A complete maniac. And as though in lieu of my planned knife attack, I felt a voice well up in me, and I began to shout at him even as I saw him scream and rave in another direction: "Poes! What the hell, what the fuckin' hell d'you think I am? Go! Go to hell! Do you think I am easier to be played on than . . ." But to be honest I don't think he even saw me, let alone heard me, or if he did see me, that he even knew at that moment who I was.

Before I could make a complete and utter fool of myself, the people around me already gawking, a policeman came up to me and stared me down, all the while pushing the crowd back, back, and as we moved backwards I came to myself. I felt my heart racing as the crowd began to clap and jeer at the madman in the middle of the city street.

I looked at the charred blackness of the shop, an ashen blackness that was once a lucrative city furniture empire, not only that, but was once the walls of my counselling-room, my love-nest, my sanctuary, my chamber of darkness. The neon sign outside the entrance to the shop hung dead, water trickling down it as though out of an animal's jaw. Above it, the shop's motto, *Golden by Name, Golden by Quality*, a curled piece of purple-grey carbon.

Then I saw a group of police – it took about six of them – grappling with and then handcuffing Uncle Harold. Once under a modicum of control, they walked him away, and as I watched his soot-soaked body being dragged off, I took the knife I did not use and dropped it to the ground. And then, knowing that for the moment there was nothing, absolutely nothing I could do, I slipped out of the crowd, making my way back to the bus stop.

Once at home, I did something I seldom did in those days: I took a shower rather than a bath, letting the scalding water pour over me until it stung every centimetre of my body, especially my head, my head and my penis, that felt so smeared in soot and mud and grime. Afterwards, without drying myself, I wrapped a towel around the waist of my now deeply burnt-pink flesh and let the orange glow from the bathroom heater keep my body burning as the water and sweat dripped from my head, my neck, my underarms, my despicable, sodden penis, my grossly hanging testicles, and noted below me, with some pleasure, some tiny satisfaction, the darkening hairs that were beginning to cluster, curly, yes, dark and curly, around my ankles.

25

The next day, Saturday, my head still heavy with the ashes of Friday's fire I was called to lunch. Reluctantly, I pulled myself from my bed, dressed, walked through the lounge, head down, and bumped into my mother as I entered the open double doorway into the dining-room. She was standing there in my path, by accident or design, carrying a strangely sunken look on her face.

"Give your mother a kiss hello," she said, reaching out to me as I walked past, but I carried on walking, almost without thinking, pushing her aside, leaving her behind me.

"Well, well!" She looked at me, a hurt look sitting around her slight jaw.

I pretended I had not heard and sat down with my father, who was already at the table. He greeted me, but almost absentmindedly, like his thoughts were lost in another place. There was a tall glass of water in front of him and he lifted it, beginning to sip it, the sip turning into one long gulp, like this water was somehow the container of his thoughts, like this water was going to sift his thoughts for him, work out whatever it was that had his thoughts so entirely wrapped up.

My mother now, with her right pinkie finger pointing graciously into the air, picked up the little brass bell on the table and gave it a sharp, vigorous shaking. A few seconds later, Beauty, the cardboard-thin, stand-in maid for Faith – who was on two weeks' leave to her homeland in the Ciskei to attend the funeral of an uncle – carried in with some pride a long silver plate of cold, ready-cut chicken pieces.

"What about the salad?" my mother asked.

The maid's stiff cardboard shoulders drooped. She hit her head with her hand, froze her lips, said, "Hau, madam, mistake!"

Ten minutes later she raced back into the dining-room holding out a glass bowl full of crisp salad.

Embarrassedly, she looked at my mother, and my mother said, "That's better, Beauty, now you're learning." The maid, crinkle-lipped, turned and left the room.

"A real Beauty that one. Always so bladdy miserable," said my father sourly. I was amazed that my father, so preoccupied, even noticed.

My mother didn't reply, just shook her head and dished out our food. Usually my father or my mother would have had something to say, something light to keep the conversation going, but this particular afternoon there was just this heavy silence, and I began to wonder if my mother was still affronted by the way I had brushed past her on my way to the table. I was about to open my mouth in an attempt to retrieve the situation, when my father, chewing on a mouthful of food, looked up at my mother and said, "Can you believe it . . .? Can you believe Harold Kleinhart would do a thing like that . . .? Burn down his own bladdy business?"

I nearly choked on my chicken bone.

"The man's turned out to be a ganef, what can you say?" my mother said. "It's hard to believe, but that's what happens when you get into politics. Don't say I didn't tell you."

"Just goes to show . . ." My father shook his head again. "You can't trust anyone these days, no one, not a soul. Not even your own family, your best friends."

"Burnt down his shop?" It spluttered from my mouth, sort of just fell out.

"Burnt down the whole bladdy thing. From top to bottom. Gone, finished, klaar." My father looked at me, shaking his head. "It was on the late news last night. And it's in all the papers today."

I was confused. "Why . . . Why would he do something like that? Are you sure it wasn't just an accident or something?"

"Why d'you think?" My father bit into the chunky chicken leg that was dangling loosely in his hand. "The insurance, of course . . . Danny, don't be such a bladdy imbongolo!" He swallowed the mouthful and I could see his Adam's apple pushing outwards to get the lump of meat down. Then he licked his fingers and launched into something of a tirade. "That's the bladdy trouble with people today: no bladdy backbone. Not even the people we're supposed to vote for! I just never thought Harold Kleinhart fitted into that mould." He shook his head vigorously, eyes wheeling in disbelief. "And to think I would have trusted that man with my life!"

"And you let him take Danny out at nights," my mother added.

"Jesus, Stel, how was I to know?" My father looked up at her, apologetically. "How the hell was I to know? To me he was always so trustworthy, a genuine pal. Might've been a bit of a playboy in his time, but you just don't expect something like this from someone his calibre."

"So, what did he teach you?" said my mother, suddenly turning to me, I think somehow venting an anger that was directed at Uncle Harold – and my father – at me.

"Uh-hem," I swallowed and held my breath. "About pricing second-hand furniture . . . and . . . and . . . how to deal with difficult customers."

"And what else?"

"And . . . to make sure the books are always kept in good order . . ."

"And . . ."

"Oh yes, and . . . how to keep your business things secret."

She looked at me baffled, shaking her head like I was crazy.

"Well . . ." I swallowed, "I mean . . . how to keep your business dealings secret . . . like not to let your opposition know how much you pay for goods 'n' things . . . so they don't know your mark-up . . ." I felt, for a moment while I struggled there, that I almost wanted to say more to her, but I knew I couldn't, and even if I could have summoned the courage I couldn't have said anything in front of my father.

"Bladdy kaffir wouldn't stoop so low," my father suddenly started again. "And I heard he was carrying on outside the shop like a madman, like a bladdy swab, worse than a kaffir. As if he wasn't in enough trouble already, apparently he was stirring up a bloody revolution!"

I looked down.

"Well, we better at least go and see Thelma," my mother said as though trying to console my father. "That's the least we can do. Poor thing, she'll be in pieces."

But my father was still mumbling to himself: "Fancy that, Harold bloody Kleinhart, Harold always-putting-himself-out-for-others Kleinhart, of all people. In jail for burning down his own shop!"

There was a dark shadow over my father's eyes, and again I wondered what he would do if he knew about us, Uncle Harold and me. At the least, I saw the whole house shaking, the bricks rattling and falling inwards, like in an earthquake, not even the chimney left standing. I watched as my father picked up his white linen serviette and meticulously wiped the corners of his mouth. Then, as if accepting what was, he threw down the serviette and said, "OK then, I suppose we'd better get going, get a cake or something?"

"Ah yes, of course," my mother said as though suddenly remembering the ancient tradition that good news or bad, you always took a cake. "We'll stop off at Fontana's, in Hillbrow, they're open on a Saturday . . ."

I used the opportunity of their planning to quickly excuse myself from the table before my mother could start on me to finish my salad.

Back in my room, sitting on my bed, I began to absorb the news, the shock at the thought of Uncle Harold burning down his business, but the more I thought about Uncle Harold, the more it began to strike me as possible. Come to think of it, knowing Uncle Harold the way I knew Uncle Harold, he was capable of anything. Anything. I suppose even this. And as I thought about it, in an inexplicable way, I felt betrayed yet again. But this time, not in the way he had betrayed me before – by making me believe one thing and then dishing out something completely different – but rather, and perhaps ironically, in the way one friend betrays another by not telling him what he is planning. Sort of in the way I had betrayed Chaz by not telling him the truth, by not honouring his friendship with the real story. Was it possible, I began to wonder, that Uncle Harold really had gone out of his way to lure Sophie? I shuddered, feeling sick, the little bit of chicken I ate at lunch swimming in my stomach. I felt abandoned. Like I had no one now. Absolutely no one. How could someone be so sensitive – as Uncle Harold always asserted I was – and yet be so thick-headed at the same time? Now I couldn't even turn to Chaz, because of the lies I had told him. Not Cyril, because of the idiot he had turned out to be, and not even Sophie, because of the way I had used her. Then suddenly in the far reaches of my reeling mind I heard a hammer knocking the hell out of my bedroom door.

"It's Chaz, Danny . . . Can't you hear me knocking . . .? On the phone . . . Yes, on the phone. What's the matter with you? Don't you listen? Danny, what are you doing in there?"

"Nothing, just sitting. OK, I'm coming. On my way."

"We're off to Thelma's now," she continued to shout through the door. "We'll be back around five, OK? Oh, and . . . if anyone calls maybe you better not say where we are. Just say out for the afternoon, and take a message."

"Yeah, sure, ma, OK, ma." *Go already, go.*

As I arrived at the phone, my mother and father were leaving. Seeing me, my mother immediately turned in my direction, her bone-thin arms stretching out towards me, but I quickly turned my back on her, pretending I hadn't seen.

Chaz was charged with excitement. "How's about coming over to my place this arvie, like? I'll tune Zilla, you know Zilla Tabatznik, and you tune Sophie, like . . . like we planned?"

"Naaa," I quickly responded, searching for a way out. "Your mom's there, and anyway I don't really feel like doing anything. I've got too much homework to finish . . . and, anyway, how d'you know Zilla Tabatznik'll even be interested? You didn't seem so sure before?" I was curious.

"I already called her, like. Last night. On your advice. So, I know she's not doing anything. C'mon, Danny . . ."

I was amazed that Chaz had actually organised his own date, but I really wasn't up to doing anything at all, and the last thing I wanted right then was to see Sophie Street.

"Naaa, I really must get this homework done."

"Shit maa-en," he said, his voice breaking into a squeak. "I just don't think Zilla'll come over if she knows no one else is going to be around. She'll probably arrive with one of her Kensington ouks, for protection, like . . . C'mon Danny, this could be a good chance for me."

On the other hand, maybe I did owe it to myself to give it one last shot. If Sophie Street was at home and was willing to come over, if she was still speaking to me, then maybe everything wasn't lost after all. And anyway Chaz was my best friend, and I owed him. I sure as hell owed him, even without him knowing I owed him.

"OK then," I said. "Cool . . ."

"Great Danny, thanks, too much, man. Too much!"

"But look, but look," I had to shout twice before I could bring him back to his senses. "My folks have gone out and there's absolutely no one at my place this arvie. Why not rather get Zilla to come over here, it'll be better than your flat, with your old girl hanging around . . ."

"Yeah, ja, ja, sounds great!" He was so full of enthusiasm, I felt like hitting him over the head with the phone.

"But remember, only if I can get Sophie to come over . . . and there's like no guarantees . . ."

"Ja, ja," he cut in again; I don't think he even heard me properly. "I'll call Zilla right now and you call Sophie, then I'll call you back in five, hey."

"OK, OK," I half shouted, knowing he had already put the phone down.

For a good couple of minutes I rubbed my chin, sitting there like Rodin's Thinker, confused and stunned, toying with the idea of pretending to Chaz that I had called Sophie and she was busy, couldn't make it. But in the end, reluctantly, I did what I had said I would. I think more than anything I wanted to hear from Sophie Street herself if she was still in the least bit interested.

* * *

As it turned out, confirming all my worst fears, Sophie Street did not sound at all keen, stating emphatically that she didn't want to come over. For a while we spoke uneasily about other things, avoiding at all costs the episode with Uncle Harold – about upcoming school exams, movies we wanted to see and her latest Lou Reed album. Then, just as I was about to replace the receiver, she said, "Well, alright then, Danny Rothbart. I'll get my dad to drop me over." I looked downwards at my toes, up at a winking Madame Tretchikoff, shocked, surprised, excited and at the same time saw I was biting my nails. It was an instant reaction. Panic.

Chaz rang back – I was sure had been trying for quite a while – sounding out of breath as he announced that everything was on with Zilla Tabatznik. And when I said it was all systems go at my end, he was over the moon. Right over the moon. Quite literally, shouting: "Too much, man. Too much. Cheers, Danny, cheers."

As I put the phone down, I looked up into the mirror above the phone and ruffled my hair with my fingers until it looked just right. It was a while since I had done that. Looked at myself that closely, put my fingers through my hair, to make sure the wave on the fringe fell just right.

Fidgety and anxious, I ambled around the house, looking for something to fill in the time, to settle me down. In the end I poured myself a bowl of Post Toasties and milk with heaps of sugar on top, then, on second thoughts, added a thick layer of drinking chocolate.

26

F inally, after half an hour of biting my nails and looking out of the lounge window, Chaz and Zilla Tabatznik arrived, dropped off by Chaz's mother. Burping up chocolate Post Toasties, I led them straight into the lounge where The Who: *Who's Next?* was playing on the stereo. For a while, from the way Zilla Tabatznik kept looking at me, her insipid, hazy blue eyes following my every movement, sort of roving around me like dull torchlights, I thought she fancied me. While I didn't want to steal her from Chaz, it brought back old, satisfying feelings of pride. Soon I was strutting about the room, swaggering my hips and swirling an imaginary scarf a la Mick Jagger, flapping my arms like ducks' wings a la David Bowie, and calling out jokes in a way that was once trademark Danny Rothbart.

While I played centre-stage, Chaz, who was sitting next to Zilla Tabatznik on the room's smaller, two-seater couch, moved slowly closer and closer to her until finally he dangled a hand round her neck. I was relieved when I saw her let it hang there – even if it did just hang there like a dead carp. She still had her eyes on me, which was very pleasing, though a little awkward, but I felt better a few minutes later when, while still looking at me, she actually took Chaz's dead-fish hand and put her hand over it. That was something that didn't happen too often to Chaz Bernstein. If at all. They must have really hit it off on the phone or in Chaz's mother's car on the way over, because usually with Chaz and girls, well, with Chaz and girls it was more like trying to push together two negatively charged magnets – nothing but repulsion. Chaz was likeable, kind and easy-going, but when it came to girls, his blotchy, red-spotted face, parrot nose, long giraffe frame, inordinately protruding Adam's apple, and an ability to tell them what he really thought of them – which was rarely very kind – drove them away. The truth was, I, we, all of our crew, wondered how poor old Chaz was ever going to make it. If anything, we always had to drag him out of places, because of the near-physical tangles he got into with girls. I was watching a near miracle.

Then Sophie Street arrived. She sat down with an audible huff on the other, larger couch in the room, and although she knew Chaz quite well, and even Zilla Tabatznik, she sat there eyeing them both with squinting, suspicious eyes, as if they might suddenly ambush her. Then she turned her eyes on me and suddenly I felt self-conscious and un-comfortable with my antics. I quickly relinquished my stage and gave up my show, but in doing so, I did make sure to plonk myself down right next to her. Otherwise I knew, if I sat somewhere else, there would be no coming back, no chance of getting close to her again, and what would Chaz say to that? So now there we sat, looking like we were together, but not saying a word to one another, hardly even look-ing at one another. Sullen-faced, we stared straight ahead, which was more or less directly at Chaz and Zilla Tabatznik, on the couch op-posite, where the two of them sat bolt upright, like corpses. Above them our orange, glowing Tretchikoff print looked down over the lounge, and in it at that moment I swear I saw Sophie Street: that same stiff-necked pride, that same sense of hubris streaking from the smirking, knowing lips, the ever-watchful, slanting cat's eyes.

Turning back to Sophie I saw her glaring caustically at me, her eyes narrowing with the kind of come-on look I had identified before and that had, in the end, completely annihilated me. The kind of come-on look that Uncle Harold had spoken about? I shivered, breathing out. It attracted me, strongly. Irked me. Made me feel nervous. *Could Uncle Harold have had grounds?* I swallowed tightly. I didn't want to think about it right then. Not about that. Wanting, as Uncle Harold said, despite everything, despite everything, to put it in the past. Amazed how, even having opened my eyes to Uncle Harold, knowing what I knew now, I couldn't get him out of my head. He always seemed to be in there, giving advice, telling me what to do, guiding me forward. Hearing The Who album wind to an end, I quickly jumped up to change it for Shawn Phillips' much mellower, much more atmospheric *Second Contribution*, and then plonked myself down again, even closer to Sophie than I had been sitting before.

On the couch opposite, below the slicing eyes of the Tretchikoff woman, Chaz and Zilla Tabatznik were now turned to one another, a little less stiffly. They were holding onto one another, their arms draped awkwardly, long and limply, around each other's shoulders. Two octopuses staring into one another's eyes, framed within the bright, gold-specked orange of the couch. But octopuses or not, at least they were touching, had made their way into each other's arms. This was definitely a change, a first for Chaz. I felt pleased for him.

I looked at Sophie Street, who glared back at me, at everything around her. I wondered why she had even agreed to come over, unless it was for this, to wreak her revenge on me, in front of Chaz. I wished now, more than ever, that I had not given in to Chaz and invited her. At this rate, I wasn't even going to get a touch, not even a friendly embrace. I could feel my face growing red and hot as I watched Chaz and Zilla Tabatznik.

In sheer desperation, it struck me, an idea that would save me from public humiliation. With statesman-like concern, I whispered into Sophie's suspicious, cold, withdrawing ear that Chaz and Zilla needed to be alone, with no staring eyes, no one around, so that they could work out their relationship, especially now, since they were getting so close. Although Sophie eyed me sceptically, in the end, hand to cheek, she nodded in the affirmative, flicking her glittery, Liza Minnelli theatre curtain eyes in the direction of the doorway. Bravely, I reached for her hand, which she allowed me to take with surprising ease, and I led her out of the lounge towards my bedroom. Looking back I saw Chaz give me the thumbs up from behind Zilla Tabatznik's neck. I winked at him, knowing that for him it was still a long, long shot.

In the bedroom Sophie and I sat on my bed, at opposite ends, with our backs to the wall, as though waiting for a bus at a bus stop. She was gazing out of the window opposite, and the room felt small and dense. I wished I could just unlock my mouth and talk honestly to her, but I found it hard to breathe, let alone open my mouth and form the shape of words.

"Why are you looking at me like that, Danny?" Sophie slapped a curl of jet-black hair behind her ear.

"Can't I look at you?"

"Not like that, it makes me feel funny."

"Oh." I looked away, out of the window, over our high security fence, onto the dull, geometric green and red tin rooftops of the houses across the road.

Silence. A long, hot, tortured silence.

And then she turned to me and said, "You'd rather believe him, wouldn't you?"

I should have known that was what she was thinking.

"No . . . no," I said softly, perhaps too softly to be convincing, looking up at her squinting geisha eyes, her sharp, angular cheekbones.

"You still believe him, don't you?" she insisted, and I felt my throat swell. I wanted to say sorry, but sorry wasn't a word that came easily to my throat. I also didn't know if it was the right word. I didn't know, wasn't sure if I had anything to be sorry about. The only thing I was sorry about right then was that I thought I had lost Sophie. Completely lost her. She moved up to me, and to my surprise, took my hand into hers. Her soft, pulpy fingers felt so warm, so reassuring, I could have just rested my hand in hers for hours, for days, forever. And then she kissed me, softly, a butterfly wing on the cheek, and I felt lifted, exhilarated, like I was rising, surging in a way I had not felt in years.

Then just as suddenly she pushed me backwards and laughed.

251

"You're such a fuckin' arsehole, Danny Rothbart! Such a selfish prick! You don't want to make love to me, you just want to screw me. That's all you ever want to do. All you care about, all you ever think about, is you, you, you. You're like a bad key on a piano: do, ray, me, me, me . . . and that's as far as you can ever go. Because that's all you can think about, you, you, you. Well, I tell you, my boy, you may as well go screw yourself!" I looked at her and blinked, but she wasn't finished yet. "And I think your relationship with this old deviant, this city councillor shit-head, this Harold Craphart, stinks."

"Kleinhart," I corrected, it just came out, tripped off my tongue instinctively.

"Well, it's Craphart to me, OK." I nodded. "I don't know what's going on, Danny," she breathed in sharply, "I don't even know why I'm saying all this, except that it pisses me off how you can take his word over mine, how you can let him rule you like you're his little pet chihuahua or some little hamster in a cage." I nodded unconsciously, my eyes spinning. "Listen, Mr Danny Rothbart, even if I was doing it with him, him and me, doing it, but I didn't want to do it, don't you think that would still constitute a violation? A rape?"

"Well, yes, kind of, like . . ."

"Well, yes, kind of, like. I think you should understand something, Mr Rothbart, that you obviously know shit about. If I let you use me, it's one thing. But if you use me, and it's not something I like, not something I want, it's *not* OK. It's definitely *not* OK. It's a violation. It's like an animal in a pet-shop cage. It may not want to go with the cruel pervert who buys it, but there's no choice. It can't get away; it can't say no. Who knows how loudly it may have screamed within itself? Only animals don't understand the process, what's happening inside, and that's the difference between them and us!"

Before I could say anything, if I could have said anything at all, she poured on: "Danny, when you've stopped playing your silly little games and taken a good, hard look at yourself, then maybe, then maybe give me a call some time."

I looked across at her, unable to speak, not even mutter; I was KO'd. She looked at me, at first I thought about to walk out – the final humiliation, the final goodbye, the final kick in the jaw – and then, I'm sure for no other reason than my beaten, wounded look, she took my hand into hers. She held it more like a mother than a girlfriend, like it was a thing cold and outcast that needed to be warmed and saved. I could not understand but I was grateful. Truly grateful as I sat there frozen, but content.

We sat like that for a long while, Sophie Street sort of studying my face and then looking out of the window, and then back again, and then something took over in my mind. With my free hand I began to stroke her arm, and then her shoulder, and then her neck and then her ears that lay buried beneath her tucked-in sweep of jet-black hair. I was feeling so warmed now, and she was looking more relaxed than she had all afternoon. I let my hand stroll back down her shoulder, then ever so slowly over her chest, touching her breast, feeling the tip through her soft neon-blue jersey. I didn't know what was wrong with me, it was like I could see exactly what I was doing, but I couldn't help myself. I gasped with relief as I felt her hand reach down, tenderly, and tickle me softly on the stomach. Then suddenly she shoved me reeling backwards with that same hand.

"No!" she said. "No!" The magic word I could not pronounce. I felt cold inside, but my fingers were burning. "I'm going. I'm getting out of here!"

"No, please, please . . . stay," it sputtered out of my mouth like a car backfiring.

She looked at me sceptically, then she said, "Well then, hold me, Danny Rothbart, don't *do* anything. Just hold me."

I sat back, my arm around her shoulders, silent, silenced. And then after a while, I said, "Do you know Uncle Harold, I mean Harold Kleinhart, is in jail?"

"What?" She looked completely dumbfounded.

"He burnt down the furniture shop yesterday, apparently for the insurance. It's in all the papers today; he's been arrested. That's where my folks are now. They've gone to see Thelma."

She looked at me stunned.

"Good God. Holy Hell." And then after a moment's silence, she said, "May that stupid old prick rot in Gehenna!"

But somehow I couldn't, even then, tell her that the day his shop burnt down I was on my way to do bloody carnage, to do him in. I couldn't tell her because I couldn't be sure that I would have even carried it out. But I couldn't tell her, also, more, much more importantly, because I couldn't tell her why I felt betrayed. So I would just have to keep my trap shut, keep it in my head, in my stomach, concealed. Yet another truth concealed. My stomach was bloated, I felt pregnant, yes pregnant with concealment. Lies and concealment.

She looked at me, her eyes suddenly velvety.

"Danny, there's something wrong. I can see, something's the matter." I looked at her out of the corner of my eye. "Honestly, Danny, you've got to loosen up, unwind. If you keep this sort of pressure up, you're going to kill yourself. Literally. You've got to let go . . ." Even she was using Uncle Harold's language now, or was it her language? Or was it just everyone's language and I had just thought that it somehow belonged to him, like he was the only one who ever could tell people to let go, unwind, relax?

"For God's sake, Danny," Sophie was almost yelling at me now, but in a whispered sort of way, so that you could probably not hear it beyond my door. "You have to open your mouth. There's something you're not telling me, I know. But if you don't tell me, I can't know. Can't do anything."

I looked up at the cold ceiling, the dull white beams. I knew she was looking at me, probing me with her eyes, but I couldn't tell her, just couldn't. I turned to her and as if a big, wide arm, bigger than both of us, were wrapping itself around us, we held onto one another, feeling our hearts softly pounding, rising and falling, softly, softly, together.

27

We awoke, what seemed like hours later, my eyes opening slowly into a beam of light that was shining into the room, and I realised just how peaceful that sleep had been. How good it felt to fall asleep in the arms of someone you could trust, someone you could really trust. It was like when I used to fall asleep in my mother and father's bed when I was a small child. It was like the whole world could collapse, spin off its axis, but whatever happened you were safe. In that hour of sleep I grew, I'm sure I grew, mentally, physically, metaphysically. I had been turned around, shaken inside-out, dropped on my head; had failed, in a manner of speaking, yet again, but in the process I had gained, through Sophie Street I had gained. All extravagant paint and make-up on the outside, on the inside Sophie Street was real. More than real. A human being. No, an angel, an exquisite, bewitching angel.

I looked at my watch.

"Jesus, it's after five! We better get up."

Quickly, we jumped up, tidied our hair, our clothes and then holding hands, almost leaning into one another we walked back into the lounge. Old lovers, old experienced lovers, who had yet to love.

There, sitting on the floor, the shaggy carpeted floor, also holding onto one another, were a dishevelled but smiling, broadly smiling, Chaz and Zilla Tabatznik. The second Zilla Tabatznik turned her attention for a moment Chaz was winking at me. At first I thought it was the old wink, the one that said, "Too much, man, I know you did it again, I know what went on in that room." But then as I looked at him and saw the wink continue, sort of like an unstoppable commotion of butterfly wings, I knew he was trying to say something else.

And then when I looked into his pink face, the broad smile, that continuing, unabated wink-wink, I saw that Chaz Bernstein, pimple-faced, half-baked, grizzly-bearded, hook-nosed Chaz Bernstein had beaten us all to the draw. Chaz Bernstein, my best friend, the most socially inept person in the whole world, who looked up to me, looked up to me now more than ever, because I had ostensibly long ago crossed the line and was first, had done it. No wonder his smile was stretching from the lounge windows to the maid's quarters outside. If only he had known. If only he knew. His smile would be stretching not just from the lounge windows to the maid's quarters outside, but all the way to Table Mountain. Above him, even the smirking Tretchikoff woman seemed to be winking with him now, at me. Even Chaz's distended Adam's apple was having a go. Eventually it grew so bad, Sophie whispered into my ear, "What's with him, what's with the winking, for Godsake?"

"Dunno," I muttered, but I knew, I knew alright and it made me think even more what a true and loyal friend Chaz really was – to give me all that unyielding praise, all that unyielding faith, when even he could've guessed the whole thing looked skew. But now, in his turn, he was unstoppable, the way I should have been unstoppable, and I just couldn't respond in the same way. I felt embarrassed at his display and ashamed of myself at the same time.

Chaz was my best friend, and I suppose that meant I should have been all over him, winking and smiling back, giving him praise, heaps of praise, but the truth was, this was a hard victory to swallow. Just doing it for Chaz was a victory, or a miracle, like finding life, real life, on Mars, but I found it hard to give him even that. He was looking so self-satisfied, so pleased, so proud that I could have punctured his head with a pick.

Something in me had died. Harsh, cruel, unkind as it may have seemed, there was a kind of death in me, it was like amid all this celebration I was at a funeral. Poor, poor Chaz, poor pimple-faced Chaz, he had just achieved so, so much – and there I sat white as a sheet, wondering if he would ever find out exactly how much, how extremely much he had just achieved.

After a while, I think when Sophie could no longer take that wide brimming grin on Chaz's face, she grabbed hold of Zilla Tabatznik with an understanding that only girls have and they went off to the bathroom together. Immediately, almost before they had even left the room, Chaz gave me the final big wink-wink, smile-smile, to confirm everything that I already knew was written all over his zit-clotted face. Thank God for small mercies, he said he would spare me the details, the squishy finer details, because – as he was quick to acknowledge – I already knew. Saying to me only, "Why didn't you tell me it was *this* good?"

Cause I didn't bloody know, Chaz, my dear silly little boy, Chaz, Chaz, Chazzie, because I didn't bloody know, I wanted to scream back at him. But instead, I just smiled, holding my shameful chin sky-high. The truth was, I could hardly open my mouth, let alone think.

When Zilla and Sophie returned from the bathroom – looking like they had spent their time doing their hair, fixing their clothes, colouring their lips, holding court with one another, anything rather than sitting on any opened toilet seat – Chaz turned first to Zilla and then to me, and said, "Geez, I really feel like a fag." And for a moment I distinctly thought he was referring to me.

Suddenly he had become a big man, and even he, he, my best friend Chaz, was casting aspersions. But when he repeated the question, probably seeing the dumbstruck look on my face, saying, "Well, d'you think I can have a smoke," I knew how screwed up I had become.

"No ways, not in here . . . my folks'll be home soon. They'll kill me," I managed to splutter in a spiteful way, happy to be turning him down.

Disappointed, Chaz sighed, looking at me as though I had given him a minor bruising. But obviously only minor, because he did that wink-wink, smile-smile thing again, that so obviously told me he could live with anything now, anything, even without the smoky old fags he was so addicted to. Then proudly, like a real man – the ones you saw in the movies – he put his arm around his new-won love's stout shoulders, like he somehow owned her, had possession of her, and when instead of looking away she smiled at him, and he smiled back confidently, I knew I had been completely and utterly beaten. I was finished. I was at rock-bottom. Although to all intents and purposes I was in Chaz's eyes, in the crew's eyes, still the champion of the world. Well, at least champion of our little corner of Yeoville. I could have stabbed myself in the chest.

A tortuous twenty or so minutes later there was the blaring sound of an old car hooting outside and Sophie jumped off the couch, saying it was her father. She offered Chaz and Zilla a lift home, and to my relief they took it. At the front door, Chaz and I, left to ourselves for a minute, looked at one another, and then Chaz's hand went up in the air, slightly bent, like an Indian brave. For a moment I looked at him askance, as if he were making some totally out-of-proportion victory salute, not sure how far this whole thing had driven him, how far he was going to rub it in. And then it dawned on me what he wanted. I lifted my own hand and it met his hand in the air for a slap of palms, a tight clinch of fingertips. Best friends in love and war, victory and defeat, best friends forever, and finally I said with my eyes what I could not say with the tongue: *You done well, Chaz.* As he turned away he flicked a cigarette into his mouth Clint Eastwood-style, I didn't know what Sophie's father would think of that, but Chaz looked like he didn't give a damn. As he walked down the front path the smoke-rings roared out of his mouth, and holding Zilla Tabatznik around the shoulders, he called out loudly from the front gate: "Shit man, I forgot that poison. I'll bring it to school on Monday." He winked at me and then he and Zilla Tabatznik smiled at one another and bounded out of the gate, almost flying, rotating, like two planets that had just discovered they were actually, really, a part of the same solar system.

At the bottom of the front stairs, Sophie Street and I embraced and I felt a tingle run down my back. Above us, though darkening, the sky was a thin metallic blue. In a low corner of the sky, the sun poked out like a motorbike light dying in the distance, a round yellow glimmer, like a halo, quickly fading around it. Perhaps it was my body temperature, but the day felt warmer than it had for a long time, like spring was finally coming.

I wanted to say something to Sophie, but I knew I could not. I guess I really wanted to thank her. But I didn't know how. Not, anyway, without overstepping that line, that dense, immutable line of concealment that I was bound to. Sophie let go of me and walked away. After a few paces she looked back and in her piercing, geisha eyes I swore I saw magic charcoals flaming in there, and then she too was gone, perhaps forever, through the front gate, and I was alone.

Turning back into the house, my orange and gold-specked sanctuary, I went first to the lounge just to double-check that the Tretchikoff woman wasn't actually winking at me. She wasn't, but she still managed an awful, squinting glare. Seeing her look, and still angry with myself, I bent over and pulled my trousers down, just like my mother had done to me in that dream, and stuck my bum out at the painting, shouting, just as my mother had shouted that night: "Kush mich in toches! Kush mich in toches!"

"What the hell are you doing?" I heard my mother's voice behind me.

Glowing, bright red-faced, I quickly pulled my pants up and turned around to see both my parents standing there shaking their heads. But although they both looked agitated, and shook their heads in disbelief, they said nothing more about my antics. It was as if they were too preoccupied, too busy with their own day's events, to pursue my latest disturbed behaviour. My latest phase.

Instead my mother announced: "The police are pretty sure he did it, and he's going to be put away for a long time. Thelma's in a terrible state, as you can imagine, but it's the kinder I feel sorry for." The words were rolling off her tongue like a drunk's. "Thelma said she had no idea, absolutely no idea. It turns out he had a lot of bad debts, you know, and it looks like the shop was heading for insolvency and it was eating at him, eating away at him, but no one could have thought he'd do something like this . . . and now everyone has to suffer . . . Thelma, the children, everyone."

Gazing at her, digesting what she was saying, something in me moved, something in my stomach and chest, sending a shudder down my shoulder-blades, a rush of pins and needles to my toes. The knowledge of Uncle Harold being put away made me feel safe, somehow lighter, like no one could suddenly come banging on the door to wake me up or bring me back to reality; and suddenly the room smelled of honeysuckle, or roses, like Sophie's sweet red-rose perfume.

My father took a seat in the lounge, throwing his weight into the armchair like an exhausted rugby prop into a set scrum. He exhaled loudly, looking down.

"It's just so hard, so bladdy hard to believe. Such a bladdy tragedy. Such a waste. He could've had an empire, that man. Could have been at the head of this town one day. The very top. And to think that I trusted that ganef with my life!" Much of his bitterness was annoyance with himself; you could see it in the dark, introspective creases that crept along his forehead, that drifted into his crinkling eyes. He sat down low in his armchair with his stocky shoulders curled over.

If it had been my mother I might have gone up to her and hugged her: put my arms around her shoulders and held her. But you didn't do that sort of thing with my father, he was just too much of a man and it was hard to show you even felt sorry for him, but I did feel sorry for him then, seeing that it was like a slice of flesh had been cut from his body. They were close, he and Uncle Harold, very close, and then it struck me suddenly, could my father have been one of those best friends Uncle Harold had spoken about, that played with one another; was this why he was so upset? I searched for a reason why it couldn't be. I just didn't want it to be possible, didn't want to think about my father in that way, my own macho-man, wrestling, tough-guy father. What would he think of me, if that was what I thought about him?

I looked at him sitting there. Surely he would never, never have allowed me to go out at nights with Uncle Harold if he knew, if he knew what Uncle Harold did? Surely? I was confused, I just couldn't put the two of them together in that way. I didn't know which way to run my thoughts, that I could even think of my father in that way showed that something in me had changed, been injured, broken. The only thing I wished right then was that I could have gone up to my father and hugged him. But I knew I could not.

Suddenly he looked up, staring straight ahead of him, and said, "How could anyone live with such a lie? How could they?"

I looked at my father, shaking my head, as if to say I agreed. *How could anyone?* But I knew. I knew only too well. And it was killing me, and all I wanted was to make amends, somehow make amends, sew up the cuts and wounds and start all over again. I turned away from my father and started to walk to my room, but my mother called me back.

"I think you're forgetting your ol' ma , what about a hug and a kiss before you go running?" she said, her arms already rising, but forlornly, to accept me into her bosom. "I know that soon you won't want me to do this any more. You think you're too big already."

I felt my stomach flush with that ancient feeling, that piercing hot and ice-dry cold, that feeling that I resented myself for as much as I resented her for; then something in me released. Even if she didn't know how best to show her love, wanted to smother rather than mother, at least I knew I could have belief in her. There were no veils, no double languages, no hidden meanings, what you saw was what there was. There were no hidden scripts, no secret codes, no secret deal-

ings and in the end, measured against that, it didn't make any difference that she didn't really understand.

This time I turned back to face her, smiled, then walked up to her
and hugged her, closely, in a way I would have liked to have hugged
my father, in the way I could remember hugging her when I was a
small child. Like I really looked up to her, believed in her, loved her,
really wanted her to love me. She gave me a long squeeze that brought
tears to my eyes, tears that, with my head buried in her shoulder, I
was glad no one could see. Before anyone – especially my father –
could see the moisture in my eyes, I quickly turned to go to my room.
Already rummaging through my twisted skull, thinking how to plan
my days ahead. That I had to somehow, somehow start all over again.

28

U ncle Harold's trial was quick and decisive. My parents and I followed the case and everything about it – for different reasons – through the newspapers, the little bits that were on TV, and whatever gossip went on around the case. I guess the truth was, deep down both of them – my mother and father – wanted Uncle Harold to be found innocent. Because somehow, like most of the people who knew him – including those who had accepted his hand of philanthropy – they didn't want to go down in their own little histories as being duped by him, made to look like fools, and that by his exoneration they could somehow be forgiven for trusting him. I, on the other hand, wanted him without question to be sent to jail for a long, long time. It seemed like the only way I could drive his shadow from my flesh, by somehow having him fully and completely out of the way. It was amazing how big the mental attachment was: I wanted him away, out of my life forever, and yet whenever I looked into my mind, I would always find him there, his voice, his words, his unfailing support. But there was also this other feeling – and to this extent I suppose I was not that much different to everyone else: although I wanted to see him put away, I also wanted him found innocent. Because then, even to Sophie, I could say, "See, he's not that bad." Talk about the logic of an imbongolo, but somehow I didn't want anyone throwing it in my face: "I told you." Or maybe even worse: "You see, I always thought there was something wrong there, Danny." I suppose, no different to the rest of them, his innocence would, yes, somehow exonerate me.

"By the look of it, I think he's going to jail for a long time," my father would say day after day as the trial proceeded. "Bloody fool, only has himself to blame."

"I can't imagine what it's like for Thelma," my mother would reply. "I wish it could be all over soon, no matter the outcome."

Everyone, the whole town, including me, seemed to be holding their breath for the outcome. But I think I was the only one who sighed with relief when the verdict was announced and sentence was passed a couple of days later. Everyone said that the five years that was given him by the crab-browed magistrate was excessive, especially for a crime that didn't really harm anyone but the perpetrator, but as the judge said in announcing sentence: "This man was a pillar of society, people look up to him and he should be made an example of."

I imagined Uncle Harold when sentence was pronounced staring forwards, stiff-necked from the dock like something out of a Dickens novel, his enormous frame a dark-cloaked mountain alone on a raised podium.

The truth was that I thought I saw tears in my father's eyes for the first time ever as he announced the news of Uncle Harold's sentence to my mother in the lounge just before the dinner bell.

"Bloody ganef, bloody thief." He looked down, watery-eyed, like he didn't want anyone to see what was really going on inside.

My mother flew straight on to the phone to Thelma and they seemed to speak for hours. I headed for my room and looked at my four walls like I was in jail, trying to imagine, really imagine what it was like to be in a prison. I felt my skin prickle, my skin that was like the cold, tight walls of this room reminding me why I should be re-joicing, why I should be so happy. And though I was, I felt like a part of me had just died. And I wondered how much it would change my life. Like that Doors song that begins with the tribute to Otis Redding, I couldn't help but sing over and over to myself: "Poor Uncle Harold dead and gone. Left me here to sing his song. Pretty little girl with the red dress on."

29

S everal things were going my way by the end of that year, but I was not exactly flying high. Here's the list that would have had most normal people jumping for joy: first and foremost Uncle Harold was in prison, second I passed my matric, third – which was really a part of the second, but I was so amazed at myself that I saw it as an entity in itself – I passed my matric with a university pass, and finally – and to me most amazing of all – I managed to avoid the army. But of course the thing I wanted most still eluded me. Nevertheless, all things considered, avoiding the army sure came a good second – and avoiding it, I can tell you, was not as easy as I had thought.

In the end, despite all of our great plans, it was my father who saved me. Looking at me as though I were more of a mouse than a man, he nevertheless pulled all sorts of strings with the vast array of people I suddenly discovered he knew in the right places, to delay my being called up. I sometimes think now, somewhere deep inside of him, even if he had no sympathy for the black kids' struggle for a better life, the events of the nineteen seventy-six Soweto uprising did affect him. I think he saw for the first time what teenagers were capable of, and his deep fear was that his mouse of a son might really end up in fatigues – and trouble – either because he would be sent to some future danger zone or, more likely, because his imbongolo son would – being such a difficult schlemiel of a teen – put himself in a danger zone.

Chaz was not so lucky. Or, rather, was lucky in another way. He was called up and could not get out of it, but fortunately he had done so well at school – as had been expected – that, with the help of relatives overseas, he actually managed to apply for, and receive, a bursary to do A Levels in England, which would allow him to go on to a top university over there.

Despite this, despite all that had gone my way, I was still bitterly unhappy and it wasn't to do with the great racial schisms in our country, or world poverty, or the Cold War, or the great threats of nuclear holocaust; it all revolved around sex. Looking back on it now, I can see I was in a depression, a constant state of depression. But at the time, even though it was becoming more and more popular to be depressed in some circles – a trend extending from the liberating sixties – in backward South Africa you still mostly put on your best face and never admitted you needed help. You definitely did not readily say you needed to see a shrink.

So, being in that state – almost constantly – not too surprisingly my first year at university, despite the joy of not being in the army, of getting into varsity in the first place, was not very bright or happy. I chopped and changed subjects in my arts course. First it was English literature and modern history, then it was art history and music appreciation, then it was archaeology and philosophy, and so the list went on until the head of the faculty told me to see a university guidance counsellor, or quit. And that meant the army. So, under duress, I made an appointment to see a counsellor who somehow managed to make me think about my future and see what a privilege it was to be at a university, any university. Of course, true to form, I didn't tell her anything about my breakdown in the watering or, if you like, hosing department, and definitely nothing about my now infamous Uncle Harold.

But with her help – I suppose, when I think about it now I was in such a sad state it must have been easy for anyone to see I needed help – I was encouraged to write everything down, all my experiences, all my feelings, then and now. And that process, in some cathartic way that I slowly became aware of, did help to give me some fresh air to breathe into my thickly tarred lungs.

Through this counsellor, I also finally settled on my two arts majors – sociology, and I suppose because of my dire need to try to figure myself out, psychology. But at least I was back on the varsity track.

Through it all I did stay in touch with Sophie Street, who was also studying at Wits, and who – as predicted – had told me after Uncle Harold's guilty verdict the year before: "You see, I told you. There's something wrong with that man." But even though at times we did get quite close, it never went beyond an innocent bit of pecking and hugging. I also, through that year, became friendly with one or two other girls and even went to some pretty wild varsity parties, but, a bit like a boxer who has been punched one too many times, I was simply too afraid to feel another one of those blows to my already well punched-in eagle snout.

In early September of that year, there was another event that showed me up for the person I had become. Steve Biko's cruel and callous death in a Pretoria prison cell after a naked ride – bruised and semi-conscious from torture – on the steel floor of a police van from Port Elizabeth left a Government security minister and probably ninety percent of whites in the country cold, but it certainly got the blood of the rest of the nation boiling. Stung like everyone else in the country by the horrendous event, I even went to the first protest day outside the university, on Jan Smuts Avenue, which was mainly a white students' affair – from straight white liberals to aspiring communists, as well as I imagine some real communists. I stood there below an anti-Government banner, in the crowd, alone. Rather than a part of the protest, I felt uncomfortably apart. A loose part. Something was still niggling and biting in me. I felt cold. Inside of me, I knew exactly what all the depraved whites of the country felt at the death of Biko, and I felt ashamed and guilty. I didn't go back to future protests.

Socially at least there was still Sophie Street, and despite her standoffishness, there always remained between us a kind of spark. Towards the very end of that year at university, the chemistry between Sophie and I did begin to change again. The sessions, though brief, with that counsellor had brought about changes within myself: turning the turmoil that was rumbling like a clothes-washer inside me into words had somehow – eventually – changed something.

For the first time ever Sophie and I began to speak to one another about issues that affected ourselves, real issues, the big issues of the world around us – the politics of our country, the death of Biko, and the problems with Black Consciousness – and though I was even deeply tempted at times in this closeness, I would still never tell her about what happened between myself and Uncle Harold.

"You know Danny I still love you," Sophie said as we sat one weekday afternoon in my room together on the bed, just chatting and holding one another, as we sometimes did.

My eyes lit up.

"Yeah . . . but . . ."

"What?"

"You still keep your distance, you're not really interested in taking it any further."

"I'm just scared. Danny, I'm just scared."

To my surprise she did exactly the opposite of what I was expecting, she held me closer.

I breathed and held her closer. We fell over on the bed, and just lay there. A long while, me suddenly becoming aware of that delicious rose perfume that still emanated from that perfectly smooth apricot skin. Unprovoked, she blew a whispery breath into my ear – I had felt that breath before, it tickled, oh how it tickled – and it made me feel nervous. But I just lay there battling not to think of anything, the thought of Uncle Harold and then a condom shooting straight through my head. I shuddered and hoped she could not feel it, telling myself not to be silly, Uncle Harold was far away, in prison.

I felt Sophie's skin like velvet now, like the velvet on soft apricots, like of the skin of the milk-white, immaculately beautiful Nordic women of my dreams, of those magazines. They too had never left me, but I welcomed their image, always welcomed their image, and as I did, for a moment Uncle Harold appeared, telling me to calm down, to relax, to go with the flow – I shivered – and then there was the varsity counsellor I had seen, telling me to ignore him and not to worry, to just write it down. I felt Sophie pulling up her thin, cotton dress, her panties sliding down, and I swear I felt something stir as I told myself to relax, just relax, go with it.

Rather than get up – and make an idiot of myself for the hundredth time – I quickly decided not to get up and undress, but to simply twist and turn and do whatever manoeuvring it took right there on top of her now half-undressed body. I know I must have felt like a funny, twisty little monkey on top of her, but she didn't seem to bat an eyelid and instead, after a short while, helped me in my twisting and turning, and it felt somehow for the first time like there were two of us there, really two of us. Two people. With my pants down now, my buttocks feeling uncomfortably pink and naked, I told myself yet again to stop thinking about anything and just relax, relax, relax. Bravely, I slipped down between her well-rounded thighs, and immediately became aware that despite my newfound feeling, not much was happening down there. I was conscious of Uncle Harold somewhere in there, yes, somewhere in there, but I wasn't talking to him, refusing to talk to him, letting him just sort of swirl around, but refusing in any way to communicate with him. My head was warping again, growing thick and damp and black, torpedoing towards explosion, and with no way round, not even through – as Uncle Harold would have been quick to point out Napoleon had said – I just let myself rest there surrounded by the rosy smell of Sophie Street.

She looked at me, but didn't talk, or roll her eyes back. A consolation. A grand consolation. I looked back at her comforted but afraid, and then down, into the pillow, fearing she was reading the old schlemiel in my eyes. Then she wriggled her body – something she had never done before – wriggled like someone had placed something cold on the back of her neck or shoulders, like a tremor going down her vertebrae, down into her softly curved bottom, and I felt the most amazing sensation I have ever experienced in my life: I was immersed in a soft, jelly-like fluid.

For a moment I wondered if Sophie Street really did possess magic, was of some foreign voodoo world. I wondered how she had managed, without really touching me, to douse me in this completely unfamiliar, freshly warmed salve. To be honest, I wasn't exactly sure what the hell was going on, except that I had never felt anything like this sensation in my life before. This was of another planet, another world, another dimension. Giant shards of gold and silver like falling stars were shooting across the inside of my skull, spreading like a fiery gas down my spine. Each time I moved I felt like I was inventing the world. I was sure, absolutely sure, I was inventing the world. Like every movement was an original idea, some profound wisdom, a great new philosophy, a new scientific advance. It was like I was orchestrating the most original score that had ever been performed, great rows of violins and electric guitars somehow fusing, somehow showing they could be one, and at the end of each riff, each bow, a pulse, a tingling, and then a pulse again. Then somehow I moved one, one fraction too much – too much to the left, too much to the right, too much straight in front of me, I don't know, I don't know, I didn't care – and the entire world sparked and a great rush of atoms or electrons, like mini-skyrockets, blasted from me into this other universe, a universe I had discovered, this other universe that was now a part of me, that was perhaps even now, at this very moment, creating me?

She smiled and lay back and I knew it was over. I knew I had done it. I had finally done it! But rather than jump up with joy I just lay there, still, perfectly still, while Sophie Street stroked my still newly invigorated flesh and drew a huge mandala from the top of my neck down to the bottom of my spine with her long fingernail. Inside of me, the troubles of the world – despite the mass bannings and the political jailings that were wracking our country of late and were still smouldering beneath the white surface of our patch of this earth – were the troubles of another planet. A long, long way away.

The truth was that it was all over in a matter of seconds. But those few seconds, be they only five or six, or even three or four, to me were forever, forever! In those few seconds I had seen heaven. Suddenly I understood why there would always be children in this world. Why there were four billion of us in the world already, and there would be billions more in the future. Why even people like my eagle-nosed Uncle Abe and my sexless Aunty Fanny would want to be a part of this procreation, why the message would always be passed on, without having to pass it on, without having to command it to be passed on, from one generation to the next, like it was said, "L'dor v'dor". I felt myself smiling, deep inside, smiling from the tips of my toes to the tips of the hairs on my head, from one side of my sunken cheeks to the other, from earlobe to earlobe. I was in love. In love! Yes, what Uncle Harold, I know, experienced Uncle Harold would have simply called "cunt-struck". But I didn't care. I didn't want to know. I didn't want to hear that voice any more.

I squeezed Sophie tightly, feeling myself glow, and I looked up at my ceiling and instead of seeing empty white square beams and bones up there, as I always did, suddenly I saw angels up there, sailing without wind, free-wheeling, dancing, gliding. I looked straight down, across my body, happy with my circumcision now. Ready to forgive that butcher, that son of a mohel!

I had done it! I wanted to shout it across the streets and across the seas so that Chaz and my brother Cyril could hear it, and even into all the jails in South Africa so that Uncle Harold could hear it. I was a man now, one of the tribe, a klutz, a dunce, a schlemiel, perhaps, but not a kid, not a shame, no one's rachmones, not any more. My head was swimming, swirling high above the world with the angels that

271

had gathered on my now lightning-white ceiling. And suddenly, lying there the most unlikely of songs poured through my head, unstoppable, floating upwards to the angels on my bedroom ceiling: "Oh, what a wonderful world. What a woooonderrrrfuuullll woooorrrlllld."

I was last, stone last, no magic moment of fame, no stage upon which my friends could look up to me in adulation. But still it was grand. Still it was grand. I really should become a priest now, I thought. Only not, definitely not a Catholic one! I laughed to myself. A rabbi? I smiled. Yes, yes, now I was ready. And would have a big family. Yes, a very, very big family!

Sophie looked at me, smiling, for once smiling. "I love you, Danny," she whispered, her warm breath tickling my ear, and then she laughed, I don't know why she laughed, but she laughed, and I just lay there, lay there unperturbed, and began to laugh too, laughing with her now, the two of us just laughing and laughing. For a moment it was like we had seen, the two of us together, that this was what it was all about, this, and suddenly it all looked so small and insignificant, so, so small yet so large and multi-dimensional, so simple yet so dark and intricate, so innocent yet so covered in guilt, so open to shame and twisting, yet so funny. Yes, so funny, so ironically, bitterly funny.

* * *

Our eyes still wet with the laughter, the warmth, the closeness of it all, I saw how much older she looked, how much older she felt than me. But young as I felt there next to her, I felt like a man. Lying back in her buttery arms, looking back on my life, thinking of the man I had become, my chest swelling, I said, "You know I didn't use anything?"

"Yes, I know."

"Doesn't it worry you?"

"No. I'm on the pill."

Suddenly I felt my heart chug to a halt, an angry, red liquid in there rising. Perhaps this was nothing for her? I was just another in a long, long, ragged line?

"Oh, so I'm not the only one?" I tried to sound casual, unconcerned, but at the same time wanting it to dig.

"As if you're such a saint, Mr Rothbart!" She looked angry. "And if you really must know, no, Mr Danny fuckin' Rothbart, you're not the only one. There've been others." I felt my jaw stiffen. Then she breathed out, and said, "Both of them finished now. Make you feel better?"

I shook my head, reeling, but happy to have her believing I was "not such a saint". In reality, my rolling eyes, my shock, probably gave it away: that I was jealous, and afraid.

Sophie looked at me, considering me, eyes half-closed, a flickering curtain-call, and said again, "Danny, I love you." And my chest swelled, really swelled this time. Then she clicked her tongue. "Arsehole!"

And all I could do was smile, smile back at her. Truth was, life looked so good right then, I could have cried.

30

About six weeks later, my brother Cyril, still living in England – I think a citizen by then – came home to visit. It was his first visit since he'd left the country more than three years earlier. Although I promised myself I wouldn't do it, I had already written to him about my good news, I just couldn't hold back. I had to tell him I knew what it was like. That I was capable. A man. He wrote back with a fraction of the enthusiasm I had written to him with, congratulating me, and again urging me to come to England where everything was "so free, especially the birds". He used that word of Uncle Harold's: birds. I couldn't believe it, but I guessed after that that it must have been an English term, even if I had always just thought it outdated.

The strange thing about Cyril's trip, even from the moment he stepped out of customs, was that he seemed so distant. There I was almost bursting to hug him and all he could do was take my hand and shake it like a typical English gentleman. I couldn't believe it. Even my father, my father, that most masculine of men, he hugged. He even wiped my mother's tears with his own hanky, and all he could offer me was a handshake and a sort of wry smile.

"The racism is so thick around here, you can smell it. The moment you step off the plane the blacks you've been travelling with suddenly have to go into their own queue," he said, as we walked alone for a moment out of the Jan Smuts terminal building, and for a while I thought maybe that was it, that it was his disgust at South Africa that had turned him so cold. But even then, when I tried to engage him about it, he fell back between ma and da', and walked with them instead.

And when we arrived home, and I tried again to take him aside and speak to him like we used to, all he said was: "I need to catch up on some of this jet-lag, maybe later, Danny." And he walked off to his old room like he had never moved out of it.

"There're some chicks I'd like to introduce you to," I enticed him one day, right at the beginning of his visit, but all he replied was: "Danny, that's not why I'm here. If I wanted chicks I'd've stayed in London."

"They're pretty cool, I think you'd be surprised," I almost begged, "and they're involved – against apartheid." But he just shook his head, and simply shrugged me off.

"God, don't you talk any more," I finally spluttered in desperation one day, just wanting to embroil him in conversation, any conversation.

"Just bugger off," he told me, as though I were still his little four-year-old brother.

The truth was, during Cyril's entire three-week visit he never seemed very happy, and after a while not only did I stop bothering him, I stopped guiltily wondering if it was me that he was avoiding. I began to think he had just become a desperately unhappy soul. I put it down to the bad English weather; he just wouldn't admit how much he missed home and least of all to his little boetie. Mainly he kept to himself, only venturing out with my parents, going with them to visit our bobbe and all the relatives, using the excuse, whenever I approached him, that he might never see them again, because he had no intentions of ever coming back.

Still, whenever the opportunity arose, I did try to bait him into some deeper conversation – usually, for example, over breakfast, when ma and da' weren't around – I would ask him what I saw as serious questions about politics in England: about the dole and how it worked, whether he felt happier in a free society and whether it was truly free. I knew he used to be interested in politics, I knew it was the reason he left "Sunny South Africa: still the best, cheapest and cleanest country in the world." It used to irritate the hell out of him how my parents and their friends always said that, but now he wasn't interested at all. I felt like I had lost him.

After he left, which despite everything was quite emotional – two brothers standing there at the airport, two men needing to shave, like old lighthouse beacons beside our ma and dad who definitely looked like they were getting on in years – I thought he was actually going to hug me too, but in the end all he did was shake my hand and cover my right forearm with his left palm, a bit like a political leader would greet a protégé. I must say, there was fair bit of warmth in that handshake, in that holding of my forearm. It felt kind of like a changing of the guard, and tears began to brim in my eyes.

Later, when I arrived home from the airport I found this note on my desk from Cyril:

> Danny, little boetie, I'm just writing this to say sorry. I didn't know how much to say when you wrote about your problem. I knew what you were talking about, but I didn't want to disillusion you with something I had, until now, found I wanted to keep from you. I also wasn't sure what your relationship with Uncle Harold was. Anyway, for better or for worse, I am going to get this off my chest now. You know Uncle Harold used to play with me. Yes, I'm sorry, I'm sorry, I never could tell you before, not to your face, and maybe that's why I'm having a few of my own problems now. I just hope your relationship with him always remained above board. But he just got under my skin and in the end I just had to get away. Let me tell you, Uncle Harold's being behind bars is a kind of freedom for me. It has certainly allowed me to come back to see ma and da, even if only for this short visit. But believe me, I don't think I could live in SA, not anymore. I think you need a certain kind of skin – and I mean in terms of density. As I said

before, I know you had mentioned Uncle Harold, but I was nervous of being misunderstood. Well, you know now. Anyway, that
aside, I know how you feel. Yep, it happened to me. Just before
I arrived here. I couldn't do it – on two separate occasions. Shit.
Maybe it runs in the family? Ask dad. Just joking. He'd blow a
blood vessel! Anyway, I am seeing someone about it, things as
you know are much more open there, and I recommend you do
too. Even though, as you say, you've done it now. Well done! Bra-
vo! Mazeltov and all that! It was good to see you again, though I
know I wasn't very good company. You must get over to England,
soon as you've finished varsity! Cheers Danny. Vasbyt!

Sorry,

Cyril.

Christ, I felt like ripping my heart out. *To get away from ma and da'
and this stupid everything-banned apartheid,* he had told me. And all
along it was because of him! I could have killed Uncle Harold right
there and then. I could have killed Cyril for not telling me. All this
time we had our wires so completely and utterly crossed. He too had
been "loved" by Uncle Harold. I felt sick. I understood that I would
never have been able to understand if Cyril had told me when we
were younger, and I would have looked at him thinking everything I
thought everyone would think of me – poofter, rabbit, nancy boy, fag.
Except when I wrote him that letter, but no, I think even then, I
wouldn't have understood: I was still too keen, too obsessed, too one-
tracked, too infatuated to think that Uncle Harold's love was doing
anything but good. I wanted to write him, I wanted to talk to him
desperately, but I could not decide what to do about it: let sleeping
dogs lie, keep it away from Cyril? Confess to him and in that way
strengthen our bond? Or weaken it?

Delaying the decision on what to do with Cyril, I even wrote to
Chaz – of course busting to tell him the truth but settling for an-

other lie, telling him that I was doing it regularly now, and not just with Sophie but with *some pretty groovy chicks at varsity*. You would think one would have learnt, but I didn't. It was like I wasn't happy until I fell on my bum and then had to lift myself off the bone-breaking surface of the granite earth again. Too full of silly little games, as Sophie rightly said. The very, very ingredients of a failure, just as ma and da' had predicted.

Anyway I didn't feel so bad when I received Chaz's reply: that he had two chicks on the go at once. As if! I knew Chaz Bernstein better than that, it just didn't happen that way. Not even in England.

And then something happened that turned my life upside down.

T W O

The End

31

Soon after Cyril's visit, soon after I had done it with Sophie, soon after I had begun to call myself a man, Uncle Harold was released from jail. Using all sorts of people with influence that he used to know to push for an appeal, Uncle Harold had apparently played a trump card – pleading a nervous breakdown that wasn't diagnosed at the time, arguing it was the riot-torn, politically motivated economic downturn of June nineteen seventy-six that was at the back of his irrational behaviour.

I was looking through the lounge window when I saw him lumbering up the front steps of our house in Isipingo Street in his mustard pants and black turtleneck jersey, his stomach and double chin looking like they had shed a good twenty-five kilos between them. Shocked, I ran to my bedroom and literally hid behind my door. I didn't want to see him and I didn't even want him to know I was there. I heard my parents greeting him at the front door, more reserved than usual, and then leading him out to the table and chairs at the back porch beside our swimming-pool. They hadn't even warned me that they were expecting him. *It was definitely time to move out of home*, I thought.

After a while, feeling curious, I opened my bedroom door and walked out into the hallway where I could pick up some of their conversation. Uncle Harold, in a very calm, controlled voice that was difficult to hear, was saying something about his nervous breakdown and not even realising he was going through one. I could see my mother agreeing, sympathising whole-heartedly, knowing what it was like to live on the brink, but I could also imagine the fury and disbelief growing in my father who thought nervous breakdowns were trumped-up mental failings, made up mainly by mental cases and women like my mother who didn't want to face up to life.

Then Uncle Harold began to speak about wanting to resurrect his business as well as his political standing, and seemed to say, quite honestly, that he needed his old friends, that "at the end of the day" they were the ones you could always rely on. A few minutes later, feeling bolder, I ventured into the adjoining room and saw, through the glass sliding doors leading to the back porch, my father and Uncle Harold standing up and shaking hands like estranged brothers who had returned from a war. The hand-clasp looked strong, eager, vigorous, and my father actually patted Uncle Harold's shoulder. My mother sat there with tears in her eyes, and I could see they were all pleased as hell to be friends again. And then I saw my father pointing Uncle Harold inside, and I knew he was being invited to say some words of reconciliation to me. I couldn't believe it. I ran from the doorway into my room and sat down on my bed panting, not knowing what to do, how to react, thinking for a minute I should fetch a chopping-knife from the kitchen, but by then it was already too late. After a quick knock, and without even waiting for a response, he was standing in the middle of my bedroom, alone. His eyes looked full of misgiving.

Starting out nervously but still maintaining that familiar rounded tone of his, he began the talking while I sat on the edge of my bed, and it didn't take me long to see that behind the sorrow, behind the plea and apprehension in his eyes, there still existed in there that deep concentrated strength of his that stunned whoever stood in front of it like a rabbit caught in powerful torchlight.

"Danny, whatever you think of me now, even if you never talk to me again," he said, "I just want you to always remember, I only ever wanted to help you. That was all. That was always my only intention. I think in your heart you know that, Danny. You came to me with a problem. It was brave, very brave of you. And I gave you what I would still like to give you: help, a shoulder to lean on, and love. I think it's more than anyone could give you, but if there has been some hurt in the process, Danny, I'm sorry, I'm truly sorry . . . there was no intention." He breathed in, I think waiting for a response, but when none came, he went on: "I just want us to be friends, Danny. It's important to me. I don't ever want to see our friendship end." Again he waited as though for some response, some sign, but when I merely cleared my throat and looked down, he said, "Or, if that's what you prefer, we can forget the past altogether and start all over again. Like nothing ever happened. Just remember, Danny, in spite of everything, I still love you. I will always love you. I just want you to know that. I . . . I . . ." He started to stumble, as though for the first time having to think through what he was about to say. "I just don't want anything that was between us to be taken out of proportion. I just don't want the wrong things to get out. You know what I mean?" He looked at me earnestly, and I nodded. "You know, Danny, if you really look around you, you have all the support you need. And I just want to reaffirm I am here for you. Everything can still turn out fine."

Before me I saw him there, in that office, beside me at that desk, twisting my arm around to him, hugging me with tears in his eyes, and I said, "Look, look . . ." My fingertips were tingling, my head was heavy, and I suppose I should have known that when it came to it my voice would stop dead, baulk in my throat. And then I breathed in, deeply, and it came out, came out, whisper-soft, what I was screaming out to him that day of the fire, that day when I saw him behaving like a maniac in the middle of the street, like a crazy, fallen Roman emperor: "What the . . . what the fuckin' hell d'you think I am? "Do you think . . . do you think I am easier to be played on than a pipe . . ."

I felt my fingers twitch uncontrollably, my tongue grow stiff like cement.

There was a dense silence in the room, a darkness, like the light needed to be switched on. And then his voice came back, softly, faltering slightly, pleading, "Please, Danny . . . please, this isn't a time for Shakespeare. No histrionics. Not now. Not now. I just . . . I just don't want this whole thing blown out of proportion. I have family; I still have a political career ahead of me. Danny, I just want to apologise for everything, I want you to know I am sorry, truly sorry, and that I love you, my time inside has changed none of that . . . I swear there never has been anyone else in my life, not like this. Only you."

I wanted to mention Cyril, and Sophie, but a small voice within me seemed to stop me, was warning me that this conversation might get out of hand, that my parents were well within earshot of anything louder than the soft tones we were talking in now, and in the end I only managed: "What . . . what about your 'other friends'?"

"That was different, Danny. That was different. We were growing up together. It was just something we did. Did better than birds. It wasn't something we did with just anyone. We were close. Close friends, that's all . . . It, it had nothing to do with love. Not like I feel for you, Danny. Not, not like this. It was just something we did."

I breathed in, feeling my throat tighten, that word love, that word love, so slippery, the way he said it, the way he pleaded so flattering. I felt like crying, recalling how he had allowed me into his life, always had the time for me, closed his shop early for me, always put me first. Looking up at him peering down at me with such pleading, such un-reserved love and sorrow in his eyes, I didn't know any longer why I was doing it. Why I was trying to thwart him. Why I had let one liber-ating book on homosexuality turn me so angrily against him.

"Please, Danny, all I am asking is that you just see things from my perspective. From my point of view." And then when there was si-lence, just a rough, unmelodic murmur in my throat, he said, "Dan-ny, look, whatever happens, I must see you again. I must. We'll both feel better for it. This isn't a place to talk."

I shuddered. I don't know why, I should have been expecting it, but somehow I thought I could stop him in his tracks, get him to say sor-ry and leave. End of story. My door forever shut to him. But not Harold Kleinhart, not Uncle Harold, not Uncle HK, he didn't operate that way, and suddenly I could see why Cyril had to leave. Only I couldn't, couldn't even move my bum from my stiff-backed position on the corner of my bed, and when I looked up into those exacting eyes and saw the confessions of love and grieving in there I felt like a little injured bird nestled in a large and warm cupped hand. I cleared my throat loudly.

"Ah-hem . . . I, I don't think it's possible, I don't think we should, like . . ." And then I blurted it out, that I had done it – in some way unable to hold back and not share the news, especially with him, and in another way hoping it would put him off, stop him from wanting to see me. He looked genuinely happy for me, smiling, honestly, widely smiling for the first time since he had walked into my room, then throwing a fist with a thumbs-up in the air like a boxer in the ring would give a victory salute.

"You see, I told you, Danny, I told you it would all happen in good time. A little bit of patience, eh, patience, that's all. I'm proud of you, boychik. Very proud of you." I remember feeling my chest swell. He held my shoulder and squeezed it. Then he stood back and looked at me in that considered, fatherly way of his.

"Now I just want you to remember this, Danny, especially while you are still young and while time and good looks are still on your side, there's a big playing-field out there, Danny, deep oceans with many fish in them, cut yourself loose and enjoy yourself."

I nodded and smiled, hoping that would be the end of it, that he would accept what was and about-turn. But instead he stood there, and with even more intent he started up in a new vein.

"Look Danny," he said, his eyes turning moist and pulpy, "I won't make you do anything. It's just hard to speak to you now, here, to be with you the way I would like to be with you. I just want to see you. I need to see you. I want to speak to you about this, openly, about so many things. Danny, please. Just this once."

I knew, seeing that focused look in his eyes, that he wouldn't let up, not ever. And it wasn't exactly like I could go rushing out and tell my parents, who had just made up with him, shaken his hand, and shown him to my room, that I didn't want to see him again – ever. How would they ever understand? And . . . I didn't even know now if I didn't want to see him again. I seemed to have so much to tell him, so much, about making it, about my studies at varsity, about other girls I had my eyes on, about my lingering nervousness, anxiety. There was still a need inside me, a desire to lean on him, then to brag, show him how in the end it had helped, it had all maybe borne fruit.

I sat there feeling like I was failing my parents, my brother, Sophie, maybe even Chaz. If only they knew, if only they all knew what a failure I had become, how weak I was. I looked up and saw him there, offering me love. Strong. Unreserved.

Uncle Harold looked behind my door and satisfied no one was there quickly closed it. He told me to get up and come to him. Slowly, I lifted myself from my bed and stepped towards him. Immediately he opened his arms and embraced me in a bear-like grip – so familiar, so warm – and just as I had felt tears in my eyes on the day my mother had hugged me when she and my father had returned from visiting Thelma, so I felt the tears in my eyes begin to flow now. On my back I could feel Uncle Harold's tears seeping through my shirt.

He let go of me and looked at me, unashamed of the tears in his eyes.

"OK," I nodded unconsciously, feeling the soupy brown thickness of thoughts swirling in my head, "OK," I repeated, as we arranged that he would pick me up from my house the next day, just as he had picked me up so many times before.

That embrace, that cruel, warm embrace, would be the beginning of a months-long re-ignition of the old fuels, the old practices – despite Cyril, despite my new relationship with Sophie – that once again I would hide from the world. Only now he would pick me up and race me to his home – at times when he knew Thelma and the kids wouldn't be there – and we would lie on his double-bed, or on the shaggy white-carpeted lounge floor, just the two of us, Uncle Harold telling me I would grow and benefit from the experience, from our time together, adding always: "Even when we have grown old and your own children have married and had children, I will love you, Danny. I will love you."

I don't know what it was, I think it was like a disease, a snakebite I had no antidote for. I didn't even love him – though on many occasions he did try to get me to say I did. As Cyril had said, I think he had somehow managed to get under my skin, only unlike Cyril I did not have it in me to run. To break free.

Now I know what it is like to feel trapped, and in defiance of all logic, despite the desire to run, despite the desire to fight back, to fall naked before the master's knees and even enjoy the lovemaking.

32

U ncle Harold was making his comeback in the Party and he wanted me to be a part of it.

Racing along the highway on our way back from Pretoria – "verkrampte Pretoria", as Uncle Harold put it when he talked me into accompanying him to "a small Progressive Party meeting" in the Afrikaner heartland – Uncle Harold looked over his driving arm, and said, "Not so happy, eh Danny? Was coming with me to a meeting with a bunch of verkrampte liberals that bad?"

I shrugged my shoulders, as we sped past Halfway House, feeling a rush of honesty that comes perhaps from being out on the open road in the countryside in the darkness, thinking that I would like to banish him from my soul, tell him it was over, once and for all.

"No, it's not necessarily that, it's just, like . . . what's there to be so happy about?"

"Jeez, Danny," he looked at me disappointed, "how many hundreds of times have I told you, an ouk like you, you've got the world at your feet. You've got the looks, the intelligence, the imagination, everything that people are looking for. Really, you should be smiling . . . Look, I know you still struggle a bit in that department," he looked down purposefully at my midriff area, and I lifted my eyes to him, "but it's getting better . . . at least now and then you have Sophie. And I promise you there'll be more, many more, just make yourself available and it'll continue to get better. Danny, there's no turning back now. It's time to look at your life and start smiling." He paused.

"You see that leafless tree on the side of the road?" He pointed ahead, and in the distance, through the darkness, in the spread of the headlights I could make out the lone figure of a tree that looked like a gnarled, crippled old black man coming up on the roadside. "Well, that tree is like the end of life, that tree is the way you don't want to live your life. Life must be like a tree full of leaves, a constant summer full of growth. Especially at your age."

He just didn't get it. He could never relate to my unhappiness. I knew he could see it, somewhere, just didn't want to see it. That I was bound to him, yet wanted to unbind myself.

"Ha, yes," I acknowledged, as the lifeless ghost-tree whizzed by. "But it's . . . it's just not the way I feel. I feel, I don't know, you know, like all the leaves have been plucked from me by some foreign force . . . by . . . like . . . like I have never really had a say in the outcome of my life, it's like things, events, have just unravelled before me, in front of me, and I've come up with a pretty bare stump . . ."

"Bullshit, Danny, bullshit." He nearly swerved into the adjoining lane and had to quickly swerve back. "You see, that's your trouble, I don't know what's happened in that kop of yours. Instead of a tree in summer, you see a tree in the winter. Instead of spring you always see autumn. You even fight against love, the love I offer you, the love your parents offer you. The love Sophie Street offers you. Danny, it doesn't help, you have to trust. You have to believe that things will come right . . . I know you're still unsure about us," I felt the hairs on the back of my neck bristle, "but Danny I'm not going to say it again; despite everything, in me you can trust. I am never going to let you down. Even if you may never feel this way about yourself, for you I will always be a tree full of leaves, a tree in the summertime."

"Like you were for Cyril?" It just bumbled out of me, and suddenly there it was somehow floating in the car between us.

He looked at me and I thought he was going to hit me, only he was driving and he had to eventually look away, using the time to think. Afraid he could still hit me with the back of his hand, knock my teeth out, I braced myself, preparing myself to block, gathering the courage to strike back.

And then he looked at me again, like he had seen something in the road, something revealing, like some higher force had spoken to him, and he said, "I know, Danny, I'm sorry . . ."

"What do you mean, 'sorry'? What do you mean?" My lip curled, all the bitterness inside suddenly finding a vent, a release.

"I mean that was different."

I glared at him, my eyes full of fire and revenge on behalf of Cyril, on behalf of myself. On behalf of Sophie.

"How, Harold, I can't believe it, what am I meant to believe? That he was just like a toy to you . . .? You know I feel like jumping out of this car, jumping out here and now, I don't care what happens to me, I, I just want to get out!" I made for the door-handle, but a big, heavy left arm came across me, pinning my chest fast against the seat.

"I mean it was different, Danny, because he was different." He looked down at me for longer than he should on this road, like he was on auto-pilot, then as though realising we were actually in a car, he turned sharply back to the wheel and the road again. "I didn't mean anything to happen with him, Danny, I just thought for a while he was a friend, younger, sure, but becoming a friend like my old friends, the guys used to be. A real friend." He looked at me again, and released his arm, the pressure on my chest, as though he trusted he had my trust, that I would not do anything blind, like I had threatened. I looked away from him, at the darkness outside.

"You know Cyril and I were very close for a while . . . like you, I used to help him with all the little problems one has in adolescence, all those little conundrums that look so big, but really are quite small. But it never happened, Danny, never happened, not like it happened with you." I looked back at him, finally, hearing his voice straining. "With you, Danny, it's always been different. Danny, believe me, if I have to tell you a thousand times, there has never been anyone like you. Never. I love you, Danny. I would do anything for you, anything. You know that."

He looked at me, the way he had looked at me so many times before, and I reeled into those eyes, confused, yet somehow secure, somehow forgiving him, wondering what I would, if anything, ever say to Cyril.

"Believe me, Danny," he said, "believe me, it's not like you are a woman, or that I want you as a girlfriend. I have a wife and you have a girl now, and I want you to have many girls. It's nothing like that. Absolutely nothing. I don't need anyone else. It's just . . . something more, something much more . . . like blood you cannot stop from flowing, like a river you cannot dam. I am that river for you, Danny, I am blood to you, there is nothing, nothing I would not do for you. The rest is in the past. History. You will always be a brother to me. More than my own brother."

I looked up at him, tears brimming in my eyes, my hands somehow limp, warm, sweaty, finding myself, like I had no control over it, whispering, "Thanks, Uncle Harold . . . I . . . I . . . appreciate it."

I stared up at him, overwhelmed, bedazzled at my own response, and he looked at me again, knowingly, as if we really were the brothers he said we were. Then he put his hand on my thigh and squeezed, and said, "Danny, Danny, alles sal regkom. Take my word." And I looked ahead at the long, black-inky road, Johannesburg a dim spark rising in the distance.

* * *

And then we were outside my house, in Isipingo Street, and Uncle Harold was saying he would come in for a minute. I nodded apprehensively, knowing, as he knew, that my parents weren't at home because they were at his house, baby-sitting. Yes, the past, all the evils of Uncle Harold's past had been forgiven and forgotten, we were a happy circle again: he, me, my parents. Thelma was at a Union of Jewish Women meeting and needed someone to look after the boys because Thursdays were the maid's night off. My parents had been only too happy to oblige, especially since their boy was going with Uncle Harold.

Uncle Harold assured me a "quick session" would be in order, because we were back early and Thelma would be at her meeting for a while yet. Meaning my parents would have a while yet before Thelma arrived home to relieve them of their baby-sitting duties, and anyway it was "necessary, for us".

In my room – where Sophie Street and I had finally made it, where I had seen heaven – I lay back, as I always did. Uncle Harold, his pants neatly folded over my little red and yellow desk, knelt before me at the side of the bed; my desk lamp casting two Caligari-esque shadows against the wall in the darkened room. I felt my blood swirling, calmly, then with pace, in my chest and loins. I looked up at the bare bones I always saw in the ceiling, that had once again replaced the angels that I had seen with Sophie, then down across the wall to where I saw my father, his head around the door that opened against my bed. Even in that dull, shadowy light I saw his eyes wheeling with incomprehension, then rolling back the other way with a kind of bull-like anger.

"Jesus Christ, what's going on here?"

I felt Uncle Harold jump, as I jumped, hearing him whisper, "Oh shit!" And then my father was gone from the door, screaming through the house, "Jesus Christ, Stella. Jesus Christ, Stella!" And we were suddenly searching through the room for underwear and pants and clothes. In the middle of this furious tearing on of underwear and clothes, a strange thing happened, all around Uncle Harold and I: time actually slowed down. Everything, our haste, our surprise, our fear, our shock was in slow motion, and somewhere in that slowness our eyes met and I waited for that smile – the one he used to give me when we were picking up the cushions and making a bed of them on that desk – but when I looked at him I saw his head held at half-mast, the smile gone, completely wiped. And suddenly he was gone – had left the room, had left the house – and my father was back in my room, the main light switched on.

He stood there facing me with eyes that looked so dark I could hardly see the pupils, his chest so tight you could hear the breath snorting from him like a real live bull. I looked down, ashamed, seeing in his hand a short stick that I had never seen in our house before, like a shortened knobkerrie, with a big round hard head on it.

"What the hell, Danny? Is that what all your bullshit is about? Is it? Tell me! Are you sick or something? Both of you?"

I looked up into his eyes and saw such a deep rage in there that for a moment I felt like shouting back at him: "Yes, yes I am." Just to shock him, to see what would happen, what it would do to his all-manly soul, but I felt myself falter at the very last second.

Only half-looking at him now I felt the whole, long, stumbling story pour out of me, thick, salty tears running down my face, as I told how Uncle Harold had over a long period talked me into this. How I couldn't escape, because I couldn't tell anyone. Assuring him, because I could see his need for assurance, that it was only Harold, only ever with Uncle Harold – my fingers jumping at my sides, my eyes darting all over the place. Still unable to tell him what started it all, what started it all. He looked so enraged and confused, his body trembling, his face white and growing whiter, that I didn't know how much he could take. Then I saw my mother behind him, a second pair of eyes, a thin, piercing rationality in them, trying to comprehend.

"I'll have that bastard. I'll have him!" My father tightened his grip on the stumpy knobkerrie. He glared at me, lifting it, and I felt myself jerk backwards in fright, feeling the blood already oozing out of my cracked skull, hearing him scream what I always thought he would scream: "You weak . . . you bladdy weak . . ."

But he couldn't finish it, what he started out to say, and I saw my mother's thin, fragile arm shoot straight out and clutch his wrist and he relaxed his grip and pulled me into his chest, holding me awkwardly, like I was a little boy again, his little boy. I felt ashamed, for having ever thought he could have even been remotely connected to Uncle

Harold in that way. And then I felt my mother, my father pulling us both, pulling everything in our house into him, protecting us from invaders, from the outside world. My mother crying into my shoulder: "Where did we go wrong? Where, oh God, where did we go wrong?"

Then my father finally took control again, put up the shield and declared war: "I'll kill the bastard, I'll kill him. I don't care who he is. Thelma will know about this! I'll drag his bladdy filthy name through the courts! It'll be the end of him!" And the circle was broken, my mother leading my father into their bedroom, blaming herself, as I always thought she would, looking up, mumbling as though in a trance: "What did I do? Tell me, what did I do?"

I lay in my bed that night seeing what I never saw before: how protective a father could be. I felt guilty that I doubted he could love. And in a hundred ways I felt pleased it was out in the open. I was just afraid of it going further, of my father threatening as he had to take it through the courts, showing me up to be the failure that I was. That they always knew I was.

Early the next morning I found my parents in the lounge. They were sitting with their coffee, as though waiting for me. They were like two different people, like people who had been critically injured, hospitalised, and returned with a different view on life. They looked serious but well-washed, like they had specially readied and cleaned themselves for this meeting and didn't want anything to go wrong. Unusually, they sat together, on the orange and gold-speckled couch, above them the Tretchikoff woman despite their solemnity smirking down on all of us.

My father did the talking, though there wasn't much of that. He told me that Uncle Harold was finished in their eyes: "May as well be dead. Dead." But they would not go to the police. They had decided after much thought and deliberation – he said it like his internal organs were being sliced slowly from his body, my mother loudly silent at his side – that "it would only bring shame . . . no matter what the truth of the story. Nothing will go further than this front door."

And although I didn't say it, just nodded as though in compliance, in agreement with their wisdom, I was completely relieved. I wouldn't have to show Chaz or Sophie Street or the crew, or the rest of the world for that matter, what a failure, what a fool I was. I wouldn't even have to tell Cyril, who was probably the only one who would have really understood. My parents, who I thought were such fools, had come to the wisest conclusion that night. And it made me happy. It would remain within the family, behind closed doors, deeply locked in the family closet. Safe until I, the bringer of all this shame, died. Uncle Harold punished through immediate and eternal condemnation and excommunication. Yes, even my father, who I once thought would throttle the both of us if ever he found out, preferred the woollen blanket of secrecy.

In my head I knew, finally, I had found safety, escaped from his clutches in the protection offered by my family.

But even to this day, whenever I look into my father's eyes, that sit under the heavy shadow of his bald head, I see a sigh in there, a sigh rather than forgiveness, a sigh that I know signifies my failure, my weakness that he can never forget nearly publicly shamed us. He wears it in his eyes like it is some sort of cataract that will eventually blind and destroy his already quickly failing sight. My mother, though we of course no longer live under the same roof, hugs and kisses me more than ever. I should have known! Uncle Harold had warned me. But I guess I have had to forever bear responsibility for the guilt I always knew she would take on herself. That she should have seen coming the day Uncle Harold invited me to go out with him and learn about the world. That she should have, as she always wanted to do, put a stop to it there and then.

Yes, a failure to all and sundry, at any rate to those who knew. Perhaps the worst kind of failure. A weakling, too afraid of the truth. Too afraid to reveal the real person inside. Too afraid of what the world might think. A coward and a failure afraid of failure. But I could live with that; I had lived with it for long enough already. Plus I had given my word to my father and mother that it would go no further than our front door. Chaz, who wrote me fairly regularly from England – where he worked for years in London as an actuary in a bank, and who like my brother Cyril never returned to bright, strange, funny, sunny South Africa, not even to show off his wife and five children – I wrote back to, always, I have to admit, with a guilty heart.

And Sophie Street? Even though she doesn't know the full family secret, she is with me still. And believe it or not Uncle Harold, Uncle HK, still calls every now and then, well on the phone that is. He wouldn't dare to actually arrive on our doorstep, especially with Sophie around, but he calls from time to time – our two teenage children think he is nothing but a business associate from the clothing store that I have taken over from my father. And when Uncle Harold does call – strange that even at my age I still think of him as Uncle Harold, though I only ever call him Harold now and have for many years – he still tries to talk to me like I am an old friend, professing in his voice, no matter what the topic, usually no more than the weather or the state of the economy, his feelings for me. The warble in his voice a kind of continual apology. Just the thought, just the picture of him in my mind, makes my hair prickle, my tongue tighten, and I begin to stammer, and yet still have I never managed to put the phone down on him. But he must feel it, must sense it in my stammering, dislocated voice. Yet completely bald and stooping as I know he is – from the odd picture I see of him in the local rags, where he is described as a well-known local philanthropist and retired elder political spokesman on democratic rights – he has still not taken the hint. I don't know what it is, I know that he still lives on in me somewhere, I still tell myself with his voice to *relax, Danny, just relax, lighten up, let go*. No, despite everything, he has never let go, still lives on in me because he has never let go, has, as he did to Cyril a long time ago, managed to get under my skin. Irremovable. I don't know what it will take to get through to him. A bullet? I don't have it in me, never did, and in the end, I see, nor did my father. But then when he is gone, off the phone, Sophie, fiery and wet-eyed, goes around the house shouting like a lunatic: "Bloody fuckin' moron, if he ever comes here I'll bash him over the head with a candlestick! Deviant! Arsehole! Who the fuck does he think he is? How do you tolerate it, Danny!"

The kids think she is crazy, always look at her stupefied, wondering whom she is referring to, but it reminds me each time she does it that maybe there is such a thing as loyalty, as trust, as true love. Just don't ask me to feel it, I can't. If it is something one can be stripped of, then I have been stripped. I wonder how Sophie can tolerate such a cold, distant being living so close to her, but I think she knows, secretly, what has happened to her soldier in this war that is life.

A failure, just as ma and da' had unwittingly implied I would become. A failure and a fool, the depths of which no one will ever really know. Except that it shows up in this constant splitting headache that I walk around with, that I carry with me to work at the shop each day, and in my body that is stiff and bent beyond its years. And that old poem, forever warping, still keeps washing up in my feeble, china-thin head: "Tyger, Tyger, burning bright, In the forests of the night; What immortal hand or eye, Could *destroy* thy fearful symmetry." The truth is, it hurts to hold it down – to hold all the lies and deceit and secrets down – but, like my ma and da', I prefer it that way. It is easier, somehow much easier, much safer and definitely more comfortable, to keep it behind closed doors, in the bottle with the cork tightly screwed in. My mind, like the name of the street I still live in, Isipingo Street – just a few doors down from ma and da's – is a ridiculous and puzzling place to be. But I am safe in it now, safely locked in, safely locked away, safe behind my high walls. Yes, in the end, Uncle Harold, as you always said, as you always said, alles sal regkom.

Glossary

bris (bris melah) – circumcision

bobbe – grandmother

boychick – little boy; affectionate term for boy or man

chrain – horse radish; colloquially used to mean "backbone", gumption

drek – human dung, faeces

Gai in drerd arein! – Go to hell!

ganef – crook, swindler

gefilte fish – stuffed fish

Gehenna – hell

g'vald – wail of sorrow

goy, goyishe – gentile, non-Jew

kinder – children

klutz – clumsy person, bungler

k'naidlech – round dumplings usually made of matzah meal

kosher – food that meets Jewish dietary laws

kugel – noodle or bread sweet pudding cooked with raisins; colloquially used to mean Jewish girl only interested in looks and material things

Kush mich in toches! – Kiss me in the backside!

Kush mich in pupik! – another way of saying the above, but more literally means: Kiss me in the (chicken) gizzards!

l'dor v'dor – (Biblical Hebrew) from this generation to the next

macher – person with access to the authorities who processes favours for his clients, big shot

matzah-ball soup – soup made with k'naidlech (see above)

meshuggene – mad, crazy, insane man

mohel – religious functionary who performs circumcisions

nebbish – a pitiful, timid man
payers – long side-burns grown for religious reasons
putsen – decorate, move little things around
rachmones – a pitiful person, "mother's shame"
saichel – common sense, good sense
schmek – smell
schlemiel – clumsy bungler, inept person, fool
schmendrik – fool, nincompoop
schmo – naive person, easy to deceive
schmock – self-made fool
schnorrer – miser, sponger
shul – synagogue
tsores – troubles, misery
vildergai – wild one, wild person
yarmulke – Jewish skullcap
zeide – grandfather
zets – smack, punch, hiding